UNKNOWN FAMILY

A Gods of Carina Novel

AMBER S CRAFT

New Haven Publications

UNKNOWN FAMILY
A Gods of Carina Novel

Amber S. Craft
UNKNOWN FAMILY
A New Haven Publications book

For information contact :
New Haven Publications
theunknownseries@gmail.com

DISCLAIMER AND CREDITS

Cover illustration by Designer Alec Williams
Editing by Rose City Editing

First Edition: November 2021

To those who encouraged me, thank you from the bottom of my heart. To my daughter, I hope I have shown you how to follow your dreams. But this book is for those that I have lost. My cousin, Phillip Beasley, who made sure he was my first sale; to my Great Aunt and Uncle who put up with my interruptions while visiting my grandma every Sunday; and to my Big Granny, who is missed every day, and who listened to thousands of stories as they rolled out of my head and off my tongue while you taught me how to cook. And to my best friend, who we lost too soon. You are all missed, and we are all thankful for the time that I had with you. Hope you are all together and happy.

FOR MY READERS

Be sure to go to www.amberscraft.com to see what I am up to, sign up for my newsletter, find me on all of my social media platforms, sign up to get firsthand news, enter discussions on my blog, and ask questions. I would love to hear from you. Please feel free to email me at theunknownseries@gmail.com.

OTHER BOOKS BY AMBER S. CRAFT

Unknown Love

TRANSLATIONS

ENGLISH / AVAAN
About - alt
Am - ta
And - nes
Answer - lax/awe
Are - da
Aunt - arhe
Bad things - cafade
Barrier - lavh
Body - niyt
Bright - kalec
Brother - dahe
But - qua
Button - neve
Can - fig
Child - meve
Confused ones - danmoc
Council - cru
Daughter - aot
Decide - tsrada

Die - mahel
Do - to
Does - tsran
Done - ser
Don't - tsrane
Earth - colern
Eat - tac
Energy - eanug
English - enlehe
Even - ge
Finish - fil
Gas - nac
Good - lohe
Granddaughter - alao
Grandmother - malao
Guide - gui
Hand - kol
Happy - hestla
Has - uke
Have - hae/ke
Heal - lehel
Hell - undu
Help - kel
Her - kea
Here - lef
Him - van
Hitman - danmoc
Human - mevid
I - le
Injured - jin
Interfere - ilehi
Is - ne
It - ti
I am - le ta

Just - ton
Know - whe
Language - ocha
Learn - arne
Life - vele
Like - laf
Little - lifda
Locked - locni
Look - flahat
Love - varela
Man - jut
Mate - mer
May - seuc
Me - ba
Memory Star - afaj
Mental - nemg
Message - sanm
Met - eme
Mother - mahe
Need - neu
Niece - syla
No - holel
On - no
Or - lu
Other - leche
Pillow - weki
Precious - precu
Pure - pre
Queen - baque
English - AVAAN
Return - sunu
Screwed - vahe
See - ve
Servant - halia

Shine - serl
Sister - meta
Skye,Skylu
So - sa
Son - raher
Sorry - solu
Spider - datera
Spirit - sko
Star - stri
Still - dahs
Symee - Saiph
Teach - vete
Tell - dat
Thank - gra
That - zha/ple
The - les
There - zeha
Things - tseil
Think - stral
This - ser
To - ka
Track - tele
Use - seu
Was - wal
Way - won
We - tem
What - wem
Who - hios
Would - jol/vole
Why,wen

"**H**annah would you please tell Sedah that I would like for her to come to dinner?" Persephone asked.

Hannah nodded to her mistress and walked out the wide doors. Persephone braced herself as she watched the servant go. This would be a disastrous dinner. She was thankful that Hannah was too faithful of a servant to question the order.

"She will not come, my dear. I have angered her once again and, as usual, she will try to punish me by hurting you," Hades said as he wrapped his arms around his wife's stomach from behind. The familiar strength of her husband's embrace centered her as nothing else could. They stood in the center of the dining room, watching at the doors their daughter had stormed through earlier, when she tried to get away from what they were trying to tell her.

The dining room also served as the receiving hall for guests or those being judged. As such, it was the hub of their home, with many halls breaking off from the room like spokes on a chariot wheel.

"How does she expect you to treat her as an adult when

she does not behave as such?" Persephone asked no one in particular as she let out a loud, heartfelt sigh. She crossed her arms, lightly gripping Hades' forearms. Sedah had just been told she would be leaving home when her mom did. Sedah was usually the child they never had to worry about lying, sneaking out, or misbehaving at all, but Persephone couldn't blame her daughter for storming out when she had been told what was about to happen to her. Sedah had always wanted to visit the human world with her mother, but for fun, not like this. It should have been great news to get out of the Underworld, but it wasn't. Instead of going with her mother, she would be living with nymphs, Persephone's enemies. Persephone knew all too well how it felt to be forced into something you didn't want. At least, with her husband, it had turned out well in the end for the most part. Asking her daughter to live with the one type of creature she despised the most made it that much harder to ask her to do it.

It was part of the same argument the family seemed to have every year, like clockwork. In just one week, Persephone would be forced to return to her mother and leave Hades behind for nine months. They both had always hated it, but it had become even more unbearable as each of the children had been born. Missing seeing your children grow up for months at a time was hard on any parent.

Just then, their peaceful moment was broken up by the sound of laughter coming from one of the halls to their right. Persephone turned her gaze from the door leading to their youngest daughter's wing, to where their three boys were coming in from the outer grounds.

"Sorry mom, we broke the vase again," Milos said, "but we repaired it," he added after righting himself from being pushed. As the eldest, and the spitting image of his father, Milos had always felt it was his duty to break the bad news and take the brunt of the punishment for his siblings.

"Only because you would have blamed me, when you broke it by pushing me into it," Sephir told Lexur with a glare.

Persephone sighed as she watched her middle son try to charm his way out of being punished. When he was a child, he would shine those huge, glacier blue eyes at her from behind that adorable mop of sandy brown hair, and she couldn't stop herself from letting him off with warning after warning. Now, as an adult, those tricks wouldn't work on her. His hair was shaggy, long, and unkempt, and the innocent smile was now a leer that spoke of more mischief to come. He wasn't half as charming as he thought he was. Still, her heart ached at having to leave him behind again.

"Again," Hades added. He raised an eyebrow toward Lexur. "If your brother didn't keep fixing it, he might have to fix you after your mother got through with you."

The boys became silent, exchanging warning glances at each other, and went to their places at the table. Persephone felt a smile quirk at the corner of her mouth; those glances had always been their code to stop angering their father while they still had their hides. Persephone turned her attention back toward Sedah's door, the boys sighed in unison.

"You know, you would think she'd be a little more yielding. She has been asking to go above with mom, without fail, for years now," Lexur said with a sigh. He sat slouched, staring at his empty plate, obviously pouting. He'd been asking, since before Sedah was born, to visit Earth with Persephone. She didn't blame him for wanting to see new things, but he needed to stay safely in the Underworld for the same reason Sedah did. Persephone would give anything for the chance to travel the human world with all of her children.

Hades turned from his wife and went to sit at his place at the head of the table, and Persephone decided to do the same, knowing this might take a while.

"She is still a girl, and a teenager: two things that add up to drama at any hour, day, or realm," Sephir told them honestly, trying to make them understand. Persephone's youngest boy of the three, had always tried to be the calm voice of reason since he first started talking. His soft feminine features kept him looking childlike, and were what helped him stay more relatable and calming to the spirits of the children in his care.

"What about girls and drama?" Melinoe asked as she and Makaria materialized into their seats at the table.

"Shh!" Persephone said, her tone telling them that she meant business. She could feel her daughter finally coming down the hall. She rose to greet her, and to let the others know Sedah was nearly there.

Hannah came through first, opening the door for Sedah to enter. At once, Sedah went to her mother's waiting arms. They hugged for a moment before turning and walking to the table together. Hannah silently closed the door behind Sedah and drifted into the shadows, where she would disappear until summoned. Sedah's small, toned frame tucked into Persephone's more feminine frame.

"Finally, we can eat." Milos said under his breath.

"Oh, be quiet," Sedah said quietly, her entire body turning red.

"And you wonder why you have to stay hidden?" Lexur smiled with a false sweetness at his sister, telepathically razzing her as she sat down in front of him.

"Could it be that I am also a human chameleon right now? I think that's the first thing they'll notice." Sedah glared back. When it had started a couple months ago, she had been excited. She had run to her mother to show her mood changing skin color, and they worked together in Persephone's garden, practicing making her emotions change to see what colors appeared. Once they had seen every emotional color, they tried to keep her skin tone the same while feeling each emotion, but to no avail. Persephone had been proud of her. She knew from experience how hard it had been for her. Her brothers had used the opportunity to make fun of her.

"Enough! Let's eat," Hades commanded, watching his daughter's skin turn from red to blue. There was more than polite verbal conversation going on, and this was not the time for it. His normally caramel complexion was reddening, and Persephone searched her mind for a way to diffuse his obvious anger. His tone indicating that their dad wasn't playing around, everyone calmed down and tried to eat, despite the tension.

"Milos, how are the judgments going?" Hades asked after a few minutes of silent eating and watching the death glares going on between two of the boys and Sedah.

"Fine, except that I'm starting to see more souls go to other places than Elysium or Makaron. The tide is turning, and it seems we have no way to tell the reason behind it, or how long it will last. The Asphodel fields still gain the same numbers though, so there is still hope out there," Milos replied, Hades nodding in response.

Milos's job as the first-born male was to work with his two uncles and aunt to judge new souls arriving at the crossroads. Every season, one of the judges received three months off, and Milos took winter to coincide with Persephone's time in Erebus.

"What about the entrances?" Hades directed to Lexur.

"Fine. Only one rogue entity evaded Hermes and entered through the back in the past two months, but it used the Horns and Ivory gate, letting us know where it was headed, so we are good there. The front is crowded as always, though." Lexur smiled, self-congratulatory pride taking over his face for catching the vampire that had been bent on getting in. Persephone shared in that pride: only one breach in two months, and that one apprehended, was quite an accomplishment. Lexur only played at being a slacker to torment Hades and Milos, but Persephone was willing to let him have his fun there.

"I will never understand someone not paying for the passage of the dead. Whether a loved one or a common enemy, it is so cruel to deny someone the afterlife," Melinoe complained.

"Yet it is something that happens too often, I'm afraid," Hades said solemnly. "Few would try to get in if they realized it meant automatically being part of the river Akheron, I am sure."

"The islands are doing as well as they always are, although sometimes I sense that some would like another chance in Elysium to prove themselves," Sephir said after silence had once again settled over the table.

Sometimes, Persephone would overhear his brothers complaining that Sephir's job was the easiest, but she didn't agree. Milos sat in a chair with his two uncles and one aunt, judging people. Lexur got to run around all the gates with his Uncle Hermes. Lexur had even left the Underworld with their uncle a few times and played pranks on humans. Sephir might have been in charge of Makaron, Atlas, and Aeo, but he did it alone. He alone dealt with the heroes sent to Makaron, and the children and teenagers on Atlas.

The only other house on the Isle of the Dawn, as Aeo was known, was occupied by someone Hades had told Sephir not to bother, under even the most severe circumstances. If his father was wary of the inhabitant, Sephir was too diligent to disobey.

Since Persephone's mother knew about them, Melinoe and Makaria's jobs allowed them to go back and forth between the two realms without fear of Demeter's wrath.

Melinoe was in charge of keeping ghosts in line while they decided to stay on the earthly plane and presided over those who wished to propitiate their ghosts.

Makaria was in charge of both reaping the souls of the blessed humans, taking them straight to their earned area to await their rebirth, and policing the paranormals by calling in the Erinyes to take care of them when they stepped beyond their limits and were not punished by their own kind. These responsibilities kept them from home, and away from Persephone, more than their siblings.

"It has been like that since its creation. I have thought on it a few times, but if I make the changes in one area, the other areas will learn and start making demands as well," Hades told Sephir. "That I cannot have. The prisoners cannot run the prison, as the humans say."

"I will not go!" Sedah yelled out of nowhere, going from a slight red to that of an autumnal fire. Everyone turned their attention to her as she yelled. Her anger had grown more and more until she couldn't contain it anymore. The thought of living with women who didn't know her, yet hated her simply for the family she was born into, was terrifying. For their precious tree, her father had traded her.

"You will, child, and that is the end of it," Hades countered somewhat loudly, yet in an icy, calm tone that belied his anger. As if he had decreed it to happen, the walls of the mansion responded to its master's mood, beginning to frost over as the air temperature went down a few degrees.

"There is no place for you down here honey. I would take you with me, but none must know you exist. You wore the helmet of invisibility when you were a child, but you hated it, We had to stop for fear you would take it off and reveal yourself." Her mother was clearly trying to persuade Sedah and calm her frigid father at the same time.

It was true that maybe a dozen or so immortals and gods

knew the total of Persephone's children, but Hades had made them all take oaths by the river Styx that they would never be able to talk about anything or anyone existing in the Underworld other than Hades and Persephone themselves. Every time one of the kids had gone above, the god responsible for aiding them had been forced by Hades to drink from the river Lethe to forget.

"Those two idiots were never forced to go to earth. They snuck up there for fun, even! What makes me so special?"

Persephone exchanged a look with Hades. After a few minutes of silent, mental discussion between them, Hades nodded in agreement, letting out a defeated sigh.

"What?" Sedah yelled at the obviousness of something being discussed about her but not shared with her. She couldn't stand the fact that her fate was being decided for her without so much as an iota of input from her.

Getting the okay from her husband, Persephone sighed and looked back at her daughter.

"You hold more of my power in you than the others do sweetheart, which is why you have begun to change colors within the last few months. That is thanks to your grandmother- a gift she gave me when I was little, for a perceived slight. Because my gifts are starting to manifest in you, you will probably begin needing the healing soil from above also. We need to feel Helios' warmth and be around nature to draw energy. If you stay here, you will begin to feel rundown all the time. My gardens will help, but not as much as you will need at first. The only place to send you while all of this is happening is into the mountains with the nymphs. They report to Artemis and she has taken a vow to protect and never speak of you. While you are there, they will teach you about Earth and the current workings of the world above. In the time that it takes for you to quit changing colors, you will study and follow whatever they tell you."

"What is the point of learning if I am just going to come back home? All of that knowledge will have been for naught. Why do I have to leave at all when I can just stay here?" Sedah looked at her mother for an answer. Her mother was here for three months at a time, and she seemed fine. There was soil and nature in her mother's groves south of the Elysium fields. Helios had even given sun to Persephone and to the shades of the holy men, as a last reward for their selfless acts when they were alive. Surely that would be enough.

No one said a word or looked at her. Her brothers all became interested in their food with gusto while her sisters looked just as lost as Sedah felt.

"What?" she looked at them all expectantly. For some reason, she had the feeling there was something much worse that she had not been told yet.

Still no one said a word.

"What is no one telling me?" Sedah began to sound frantic, going into multiple colors as she looked from her mother, to her father, and back.

"A deal has been struck," Persephone said in little more than a whisper, her eyes tearing as she looked at her daughter. She turned her head to glare at Hades for a second, long enough for Sedah to catch on that this was his doing and not her mother's.

"What is it then? What deal have you made for your *youngest* daughter, without even consulting her, Father?" Her skin took on a dark bluish hue to add to the multiple colors of red swirling through her skin like a kaleidoscope. She was glad only her mother knew each color's meaning as she heard her mother gasp from her place at the table.

"An alliance. You have until you stop changing to find your own love, or you will serve one of Poseidon's children," He replied.

"I must become a mermaid servant? Oh, this is too rich!"

9

Sedah banged her fists on the table as she looked at them all, "You all know for a fact that I hate the sea!" She looked around, hoping this was some sick joke.

"It will be Poseidon's choice of land or sea, as well as whether it be his son you marry or one of his daughters you will be serving." Persephone had no idea how Poseidon and her husband expected a grandchild of the harvest to live under the sea. This whole second agreement with Poseidon seemed . . . fishy, for a lack of a more appropriate word. She put her hand on Sedah's leg to try to give her some show of support.

"And when do I get shipped off, Father? Now, or do I have time to pack?" She asked, her tone as barbed and icy as his. A chill rolled into the room on a wave of fog so thick that Sedah could actually see her breath.

Her mother cleared her throat. "You leave with me, dear. I will drop you off with them on my way back to mother. I do not trust your father anywhere near those nymphs. We need no more trees around Erebus, do we dear?" She turned to her husband. Her mother always got an odd smirk when she talked about that tree, the only symbol of what her vengeance could create. It was a lesson to anyone else who tried to warm her husband's bed again while she was away.

"No, dear." Hades rolled his eyes. She would never forgive his one discretion since they had been together, nor let him forget that she hadn't.

"So, which are you hoping for?" Sedah suddenly asked, her head down to hide the tears threatening to escape.

Hades sighed. "I care not, my child. The deal with Poseidon is done. You are grown, and it is time you acted like it. What better way than to learn the world above that you will have to engage in?" Hades sighed again, harsher this time. *"Why can you not see that I am doing this for you, not against you?"* he blasted mentally so that everyone could hear him.

"Don't answer that sweetheart," Persephone warned, though to which person that she was warning at the moment, Sedah was not quite sure. She looked at her father, her eyes pained.

"Why must I serve one of Poseidon's snobby mer-kids like a common servant when I can just live my own life?" Sedah's confusion was easily read on her face, even if she hadn't slowly turned from blue to a reddish yellow to prove it.

"The reasons do not matter. It has been decided by my brother and I, and it will be carried out. Thank your mother for the little time that you do have. I didn't want to give you even that, but if you are going to marry or serve someone up above, she is right that you will have to be up to date on Earth, its ways, and technologies. Otherwise, you will face communication issues between you and either the prince or whichever princess that you serve."

"For what it's worth, Poseidon said you would have full capabilities to go between sea and shore whenever you need to," Milos told Sedah. She glanced over to see a genuine smile, clearly trying to help calm her down with a bright point. It did the opposite.

"You knew about this?" Sedah yelled across the table to him, slamming both of her fists down again. Sedah went blood red faster than she had ever changed colors since first becoming a chameleon. Slowly, she noticed that all three of her brothers looked guilty in their own telling ways. Milos took on their dad's stern expression, Lexur bit his bottom lip, and Sephir had the decency to look down in regret.

"You *all* knew? How long has this deal been made?" she yelled, eyes wide with disbelief as she looked at her father incredulously.

Milos' voice became harsh, taking a tone he normally used when he tried to explain something that he didn't think needed to be explained in the first place. "You will be allowed

to come home when mom does, once you start your steward-
ship. Otherwise, all holidays, you have the choice to come
home, or to stay at Poseidon's Palace. It's more than I would
have done if I had been the one making the deal instead of
Dad, so you should be thankful."

"So, do I get to come back for my things before I go to
the ocean, or does it all have to go to the jungle with me for
as long as it takes to quit being a chameleon?" Sedah was
beginning to turn grey as she looked to her mom for an
answer.

"Honey, all of your questions will be answered as they
need to be. If you're done eating, go to your room and start
packing. To take you to the nymphs, we have to leave a few
days early so that I can still be back at mother's on time."
Persephone stood, walking around the table to where Sedah
sat. She lifted Sedah's chin to look up at her. The chandelier
of candles behind her mother made her strawberry blonde
hair glow like a sunrise.

"Is there not the option to stay with grandma Rhea? She
has never told anyone about us. I could stay in her cottage
with her, instead of with the nymphs. What would be the
difference? They're both in the mountains away from
humans."

"You are more like your mother," Hades told her, "which,
in time, will only remind her of the past. That would do
nothing but cause both mortals and immortals alike untold
grief and harm."

"Can't blame a girl for trying," Persephone muttered
under her breath as Sedah rose from her seat, going back to a
more normal color for her. She waved goodbye to her
brothers and left, Hannah opening the door for her and
following her out.

"I WILL NEVER UNDERSTAND WHY CHILDREN CANNOT JUST mind their parents without a fight. We are many centuries older and therefore wiser, so fighting is futile." Hades sighed, the exhaustion evident in both his breath and his stance.

"She fights because she does not understand. All she ever hears is that she is like me, but she does not understand that may mean the powers too," Persephone defended her baby girl, putting her hands on her hips, staring her husband down.

"You'd think she would see that since we have versions of dad's power, it makes sense she would have some of yours like Melinoe and Makaria do," Sephir said aloud to no one in particular.

"The time in the mountains will teach her how to control her emotions better, Mother. If more of your powers come out of Sedah during that time, she will be in the right place should she need help controlling them, or should something go wrong," Milos added.

She relaxed a little. "She'll be fine. Let her vent all of her rage at us hiding something so big from her for so long, and I will bring her breakfast in the morning to talk it all out with her." Persephone kissed her daughters, then each of her three sons on their heads as she passed them. "Goodnight children. See you all in the morning."

Now that dinner was obviously over, the kids got up silently and left for their sections of the Underworld, while Hades joined his wife for the hours she needed to sleep.

Being one of the twelve great Olympians, routine sleep was not a requirement for Hades and his children. While Hades and his sons still needed sleep, they only needed one night every year to keep their powers at their fullest. Persephone however, was different since she was born in the sun. Her body needed one night a week, at least, in order to keep her body and powers at full capacity.

Persephone hadn't yet fallen asleep when she felt Hades

running his fingers over her body. To all others, Gods and humans alike, his was both a name and a realm that one did not dare speak of. It was so ingrained into each person from their conception, that it had taken trickery to get her as his wife. One desperate act had sealed both of their fates forever, but it had been worth it, looking back now.

2

A red bodied Sedah burst into her parlor, thrusting the doors open with a fury and force that slammed them into the walls, making them ripple like water to better absorb the impact. The windows shook, but also held strong. Being the Underworld, everything was crafted around emotions. The palace absorbed all of them and turned them into electricity and power. The palace came alive to absorb the positive and negative feelings of the people in it. Sedah was proud that she had a house that could absorb her worst moods and use it to get even stronger. It was like a friend that she could vent her frustrations on, and it would still be there afterward, ready and waiting for more.

"I can't believe I might have to serve a spoiled rotten, fish eating, mer-thing! How am I supposed to find my own way, enough to fall in love, at the very least, if I have a deadline hanging over my head?" Sedah shouted to the ceiling. Striding to the right wall of the parlor, next to the archway leading to her bedroom, she opened up the armoire that held weapons instead of clothes, selecting a crossbow and bolts.

"Target Range!" she yelled, even as she closed the doors. A

wall panel to the right, about five feet from the armoire, recessed itself and slid left to reveal a number of targets. Barely giving the wall time to slide to a stop, Sedah shot off bolt after bolt as she complained aloud.

"Now I have to add to that horror by staying with a bunch of nature loving, animal hugging, green thumbed pansies so I can learn how to control my mood and how, the world works? How stupid does that sound to you, Hannah?"

"Well ma'am, I honestly think it's a good idea. If I went back, I would be bewildered at any new advancements other than equipment run by hand, yet I hear your brothers speak all the time of tokeners coming through, speaking of things in which I cannot fathom, such as motorized things in the sea and the skies. I think it would take time to become used to this new world so that you are not wrongly branded, judged, and cast out." Hannah's tone stayed thoughtful and steady, as it always did.

"Hannah, if I wanted common sense, I would have asked my mother." Sedah couldn't help but smile, her color slowly changing back to normal. Hannah had been with the family longer than anyone could remember. Some say she had been her father's first maid as he built his kingdom. She was probably the only person not afraid of Hades, other than Persephone.

As Sedah's coloring went back to its normal alabaster tone, there was a knock on the door. Immediately Hannah snapped her fingers, the wall starting to move into place, as Sedah picked up her remaining bolts and crossbow and returned them to the armoire.

"Come in, mom," Sedah said as she shut the weapon closet's door. She had really hoped for more time to herself before anyone else came to try and calm her down.

"Thank you for that," Sephir said as he entered, smiling.

"Mom is the only one that knocks. If I had known it was

you, I wouldn't have put up my weapons," she huffed, her skin going gray to show her disappointment.

"Knowing how you think *was* the reason that I knocked. No need to have those things directed at me. Now, I can leave and you can go through the trouble of getting it all back out, just to have to stash it again when mom does get here, or you can just cool off, sit down, and talk to me for the few minutes I have." He sat down in one of Sedah's royal purple plush velvet chairs. It was by far his favorite piece of furniture in the house. After she had gotten an artist and an interior decorator to come in and do her room in what the ghost had called a Parisian influence, he had fallen in love with the chair he was currently sitting in, and had gotten a red one for himself as well.

Sighing in defeat, Sedah jumped over the back of the more normal chair facing him, landing with a puff from the seat and a giggle from Sedah.

Becoming snow white from pure happiness, Sedah smiled at her brother. "So, what has you knocking on my door tonight, o brother of mine?"

"I wanted to see how you were handling the news," he answered honestly. Out of her three brothers, Sedah had to admit that Sephir was by far the nicest. When she was younger, she had thought it was because he had to be, due to his position as caretaker of the children on the fortunate islands. As she got older, however, she began to realize that his disposition is what got him put in his position instead of the other way around.

"How do you think I'm handling it?" she raised her eyebrows daringly.

"I only know what you tell me."

"I'm your sister, remember? You're the one with empathy in the family. It's part of the reason all of us girls go to you when we want sympathy and logic. Not to mention, I change colors right now, anyone and everyone knows my moods."

"Your mood does not betray exactly what you are feeling though, am I right?" he smirked, knowing the answer as his eyes met hers. The light from the room flickered in his magenta ones.

"Yes, you're right as usual," she sighed. "I guess the best word would be that I feel . . . bamboozled honestly. And not just by one of you. Every single one of you boys knew. How long have you known for?"

"A month or so." Sephir had the decency to look down in shame. His shoulder length hair came down to cover his face.

"What! It's worse than I originally guessed!" Sedah groaned, going slightly gray as she hit her forehead with her palm.

"It was up to father if, and when, you were told, Sedah. We may be your big brothers, but we could do nothing but give him counsel! Why you act as if you don't already know this is a mystery to me." Sephir shook his head. "He's doing the same thing to me, Sedah. There's something about the person living in the second house on Aeo that I'm not supposed to know. I asked Father, but he told me to keep to my own business on that matter. Aeo is my business, and he doesn't trust me enough to let me handle my own job fully. It happened again when I found out Lexur had gone to the human world without permission. Father denied that it was possible, but it turned out to be true. We all found out when Makaria and Melinoe brought it up like it was old news. It's why the girls aren't here that much. They don't like deceiving you, and Heaven knows they cannot keep a secret, so they stayed away. There's more to this than they're telling us." He threw his hair back and stared out her window as he sighed. "What do you mean?" Sedah asked. Her brother continued to stare out the window.

"What do you mean?" Sedah asked. Her brother continued to stare out the window. "Sephir, what are you saying?"

Sighing once again before standing up, Sephir looked down at his baby sister who was about to learn more than she would probably want to about life.

"Sedah, I worry for you. There are things that are unknown, even to humans in this world, that you are about to enter, things which are never allowed to enter our realm. You'll need to grow up fast once you get there. Earth spares no one and shows no mercy to the ignorant."

"So, you're saying in a nutshell . . . what?" she looked up, confused at his solemn words and the worry in his eyes.

"Soak up everything and ask as many questions as possible, no matter how stupid they may seem. The nymphs are smarter than you think. Give them their due." Saying all he could, Sephir got up, bent down to kiss Sedah's head, and silently left her to think over everything that he had said.

Hannah came from the bedroom, leaning against the door frame, watching Sedah with an expression more worried than the one Sedah was used to seeing, but still filled with the grandmotherly love she always showed. "Keep changing colors so quickly and you will become a permanent rainbow." She laughed, her voice thick, as she quickly swallowed her emotions, walking forward and hugging her charge as soon as Sedah had stood.

"So, do I start packing now, or what? Have you been told anything? I have so many questions about all of the practical things and no one is here to answer them." Sedah threw her grey hands into the air and looked at Hannah for answers. Everything that had happened at dinner and before, had left her feeling lost and drained. Hades and his sons fed more on the negative emotions of the Underworld, while Sedah fed on the positive.

"Your mother will answer any questions that you have when she wakes up. Just relax." She put her hands on Sedah's shoulders. "Look at me, and take what you need," she volunteered.

"No, Hannah, I'll wait for Mom. I can calm down on my own. If not, I will take a walk or something." Sedah began toward the arch leading toward her bedroom. She tipped sideways as she walked and placed a hand on the wall to steady herself.

"Yes, but you are more drained than that. You have much to do, very quickly, and have no time for a walk. You need your strength, not to forget about your hunger with Lethe water. I'll go to the islands with your brother and get my strength back once you leave, so don't worry about me." Hannah pushed as she followed.

"Fine, but just enough to keep me going. Agreed?" Sedah had always hated how they needed to live. Where humans needed food for their life-giving energy, her family needed emotional energy. It was a curse that they had been born with, and had to be taught to use properly. If they took too much of a person's energy, they could put them into a coma until their bodies were replenished with oxygen. Her mother had warned her that if she must take from a human, to take only what was needed, or take from a person already close to death so as not to disturb the balance. Water from the pool of Lethe helped in forgetting about the hunger and kept it at bay.

Knowing Hannah was right, Sedah turned back, making Hannah stop also. "I'll take some now and some before I leave, so you will be unaffected until Sephir can take you to the islands with him," Sedah said seriously as she stared into Hannah's green eyes, looking for any doubt.

Hannah closed her eyes and waited with the complete trust Sedah had earned over time. With the reassurance that she could not kill her already dead servant, Sedah calmed her racing mind. Reaching within herself, she felt her power expand to surround her. Laying her hand where Hannah's heart would have been when alive, Sedah let her power flow down her arm, through her hand. Hannah's energy responded, and Sedah's fingertips tingled as the first strand of power sought out Hannah's energy.

Instantly, the flow of power connected the two women together like a hand grabbing rope, pulling that rope of power into Sedah. She watched Hannah and determined how much she could take based on Hannah's essence. A few strands of her beautiful, waist length, blonde hair stood on end as Sedah's energy began to pull at hers.

Once she had taken all that she dared, Sedah slowly broke the connection physically, willing the strands of energy to naturally break apart. Pulling the power slowly back within herself, she effectively shut the power box off for the moment.

Sedah watched Hannah open her eyes and look at her body. She was barely translucent. "You could have taken more, Miss."

"I'm good for now, Thank you though," Sedah told her friend. "Could you go get me some regular water though?" Nodding, Hannah left to do her mistress's bidding.

"Let my brother know that you will need to go with him whenever he decides to return," she told Hannah when she came back with the water. Seeing this as her cue, Hannah bowed and silently left her charge.

Never really needing sleep, there were endless hours of time, so there was no reason not to do something whenever you wanted. Hell had no way to distinguish day or night. Different parts of Hell had different climates, but nothing more. The grounds around the castle and Erebus had a constant, gentle breeze with a sky that Persephone had once said, resembled the human world at dawn and sunset.

Still feeling somewhat melancholy, Sedah went to her grand piano and began to play. She knew how to play many instruments thanks to the inhabitants of the realm. Any time she had expressed the wish to learn any subject, hobby, skill, or instrument, her father had found someone either in Elysium, the fortunate islands, or even the Asphodel fields to tutor her until she was either satisfied, bored, or wanted to learn something else. She was beginning to wonder why she had never had teachers from this new, modern world she kept hearing about.

Starting out playing some Beethoven, then flowing into Bach, both of whom had taught her personally, Sedah eventually heard a knock on her door. This time it would be her mother. She changed into Persephone's favorite song as a way to tell her mom to come in without having to say the words.

Entering silently, her mother walked over to the piano, listening to her daughter play before acknowledging her mother's presence. She smiled at Persephone as she played the last note.

"Thank you, sweetheart. I always love to hear you play, and dream about it often when I am away. Your brothers only wanted to learn history. Your sisters had to study humans and had time for nothing else. You always were my little artist." She sat down on the stool beside Sedah and gave her a reassuring half hug. "I heard you had some questions for me."

"Yes. Quite a few, actually," Sedah admitted nervously.

"Well, I won't be able to answer all of them, probably, but I'll answer what I can," she told her daughter. She never liked to lie to her children, and she didn't now. Sure enough, Sedah turned red and bolted up in frustration. She walked around blindly as she considered what she needed to know the most.

"Guess I'll start off with the practical questions then. Might as well get those out of the way. When do we leave?"

"Thirteen meals if you eat all of them. Four days in human terms."

Sedah paced back and forth between her piano and the nearest window and she decided which of her questions to ask. "How do I pack? Is it one case for each place, or do I have to pack it all and let it sit in the woods for an entire year?"

"One for each place, although the nymphs will want you to wear their more natural clothes, so do not pack too much for there. Your trunk for Poseidon's palace will be delivered, but I would pack it now, unless you'd like your brothers to do it for you." Persephone frowned, walking over to sit on the sofa.

"Like Hannah would let that happen! How long will I have to stay with the nymphs?"

"I was this way for a year, so probably the same. I know the concept of time means nothing here, but you will become used to it after a while." Sedah stopped pacing to turn and stare at her mother in abject horror. Persephone continued quickly before Sedah could speak. "More of my powers will also emerge within this year if you follow in my footsteps. Once you stop showing your emotions as color, you will go to Poseidon. That includes any other powers that you may come into. The nymphs will judge whether you are ready or not."

"Will I know which of his children I am to serve before my teaching is over?" Sedah sat on the floor, deflated, facing her mom.

"That will be up to Poseidon dear." Persephone's jaw tightened. "Your father made the deal while I was away, knowing full well that I would not approve.

"What about finding love in one year? Are there any specifications, limitations, or loopholes that I should know about beforehand?" Sedah threw her body back to lie down and look at her ceiling. "We all know how the Gods *love* those!"

"Those, I must see about myself." Persephone sighed. "All I know is that the one you love must not only truly love you back, but profess that love openly. Otherwise, the deal is not complete, and you are still bound to servitude or marriage."

"In other words, don't be pushy if I do find love. Got it. But if or when I do find love, do I get to return home? Will I stay on earth? What?" She sat up on her elbows, looking at her mother with hope.

"That would be determined by the manner of the . . . person. Olympians could return, but you risk being found out eventually. Humans could not if they are fully human. Like I said, we will see when or if it happens. You never know what the fates have for us. They know all, though others do not."

"Why was this deal struck in the first place, Mom?" Sedah stood, frustration outweighing despair.

"Basically, Poseidon saw Lexur when he went above. He needed help and agreed not to tell Zeus about you children if Hades helped him out. As the daughter with the powers most like mine, you are going to start having complications living down here. I had already told your father that you should be able to experience earth like a teenager instead of toiling your days here. Your brothers have duties. Your sisters are allowed above because Mom knows about them, and they can cloak themselves while performing their duties if they need to, but you do not have either of those. I guess the deal with Poseidon was a way to handle you going above so that you would not want to go native. We both know how your dad and uncles feel about mortals."

"Seems unfair, but thank you for thinking I'm grown enough to handle going to earth on my own." Sedah walked to her bedroom and touched her trunk at the end of the bed. Instantly, a replica of it appeared beside her chair that was located in the middle of her parlor. As they talked, she went about the bedroom, touching things that would be instantly replicated inside of the trunk. A nice spaghetti strapped top, and her favorite leather pants were some of the first to go in.

"Do not get me wrong, you will have difficulties, as well as meet beings you have never heard of before. But you are the daughter of a God and Goddess. As such, you will have powers to aid you, should you have need of them. Do not let anyone disrespect you. You may have to be careful for now, but you should still be respected as the Goddess that you are."

"Father isn't going to cap my powers, is he? Or give me a bodyguard?" The last thing Sedah needed was to get caught talking to a guard and have someone saying she had imaginary friends, or thinking that she was crazy.

"He said that he would not do either one unless he needed or was forced to. But you will have to come up with a cover story for when you meet new people. Having a friend there to back you up doesn't sound like a bad thing. I'm not fond of the nymphs, as you know, but I much prefer you to be in their care than on your own."

"Apparently, I have a year to think about it. We'll see how well I become acclimated to everything." Sedah sighed in confused defeat.

"Well, I'll let you get packed." Persephone gracefully stood and walked over to Sedah, who stood motionless in front of an open dresser drawer. Persephone kissed Sedah on the back of her head, materialized a tray of eggs and toast on the piano stool, and left as silently as she had entered.

Sedah remained at her dresser, reflecting on everything imaginable. She still had many questions needing to be answered, and not a single person to answer any of them for her. She could have asked her mom, but they would have been there for hours, which was not fair to her mother, who had packing of her own to do. Then there were the questions she had still been too shocked to even think of asking: simple questions about the earth itself, like the climate, temperatures, elements, clothes, and seasons needed answering so that she could better pack for the journey. Then were questions about the culture, people, technology, and laws, which she guessed the nymphs would have to answer for her.

Nymphs, for all their forest living, were very up to date on everything that happened in the populated areas around them. They had to be, to have kept their forests safe and animals from becoming extinct for millennia. They really weren't given enough credit in the Olympian society, from what her grandmother had once said.

Then there was this business with Poseidon and children to contend with. Poseidon was just like any of the Olympian Mega Gods, all six or seven of them—she wasn't really sure the number. He cheated on his spouse regularly with humans and immortals alike, just like his brother, Zeus. Some had come to have hundreds of sons and daughters through these unions. Who knew which of the children she would end up serving if she had to live on land instead of in the sea.

She was thankful her mother had nipped that in the bud, quite literally, almost immediately upon being bound to Hades. Sedah hated to think of all those half siblings everywhere. She had enough to deal with, with three brothers and two sisters.

As far as her studies told her, Poseidon had about fifty children in total, but only eleven to his wife Amphitrite. Of those eleven, ten were girls and only one was a boy. She knew nothing of their ages, rank, duties, birth line, or demeanor. These unknowns left an entire list of questions all on their own, which was so long she had no hope of ever asking them all.

Better to put that list in the back of her mind until reason or time came to pull it back out. Sedah smiled as she got the image of a mental trunk gobbling it up and locking it away for later.

Realizing that she was smiling, Sedah pulled herself out of her thoughts and resumed packing. Her grandmother made the world cold and frigid when Persephone was here visiting, so she assumed it would be warm and peaceful when Persephone was back. She missed three meals with the family while she took her time alternating between packing her trunks and getting lost in one train of thought or another. Hannah brought them to Sedah's wing to eat when she desired.

The next two meals were spent in silence, for the most part. Lunch had been silent, her father and mother speaking with their eyes. Dinner was spent with her brothers and sisters trying to cheer her up, but giving up eventually when nothing could seem to draw her out of the protective bubble that she had firmly locked herself in.

Sedah had no idea of what lay ahead, and only glimpses of what the earth had at one time looked like from the river of memory, which bordered her mom's gardens. She locked herself in her room for the next day and a half, dividing the time between all of her instruments.

The morning of the fourth day brought mixed emotions. She took a walk around Damos Hadou, the Dominion of Hades, passing through the orchards as she tried to sort them out. First and foremost, she was angry at being kept in the dark. Not having a say over your own fate was infuriating. Looking out over the many different areas of the Underworld that her family held rule over and kept safe, she wondered if she would ever see it again. That thought just brought on a wave of sadness that had her struggling not to break down and cry.

On the way back to the palace, she took the long way

around, cutting through the Stygian Marsh to gather big branches for the dogs. Cerberus lay on their side, resting, yet ever watchful. The second Sedah turned the corner, one of the heads turned her way.

"Hey boy! How are you this morning?" She smiled. Cerberus rolled and stood, two of the three heads turning her way, while one stayed forever vigilant. The dogs' black coat gleamed in the light, causing Sedah to smile at the dirt it shook off as it stood.

"Lucy, Lila, here you go." She tossed the two heads their individual logs to munch on. "Lila, will you take over so Tom can have his?" she asked the middle head. Lila immediately obeyed, log staying firmly in her mouth. His duty covered, the left head turned to Sedah, tongue hanging out in expectation of a treat.

"Hey Tom, are you being a good brother? Don't let these girls boss you around." She said. Tom nodded his head as he hung on to his log. "Well, I've got to get back. I just wanted to spoil you three one last time." She took a few steps back to better see all three heads without having to stare up.

"Cerberus!" she said loudly enough for them to hear over their snacking. Instantly, all three heads focused, turning towards her, as one unit. "Take good care of the family. Do your job flawlessly and I will see if I can bring you a treat back with me, okay?" As one, as Cerberus, they barked in understanding.

"Good dog." She said, reaching up and patting the dogs' stomach before she walked toward the front gate and to the dining room where her family was waiting.

"THERE YOU ARE, YOUNG LADY!" HADES BELLOWED AS SOON as she came in the front door. "Your mother is leaving here early, so that you can be escorted to the forest safely, and you have the audacity to show up late!"

"Pluton! It is of no importance." Persephone snapped at him.

"Your time here is cut off shorter than usual, and she doesn't even care." He gestured with his hand in Sedah's direction while looking at his wife. If he didn't want her to leave with him in the doghouse, he needed to calm down. Calling him "the rich one" told him he was on thin ice. It wasn't the first time Sedah had seen her mother pull that card, and it certainly wouldn't be the last.

"I just took a last look around and said goodbye to the dog! Who knows when I will be allowed back! If you have your way, I may never come back home!" Sedah yelled back to her father. She could barely see through the tears that she refused to shed in front of him.

"Of course, you're allowed home! Mom will check on you and give you a way to come home when the nymphs or Poseidon allows it. If there is an emergency, Hannah put some coins in both of your trunks for Charon to ferry you across." Milos straightened to his full six-foot, two-inch height as he defended their father. His blue eyes flared with an immortal light at the audacity of his sister questioning their father.

"I hate to rush you sweetheart, but the forest near Edgemont is a long way away. It will take a full day to get there, because I want to travel like a normal human would, so that you can get a small look at Earth and its technologies. Tell everyone goodbye while I talk to your father." She pulled Hades away from the children.

"You came close to being on my shit list," Persephone kissed her husband goodbye while chastising him.

"I know, my love. My mouth runs away with me. I knew she was leaving, yet I couldn't stop myself. I'm sorry sweetheart." Hades held his wife hip to hip, needing to be as close as possible for whatever time he had left with her.

"She just needs time, Hades. None of us know what is going to happen. All we know is that the fates told us we needed to do this, if we wanted her to live and the children to stay secret. I assume that somehow, if we don't, the children will be found out, a fight will ensue, and our daughter will be lost to us. So we will do this, and we will make it as easy a transition as possible, understand?" She eyed her husband pointedly.

"Yes, I get it." He smiled and gave her a final kiss as Sedah walked up with her head down.

"Goodbye sweetie, I'm sorry I snapped at you for something so small. Do you forgive me?" He looked down at his little girl, the one he'd told Persephone the night before had become a woman right in front of his eyes. She silently nodded, going to him for a tight hug. He returned it wholeheartedly. Who knew when he might hold her again?

"Baby, we have to go, or we'll be late," Persephone reminded her husband. Reluctantly, Hades let Sedah go, kissing her forehead as she stepped back. Persephone shrunk Sedah's clothing chest and slipped it into the pocket of her long, flowing blue dress.

Hades, Milos, Lexur, Sephir, Melinoe, Makaria, as well as Hannah, in the shadows, watched their family members walk out of the hall.

❈ 3 ❈

There were more tunnels leaving the Underworld than Sedah knew, and that was saying a lot, since she had lived here her entire life. She had walked every inch of the place, or so she'd thought.

They had passed Cerberus and gone down to the dock to be picked up by Charon. Instead of taking the usual route to the main entrance, he poled to the right, down the river Archeron. Since her mother did not correct him, Sedah said nothing.

They turned right at the fork before reaching the Restless Dead, and Persephone pointed. Seeing her intention, Sedah gathered her things and prepared to dock on the shore. The boat slid silently against the coal colored sand. Still saying nothing, Persephone stepped out of the boat, and waited for Sedah. Once she was out, they continued walking; Sedah still had no idea where they were headed. There was a worn-down path from the beach, going all the way up and around a huge hill with an old house on it. Just when Sedah was about to complain, she saw a split in the path and a guard standing at attention.

"We wish to pass, by order of Hades, Ruler of the Domos Underworld." Persephone said to the guard evenly as they walked up to the split. With these words, the guard was forced to obey. Without saying these words, one touch of the guard's spear would send a being right into Hades's grand hall for punishment. If only Persephone had known that when she'd first attempted to escape. She laughed to herself. This exit was placed here by Eros so he could come and go as he pleased, though he did not have to recite the words since he had helped create everything here. The blue gate that resembled an eye glowed in recognition whenever he came near it.

"The right path, My Queen, will take you to the exit point you seek," the older guard replied formally. Sedah wondered, looking at his armor as he spoke, if he had been part of the Hungarian war against Conrad the Second. He certainly had the accent.

"Thank you," Persephone said as they continued, choosing the direction that the guard for Eros indicated.

"Now Sedah, when we get to the door and enter Earth, there will be many things that will seem very overwhelming at first. Take it all in slowly. Once you are adjusted, we will continue. I will try to explain what I can as we go along but you are bright enough to understand at least the basics of what it all does." As she finished speaking, they branched to the right and reached an old wooden door set into a rock wall. She looked at her daughter in expectation.

Not sure she was ready, but knowing she had no choice, Sedah took a deep breath to calm her racing heart, letting the breath out slowly as she nodded to indicate that she was ready.

"Here we go," Persephone said as she opened the door and stepped into the blackness. Taking a huge gulp, Sedah followed. "All of our exits come out at different areas of the earth, and always through a door to somewhere not overly stimulating, like this alley, as it is called. Never go into one of these without someone else with you, or you might get hurt." She told Sedah as she followed her mother through the briefest patch of darkness into the alleyway.

"So where are we exactly?" Sedah looked around and above her, confused. The opening was just big enough for Cerberus to walk through. There were brick walls on each side of the alley, rising almost as high as their palace back home. *Why would two palaces be built with so little space between them?*

"This is the back entrance to a small pizzeria that I love. To be more exact, though, we are in a part of America, which is a country on Earth, in what is known as the Smoky Mountains. This town is called Pigeon Forge, Tennessee. I picked it because it's a tourist town. Your looking around would not seem so out of place here."

"So where are we heading?"

"We are going to the Nantahala National Forest. I wanted you to stay someplace beautiful, and this is my favorite. There is a river nearby that people frequent, so you can use your lessons and mingle with humans once you are ready."

"How long will it take to get there from where we are?" They began to walk to the opening of the alley.

"Around two hours or so. I want to stay here today and spend the night. Then we will rent a car and drive to Nanty, as the locals call it." She stopped at the opening to allow Sedah to get acclimated.

"Is this how the world looks?" Sedah studied everything around her.

"Today, these buildings are over a century out of date. This is the tourist area. We will walk around here so that later tonight, you will understand a little better where the current technology evolved from."

"What is this tourist place called? What makes people

come here other than its beauty?" She took a few tentative steps forward.

"To these people, it is the beauty and the curiosity of the past, while being able to use their technology of today." Persephone said as they started off, pointing out the people walking around with flat, rectangular things in their hands that they tapped with their fingers.

"So, the place in front of us here is a mill? What are they now if this is considered old?" Sedah looked at her mother after reading the information sign.

"Now, there are things called factories. Instead of that General Store," She pointed out as they walked, "there are stores that sell just clothes or food as well as stores that are as big as one thousand of these general stores." Persephone walked around Thunder Gap and other places in Dolly-World, explaining what the buildings were and how they related to things in today's world, until it was time for the park to close.

"Where do we go now? Do we have some place to stay?" Sedah turned around, looking at her mother in worry.

"You rode in the train going through the park, now you will experience something called a car. The yellow ones are called a cab or a taxi, where you pay for someone to take you where you tell them to go. Never get in one without money, or knowing where you are going, okay?" She held up her hand to wave down a nearby waiting taxi. Sedah noted the method of flagging them for later use.

Sedah waited patiently behind her mom's outstretched hand holding her back, until the vehicle stopped. Persephone opened the door and Sedah got in, but only after her mom's signal.

"The nearest hotel from here is fine," Persephone told the cab driver once she had followed her daughter into the back seat of the car.

Once they had been dropped off, Persephone got them into a hotel and settled for the night. She spent hours explaining anything she could or that Sedah had questions about. She also gave her daughter a one, five, ten, twenty, fifty, and a one-hundred-dollar bill to have so that she could replicate them for living expenses.

By the time they had checked out of the hotel the next morning and gotten into another cab, Sedah had a good head start on being prepared for the human world once her powers were under control. At the least, the nymphs wouldn't think her as naive as she actually was.

The cab driver drove the women down US-441 and all its small, winding roads once Persephone proved she had enough cash. Suddenly Sedah realized something, letting out a sudden gasp. "Mom, I haven't changed since I have been here!"

"You didn't lose it honey, *I've just . . . fixed it, for now. I still see it, but no one else. You'll get it back in the forest, once I leave,*" she explained mentally after catching the driver's apprehensive glance back at them.

"We're here, ladies," the cab driver announced. "That will be $232.58." He waited expectantly. Replicating the correct bills out of sight, Persephone thanked the man and got out.

"We'll be secluded enough by nightfall that no human can find us. That is when the nymphs will show themselves and I will take the cover of normalcy off you," Persephone explained as they passed the sign that signaled the entrance to the forest. Even though it wasn't necessary, they walked most of the way, deciding that it was nice enough out to do so.

Dusk settled. Deciding to stop, Sedah set out her small bundle of possessions. She sat on the ground and leaned against a tree as Persephone finally took the glamor off her daughter. Looking at their things, the women both willed them to expand back to their original size. Sedah sat down on a fallen tree trunk.

"Should we set up a fire to let them know that we are here?" Sedah asked as she looked up into the canopy of the trees.

A woman seemingly appeared out of the sky, causing Sedah to jump and fall backwards off the trunk she had been sitting on. Once the woman landed, facing Sedah, others descended the same way, landing just as silently as the first. This time, Sedah saw that they actually came from the huge trees above her. Looking over to her mother, Sedah realized that, at some point during all of this, Persephone had instinctively gotten up and into a defensive position.

Once it became clear that these were just the nymphs, Persephone leaned back against the tree, appearing relaxed. She kept her piercing glare on the leader of the nymphs.

"A signal will not be necessary. We know all and see all that comes into our forest," the first woman said slowly, never taking her eyes off Sedah. Sedah stared up at the woman. She had piercing green eyes, as did most of the nymphs, it seemed, with jet black straight hair that was braided down past her butt.

"There was no need to scare my daughter, Jade. She knows very little of this realm." Persephone took a step toward Jade. Instantly, the women around them also took a step, making the circle smaller. Jade raised her hand to signal a halt before ever turning around to look at Persephone.

"She will not hurt me, sisters; we *are* trading daughter for daughter after all. I will do as I said, and you will return my daughter to me as payment. But while here, your daughter will hunt prey and do the things required of other nymphs. If you have any objections, then take her and go. If not, we will return for her at dawn. I suggest you say your goodbyes before then." Using the log Sedah had fallen from as a platform to launch herself into the canopy above, Jade and the others disappeared into the trees as silently as they had appeared.

"Well, she's a cyclops of a nymph," Sedah spat out as she turned red in anger. She slowly got to her feet and wiped the dust and dirt off the hem of her shirt. "So now what?"

"Well, here are coats for the chill of the mountains at night." Persephone expanded the small objects to their original size before handing one to her daughter. "I'll set up an ethereal fire to keep us warm, which won't harm the land. That should make Jade happy, since she has someone watching us."

Persephone pulled two small, cylindrical objects, out of her pack. Placing one on each side of the floating green fire, Persephone slowly grew the sleeping bags to their true size. Sedah untied hers and quickly crawled inside with her clothes and coat still on. This place had warm days and cold nights, but Sedah was used to the Underworld's constant warmth. The only place hotter were the punishment fields of Tartarus.

Sedah started thinking of the tepees that she had seen on the way there. Her mother had explained that the native people had lived in the cone shaped shelters to keep them warm at night. Closing her eyes and imagining being warm in one of those, Sedah could feel herself growing warmer. She was almost asleep when she heard her mother gasp.

"What?" Sedah groaned, stretching the word out in annoyance.

"Did you do this, Sedah?" Persephone sounded a little worried.

"Do what, Mom?" Sedah snuggled further into her sleeping bag without even bothering to look.

"Well, open your eyes and see!" Her mom's annoyance with her had Sedah reluctantly obeying and sitting up on one elbow.

"What? How did this get here? Wait, how'd you know what I was wishing for?" Sedah looked up, her skin going white and yellow in both happiness and alarm as she looked around her. They were inside a cone of wooden poles, encircled in a fabric of some kind, keeping in the heat.

"Trust me when I say, I didn't. I could be wrong here, but it seems to me either another power has emerged, or your replicating skills has evolved in this realm. Either way, I think your need for warmth activated something in your powers." Her neutral tone made Sedah wonder whether the manifestation was a good or bad development. Unsure, she said nothing, laid her head back down on the sleeping bag and went back to sleep.

❦

NOT KNOWING WHETHER SEDAH HAD GAINED A NEW power, or her current ones had evolved, Persephone left the incident alone. She would know, soon enough, by keeping in touch with the nymphs through Apollo. It would be her only way to keep tabs on Sedah during the months with her mother. She could ask one of her sisters, but her older sister, Athena, was a daddy's girl. Her younger sister, Aphrodite, was still pissed off for making her drink Lethe water to forget the kids and was not speaking to her, even though she didn't know why. Apollo hated his parents and had drunk water from the river Styx to ensure he kept the secret. He had always loved his niece and helped when he could. Her curiosity would have to be enough for now.

Not able to fall asleep now, Persephone spent all night watching her youngest child deep in slumber, colors gently shifting as she dreamed. Whatever life would bring to her next, Sedah would face alone, and that scared Persephone to death.

Persephone shrunk the tepee down to fist size and set it in her bag as the first few rays of sun began to paint the morning sky. When it was time to get up, she pecked small, quick kisses all over Sedah's face and head until she had her daughter giggling.

"Why do I feel so sleepy, Momma? I hardly ever sleep at home."

Sedah groaned as she turned over to look face to face. "Will I get to see you again?"

Persephone pushed a piece of hair out of Sedah's eyes. "Your body is adjusting to this realm. You will sleep like mortals do now, as well as get cuts and bruises that will take time to heal. You should not tire out like a mortal, but practicing can drain you here, so stay replenished with sleep. Learn from the nymphs, even when you are not being instructed, because you never know what could be of use." Falling into silence, mother and daughter stared at one another while the morning sky changed above them.

Sensing that the time was at hand, Sedah and Persephone got up and packed camp. "No pun intended sweetheart, but please don't be so blue. You'll see me in eight months, but I will be keeping tabs on your progress if you truly need me. I leave Mom now and then to accept great people into the Underworld. If you need me to, I can swing by and check on you."

"No, Mom, I'll be fine. I asked for time away and you've given me that chance. They will keep me from harm, and knowing you're checking in on me is reassuring if I get scared or worried. I'll be fine, really." Sedah hung on to her mother's hands. Persephone knew that face: the one Sedah used when she was trying to convince herself as well as her mother.

"I'd say that you are just trying to make me feel better, but I see you're not as blue anymore; more baby than navy blue is a better look for you too."

"That I'll take as a compliment, I guess. This is one thing I wish I hadn't gotten from you, no offense."

"None taken; that is actually a gift from grandmother D, not that you can go and tell her what you think about it and her. I'll give her hell for you while I'm there this year." Persephone smiled, causing Sedah to laugh at the thought as she launched herself into her mom's arms.

"Isn't this a nice picture? The Iron Queen, hugging her daughter of the damned. One that she can't even be proud enough of to take home to mommy," a different nymph from yesterday stated, causing both women to jump.

Persephone and Sedah turned as one to face the nymph standing in front of them, with a smirk on her face and her arms crossed in front of her. Although she seemed young in appearance, she exuded a feeling of being older. She looked like a pissed off Fury standing there, looking down on them from the tree limb. She had bouncy, jet black hair that came to about breast level, with a severe right-sided part that hung forward to partially cover her eye, and for good reason. Closely set almond shaped eyes showed a vertical slit composed of an array of diamond shaped dots that reminded Persephone of a gecko.

"Okay, before you say another word, tree hugger, let me warn you that if you don't shut your mouth, either my mom will use her powers and turn you into something without a mouth, or I will just beat the fire and brimstone out of you until you can't talk," Sedah warned, turning crimson red with pent-up fury at this girl's mockery.

Just as the girl pointed her finger and was about to say something else, another girl, looking closer to Sedah's age than the first nymph's, dropped behind the girl, putting her hand on the other nymph's shoulder. "I would heed her advice, unless you want to join Leuce in the Underworld. Jade said to play nice and bring her back. How do you plan on doing that as a tree?" the blonde-haired nymph said to the mean girl.

Looking rather perturbed, the rude girl muttered something under her breath, took a running leap, and landed on a low hanging branch. She looked back and glared at Sedah once more, before turning to disappear into the canopy of branches. Sedah visibly shivered.

"Sorry, guess I don't have to warn you about Onyx now. Her attitude is as black and hard as the stone she was named for; stay away from her group and you'll have some fun here."

"Thank you, though it really wasn't needed. And you are?" Persephone questioned as she smiled at this young nymph girl who'd come to aid them.

"Sorry, again. I am Caprika, daughter of Dionysus and Pewter, who is one of the 'Original Daughters' like Jade." She used air quotations to indicate the name all knew to describe the twelve daughters of Mother Earth.

"So Jade is expecting us?" Sedah's confusion showed throughout her skin tone when she caught the nymph's forest green eyes as they widened. Though Caprika wouldn't know what the color meant, Persephone certainly did.

"That's cool! No wait, sorry, you're a human lie detector, so that actually sucks, I guess." Caprika quickly corrected herself when Sedah got a tinge of red and a scowl on her face. "No, you say your goodbyes here and come with—I guess me now—back to camp."

Caprika stayed on the side, silently, as Persephone exchanged goodbyes and heartfelt hugs with her daughter. Persephone nodded when they were ready. Nodding back with a smile, Caprika waited for Sedah to grab her few belongings before they started walking down a path that had not been there moments before.

A FEW STEPS ONTO THE PATH, SEDAH LOOKED BACK JUST IN time to see her mother shimmer into transparency and glide back the way they had come the day before. Pulling in a deep breath to keep the tears at bay, she let it out slowly as her mother disappeared fully from sight. Like it or not, she had gotten her wish and was here now, so she had better learn to make the best of it.

4

The girls began to get acquainted as they walked. Plants and vines retracted as they approached and refilled the vacant spaces in their wake.

Sedah looked behind them in awe, "Is that normal?"

Caprika laughed. "For us woodland people, yes, I guess it is. For you, it would be abnormal if you were alone, so don't expect it. We have a link to every plant, body of water, and animal in this forest. We feel everything that they do. The plants moving is a show of respect for all that we do to ensure their survival."

"Is that why they do not move for humans?" Sedah deduced.

"Essentially. Humans harm them. Since you're in a human body, they'll respond to you the same way. Maybe after you've been with us for a while something could happen, but I doubt it." She laughed under her breath as she spoke the last words.

"How many of Gaea's daughters live here?"

"Only Jade for now. In the winter, they all will come together for the winter solstice and rotate mountain groups. We stay where we are, and our mothers move around according to Demeter's seasons in the different regions. There are twelve mountain regions, and twelve daughters to care for them. Demeter picked that to coincide with the months of the human year when the Olympian brothers were deciding who would rule what. But then, Hades pissed her off by kidnapping your mother. Since Zeus allowed it to happen, she took it out on the one thing that they had loved together other than your mother, Earth." Caprika filled in holes she doubted that Sedah knew or had ever even been told.

"So, let me see if I remember their names: Leuce, Pewter, Char, Sol, Hema, Pyr, Baux, Lapis, Jade. Who am I missing?"

"Only Mag, Fawn, and Air. Pretty good otherwise though," Caprika acknowledged. "Once we get inside camp, sit where I tell you, don't make eye contact, and don't stare at anyone, although they will all probably be staring at you. If someone likes you, they will come to you and speak first, okay?"

Sedah nodded in understanding, suddenly finding herself a little afraid of what was coming next, and the uncertainty of it all. She had to remind herself not to not be afraid, lest those like Onyx and Jade see it and use it to their advantage.

Caprika stopped at the edge of the camp, giving Sedah a moment to take it all in. Few of my sisters will give a myk'tu, which is what we call a newcomer, a chance. It's nothing against you, but few others have ever been allowed to see woodland creatures, much less live among them and learn from them. Some will see you as a gift, but most will see you as nothing more than an interloper they must put up with in order to get a fellow sister back."

Sedah looked up at the veil—shimmering, like diamonds being suspended in a rainbow of color, moving with the wind. The barrier tingled as she walked through it, making her feel as if it were sticking to her and being across her skin as she walked through. Had she not already walked through a portal when she left the Underworld, she would have been afraid that it wouldn't allow her entrance. With only a little resistance, she felt the barrier give way as they walked over to a fallen log a few feet within the barrier.

"Sit here for now, I'll go see where you will be staying while you are here." Caprika walked off without waiting for Sedah to react.

Sedah hoped that no one would come up and approach her right. She wanted to have at least one day before being bombarded by girls she did not know. One hundred and eighty years of knowing everyone around you made it hard to be receptive to new people. The Caprika girl seemed alright, but the other one was proof that they were not all so nice.

Just as Caprika had predicted, though, every person in sight stopped what they were doing and stared openly at her as she sat down, once Caprika walked away. Some faces were an open book, while others were either blank, or trying to remain so. Sedah began to turn yellow as she grew uncomfortable with all the stares aimed her way. It was a full minute or so of silence before a bird's squawk from the air seemed to startle everyone into motion again.

Even with everyone going back to their chores or jobs for the moment, Sedah still felt that she was being watched. Just as she was about to pick up her head and look around, something suddenly dropped onto her from above, causing her to fall backwards off a second log that day. With her head back on the ground, she couldn't see the heavy object squirming in her lap.

"What the—" Sedah got out as she opened her eyes and got her breath back. Nose to nose with her was a small girl, with what appeared to be an infant monkey in her hands. The first thing Sedah noticed was the weird eyes again. Gasping, she pulled back quickly. Other than the weird eyes, the little girl was otherwise normal, with a pear-shaped face that currently radiated fear and an olive complexion that went well with her dark brown hair.

"I'm sorry, I tried to float, but I only know how to float myself! Are you mad at me? Please don't turn me and Harold into a tree please!" The little girl looked fearfully at Sedah.

"Honey, what makes you think that I would do such a thing?" Sedah held onto the child as she took her legs off the log and crossed them in her lap while placing the two little ones where they could all sit more comfortably in her lap.

"That's what Onyx and her friends told me and some of the others. They said that when you get mad and turn red that you will turn us all into trees like your momma did to Sister Luece! When I fell on you, you got red." Her bottom lip quivered as unshed tears began to show in her eyes, despite her bravado.

"No sweetheart, I cannot do that even if I wanted to, which I do not. I might be able to one day, I think, though I would never do it unless someone really deserved it. Don't believe anything that you hear about me unless it comes from Caprika or myself, okay?" she tried to reassure the little girl, letting her see the truth in her eyes. "So, if this is Harold the monkey, what is your name?" she asked as she poked the little girl's belly button, making her giggle.

"She's Dustie, my youngest sister, at the moment. And she is also in trouble with me right now." Caprika walked up with eyebrows raised as she stared down at her sister. "Come on, what happened this time?" She crossed her arms, waiting.

"I couldn't float us both! He was in the middle of a jump when a bird squawked and scared him out of focus. He lost his train of thought, I guess, and didn't make it to the branch. I tried to catch him and float us, but I couldn't. She broke our fall and we saw her turn red! Onyx said that 'the outsider' would turn us into a tree like Leuce, but," she pointed at Sedah, "she said to only believe whatever her and you say about her. Now I am just confused." Dustie frowned and her brow furrowed together. Caprika bent down and looked into her younger sister's reptilian eyes.

"Well, you know better than to believe Onyx about anything, so why you listened in the first place is beyond me. Just because her mother is the one currently in charge, doesn't mean she suddenly knows more, nor has she suddenly become honest. Now get back to work and you can visit with Sedah later. She is staying in our hut, so you will be seeing her a lot."

"Yes! See you later, then. Thanks for the cushion to land on!" Dustie jumped up and ran off with Harold still in her arms.

"Work? She is only a child. How young do they start earning their food here?" Sedah couldn't keep the sarcasm out of her tone as she asked. Caprika helped her to stand.

"Fifty, why? Does that seem too old? How old were you when your mother and father gave you chores and duties to earn your keep?" Caprika indicated which way that they needed to go.

"I don't have any chores, jobs, or duties. My brothers all have very crucial jobs in the Underworld, and my sisters work is both above and below, but I never have."

"Then what do you do with your days?" Confusion came through Caprika's voice.

"There's no separation of day or night, or even of time passing in the Underworld. I spend a lot of my time with tutors learning anything that I wish to know. Since all of the great thinkers are dead, they make for great teachers while awaiting their next chance at life on Earth. My sisters like to go above often and cause mayhem when they can."

"So, you don't sleep or work, just learn?"

"My sisters and I need sleep like my mother, though not nearly as much. My brothers are like my father and have no need to sleep at all. That is part of why I am here, apparently, to see if my powers are going to be more like my mom's or my dad's. The second I began to change colors, the decision was made for me to come here just in case."

Caprika laughed. "Jade decided that since we hit it off so well today, that you could stay with Dustie and I. I think she meant it to be torture, hoping I would hate you." They stopped in front of a house. While others were simple, this one was bigger, with a shed and stalls attached to the side.

"What, no tree house like the others have?"

"Dustie's job is to care for orphaned animals so we need more room than the others do. Come on, let me show you around."

"If everyone has a job, then am I hindering you doing yours?" she followed Caprika through the front door.

"Normally, I would say yes, but Jade put my duties on Onyx for the day to punish her for her rudeness. She is old enough to know better."

"How do you age here? For me and my siblings, we only age one year physically for every ten years on Earth. Once we hit eighteen, or one hundred and eighty, depending on how you choose to look at it, we stop aging all together," Sedah asked out of curiosity. Her eyes slowly adjusted to the indoors and she surveyed the hut. To the left was a very small dining area that flowed into the kitchen. To the right was a living room with what Sedah could tell was all handmade furniture and pillows. Behind that were a few cribs, a hammock attached to a tree that was growing through the house, and the wall. Above the tree and hammock, a loft was situated over the first floor. Sedah couldn't see a second place to sleep and assumed the second level held bed for Caprika.

"Well, for us, we also do the ten years for one physical year of aging, but it goes on until we're twenty-five. Then the ten becomes one hundred," Caprika explained.

"Wow! So how old are you, then?" Sedah asked, trying to judge Caprika's age.

Caprika laughed. "I'm one hundred and ninety, if we're being exact. You?"

"One hundred and eighty overworld years, According to my mom. Only she keeps track, since she's tied to Earth time. We just see the subtle differences in ourselves over the years."

"So, back to the present. Here's where you will sleep. We'll put one up farther for Dustie to take." She pointed to the hammock. "I'll leave it up to you if you decide to switch or something. You'll work wherever you are needed, but you are my responsibility now, so once you're done with the day's work, then you'll have chores around camp. I, along with a few others will instruct you on the outside world and what you'll need to know."

"Great." Sedah drew out the word sarcastically. "So what do we do today?"

"I'm going to take you around the camp and show you all of the jobs that you will have to help out with at some point or another. There are point people that you'll report to when you're told to go do a job. As long as you are nice, respectful, and open to learning and suggestions, I see no reason why almost everyone wouldn't grow to accept you."

Nodding, Sedah allowed Caprika to introduce her to person after person, who quickly explained their jobs and answered any questions that she had for them. They visited all the nymphs that were working within the housing area. She guaged how they felt about her and her being here. Some of the questions they had for her explained the misunderstood gossip that had gone around camp already.

"Why do you know nothing of vines, weaving, weapon making, or fog? Do you not have these things in the Underworld?" a woman asked as she was instructing Sedah on how to soak reeds, so they would be flexible enough to make a suitable basket.

"These vines do not grow in the underworld since we do not have a sun or moon. There are only a few trees anywhere except for the Fortunate Islands, or in my mom's personal garden. Weapons and clothes are made for us or brought from the human world by mom so there is no reason to make our own."

That seemed to satisfy the woman, and the two girls soon moved on to the next person for yet another introduction. These women knew very little of the Underworld, which was understandable, since her father's realm was one that no one willingly spoke of unless faced with their own mortality. "Some of the ignorance you've seen today is a lack of information, but a lot of it has been the lies of Onyx and her friends," Caprika confided in her.

After a small, quick lunch of berries and greens, they walked through the outskirts of the forest. Sedah's limbs felt heavy. "Can we sit for a while?"

"It is just you having to get used to the difference in the gravity and altitude of the mountains. Plus, you're actually using your muscles, which I'm going to bet they're not used to," Caprika, with hands on her hips, told Sedah, when the young Goddess had stopped walking to lean against a tree.

Sedah slid down the trunk to the ground. "I don't care what the reason is. I am tired and want to either slow down or stop for a while and rest."

"Look, you need to learn all of the important things today so you don't make a mess of them or need someone to constantly come to your rescue. There are some plants and animals in the forest that could, and probably would, be dangerous to you, should you happen across any of them on your own in the future."

"I would rather learn tomorrow than overdo it today." Sedah mumbled, turning gray.

"I don't understand you! How do you know so much about so many other things, but know nothing about the place that you knew you were coming to? Did you not take this seriously at all?"

"All my information comes from books and talking to the newly dead in Elysium. I learned the name and descriptions of many things, but I have never actually held them or seen any of them myself if they were not in my mom's garden. There is a vast difference between being told or reading about something and actually experiencing it, am I wrong?"

"No, you aren't, and I got it. Well, I think that, other than Dustie, I've shown you those who fertilize, heal trees, animal healers and tenders, water cleaners, air cleaners, and revivers of the burnt earth. My job is to heal and fertilize in a way, too. I look at the soil and determine what it should have to be at its best."

"So, you mean you decide whether a forest lives or dies?" Sedah's mouth dropped open.

"What? No! Well, if I didn't do what I do, it eventually would, I guess. I meant that I see what it needs in order to thrive." Sedah tipped her head in confusion. "It's like this. Soil, dirt, is made up of many kinds of nutrients. It takes a certain balance of them to keep a forest healthy and thriving. When a forest slows its growth, I find out what the soil could be missing. If that still doesn't fix the problem in the area, then I know at least I did my job and then it is up to another sister, or even the Mother to handle."

"Gaea is basically Zeus, but of Earth itself. Why should she be bothered to have the final say?" Sedah was confused. She had always thought that the Gods did not deal directly with what they were the protectors of, but rather had their children and other minions take care of the problem. That way, there was always someone other than themselves to blame if or when something went wrong.

"It is a complex thing to comprehend and is best left alone," Caprika warned. "If there are parts of your family hierarchy you don't know, I don't want to be the one to piss off the gods by spilling their secrets. The part you need to know, because it's integral to our life here, is that we're all connected through Gaea. Her children were the actual beings that made the earth. Her own brother is Tartarus itself. Everything comes from her and flows through her." Once Caprika stopped talking, she raised her finger in a sign to wait, then held her arms out, palms up. Sedah would get no further answer, so she wisely shut her mouth and watched.

"As with all the others, my gift is through touch." Caprika closed her eyes, took a deep breath in and concentrated. Sedah watched as the nearby grass and weeds wrapped themselves around her legs as if giving Caprika a welcoming hug. Caprika smiled and laughed as the plants slowly unwound themselves back to normal.

"It always tickles. They say that the other side of the park area needs a little help controlling bugs, so we'll go over there and add minerals that they won't like."

"Will it not kill the bugs?"

"If Arahel doesn't get them to move on or break down into smaller groups to go to different areas of the forest, then yes. The plants say she's been there twice. If they are telling me that I'm needed, either the damage is already done, or the animals refuse to listen. Better to kill bugs than my sisters. I'll take you back to Dustie, since you say you're tired, and you can help her until dinner."

Sedah panicked at the thought of dinner with only one friend in the entire camp there. She'd met many women that day, but who knew which of them really hated her and who would simply tolerate her? "What if I wanted to go with you to see you work? Could I come with you?" she asked while getting to her feet hastily, forgetting how worry and fear would show in her skin color, so Caprika would know how she really felt.

"To get there safely, I have to take to the trees, and you can't do that yet. You said that you're tired, and I don't have the time to teach you today. We'll start on that first thing in the morning, unless something comes up," Caprika planned aloud as she turned back in the direction of their home.

"I assume that people flying through the trees are not a common occurrence, even in the forest, correct? So how do you keep from being seen by the humans?"

Caprika laughed, "No, it's not, but that's from being one with nature. The trees hide us most of the time, and we're camouflaged if someone should see through that."

"Is that why all of you have weird eyes and wear outfits made of leaves, vines, twigs, limbs and bark?" Sedah asked, gesturing up and down at Caprika's outfit. She loved the way the reeds intertwined with vines to make a basket-shaped skirt that was flexible as well as durable. "Did I see some nymphs with it growing out of their skin?" Sedah had to ask now that they were alone.

She began to note the differences between the women as she had been introduced to them earlier. Some had seemed like the vines and bark were actually growing out of their skin, while some just wore it as clothing. She had noticed Onyx and Caprika's outfits weren't attached, but had thought better of asking until now. Caprika seemed almost human compared to some of the women.

While Caprika had long blond hair that reached the top of her thighs and an hourglass figure, under her amazing dress, some of the other women in camp had hair made of weeping willow, full gowns made of leaves, or arms and legs that looked like tree trunks with only their hands and feet visible.

"Yes, they are growing out of my sisters." Caprika laughed. "The green hair and clothing not only helps us blend, but is actually an extension of the tree we belong to. I am a mountain nymph, or Oreiad. My tree is a pine." She stopped walking and closed her eyes. In a cascade, blonde hair shifted into dark green pine needles before Sedah's eyes. After a few moments, she reversed it and the blonde hair returned. "It helps to blend if I need to, but it gets prickly and uncomfortable fast. Since we're on the edge of the forest, the meadow nymphs choose to live among us, sharing our camp. They share clothing and food with us, so we can be more comfortable.

"Our skin is also unique. Every cell is like the bark on a tree, or the scales of a deep-diving fish. They're reflective and turn brown or green if we feel like we're in danger. It helps us look like a ray of sun shining through the canopy or as part of the foliage if someone's too close."

"So how do you hide your homes from them? Or yourselves when you are in the camp?"

"Why all of the questions about us suddenly?" Caprika countered as they stepped over a rather large fallen limb to enter the camp and continued toward the cottage.

"If I get seen, I need to know if I will be the only one seen or if any of you will be seen with me.

"Guess you got me there. Now I have to answer you, where I'd planned on just ignoring you." Caprika grinned. She had a sense of humor? Sedah chuckled without thinking. "Like now, with you, I could choose to be seen or not. Those same flakes or bark are controllable. We don't do it often as it drains our energy, but it would depend on the situation and who you were with," she finished as they reached the cottage.

"Or we could simply disappear into a tree, depending on the species of nymph.

"Okay, what about the question of how the camp is hidden?"

"If you didn't notice as we entered camp, then you'll find out another day. You should've been able to answer your own question on that one."

"Answer your own question on what one, Caprika?" Dustie asked innocently as she walked out of the cottage.

"How we keep home a secret," Caprika informed her little sister before turning to address Sedah. "I should be back before dinner. If I'm not, listen to Dustie; she'll instruct you in protocol."

"Bye," Dustie said impatiently, taking and pulling on Sedah's hand as Caprika turned to go. She couldn't be sure, but Sedah thought for sure that the corner of Caprika's mouth turned up as she turned and walked away.

"Where are we going, little one?" Sedah asked as she realized they were not going in or staying near the hut.

"To collect a hurt animal that a sister told me about. One of the brothers is helping me out."

"I didn't know there were men here! Have they been out all day? Is that why I haven't seen any of them yet?" Sedah's questions came rolling out, one after another.

"They have their own encampment somewhere in the forest. They can never find our entrance twice and we can't find theirs. It's a protection by the forest. It plays games to keep us safe, even from others of our kind, so that neither can invade or dominate over the other."

"Do they ever hide your entrance from you? I would hate to get locked out and lost."

"While you're a stranger, you should never be alone."

"So what animal are we helping that we would need a man's assistance?" Sedah changed the subject, not wanting to think about the length of time that she would be forced to be here.

"A baby cougar."

"How is it hurt?"

"Not sure exactly. She said it was a kitten. The mother could not help it back up the mountain and sent a distress call. When Amy got there, a male cougar would not let her get closer, so I sent a call to my brother counterpart."

"Aren't you a little young to be handling dangerous creatures though, even if it is a baby?"

This caused Dustie to giggle. "I was considered young at twenty. I'm on my way to being a pro now."

"How old are you then? You can't be more than eighty if you are still getting and practicing your powers."

"Try one hundred and twenty, sister." she scoffed.

Sedah's eyebrows lifted in surprise. "So, how long have you been doing this?"

"Everyone comes into their first sign of their particular duty at around fifty years old. The mother gives you the gift at birth. Between fifty and sixty, it begins to show itself, and at one hundred, it begins to emerge."

"How many are there that share your duty, then?"

"It varies, really, but we have three, including myself, at the moment. The mother takes and gives life for different reasons, but there are always enough of us to handle it all." Dustie took two more steps before stopping and holding up a hand to signal Sedah to stop as well. "We're close now. Amy says that they just raised their heads, so they can sense us."

"What do we do?"

Just as Dustie turned around to answer her, Sedah felt something hard press up against her, like a second skin, from shoulder blades to buttocks. Surprised, she tried to turn around only to have two large, powerful hands grab her shoulders firmly from behind. She tried for a few moments in vain to lessen the hold, but they only increased their pressure until she was forced by pain to cease her attempts.

"You could keep doing that, but then we would have to send the little one away," a husky male voice whispered into her ear.

"Kohl! Quit scaring her. We have work to do." Dustie glowered at the male, her arms crossed at her chest in impatience.

"Do you really think you could stop me?" He stepped back from, then around Sedah, stopping in between the two girls. "So, what are we doing today? I feel male aggression nearby."

"One of your males won't let us near the female and the female won't let him near the kitten."

"Sounds like he was trying to kill the kitten. Either the baby's a male that the adult sees as a threat, or the female's simply in heat."

"Well, cougars are so endangered, the kitten will be saved either way. The male will just have to back off this time. I take care of infant animals, so go deal with your male."

"And where will you be while we take care of this?" Kohl turned his full gaze onto Sedah.

"She will be a safe distance away and tucked behind a tree, in case any of the cats decide to climb instead of run."

"Fine then, let's just do this." Kohl sighed dramatically.

Only after Dustie told her where to go to safely stand and watch did Sedah let out the breath that she had been holding in for the last few minutes. As she watched the two work, she thought over what had just happened.

This Kohl guy wouldn't know it, but he was her first male physical contact on Earth. Having his body firmly against hers had sent shivers down her entire body and a range of so many emotions at once that she was sure she probably looked a bit like a rainbow.

When he passed her and she got a good look at him, she was a little confused. His ears were more pointed than the female nymphs. He was bare chested with only pants on, made of sackcloth material. She almost gasped at the strange, long horse tail that he had. He was a handsome male from the waist up, but he did not cause more of those shivers when she looked at him in full.

Growing up with only her close family and spirits for male company, her father and brothers were the only males that she could physically touch. All of her teachers and the servants tingled if she touched them, that numb feeling a person gets when a leg or foot falls asleep. Hades would give the tutors a dose of his energy so that they could help Sedah with her lessons for as long they needed, but once the energy was depleted, the spirit would become translucent once again, and leave.

The feelings that Kohl gave off made those pins and needles feelings seem tame. This guy was taller than she was, with wavy black hair and visible muscles that were now taut as he spoke to, and warred with, the male cougar.

She watched as he coaxed the male a small distance away from the female and kitten with fluid motions of confidence that could only come with practice. Once he had the male at a distance that seemed safe, Dustie stepped in, grabbed the kitten and began to walk toward the tree that the nymph named Amy had apparently been in the entire time. Once Amy jumped down and took possession of the kitten, the female cougar yipped toward her before running off with the male. Kohl smiled as he watched the pair run off. He turned to the girls as Sedah stepped out from behind the tree.

"Why were you not down here to help them?" Sedah asked Amy, surprising even herself at the reproachful tone in her voice as she held the nymph's almond shaped golden stare with her own.

"I was watching in case things went the other way, myk'tu, not that I really even need or have to explain any of this to you." Amy swung her long brown hair over her shoulder. Sedah winced. Amy was rightfully defensive at Sedah's tone and the implication that she had not been doing her job.

"I'm sorry, it just seems too dangerous for only two people to hande. I didn't see you up there until after the incident was already over. Look, let's change the subject. Why did she abandon her kitten? Is that why they are almost extinct, because they just don't care about their children?" She looked from one to another to see who would answer her.

"She'll come later for this little one. They are just going to have some fun together," Amy answered, hiding her slight blush by playing with the kitten.

"Since she had a girl, she needs to take advantage of a male being in the area while she's in heat again. There are so few, they can go years without seeing another of their kind," Dustie said matter-of-factly.

"They'll go romp and play at least a few times today alone." Kohl said. His voice husky, his eyes seemed to devour Sedah as he took a smooth step toward her.

Apprehensive, Sedah took a step back. Amy stepped over to her as if Kohl were not there, giving the small animal to Sedah. "Time to earn your keep, myk'tu. You'll need to find her a place in the camp until I can find a Mountain Lion or another cougar that will take her in if her mother doesn't come back for a little while." She looked over her shoulder at Kohl, "Thanks, but we will take it from here."

The dismissal obvious, Kohl gave her a look of disgust. "Sure. I will be seeing you again, new girl." He grinned with a sinister sweetness that never reached his eyes toward Sedah before turning on his heel, galloping, and disappearing northward into the foliage.

"I'll go talk to the few large females cats I might be able to track down before supper," Amy told them before going in an eastern direction.

"Well, let's get going or we'll never make it back before it gets dark." Dustie started walking, Sedah keeping pace easily with her much shorter frame.

"So, what does the little one need? Can we name her?" Sedah asked once they had gotten back to camp.

"At the back of our cottage is the cow. Go collect some milk and bring it back out. I'll take the little one with me to get our dinner and meet you back over here." Not waiting for her to either agree or disagree, Dustie and the kitten headed off, leaving Sedah no other option but to do as she had been told. After an hour of fighting with the cow and getting no liquid to show for it, she finally had to ask another sister to show her, which the girl did with a silent attitude, before stomping off once she saw that Sedah could do it.

Caprika joined them during supper. As the meal and the night wore on, the girls chatted about their day while showing Sedah all of the nightly chores both around the encampment as well as in their cottage. If today had been anything to judge from, Sedah would be falling into bed, and asleep, before her head even hit the pillow on a nightly basis.

THE NEXT MORNING CAME MUCH TOO QUICKLY FOR SEDAH'S liking. She was just coming out of a sleep induced fog when she realized that neither Dustie nor Caprika were in the cottage. Dressing as quickly as possible, in the same clothes from yesterday, she stepped outside, splashed clean, cool water on her face from the basin, and began scanning the camp for either one of the girls, or someone that she knew to be friendly.

She did not have long to look, as Caprika came around the corner at that moment with a bucket of milk. "I did it for you this time since you wouldn't wake up for some reason. Some of the elders said that I should let you sleep this week as you get used to hard work and more oxygen." She gave Sedah the bucket of milk as they met each other's stare. "But I warn you now that it'll only be for this week. Afterwards you'll be expected to get up when we do, sleep when we do, work as hard as we do, and follow every rule we do, do I make myself clear?"

Flabbergasted as to what to say, Sedah simply nodded her head and mumbled a reply.

"Good, then take this bucket up the tree to the hall. You can eat after you give this to any one of the women up there. When you're done eating, I'll have someone for you to work with. At the end of the day, we'll work on your balance." Having said her peace, Caprika walked away with purpose, probably to do her own duties for the day.

Sighing, Sedah decided to just get the chore over with and do as she was told. Walking up to the base of the tree, she stopped, trying to figure out how to make the steps slide out of the tree and into place like the nymphs did.

Nothing was coming out automatically, and no one was rushing to offer her advice. Sedah thought back to what Dustie and Caprika had told her about the forest and its trust in the women. Sedah took a deep breath in before stepping with one foot into the air as if she could see the step in front of her. She quickly exhaled her held breath when her foot touched wood at the last second before she would have fallen on her face.

Looking down and seeing wood under her foot, she gained a small bit of courage. She put her full weight on the step and did the same with her other foot on the next step. A squeal escaped her lips when she was met with another step instead of air. Realizing that the tree was going to be nice, Sedah began the ascent a little faster and with more confidence until she was almost at the top. She was roughly four steps or half a trunk away from the top entrance of the canopy when a shove from behind sent her tipping forward.

She fell, instinctively throwing her hands out in front of her to keep herself from toppling off the unrailed stairs, releasing the full bucket of milk into the air. Sedah threw a hand out and tried in vain to scramble for it as it fell.

"Oh Goddess no!" Sedah cried out as she watched the

bucket go sailing down towards the ground. Suddenly, only a foot or so from the ground, the bucket stopped, a second before hitting the ground and making milk fly everywhere. Thankfully, only a small amount slipped over the edge as the liquid settled into the basket.

"Look at what you've done! Watch where you are going myk'tu!" the woman growled at Sedah as she lay sprawled out on the steps.

Not sure what had happened, she watched as Dustie came running up and grabbed the bucket of milk from the ground. Without losing a step, Dustie continued running with the still full bucket, up the tree steps. She stepped over Sedah to take the bucket to the landing before coming back to pry the terrified goddess off of the stairs. Shaken, Sedah had a death grip on Dustie's arms for the last eight steps.

As soon as they cleared the landing, Dustie turned around and laid into the culprit. "Lilac, what the hell? Not only could you have injured someone with that bucket, you could have hurt Sedah when you purposely knocked her down. She could have fallen off of the tree entirely! What do you think would have happened to you if you had killed her? How big of a dumb ass can you be?"

"Look, it's not my fault that she can't look where she is going enough to keep from falling on her face," Lilac told Dustie in defense. Going up the remaining steps to meet them at the landing, she caught Sedah with a cold stare before taking two slow steps toward her. Sedah matched her with two steps back. "Watch where you are going and stay out of my way, ugly outsider. I have too much to do to be bothered with you," she said in a low voice. Lilac straightened up and walked away with a scowl on her face.

"Sorry about that. Are you okay?" Dustie asked a wide eyed, visibly shaking Sedah.

"Why does she hate me enough to hurt me?"

"That was Lilac. I'm sure that she just has a lot on her plate. She's not like Onyx or Jade, just a bit blunt when she's stressed."

"Why is she dressed like that? No other nymph I have seen thus far has been in human clothes," Sedah asked as she watched the nymph walk away, wearing a fitted suit and carrying a satchel of some kind.

"She is our liaison with the humans, so she often has to dress like them and have meetings with them in order to protect us. You could go ask her yourself though." Dustie smiled at her own joke before turning and picking up the milk. "What were you supposed to do with this?"

"Take it to one of the women, eat and then see who Caprika has for me to work with today."

"If you are going to eat, go now and I will get this to the right person. Then I'll take you to Sandy. You're with her today." Dustie smiled reassuringly as she disappeared around the corner with the milk.

Eating the bowl of mush as fast as possible, Sedah was able to be ready when Dustie came back from around the corner to meet her. With a nod, they headed back down the tree trunk, Sedah's legs still shaking, and over to where Sedah would be working.

"Sandy, you remember Sedah. She's here to help you until around three o'clock. Caprika will either come for her personally, or someone else will come tell her where to meet one of us, okay?" Dustie looked from Sandy to Sedah, who nodded, and then left to do her own duties.

"Okay then newbie, let's get to teaching you about what I do to keep our sand and waters clean and healthy," Sandy started with a warm smile.

"So, what are you going to be doing as far as teaching while still having the myk'tu work to earn her place here?" Jade asked Caprika.

Caprika had been waiting for this meeting since she had first been given responsibility for the myk'tu. She had expected a meeting the day before because of the way Onyx had acted, but that had apparently not been that big of a deal to their current leader.

"I showed her the jobs Dustie and I normally do yesterday, as well as taking her by every sister so that they could show her what duties she would be learning. I figured I would let her work at a different place every day, until certain people ask for her again, or we determine that she is better at certain jobs than at others. I will start her teachings at three o'clock every day and we will work until the night meal."

"What teachings are you starting with today, then?"

"I am going to take her around on fallen and leaning trees to determine her balance. If it is good, we might even get her into the trees and see if she has the strength to jump from one branch to the other."

"Okay, what do we know of her powers? Do you think that she is dangerous?"

"Well, I don't know anything about her yet, other than the fact that she changes colors with her mood."

"Onyx said that when she went to bring her in, her mother was making things smaller, shrinking them down in size. Have you seen this for yourself?" Jade countered.

"I have not seen this or any other abnormality, ma'am."

"You will tell me when you see her do anything that is abnormal for a human, or anything that we can't do."

"As you say, O Daughter."

"Thank you. You may go to your duties now," Jade said, seemingly bored.

Caprika rolled her eyes after turning her back, to get

some work done for the day. Jade obviously had Onyx in her ear, telling her lies to make Sedah seem like a danger to the clan. She was more than likely looking for a reason to break off the deal and send Sedah off to another part of the world, to another clan. Sending Sedah away would hide her from her mother, and make her a bargaining tool to get Leuce back. It made sense that she would do anything in her power to get one of her eldest children back. Caprika was no longer sure that she would tell the Daughter anything that would put Sedah in danger.

"So now that you have done this for yourself, do you think you would be able to do it alone?" Sandy asked Sedah.

"I think that I could tell by the feel of the sand and mud if it needed a few additional things. Without your intuition, I doubt that I could get anywhere near knowing how to make it better."

"Just stick your bare feet in and if it is good enough, just relax and get yourself a pedicure."

A soft laugh from the nearby canopy told them another nymph was near. Sedah glanced over to see a familiar face. "Oh, the number of times I've done just that after a long day." She looked past Sedah to her sister nymph.

"Is there something here that I can help you with, Amy?" Sandy asked politely.

"Ah, yeah, sorry. I'm here to collect Sedah for her lessons with Caprika."

"Oh, well, I guess we're done here for the day. My, how the time sure does fly when you are talking about something that you love."

Amy and Sedah waved goodbye to Sandy and headed out

of camp. "Hi, I'm Sedah, but I guess you already knew that. So, where are we headed?"

"Somewhere. And I'm Amy," Amy said tensely.

"What am I going to be taught then?"

"I don't know."

"Is Caprika at least going to be there?" Sedah asked, even as she started changing into a pinkish color.

"That, I can answer yes to. Caprika will be teaching you, with my help and possibly even Dustie's, though I have no idea what she would help you with. At any rate, we're here." Amy smiled as she jumped onto a fallen limb and somersaulted back to the ground.

"Showoff!" Caprika laughed as she stepped into one side of the clearing at the same time Sedah did on the other.

"Sorry, I love doing that. Helps the back stretch and keep me limber."

"So what are we doing that Amy could not tell me about?"

"Nothing that you couldn't be told about, technically. But I thought about it, and discussed it with Amy, and we believe that, for most of your training, it should be only Amy and I. You also won't know what you're going to be taught daily until you're with us, and you can't talk about what you're taught, other than the nymph skills we teach you so you can live with us. Anything other than that is to be only between us three. Think you can do that?" Caprika explained to her.

"I guess so, though I do not see why. I can't even discuss it with Dustie? She's an innocent kid."

"And one with a big mouth. Trust me, I'm her sister and she can absolutely not keep a secret."

"So what am I supposed to do if she wants to come with me when I train, or asks us what we were training on?"

"Just tell her to ask me, I don't mind telling her that she's not gonna go," Caprika said as she smirked.

"Okay, then. What are we doing today?" Sedah looked

from one girl to the other to see them looking at one another.

"We . . . we decided to work on your powers," Caprika started hesitantly.

"If we work on them as you discover them, then we can keep them under control. Then you'll know how to handle them better in the human world," Amy finished.

Nodding in agreement, Sedah thought about the powers that she was aware of. "So are we talking about the powers that I have naturally, or the ones that I have come into recently?"

"I think we need to see them all. Then we can decide which ones you need to conceal, and which are considered normal, or just need to be used sporadically."

"So do you want me to show you all of them or just tell you?" Sedah grinned as she sat down cross-legged right where she stood.

Caprika followed suit and Amy sat on the log that she had flipped from earlier.

"Why don't you just tell us first. We'll decide if we need you to demonstrate them for clarification, or if we need to see the limitations of a power," Amy suggested.

"Okay, well as far as the powers I have always had: I can concentrate and make things duplicate if I am touching them, I have horns that occasionally come out, and I can kill and revive animals. The color change thing comes from my grand-mother, who gave it to my mom when she was younger."

"Okay, and I assume you have a handle on all of these with the exception of being a kaleidoscope. Since you're here, that tells us it's something that even your mother could not stop. Being able to revive animals is a great thing living amongst nymphs, although we generally don't do that sort of thing," Caprika thought aloud. "Anything new since you've been here?"

"What's a kaleidoscope?" Sedah sounded it out slowly so she could say it correctly.

"A tube that lets you watch colors change the way your body does. Now answer the question," Caprika said.

"So far, my need for energy has mostly come from the false sun we get in Erebus and what I drink from others, but I am needing more lately. Mom said it would be from exerting myself more than I do at home. I didn't tell mom when we got here, but I started to feel the weather and know when it changes before it happens, like it is calling to me. And, according to her, I think about something and it appears."

"What do you mean?"

"I don't know exactly. I thought about how a tepee, like we had seen on the road here, would make me warm on the night that we stayed in the forest. When I woke up, there was a tepee around us."

"Why was it not there when I came and got you?" Caprika was surprised.

"I think it surprised Mom as well, so she miniaturized it and put it away."

"Gotcha. Then I think we need to start with that. Let's see what exactly makes things appear, and to what level we have to get you before it happens. Sound good?" Caprika asked both girls, standing up in excitement.

"Sure, sounds like as good a place to start as any," Sedah said, standing also.

"Let's get to work then," Amy concluded, standing as well.

❧ 6 ❧

"So what are we going to work on tomorrow?" Sedah asked as the three girls entered the camp a few hours later.

"I think we're going to finish on what we were working on today, then look into the things you can do without bringing attention to yourself, in case you do get into a bind and need to use them when a human is around," Caprika thought aloud.

"Just remember what we said about not telling anyone," Amy reminded her.

"I got it." Sedah laughed as Dustie came running up to them.

"Did you have fun today Sedah? Caprika said that I couldn't come but it only took me an hour to do my rounds, so I—" Dustie began to argue.

"Still couldn't come. And as far as Amy and I are concerned, you are going to take over more of her duties since she will be helping me with Sedah's training," Caprika finished.

Dustie scowled at the three girls before walking off in a huff.

As Dustie left with a dejected pace, Sedah felt like garbage for being the cause. Amy put a hand on Sedah's shoulder. "Don't worry, she'll get over it."

"She'll be happy when you show her the duties that you're letting her take over. Come on, let's get some dinner so we can start on the nightly chores. I still have to determine where you'll be working tomorrow," Caprika confirmed.

Amy and Sedah followed Caprika up the stairs of the tree to the dining hall. As they entered, the slight buzz of conversation fell to a low murmur. Caprika and Amy looked at one another in confusion before simultaneously turning behind them to look at Sedah, who was turning a combination of gray and red.

"Oh get over yourselves, there is nothing new to see here!" Amy yelled at the group of women. Immediately, all the women turned back to what they were previously doing, and the hum of conversation increased in volume.

"Is it because it's the first night Amy has eaten with us, showing that someone here likes you, or did something happen today that we don't know about?" Caprika asked as the three sat down at a table with their food.

"Both maybe?" Sedah hedged.

"What happened and when?" Amy asked curiously with a smile.

"I kind of had a run in with Lilac today. It was nothing really."

"Like I believe that for a minute. Spill," Caprika pushed.

"Nothing, really. I figured out how to get up the stairs to the hall by myself today. Took a little courage, but I was almost to the top when I got shoved from behind. Apparently, Lilac thought I was holding her up and decided to push me out of the way. I managed not to fall off and go splat, but the milk fell."

"So if the milk fell, then how are we eating bread right now?" Amy asked in confusion, waving the bread in her hand around.

"I never thought about it honestly, I was too worried about not falling down the stairs and dying!" Sedah looked at Amy incredulously.

Curious, but not questioning it for the moment, the girls put up their plates and started back down the stairs. They waved bye to Amy and went to their cottage to start on the nightly chores of settling the animals and getting ready for bed.

When Sedah came up to the side of the cottage where the buckets used to feed the animals were kept, whispers coming from inside stopped her in her tracks beside the window. Remembering what her mother had said about listening and learning everything possible, Sedah's body might as well have become stone in order to listen to the hushed conversation going on inside.

"So, what exactly happened today Dustie? I want the truth, too."

"She got pushed by Lilac. Mother O knows Sedah took long enough to get up the stairs between being scared and not letting herself drop the milk, but Lilac still had no right to knock her down. I mean why—"

"That's the other thing that I don't understand. If she dropped the milk when Lilac pushed her, how were we able to have bread tonight?"

"Because I picked up the bucket of milk off the ground and took it up the stairs to the sisters."

"How did it fall from three stories up and still manage to be full enough to make enough bread for all of us?" Caprika asked more to herself than to her little sister.

"I honestly didn't think about it. Good question though, as well as who stopped it an inch or two from the ground," Dustie said.

"Come again?"

"When I picked it up, it wasn't lying or sitting on the ground. It was, I don't know, hovering at about ankle height or a little higher." Dustie shrugged.

Deciding that she had probably heard enough, Sedah collected herself as she walked around the house and to the front door.

"Oh man, am I beat. Are we done for the day?" She smiled weakly and acted weary, despite her mind going in many different directions at the same time.

"Night, girls," Caprika agreed as they all got settled into their beds.

As the night wore on, Sedah couldn't sleep. All she kept thinking about was everything she had to absorb now, just to learn about the outside world later. When she finally fell asleep, it was with the determination that she would prove the women here wrong and make her mother proud.

※

AFTER BREAKFAST, AMY GOT RIGHT TO THE POINT OF teaching Dustie her new additional duties and Caprika reintroduced Sedah to Aqua, who worked alongside Sandy.

Having just worked with Sandy, as the day progressed, Sedah seemed to do better at understanding Aqua's job. By the time Amy came to pick her up, Sedah was working with, instead of for, Aqua. Both women were laughing and chatting as Amy jumped to the closest branch to watch, before announcing her presence.

"—and I was so pissed! I just stood there as he spun round and round in the whirlpool until it made him sick. Seeing the green of his skin was so funny that I laughed until I couldn't hold the magic any longer."

"As long as I turn green for other reasons, *I* will be happy. If I make you mad, I'll know not to get in the water," Sedah replied with a giggle.

Amy decided to collect her at that point, and gracefully swung down from her branch walking to the side of the bank. "Time to go."

Sedah sighed and waded out of the water, slipping on her shoes. "Caprika had an emergency on the other side of the mountain, so I will be teaching you today," Amy explained as they started walking away.

As they started into the forest, Amy noticed that Sedah had not spoken at all since they started walking. "You don't mind that it's just us, do you?" she asked.

"What? No, no it has nothing to do with you Amy. I'm sorry."

"Then what's wrong?"

"I hadn't really thought about it, or I guess I just wrote it off, but I overheard Dustie telling Caprika how she found the bucket of milk that I had dropped when Lilac pushed me yesterday."

"I guess I'm not understanding something. What is the issue?"

"I guess I just can't stop wondering if it is something that I did or if one of the nymphs helped me out, trying to be nice, and just doesn't want to say anything. The bucket was hovering an inch or two from the ground when Dustie found it, like someone was levitating it."

Amy thought for a moment and tried to think of all of the women and their powers. "As far as I know, there is no one with that type of power yet, so I would have to say that it was you. Dustie is coming into it, but she's not there yet."

"But I don't even know what I did or how I did it," Sedah said, sounding somewhat panicky.

"Okay, then that's what we'll work on today. We'll see if we can figure out how to stop something in midair, in mid motion, and what emotion we have to get you to feel to make it happen. It may not even be linked to your emotions, but it makes logical sense that it would be. It'll be okay."

"Are you sure? You seem so confident that it will be an easy thing to figure out."

Amy wrapped her right arm around Sedah and gave a light squeeze of reassurance. "Because I am. I have complete faith in you."

"Then let's do this," Sedah said with more gusto than she felt at the moment.

"I have a feeling that it was more of a subconscious thing to save the milk than anything else."

"What are you talking about?" Sedah giggled nervously under her breath.

"Like when you said you thought about wanting to be warm and the tent thing popped up to shelter you. I think when you fell, you thought about the milk spilling everywhere right?"

"That, plus how mad Caprika and all of the other girls would be if they didn't have any milk. In my mind, I just saw it hitting the ground and going everywhere."

"Right! Is it the fear of disappointing someone or determination to save it? That is what we need to figure out."

"So how are we gonna figure that out, O Wise One?"

"Well, we'll start on the ground and, if you get the hang of it, we'll send you higher and I will tell you if you do or do not stop an object. Sound good to you?"

"Sure. What are we going to practice with for me to try to stop midair?"

"Let's try a light object." Amy looked around them and spotted what she was thinking about. "This pine cone will work for now."

Sedah gave her a wary look, thinking she was crazy but willing to try anyway. They had worked on her materializing objects the day before, which Sedah hoped would aid her in making things stop in their tracks. Amy threw the pine cone into the air for almost two hours without a single positive result.

Frustrated, they took a break so Amy's arm could rest. Sedah walked a few steps away to gather her thoughts.

"I just don't get why I can't do it when I try, but I can subconsciously do it when I need to. It just doesn't make any sense to me!" Sedah growled in frustration, forgetting for a moment everything around her as she turned gray. It wasn't until Amy gasped from behind her that she returned to reality and looked to see what had made Amy gasp.

"What?"

"You didn't see that? Okay, okay, what were you just thinking about?" Amy started to get excited.

"Being frustrated, why?"

"That's it then! That is the key to making you do things! While you were just off in your mind, you just made this pine cone, and every other one around us, lift off the ground about two feet." A squeal of delight escaped from both girls simultaneously.

"Okay, so we know what it takes. Let's try it again." Amy held the pine cone in the palm of her hand, out towards Sedah so she could concentrate on lifting it.

ABOUT THREE HOURS LATER, CAPRIKA WAS WALKING BACK towards where the girls should be practicing when she heard yelling coming from up ahead of her. Afraid of what might be going on, she took off running until she burst through the bushes that surrounded the small clearing they had found to use for practice.

"Ooh boo hoo! So it's a little tougher! You make me sick! You're *actually* saying to me that a pine cone was easier than this? It's a boulder! It's *going* to be harder, you dummy!" Amy was yelling.

"What in the name of her Father are you yelling about?" Caprika directed to Amy before looking past her to a pissed off Sedah. "Why is she yelling at you? You're red as an apple!"

"It's okay. It's part of the training. We'll work on her trigger later. Just go somewhere with cover to watch. Hush till you see what we've accomplished today." Amy pointed toward where Caprika had just come, to a tree with another, older fallen one, in front of it. "There would work."

Curious, Caprika sat where she had been told and waited.

"Okay, are you still pissed at me? You're not that gray anymore," Amy asked.

"If you know the answer, why ask it?" Sedah replied.

"Fine, be a bitch and let everyone prove Onyx right." Amy barely had time to shrug. Almost instantly, a growl ripped through Sedah. With that anger came a spray of dirt and small rocks towards Amy, causing her to duck knowingly. "Is that all you got? Do you really think some dirt will keep people off your case?" She recovered and stood up defiantly, staring Sedah down. "Again, you baby! Hit me!"

Caprika stood in disbelief as boulders of different sizes around the small clearing hovered at waist level. Some of the smaller ones flew towards Amy, almost striking her, while the bigger ones seemed to only have enough strength to roll a few feet towards her.

Amy smiled in pride and Caprika put a hand on her

shoulder as she walked up to her. Just as Caprika was about to comment, they both watched in shock as Sedah fell to one knee, supporting herself from falling further with her hands on each side of her body.

"Oh my goddess—"

"Are you all r—"

They were both running to her in a second, helping her to stand and walking her over to sit against the cliff wall a few feet away.

"I'm fine I think, just extremely tired. I just need to rest a minute."

"Okay, so what just happened here?" Caprika finally asked.

"Apparently part of her new powers is to be able to move things telekinetically. The only issue is that she has to be . . . emotional first. That's the yelling that you heard. I had to get her upset."

"Hence the grayish black color you saw. Mad is red, and frustration and disappointment is gray." Sedah finished the explanation breathlessly.

"So why are you so tired? Too much practicing?" Caprika became concerned.

"It is the first time she's done this." Amy directed at Caprika before turning to Sedah. "I haven't pushed you too far for your first day of practicing it, have I?"

Sedah just sat for a minute, probably assessing herself. "I think that I need some energy."

"Well let's go back and we'll see about getting you some extra bread or a snack before dinner." Amy thought aloud.

"*My child needs the sun or your life energy.*" Caprika heard a female voice in her head. She startled, looking around for the source. Used to talking telepathically to her mom, she answered as she would then.

"*I am not letting her make me weak. What do I need to do?*"

"No that's not—" Sedah began to explain.

"What you need, I was afraid of that." Caprika sighed.

"Take her where there is the most sun. The rest will take care of itself." The female said.

"You know what I need? How?"

"Your mom, I suspect." She held up a hand to stop Sedah when she opened her mouth to speak. "I just got told mentally, in another woman's voice, to take you out of the canopy. I'm assuming it is your mother since your grandmother knows nothing of your being here."

"Probably. Okay girls, help me up."

Caprika and Amy both took a side and helped Sedah stand up. When her knees buckled on the first step, they put her arms around their necks, helping her walk in the direction Caprika indicated.

"It's just right up here. What do we need to do?" Caprika inquired.

"Just sit me down once we hit the sunniest spot."

"We're just . . . there we go; I knew we were close," Amy chimed in.

"See those strong rays, put me there." Sedah nodded toward a certain area with a large rock, one side flat from cracking in half as it fell.

Doing as she said, the girls helped her to sit in the sun against the rock she had indicated and backed up a few feet to relax against the nearest stumps.

"So, what now?" Amy said to Caprika, who sat beside her.

"We wait, I guess."

"For what?"

"I don't know, I only got told where to take her." Caprika rolled her eyes.

"Hmm, I see." Amy said with a sigh and turned back to watch and wait.

The two girls waited around ten minutes with seemingly nothing happening. Just as they were about to give up, they were suddenly forced to shield their eyes to the light that seemed to suddenly radiate from inside Sedah, bursting outward to the point of being able to hear the hum of the energy rippling through the air.

"Should we—?"

"I don't know." Caprika whispered.

"What do we—?"

"I don't know." Caprika said louder in frustration.

Watching, they could do nothing but wait.

SEDAH ON THE OTHER HAND, WAS WISHING IT WERE OVER. She felt completely drained from practicing with Amy. She had just had no idea how bad it was until she collapsed after the last, hardest try. While she was elated to have brought some nice sized boulders off the ground, she found that she hated being drained almost as much as she hated having been sent to the nymphs in the first place.

She was actually relieved that either her mother or Apollo had been watching her at that moment, knew that she needed energy she could not get herself, and had communicated that to Caprika.

When the girls had sat her down, she just lay back in exhaustion. She had lain against the rock like that for a few minutes, letting the sun slowly sink into her pores when the heat started within her.

At first it was just slightly hot, like on the trip to the forest when the taxi they were in didn't have working air conditioning. Then, slowly it turned into the feeling of a second-degree sunburn, before reaching the point of a burning flame that radiated from her chest, outward to her extremities. She closed her eyes as the pain overcame her ability for coherent thought, becoming so excruciating that she bit her tongue until she tasted blood to keep from screaming aloud for all of the world to hear. She howled inwardly for someone, anyone to come to her aid as she lay there in agony.

What seemed to her to last forever, really only lasted a few seconds. It seemed to give Sedah more energy than she had ever gotten from one person or any other energy source before. As the heat went from excruciating to subtle within her, she slowly sat up, not quite understanding the new feelings coursing through her body.

Opening her eyes, she caught Caprika and Amy staring at her in both awe and worry. She felt a type of humming from within her entire body. She raised her hand, watching as her fingers moved in a flowing motion in front of her face. An invisible electric pulse or current could be felt jumping from finger to finger as they moved.

"So how are you feeling?" Caprika approached her hesitantly.

"I'm not sure, to be honest."

"Is that not something normal then?" Amy seemed confused and frustrated.

"Nope. It's usually a gradual draining that I suck out of something or someone, like a tube."

"Well, are you okay to get up and head back to camp? That's why I was checking on you. It's starting to get late." Caprika reminded them.

"So . . . what do we say about the glow that I seem to have going on?" She slowly got to her feet.

"What glow? You mean the blinding light that you cast for a few seconds?" Caprika asked.

"Sorry girl, I don't see a glow. You seem a little tanner but that's it." Amy agreed.

"So you saw a bright light for a few seconds, but you don't see the glow now? I feel like a freaking lightbulb!"

"Nope."

"Nada, babe."

"Hmm, weird." Sedah shrugged and started walking off. Looking at each other and making faces, the girls jumped to catch up with her to walk to camp together.

7

As she lay in bed that night, Sedah could still feel the buzzing within her, even though it had been over five hours since it had occurred. She had refrained from touching anyone directly, in case the electricity she felt coursing through her fingers was not just in her mind, like the glow of her skin.

She had come into the camp with the girls, expecting everyone to turn and stare at her strange glow. When no one reacted, she began to believe that Caprika and Amy's earlier claims were true and no one else could see the internal glow as Sedah could.

The more she thought about it, the more she was convinced that Helios had to have been there, too. He was the God of the Sun and Healing, after all. It would make sense to heal her with the sun, since the energy seemed to have been so powerful that she was left with an ethereal glow only she could see. It had to be directly from the Gods. That meant that her uncle was keeping tabs of her like her mother had requested, which was both nice and creepy all at the same time.

She wished she could actually talk to him. Maybe he could tell her what the future held for her, if any. He was not the fates, but he could still see what was to come. His own future, and that of those that he loved, were blocked from him. Which meant that she had about a fifty percent chance of him seeing anything at all.

Sure, he was kin to her and looked after her as a favor to his cousin, but that did not mean he cared enough about her to be blocked from seeing her future. Now that it was night he was on the other side of the world, so it wasn't like she could even ask him. Sedah debated with herself for an hour before she'd had enough with all the speculation about this next year flitting through her head.

Deciding to give it a try, and calling herself crazy even as she was doing it, she called out to him in a whisper. "Uncle, I feel silly, but I am scared, so I feel that I have to at least ask. If you see anything, or if the Fates come to you or mom about me, will you let me know somehow? I'm not sure how you would show me, but I guess I'll leave that up to you. Thanks, if you heard any of this." With hope in her heart and a smile on her face, Sedah finally drifted off into a peaceful sleep.

۞

SHE WAS IN THE AIR, SUSPENDED AND TRAPPED SOMEHOW. *Panicking, she looked around and tried to stand, but for some reason couldn't. Trying to focus, she felt her hands, her fingers grasping something familiar: vines. She was in the forest, in a net of vines suspended in the air. She fought at them frantically to try and get free, to get down. Every time she moved and was about to be free, the vines would move or grow, to keep her from gaining any ground. She was getting frustrated and making noises to herself in irritation when she was silenced by the voices getting louder below her. Slowly, she managed to get her body turned in a better position to see the ground, despite the growth of the vines. Her next hurdle was to try to identify the people below through the thick fog. Just as she was about to make out one figure, a pain suddenly pierced her head, making everything fade to black.*

Gasping hard, Sedah woke with a start, sitting straight up. Catching her breath, she flopped back down and tried to think about the nightmare she had just had. It was weird, unlike anything she had ever dreamed before. Her life was generally easy, so she had no real reason to have nightmares unless she picked up on a person's emotions as she was feeding. Deciding it was just a weird dream from all the fresh energy, Sedah stared at the ceiling until she eventually fell back into a restless sleep.

DESPITE THE WEIRD DREAM, IT WAS SURPRISINGLY EASY TO get up, do her chores, and go through training until noon with a new nymph and a new abundance of energy coursing through her body. She would probably never remember the name of the nymph because she wasn't even a little nice, but her job coincided with what Aqua did, which meant Sedah had to learn it.

After the lunch break, Caprika and Amy both came and took her to train. Despite the ground that she had covered, they all decided not to push her on practicing one certain ability for too long, in fear of draining her energy reserve. Still, the girls had her a little confused as they started walking.

"What are we going to do, since you don't want to see if the extra energy will magnify my abilities?" Sedah asked curiously when they walked past the usual training area.

"We were thinking of just walking around today and see what happens. You may have questions about us or the world so far, or if we come across something that might spark a question about something else. To be honest, we—" Amy started to tell her, only for Caprika to butt in.

"—weren't sure if we should give you a few days to rest before trying again, and we have trained you this week on everything else."

"So you basically just decided to wing it," Sedah guessed with a soft giggle.

"Pretty much." Caprika laughed too.

"Well, I do have a few questions, so I guess it makes sense for it to be part of our training. I don't want to be too ignorant of the way the world works when I get out in it."

"See, it does make sense. So, what do you want to know?"

"There are too many questions going through my head at once, to be honest. I'm not even sure I can find a place to start."

"Okay, let's break it down and focus on the questions that have to do with going to Poseidon to serve," Caprika suggested, shrugging carelessly as they walked.

"My, you two are ever the problem solvers, aren't you?" Sedah laughed. "But it's okay, compartmentalizing it into different areas does actually help."

The girls walked in silence for a few minutes, letting Sedah gather her thoughts and decide what to ask.

"Well," Sedah asked when she had finally decided, "I guess the first question would be if you know when I will have to go?"

"Whoever is the leader at the time will tell us," Caprika guessed, shrugging again.

"How long am I supposed to stay?"

"That is up to you, I think."

"Do you know how many times I will have to go?"

"I haven't been told much, just about our part," Caprika admitted.

"Honestly, I don't think I will have that long," Sedah

muttered under her breath. She couldn't explain why, but she had no faith in Gods keeping their word.

"What?"

"Nothing, it's not important. What do you know about the deals that my father struck with Poseidon and Mother Earth?"

"No idea about one with him, just with Mother Earth and Jade. Jade is Leuce's eldest daughter, so of course she agreed to our camp training you, but past that, you are not our problem."

"Wow. Sorry that I'm a problem. And here I thought we were becoming friends." Sedah could not help but turn gray with disappointment at thinking they were closer than the girls really felt.

Immediately, Caprika felt horrible. "That is in no way what I mean, and I thought you would know that. I do consider you a friend, but not to the point of life long yet. I mean I've known you a week at this point!"

"I barely know you, but I like what I have seen from you so far. If I didn't, I wouldn't have agreed to keep our training a secret," Sedah countered back, a little offended.

"She has a point, Cap. Personally, I like you and hope we keep in touch no matter what, despite only knowing you for a few days. I've known Caprika for seven hundred years and she wears on my nerves sometimes." Amy laughed at the looks on both of their faces.

"Whatever, next question please," Caprika said, not even caring that she was showing her frustration.

"Fine. I know I am supposed to be here until I am no longer changing colors, but will I get to see if I am making any progress by talking to any outsiders before then?"

"We haven't decided that yet. Since we are so close to Nantahala Lake though, it might be doable, if for no other reason than to have an excuse to get away for a little while." Caprika shrugged.

"You would have to either have a control on your kaleidoscope thing, or do it after you are not one anymore, though. Otherwise, we would have no way to explain it," Amy chimed in.

"The best I can figure it, I have seven months until the color changing goes away, if it lasts as long as it did for my mom."

"Well hopefully we won't have to wait that long, and we can do something fun to get you used to people before you have to leave."

"Okay, next question. Who will take me to the ocean?" Sedah heard a slight noise in the distance and decided to head in that direction as they talked.

"I believe your mom has someone doing that. I wasn't sure who, since it was nobody from here, but I guess if there are more deals in place other than the one you have with us here, then probably someone from that end."

"So I won't know until I get told to go there?" She continued toward the noise that she could now tell was running water up ahead.

"Pretty much."

Wondering if she even wanted answers to any more questions with the way these had been going, Sedah took two big steps up a small incline and gasped. Coming up beside her, the girls exchanged looks at one another before looking at her and smiling.

"Beautiful, isn't it?" Amy almost whispered.

"Where are we?"

"One of the waterfalls that leads down to Nantahala Lake."

"It's amazing."

"It's one of the rivers that comes down from a lake north

of here, it only becomes narrow here because of the dam that was put up. It made the river flow slow down and carved out this waterfall that goes under the street just through those trees." Caprika pointed east

"Can anyone see us?"

"Not here, but they can if you go any further. The path below us is visible from the street."

"Have any of the nymphs ever been spotted, despite the shiny skin thing?"

"Lilac spends half her time with Humans. There are others here and there, but nothing that's really ever a threat. A great thing about the mountains is that we can be explained away as hikers in the distance. Even better are the "tree huggers" that get the blame for running around acting goofy." Caprika used her hands to do air quotations as she explained.

"Are there as many satyrs as there are nymphs?"

"Sure, there is a male satyr equivalent to every nymph I've introduced you to so far. That is how the entire forest gets taken care of. Nymphs do one side, and satyrs do the other, unless they need back up. Then their counterpart is called, and if both can't solve the problem, others are called in."

"So how do you call each other if you live in separate camps that are unknown to the other sex and work on opposite sides of the mountain?"

"We can talk telepathically to our male counterpart, and to our parents, but that is it."

"Makes sense, I guess."

"Where did those questions come from? I thought we were answering questions for you about going to Poseidon," Amy asked with a grin.

"You said that questions might come up with the scenery too. Why can't they start with the scenery and continue naturally from the answers that I get?" Sedah smiled playfully.

Amy shrugged. "No harm, I guess. Just a little surprised."

"Tell you what, lets chill here and see if the calming effect of the waterfall helps you focus on the boulders instead of having to use your emotions. Maybe doing that will help you use less energy."

"I never thought of that. Makes sense though."

"Amy got to thinking, as she often does, and decided that going by your emotions might be good now, it won't help when you go to the Palace. If we're going to help you understand them, and make them come out, then we also need to make sure you can use them in a peaceful and emotionless state, so you can control them better." Caprika rolled her eyes.

Sedah smiled at Amy to reassure her. "I knew there was a reason I liked you."

"Well then, let's get to work. We only have an hour or two left to practice today."

"Now I see what you mean about the barrier. How did I miss that before?" Sedah laughed as the three girls crossed the threshold into camp.

Deciding that Sedah needed focus, the girls had decided to let where she worked for the day determine where they would practice. They had even decided to let a few of the nymphs, the ones they knew would report to Jade, see them practicing some days, so Jade wouldn't start to question why Caprika hadn't come and given her an update, or why Amy and Caprika always took Sedah away from prying eyes to practice.

As the girls were talking, and about to go their separate ways for the day, Dustie stormed up to them in a huff.

"What's up that has you so mad, little one?" Sedah asked through her laughter.

"I heard about what you were practicing with them today," she shot at Caprika and Amy. "Why can't I be a part of it, if all you're doing is working on her balance and strength?"

"It's just not feasible for three of us to train her," Caprika defended, looking around. Nearby nymphs had heard and slowed down to listen.

Amy started glancing around as well. "It is also not feasible for all of our duties to go to the wayside, or not get half done. You have my duties added to your own in the afternoon, and Epipe has Caprika's."

"So! What about it?" Dustie crossed her arms and a pout formed on her face.

"Well, with all of our work, what would happen if we slacked off? How long and hard do you think we would have to work to catch back up?" Amy leaned down to look Dustie square in the eyes. "How long do you think it would take for our slacking off to affect the animals and, in turn, our sisters and their jobs? Do you see what I'm trying to say?"

Dustie looked at the floor. She had been thoroughly shamed. "Yes, I understand. I just feel like I'm being purposely excluded."

"Well, you're not. We'll let you know when you can help later on. Now go to your chores if your work is done for the day," Caprika told her a little harshly, looking at everyone around.

The small crowd dispersed, and, with a nod, Dustie ran off.

"That was eventful." Amy leaned in toward Sedah to say in a hushed tone.

"What do you wanna bet someone baited her?" Caprika mirrored her.

"What do you mean?" Sedah asked, looking back from one to the other.

"There might be a few things you don't know about politics around here. You know you have some girls that don't like you and would try to make you look bad, to lose the few friends you do have. Looks like they used our practice today to get influence Dustie," Amy hurriedly explained.

"But she's young, easy to manipulate. I should have told you to expect it. The problem is that they might not stop there." Caprika sighed.

"That's so petty!" Sedah threw her hands up in the air in frustration.

"Anyone you get on your side will become a target to use against you. Sandy, Amy, Aqua, even myself. Onyx and her friends will do the same, so you need to watch your back, starting now."

"Don't you think that's a little dramatic? These are grown women we are talking about."

"Trust us—" Amy started.

"It will happen," Caprika finished.

"Fine, I'll watch out," Sedah growled before walking off toward the side of the cabin. She grabbed the water bucket and walked in the direction of the river to get enough water to properly clean up for dinner.

"Are you mad at me?" Sedah asked Dustie when she returned to the house with the water.

"No. It's not your fault whether they include me or not. You don't know what they are going to teach you from one day to the next," Dustie huffed as she cleaned up the cottage while waiting for her turn at the water bucket.

"Who are you mad at then, Caprika or Amy?" Sedah shook her hands and stepped aside.

"I guess thanks to what Amy said, I'm just disappointed now." Dustie started cleaning her face.

"Well, I promise we will let you know the first available second that we can use you."

"Do you promise? Caprika says things sometimes just to make me happy or to get me to shut up. I know she did it this time so I would quit causing a scene. But I trust you for some reason. Do you really promise?" She turned to stare at Sedah with hope in her eyes.

"Yes, I really do promise, Dustie." Sedah gave Dustie her warmest of smiles, barely having time to keep herself from falling backward as Dustie threw her arms around Sedah's middle in an extremely tight hug. She held Dustie until the young girl unwrapped herself from Sedah, grabbing her hand and pulling her outside toward dinner, laughing. Sedah happily followed, giving both Caprika and Amy nods and a smile as she passed.

THE NEXT DAY, SEDAH WAS SENT TO WORK IN THE FOREST with a woman named Freil, whose job was done within the canopy of the trees. She was a quiet girl that liked to keep to herself. She wore a short dress, made entirely of English ivy that seemed to wrap around her. When she turned, the ivy seemed to come from under her hair as the vines created an intricate cowl neckline.

"If Caprika keeps them alive and healthy, what do you do?" Sedah asked. "Sorry, I know that sounds mean. I am genuinely curious. I never knew there were so many different sides to one job," she hastily added at the hurt and slightly disappointed look on Freil's face.

"She makes sure that they have the best chance to live from the second they are born. Once they have reached maturity, though, they become my responsibility," she explained.

"Okay, so why do you have to do your job way up in the canopy?" Sedah asked as she watched Freil jump up to a low-hanging branch on the tree in front of them.

"I make sure that the leaves are in good condition, that the trees are not being overrun by insects and animals that could hurt them, that vines are not slowly sucking the life out of their limbs. If any of that happens, a sister could die. Every nymph looks after her tree, but if the tree dies, she dies. It is the one thing that will kill us the fastest. Get up here so we can get to work. I have a lot of acreage to cover today." She stood on the branch, looking down at Sedah expectantly.

"I don't know how to climb a tree." Sedah's entire body turned a shade of pink in her embarrassment.

"Are you serious?" Freil asked. "You are! Look at you," she added when Sedah turned even darker pink.

"Okay, you don't have to seem so surprised about it. The only tree in the Underworld is the one that Leuce became, and climbing on her would just be too weird. So no, I haven't ever climbed a tree!" Sedah yelled up in defense.

"Oh yeah, bring Leuce into this! Fine. Walk that way." Freil pointed in a north western direction. "There is a section of forest with lots of vines, I will get them to help you into the canopy and we can see if you can travel once you are up here." She let out an aggravated sigh. Without waiting, Freil headed in the direction she had indicated, while talking telepathically with the vines ahead.

By the time that Sedah had gotten through the under-brush to the area where Freil was waiting, she was already thoroughly tired. "Okay, what now?"

"I can't believe they didn't teach you this before they gave you to me." Freil sighed. "Step on the vine that is on the ground and it will lift you to a branch for you to step onto."

Trusting that Freil would not let the vines do anything else, Sedah did as she had been told. She held onto the vertical sections of the vine to brace herself. She tried, in vain, not to think back to her dream of the vine cage.

Even though she had been told what would happen, she

was still shocked enough to squeal in surprise when the vines started to move beneath her hands like a snake. She glanced down in time to see her feet leaving the ground, panic rising.

Realizing that she had a fear of heights, Sedah closed her eyes and began shaking her head back and forth, warring with herself about how irrational fears were. She was still holding on for dear life, with her eyes closed tightly, when Freil's voice finally broke through the voices yelling in her head.

"Hello, earth to Sedah! For the love of Mother Earth, would you say something already?"

"What?" Sedah said shakily.

"You have to step off the vine and onto the branch if we are going to do this. I don't have all day, and the vine is getting tired of you having a death grip on it."

"I don't think I can do this Freil."

"Are you afraid of heights?" she asked, disbelief filling her tone.

"I think I am," Sedah admitted.

"Oh, for the love of all the Gods! Fine, I'll come help." Freil sighed, hopping over the three branches that separated the two girls. "Alright, I'm here. You can open your eyes." She stood on a branch that was in front of the one Sedah needed to step on.

Opening her eyes, Sedah looked down to the branch and then up to Freil. "Okay, now what? I don't think that I can let go."

"Here then." Freil held out her hands. "Give me one hand, take one step off, and then the other. If you need both hands, I have them . . . as long as you don't make me fall too," she giggled.

"Fine, here goes nothing," Sedah said with a deep sigh to calm herself before slowly placing her right hand into Freil's. She looked up into Freil's eyes and kept them there as she took a step, followed rapidly by the other foot, in fear of the vine moving under her foot and suddenly deciding to grab her ankle and toss her to the ground.

"See, you are fine. Those ballet flats you're wearing will help just as if you had no shoes on. You should be able to balance fairly well. Try to walk the length of the branch and see how you do. I'm here if you start to fall."

Trying to turn her entire body and walk forward down the length of the tree limb was not only intimidating, but seemingly impossible, as far as Sedah was concerned. She could barely take one step without losing her balance and having to reach out for Freil's hand or shoulder to keep herself from falling out of the tree.

"Obviously you need some work to walk like we do. Try to walk sideways now." When she saw Sedah's confused look, Freil walked down her own branch to show her what she meant. Seeing that, Sedah was able to imitate it down the branch and back with almost no help. "See, you are better at walking that way. Okay, let's see if you can travel then, because I have to go check on some things a ways away. It'd be a lot easier if you could get there the way that we do."

Sedah slowly made her way limb by limb. Freil turned back to face her when there were eight branches and two complete trees between them. "Okay, now see what you can do, and how far you can get."

Looking incredulously at her, Sedah took a deep breath and took a step onto the first branch carefully. Seeing that she could keep her balance somewhat, she tried taking the next few a little faster and a little smoother. She almost made it.

❧ 8 ❧

"I don't care, it hurts." Sedah barked at Freil.

"I told you, it's not broken so you'll be fine!" Freil was saying in frustration. Amy and Caprika broke through the brush at top speed into the small clearing. Both were panting..

"What happened? What's wrong? We could hear you yelling half a mile away!" Amy asked the two girls sitting on the ground, Sedah's right hand in Freil's lap.

"She got cocky and—" Freil started while wrapping a leaf bandage around Sedah's injured hand.

"I most certainly did not! I was trying to take two steps instead of just one, to see if I could maybe travel more fluidly, but I overshot my step and hurt my hand when I fell," Sedah defended herself to the three of them.

"So you fell on it. Great. Guess it's a good thing it's lunch then huh?" Caprika laughed. When Sedah turned red and glared at her, Caprika only laughed harder.

"Fine, laugh it up. What are we doing today? Can we go already?" She got up as carefully as she could without injuring her hand more and stomped off in a westerly direction. She turned back to see all three nymphs doubled over in laughter.

"We should probably go after her." Amy said once she could speak through her laughter.

"May I suggest some lessons in balance. She is fine until she looks down, then she freaks out. That is how she lost her balance earlier," Freil explained.

"Thanks, we'll add that to the list," Caprika told Freil. Waving goodbye, Freil disappeared into the canopy. She'd had enough of being laughed at with her brothers, and she wasn't about to start again here. She spun on her heel and continued storming off.

"Sedah, stop already!" Amy yelled.

"You've gone far enough!" Caprika added when Sedah still didn't stop.

Sedah was choosing to ignore them both. She was so frustrated, at both them and herself, that she just walked blindly, not really paying attention to where she was headed.

"*You might wanna stop,*" a voice whispered through the trees.

"What the?" she asked aloud, looking around her for the source while still walking forward.

"*Go much further and you won't be able to find out,*" the voice whispered back, closer somehow.

Startled, Sedah stopped walking and inspected her surroundings for the first time.

To her sides, and even partially in front of her, was nothing but thick forest. She turned to see where Amy and Caprika were coming from and then looked back at the path in the direction she'd been walking. If she had gone much farther, she would have dropped down a very wide fissure. The question now was: who had stopped her?

She almost jumped out of her skin when Caprika's hand landed on her shoulder, startling her out of her thoughts.

"Why didn't you stop? We were calling you. You almost didn't stop!" Caprika asked, sounding frantic with worry.

"Sorry, I heard you but, at the same time, I didn't. I don't know." Sedah threw her hands in the air in surrender to her inability to put the concept to words. She had no idea what or who had told her to stop, but thankfully they had, or she might be dead or hurt right now. Something inside her didn't want to tell them that a voice had been what had made her stop and look around.

"Man, I've heard about being mad out of your mind, but damn girl, not listening could literally kill you. Do you wanna go home that bad?" Amy laughed nervously.

"No, and I stopped, alright? So just drop it. What are we doing today anyway?"

"We're going to have lunch, here I guess, then we'll decide on what to do since you're hurt. Freil said that you need more lessons on balance, and getting over a fear of heights, apparently. Maybe it's a good thing you unknowingly walked this way." Caprika sat down cross-legged and handed Amy and Sedah each a piece of bread.

"What do you mean by that last part? What does the hole in the ground have to do with my fear of heights? Are you planning on pushing me off or something? In case you didn't know, I can't fly like a bird." Sedah was near hysteria by the time she finished. She took a long breath as she tried to calm down.

"No, but you can walk." Caprika looked at her with a mischievous look.

"What are you up to Caprika?" Amy asked, dragging her words out as she asked suspiciously.

"Nothing really. Just to tie a rope around her waist so that she won't fall over the cliff when she stands at the edge of it."

"Why would I stand on the edge of it, pray tell?"

"To get over your fear of heights, of course," Caprika said

in a cutesy voice. "There is no way to work on your balance if you can't even get in a tree without being scared that you'll fall." She batted her eyelashes with an exaggerated flourish.

"I guess you have a point. I'm not sure I like the method, though," Sedah acknowledged.

"You don't have to like it. Just do it. Are you done with your bread?"

"Guess so." Sedah got up carefully, using her uninjured hand.

"Okay, so here is what we are going to do," Caprika said as she walked over to a tree and placed a hand on it. A soft, warm yellow light radiated from her hand. It grew brighter for a few moments, and once again faded as she took her hand away.

"What was that for?" Amy asked in confusion.

"Help," She answered as vines slowly slithered down the tree, making their way past the two nymphs, toward Sedah. She was beginning to freak out, but also trying to stand her ground and act more confident than she really felt. The instant that the first vine touched her toe, however, she could contain herself no longer, and let out a yelp in fright as she jumped away. Again, dreams met reality and Sedah was mortified.

"Be calm, Sedah. It won't hurt you. It is attempting to climb up you to wrap around your waist. Either let it happen or pick it up and do it yourself, so we can get started."

Hearing the parental tone in her voice, as well as the frustration, Sedah decided to comply without any further complaint. Steeling herself, she snatched it up with her good hand and spun around twice so that the vine was wrapped fully around her body. "I can't tie it with a bad hand."

Without saying a word, the vine wrapped around her waist before the end of it tied itself together.

"I do love it when they're listening. Thank you, boys,"

Caprika directed to the trees. "Okay, so the vines have you. Walk to the edge of the cliff."

"What if I can't."

"GO, NOW!" Caprika yelled and pointed.

"Fine. I'm here." Sedah stopped at the edge. "Now wha —!" she screamed as she was pushed, before she could turn around.

Caprika had shoved her hard enough to make her stumble forward to the edge of the cliff. She was tipped so far, her upper body was entirely over the cliff. Her toes on the ledge were the only things keeping her from sliding down the cliff wall.

"Caprika, you bitch! Help me up or I'll make sure you go to Tartarus for this!" Sedah flailed her arms around, momentarily forgetting the pain in her left wrist—the fear of falling thousands of feet to the ground below taking over.

"Aw, you're so sweet to call me a bitch. I'm glad that you think so highly of me. Now shut up and look down. Look down, up, and all around you, until that scared-out-of-your-mind feeling is gone and you can actually think straight about something! You knew that we were going to do this, so get to it!" Caprika said, getting louder and more frustrated the longer that she spoke.

"Caprika, perhaps this isn't the right way to go about this. It's one thing to face a fear, but an entirely different thing to traumatize someone." Amy started to look worried, watching the conversation and the attitudes of the two girls play out in front of her.

"If we always coddle her, she will never learn on her own. Come on, how are you doing Sedah?" Caprika asked.

"Waiting until you go to sleep tonight, so I can send you to see my father, that's what."

"Are you able to think about things other than your fear?"

"No."

"Too bad," Caprika said. The vines grew a little more, making Sedah scream as she leaned farther forward. The vines stopped when she was almost fully horizontal.

"Caprika let me up! This isn't funny!"

"I'm not laughing. Look down!" Caprika crossed her arms in determination.

Sedah did as she was told, making herself sick. "Okay, I looked down, now let me the Underworld up!" she began to whimper in her fright.

"Caprika, let her up before I go to Jade. This is going too far!" Amy commanded. "Caprika!"

"Fine! Let her up!" she directed to the vines with a loud sigh.

Sedah continued to whimper as the vines slowly receded into the trees, pulling her up in the process. As soon as she was on the ground she backpedaled quickly from the edge and broke into hysterical sobs. The vines unwrapped themselves from around her waist and continued back into the canopy. Immensely shaken from the ordeal, Sedah dropped to her hands and knees, as her sobs racked her body. Amy rushed in, wrapping her arms around Sedah to try and comfort her.

She stared at Caprika over Sedah's head. "You should be ashamed of yourself."

"I did nothing wrong. She needs to learn, and I'm tired of everything taking so long just because she's scared."

"She has never done any of the things that you and I find natural. She told you this in the beginning!"

"All the more reason to hurry with the basics so we can get on to the more important things she needs to be taught," Caprika defended, crossing her arms over her chest in defiance.

"You are beginning to sound more like the sisters we detest, and less like yourself! She is not the enemy!" Amy yelled at her friend, before turning her attention back to Sedah. "Do you think you can walk? We'll go to the stream nearby and get you cleaned up." She spoke in a soothing voice that was like a parent speaking to an injured child.

Not sure her voice would obey her, Sedah nodded, her sobs and her shaking body calming down slowly. Amy helped her up, careful of Sedah's injured wrist. With a last glare at Caprika and a tentative glance from Sedah, the two girls passed her in silence. Caprika followed in silence.

"Here, sit down right here and I'll gather some water. Hopefully Caprika won't decide to cure your fear of heights by drowning you. Good thing there isn't a bigger waterfall nearby," Amy said without emotion. With no responses, she quickly walked away.

After a minute of silence, Caprika opened up. "I'm sorry for the way that I treated you back there. But I wasn't sure how to go about it. Jade, Onyx, and a bunch of others aren't happy you're here, and they're hoping like the Underworld that you'll fall on your face. Jade's personally breathing down my neck for fast results."

"But why take your frustrations out on me? Why take it to the point that I get hurt or end up hating you?" Sedah almost whispered.

"Jade ordered me to tell her any and every aspect of your powers, and where you excel and fail. Of course, won't do that, but it infuriates me more than I'd originally thought, I guess. I am sorry I took it out on you. Will you forgive me?"

"I suppose I have no choice. Whatever your reasons, I'm glad you're not outing me or our training though."

"I have my own reasons for that, but you're welcome. I've been outside these woods. I know the world outside of this one. Others haven't, and most that have, have only seen it in a way that benefitted them."

"Okay, what was said while I was gone? Did you two make up?" Amy returned with water.

"Yeah, we did. I told her something I should have told you, but wasn't sure how, or if I even should." Caprika wrung her hands together.

"For Mother Earth's sake, what? That sounds very serious." Amy sat down beside Sedah, handing her the bladder of water absently as she looked at Caprika expectantly.

"Unfortunately, it is," Sedah answered, taking the water.

"You knew about this!" Amy sprung to her feet, glaring at both of them.

"It's what I just told her, A. Chill and sit back down please," Caprika said quickly.

"Then what is it?"

"Jade had a talk with me," Caprika started, telling the girls everything that had transpired between her and Jade.

"Remember not to treat them any different when we see them around the village, not that any of us really pay their bunch any attention or treat them with any deference. But we still have to show Jade respect as if the two of you do not know what she said to me," Caprika warned as they all neared the entrance to camp.

"Don't worry, we know better than that. We'll help in any way necessary if there's a need for it," Amy offered.

"What I would give just to be able to—" Sedah started.

"Quiet!" Amy warned under her breath as they entered the barrier into camp.

The picture that the girls walked into was a scene of controlled chaos. Everyone rushed about as they went about their chores.

"What's going on? Why is everything just a little cleaner than it usually is?" Sedah asked as she looked around. She had no idea a forest could actually look clean, yet it did somehow.

"Is it that time already?" Amy asked.

"Has to be. No wonder she had that talk with me. Her time was up here," Caprika agreed.

"What are you two talking about? Whose time was up where?"

"That has a double edge sword to it this time, with *her* here. If she puts Onyx in charge, life will be worse than it already has been," Amy admitted.

"Why would Onyx be in charge?"

"At least it will only be for a month and a half," Caprika sighed.

"Who's set to come next?" Amy wondered aloud.

"Will one of you tell me what in the Underworld the two of you are talking about?" Sedah sighed in frustration at not being answered for the third time. She wanted to growl, she was so tired of being ignored. Hearing a noise, she ducked as a few falling pine cones hit her on the head. It said something to their concentration that neither girl noticed.

"I think Fawn or Baux. I'm not really sure, under the current circumstances," Caprika said.

"What circumstances!" Sedah could stand it no longer. She finally growled, causing both girls to look at her.

She had not realized, in her frustration, that she had also yelled, until she heard a few gasps from some of the girls nearest to them. They must have started paying attention to her when she made the cones fall and most likely started changing colors. Her arms showed that she had indeed turned red. After what Onyx had told Dustie when she had first gotten there, Sedah was sure that they were all just waiting for her to do something to hurt someone. She looked at Amy and Caprika for assurance.

It was Caprika that spoke up. "Yeah, we're thinking that

they think what you think they're thinking. She's bound to have said something to more than just Dustie. Just calm down and they'll have nothing to fear."

Doing what she said, Sedah closed her eyes and focused on calming down like they had been practicing. It was difficult, with hundreds of pairs of eyes on her, but she was finally able to do it. When she opened her eyes, everyone else had gone back to their own business. She could only thank the Goddess that her horns had not come out, or that things on the ground hadn't started to move.

"Guess it's all about what color that I turn, whether they are all scared or not, huh?" Sedah asked sadly.

"Seems like it, unfortunately," Amy agreed. "At least you didn't levitate anything," she whispered.

"Okay, so back to what you were talking about before you made me red. Will one of you please explain to me what is happening around here now?" Sedah asked Amy.

"Fine, let's go sit down by the campfire at the edge of the village and we'll explain it all as best we can." Amy took the lead, without waiting to see if the other two girls would follow. Dustie and Freil were already sitting there.

"We knew she would be asking questions. Anyone would. Then we heard the ruckus just now, so we headed this way to meet y'all," Dustie hurriedly explained when Caprika pointed for her to go back to the house.

Freil jumped in to help diffuse the situation. "I like her somewhat and, after today, I know that Onyx has been lying. I wanted to be here to help with the warnings."

"Fair enough on both accounts, I guess," Caprika said, sighing in defeat.

"Okay, so what's the story?" Sedah asked in an excited tone.

"Remember how I told you about the Original Daughters and how they move around within the twelve regions around the world? About how this fall you will see my mother when they all get here?" Caprika started. She had been the first to give her some insight to their world here.

"Yeah, we talked about how many of the names I knew and who I had missed. What about it?"

"Well, we didn't discuss the logistics and the time frames for each of the daughters. That's what is happening now."

"So Jade is getting replaced by another daughter already?"

"Not exactly," Dustie supplied.

"All of the daughters rotate every three months from region to region. Sometimes they go in the same order, and sometimes they trade off, so we have an idea of who is coming."

"That's why you said it should be either Baux or Fawn."

"Right, they often trade off to break up some of the monotony since it is pretty much the same routine for them every year."

"When is the tradeoff happening?"

"In a month and a half," Freil supplied this time.

"What is all the extra sprucing now?" Sedah was confused.

"The Daughter has to split her three months between us and the men's camp. The cleaning up is for a party tomorrow to celebrate and officialize her nomination of the person to lead us while she's there. The guys' leader will leave for her next post, or come back here, tonight, and they will have Jade until she leaves for the next region, a month and a half from now, when Fawn or Baux takes over here," Amy took over explaining.

"What did you mean about *her* being in charge? Who is Jade going to pick?" Sedah asked.

"She has picked Onyx every time, since she reached her majority age of twenty-five, which is the youngest someone is allowed to be to be chosen. Before that, it was Onyx's older sister, who has moved on to another region." Freil explained.

"So, you think it will be her again. It makes sense, I guess."

"Yes, that's what we were talking about as a double-edged sword. She usually spends her time making everyone miserable. Those who've pissed her off recently seem to have it even worse. Since she has issues with you—" Dustie said.

"She will probably make my life as miserable, or even more so, than she does with all of you," Sedah finished for Dustie. "But it has the benefit of making her lay off the rest of you."

"See, I knew you would get it." Caprika smiled ruefully.

"They're cleaning today to get ready for tomorrow night's party," Freil chimed in.

"What happens at the party, other than Jade saying Onyx will be leader and leaving for the guys' camp?"

"It is a ritual. It starts out as a party here, then we go out as a village and meet the men in the forest where the event will already be set up. From there, she makes Onyx the new leader. After that, we party," Caprika explained.

"Some, like the nymphs one-hundred-sixty and below, aren't allowed to go to the party in the forest, we have to clean up and prepare a couple things for the new leader," Dustie said, the aggravation clear in her voice.

"Don't fret, you'll be there soon enough, and others will take your place." Amy smiled, rubbing her back.

"Why are you made to stay behind?" Sedah asked, not really understanding why there was an age limit for the party.

Freil looked at her like she was tempted to slap some sense into her. "Have you never been to, or read up on, or even talked to anyone in the Underworld about parties and what happens at them?"

"She probably hasn't, Freil. She's led a structured and easy life. That probably never even crossed her mind. As anyone other than her family was see-through or dead," Caprika stated.

"Then I guess I won't be the rude bitch that I would be to anyone else of your age for being as clueless as Dustie. She may even know more than you at this point. How do they expect you to find a man, or to go with Fish Boy, if you do not understand the fundamentals between a man and woman?" Freil admitted bluntly.

"Dustie, go check with Jade and see if there is a special place that she wants the animals, and how much food she will want, since we have to give them the milk and possibly even make some cheese," Caprika said to her sister quickly, before another word could be spoken. Dustie did as she was told and set off to find Jade.

"So, what is it that you can't say, and obviously can't happen with Dustie around?"

"Oh, I don't know. Do you ever watch your parents run off to have a little play time alone?" Freil asked. Sedah felt herself blush at the thought. "Of course not. I didn't think so. It is one of the few times that we get to openly be around satyrs other than the brother component to our jobs. We use the time to chat, hang out, and sometimes even have a little alone time."

"It is the only time we don't have to worry about our work the next day, or getting in trouble for having fun before our work is completed for the current day. No girl and guy can be considered, or consider themselves, a couple like in the human world. But some have only one person that they will go off with repeatedly. It's understood yet unsaid."

"What do you do if one of you gets pregnant?" Sedah asked, dumbfounded.

"They go to another region to carry and have the child so that the male does not know. Then they either raise it there, or come back and leave it there to be raised by others. That is our custom," Caprika supplied for her.

"Do you even give a crap about how they turn out, or do you just recover and never look back?" Sedah asked in a frustrated and sarcastic manner, unsure of why it bothered her so much.

"Listen, myk'tu, it is the way that we have always done things. It is the way that we were raised when we were born, and the way that we have done with our children. There is no such thing as a familial bond. Everyone is family and must be looked out for." Freil explained, the tension of someone defending themselves filling her voice and the clearing.

"What are you saying? That it was done to you, so you will do it to your children? Do you even know who your mothers and fathers are? Did your mothers even care to check up on you once in a while?"

"Yes, we see them every year, and we have a telepathic bond with them if they, or we, get into any serious trouble. Our fathers never know who we are, but we do know their name so that we know not to sleep with them later on down the road," Caprika retorted.

"Do your mothers even name you, hold you, or any other motherly thing before they leave you to someone else to be cared for?"

Freil stood up furiously. "The nymphs who have hamadryad children have to keep the child near their tree for the first fifty years. After that, mothers can either stay, or need to go back to their own tree. If they leave, they still know of all of our milestones. Some pick our names, others don't. I named my daughter. I can go visit her whenever I want. She can choose to come here to live when she has to move on, I can reach her telepathically, and vice versa, whenever we want. Everyone is different, so stop judging." She stormed off.

"Now do you see? We have fun and converse with the guys every month and a half, have sex if we want to, just have normal fun if we don't, and have the day off afterward, unless there are forest emergencies. We haven't judged you and the way you live in your safe little cocoon in the Underworld, so don't sit here and throw stones at us when you know nothing about the world and how things work outside of your own family, understand?" Caprika asked Sedah pointedly after Freil was out of earshot. Having said her peace, Caprika stormed off as well, leaving Amy there to deal with Sedah.

৩১৯

"YOU KNOW I DIDN'T MEAN ANYTHING HURTFUL BY THAT, don't you, Amy?" Sedah asked some time later. After sitting there for a few moments in awkward silence, Amy had called out to one of the girls walking by and asked if she needed help with the large bundle of furs in her hands.

The nymph did, and Amy and Sedah had jumped in to help gather any and all extra skins as women threw them down. They took them out of camp to the area where they were being cleaned, and put them down to cover the ground for the party.

"I know you weren't trying to hurt anyone's feelings, but you have to understand that different cultures have different ways of living their lives. You know of our way now, but other people do other things as well. Humans give their kids away like we do sometimes, and some of them do it because they don't care at all. Others, still, do not want their children, and kill them before they're born. Some places and people sacrifice their children to their gods, even put restrictions on how many children that the adults can have. These are some of the uglier truths of the people you are about to go to, but examples nonetheless."

"So there are things that I need to learn about before opening my big mouth is what you are telling me. I get it now. I will apologize as soon as I see them."

"Good. Now help them beat these skins and get them cleaned up. I have kitchen duty tonight," Amy said briskly before walking away.

Knowing that it would take more to get them to truly forgive her stupid mouth, Sedah did as she was told, helping to beat out the pelts and then brushing them out to make them smooth again.

⚜

THE GIRLS HAD GOTTEN A PRETTY GOOD ASSEMBLY LINE formed after a few hours. Sedah was on her hands and knees, brushing out any stray pieces of dirt or leaves that she found on the skins once they were put down in their place on the ground. She suddenly felt as if they were not alone.

Looking around, but not seeing anything, she positioned herself to get up, but screamed when she was forcefully shoved back down, before being yanked up just as quickly. Someone's arms were around her to keep her from falling as she bounced up and down in the air.

By the time she had stopped flailing and was set down again, she was as red as an apple in embarrassed anger, and ready to kick some ass. She stood as soon as she was able, and started trying to jump and hit the guy that was still bouncing up and down on a vine, laughing at her.

Around her, the other girls had started to scream in delight as they saw some of the men, some exchanging hugs, while others were being chased, in good nature, by the boys.

"Aw, come on, don't be mad, Bad Apple. We were just having a little fun." The guy bouncing above her laughed as she tried repeatedly, in vain, to hit him.

"My name is not whatever you just said! It is Sedah, and you are going to get paid back for that as soon as you come down from there!" she yelled, putting her hands on her hips as she finally decided to give up, for now, and wait until he wasn't expecting it.

"Ohhh, I can't wait," the guy teased. "Kohl, we got a live one over here!" he yelled to the other man who was a few trees down. Catching a branch, he hopped down just out of her range. His yell, had caught every other satyr's attention as well, causing most of them to stop in their tracks and come see what all the commotion was about.

With the attention solely on her now, Sedah watched Kohl come through the crowd of excited men and peeved women now staring at her.

"I remember you, from when the female was trying to protect her cub, when she most certainly wanted to go off and get it on with the male that was propositioning her instead," Kohl said as he walked toward her casually. His tone and words also seemed casual, but his eyes seemed to hint to something altogether different that Sedah could not quite figure out.

"Yeah, so we took the cub and she went with him." Sedah didn't try to hide her confusion.

"Are you going to be attending and partaking in the festivities here tomorrow night?" he asked suggestively.

"Why would I not? I am living here just as one of you, so I am doing everything just like everyone else here is."

Kohl glanced back at the guys with a smile. "Sounds like I just found a reason to come tomorrow night," he directed towards her. Taking another step closer, he used the back of his hand to run it down the side of her face. "So beautiful," he whispered. At her answering shudder, he smiled, turned, and with a motion to the other guys, left; the men following in mass exodus. Sedah had no clue why her body responded to him when she didn't really like him. He was too sure of himself for her liking.

Hearing multiple sighs from all of the ladies around, Sedah was still confused as she and the others returned to what they were doing. Finishing within the hour, they began walking to camp for dinner, some talking, while others had disappointed looks on their faces.

As soon as she entered camp, Dustie, Freil, and Sandy came running up to her, all speaking at once.

"Did you really talk to Kohl?" Dustie asked.

"Was it really as sexy as they say?" Sandy asked.

"How could you? Do you know what Amy will think?" Freil crossed her arms over her chest.

"Whoa, I can't hear you all at once. One at a time please. Yes, I did talk to Kohl. More than just two words this time."

"I asked if it was really as sexy as the girls said?" Sandy clarified.

"And I asked, how could you?" Freil asked, the distaste clear in her voice.

"I guess I don't understand. All I did was talk to him."

"Amy has liked him for a while now and is planning on—," Freil glanced to Dustie, "—going off with him again at the party. Now that you've talked to him, everyone will expect it to be you that he . . . parties with instead of her. If they were to go off together, it would be seen as her doing it to spite you."

"How could all of that happen with me just talking to him? I don't even know why anyone would think it was sexy. He asked a question, and I answered the cocky brat."

Too frustrated to try to explain it, Freil just let out a growl, turned on her heel, and walked toward dinner, mumbling to herself about how a myk'tu should never be allowed to stay with them.

"Don't worry about her. She's right, but I don't think that

anyone will take it that far in their thinking. You're a myk'tu and wouldn't know." Sandy smiled as they followed more slowly to the tree.

"Do you think that Amy will be upset with me? I mean, I didn't know, after all, and I don't plan on going off with him at the party, so there should be no reason for her to think otherwise." Sedah was actually worried.

"I guess we'll have to wait and see, but I don't think she will be, since it was an honest mistake," Dustie reassured her with a smile.

Hoping she was right, Sedah ruffled Dustie's hair with a smile before heading up the tree to eat.

Amy either had not heard about what had happened or chose not to show it. She acted happy and cheerful throughout dinner service and clean up. Choosing not to push her luck or have an audience if Amy decided to confront her, Sedah played along. She went straight to her nightly chores and was in bed before Amy had the chance to clean up or come down for the night.

"Do you think she's mad at me?" Sedah asked Dustie as they fed the animals before breakfast.

"She might not know yet." Dustie said in hope.

"Oh, she knows," Caprika said as she came in, causing Sedah's hopeful expression to go despair, as well as her skin color to go gray

"Cheer up, I'm not mad at you." Amy came in behind Caprika, smiling.

"Oh, thank the Gods." Sedah sighed in relief.

"If certain people had their way, I would have beat you to a pulp last night in the dining hall. But because it was you, I brushed it off and asked a few more reliable people that had been there, who hadn't been preoccupied with the men, when it all went down," Amy went on to explain. "If it hadn't been for our talk the other day, when I found out how clueless you are about the opposite sex, I might have thought you were being coy, and not just oblivious to his underlying suggestions."

Sedah laughed. "While I do hate being called stupid, I understand what you mean." Sedah exhaled. They were okay and she hadn't accidently pissed off another friend. Sedah gladly went to breakfast with Amy, Dustie, and Caprika.

"So, since it is the day of the party, what time do things get underway and how the events unfold?" Sedah asked the girls as they were eating.

"There really is no order, per se, just that Jade gets all dressed in this fancy outfit, we follow her to the area that you and the girls prepared in the forest yesterday, Anoi will have done the same with the men following her there, the change of guard will happen from Anoi to Jade and Anoi will immediately go back to her post. Then Jade will do the same to . . . whomever she chooses and will leave to go to the men's camp, either alone or with a man, if she wants. After that, we are free to eat and party for the rest of the night," Caprika explained as nicely as possible.

"What time does this usually start?"

"They have to do the change from Anoi to Jade during sunset when Mother E can bless the change and decide who will be fertile or not for that event," Amy answered.

"How can the man possibly not know that he has fathered a child when the last person that he had a party with suddenly disappears?" Sedah was now confused.

"Some will have multiple people that they hang out with in one night, and there are usually anywhere from one to three parties held before the woman will go away and another replaces her. A guy may guess, but he will never know if he is the father or not for sure," Freil said as she sat down with them.

"So, not to upset you again, or push my luck, but I really am trying to understand this. If that is the case, how do you know, as the mother, who the father is out of the two or more men from that night?"

"Oddly enough, the Mother also lets us feel that we are fertile, which is why we will have multiple partners, to ensure that we become pregnant. The second one man has done the job, the Mother will mentally tell us by way of an invisible mark, only seen by other women who have had children before."

"What is the mark?" Sedah asked, becoming excited that Mother Earth had so much help in the overall process.

"The initial of the man that has fertilized us." Freil winked.

Breakfast being over, the girls walked to the stream.

"I don't have a bathing suit!" Sedah tried to tell the girls as they started to jump in, reed skirts and all, then turned and urged her to follow them in.

"Why do you think I told you that you needed to start wearing our clothes?" Sandy laughed before jumping into the creek as she came to join the girls, as they always had, before Sedah came along.

"But they are just so revealing," Sedah whined.

"But you're around others dressed this way. They already think you're weird for not dressing like us," Freil retorted in camaraderie.

"It might go in your favor a little way in helping some see you as one of us, since Onyx can't be nearly as influential as Jade is, though she is just as mean," Caprika chimed in.

"Just don't decide to change outfits until after tonight though, huh?" Amy said in a voice that matched her smile. They all knew that she was referring to Kohl and his statements.

Nodding in agreement and mutual understanding, Sedah decided to change the subject and started asking Dustie questions about all the animals that she had to take care of over the years that she had been there.

The girls hung out in the water for the rest of the day, swimming and being typical girls, taking turns making jokes and splashing one another with water. They were having so much fun they didn't even go back to camp for lunch, choosing to kill and cook a few fish over a handmade fire. They were still laughing and joking as they all returned to camp ten minutes shy of the gathering time.

WHEN THEY ENTERED THE CENTER OF CAMP, MOST OF THE women had already assembled, either standing or sitting, at the base of the tree designated for the current leader, in this case Jade, to occupy. Ten or so minutes later, everyone stood as Jade came out of her hut and descended the stairs to a balconied landing, several yards above the forest floor. Those few women that had helped her dress stood behind her as she addressed the crowd.

Where the normal attire of a nymph was a nature created outfit of various lengths, types, or materials, this ceremonial outfit was as out of the norm as Jade was from the other nymphs. Sedah had noticed the colored, patterned, or flora skin, as well as hair on others, but she had yet to see anything quite like Jade.

Instead of hair, limbs grew from her skull to form their own tree. Moss covered her upper body to form a long sleeve. Small vines like those Sedah had used with Freil, covered Jade like a corset before growing bigger at her hips to flare out in a long gown, reminiscent of trunk roots.

Surveying the women below, Jade held a long, appreciative look with most of them while barely looking at others. Apparently seeing what she wanted from her appraisal, she kept her eyes on them all as she slowly descended the final stairs. Once at the bottom, she strode toward the center of the crowd, forcing them to part for her, lest they keep her from moving forward.

With each woman that she passed, they each bowed in a respectful manner, whether they liked her or not. Once Jade passed, others began to follow behind, beginning a somber song.

If I find a way to stay, I will never be the same
As time marches on, so must I make another move
For the good of the many, before I can dare damn any
Be I flying in the wind, may I find peace in the night
Mother give her our strength, may her move give her light
We've done everything we can, her time here is sand
As the men take our light, pray keep her at her height

PRETTY AS IT SOUNDED, SEDAH DID NOT UNDERSTAND A word. Knowing better than to ask then, she followed the procession along with her friends to the forest where they had done all the preparation work the day before. Sedah watched as the men came from the western part of the forest, singing the same song behind who she could only assume to be Anoi, in another ostentatiously strange outfit. Anoi's hair was bright green, like the leaves budding to life in the spring. Her dress was made of briar vines, covering her in the front, yet showing a small amount of her midriff and most of her back, before coming together at the top of the dimple of her buttocks to drape to the ground in a ball gown fashion. The two leaders reached opposite edges of the pelts at the same time the song came to an end.

In the middle of the pelts, stood a statue that had not been there the day before. Walking in unison, the two women went toward one another, coming to a stop on each side of the statue. As if on cue, everyone but the two women sat down wherever they had been standing. Sedah quickly did the same to not draw attention.

Everyone sat around her in rapt attention to the statue as

if they were seeing something she wasn't. Sedah found herself bored as she watched and waited for something, anything, to happen. When it finally did, it made her jump.

Slowly, a glow emanated from inside both Jade and Anoi. Each woman gasped as a piece of their essence was taken out of them. Anoi dropped to her knees, but Jade stood tall, a testament to her power. The essence floated into the statue, and then out to Jade, causing a second gasp and lifting Jade to the tips of her toes.

As the two women came to themselves, everyone slowly got up, yet kept their heads bowed. They stayed this way until Anoi acknowledged the statue with a bow of her own. Standing again, Anoi slowly disappeared into a softball sized glittering orb, hovering for a minute before shooting straight through the forest to the west. Jade now stood alone in front of the statue, her back to it as she addressed both sexes.

"By tradition, as I leave the females, I must leave someone to watch over them until the next sister can take my place. This must be a person that I inherently trust above all others. For this rotation . . . I have decided to choose Lilac." She smiled, watching all the reactions crossing the nymphs faces.

Not surprisingly, many of the women, mostly those that Sedah called her friends, tried in vain to hide their gasps of surprise at the new and fresh choice after so many of the same, year after year.

Stepping forward, Lilac took her place in front of Jade, facing the statue.

"As Daughter in charge, I now give you a small piece of Mother Earth's power so that you may call if you have need of me," Jade said, indicating for Lilac to step forward to the statue.

Putting her hand in the palm of the statue, some of the same energy from before flowed into her hand like water. She let it rest within her own palms for a moment before the light soaked into her skin slowly. Lilac's breath deepened as the light seeped in, her skin taking on a glow as it spread throughout her bloodstream. After giving her a moment to recover, Lilac and Jade faced their people in unison.

"Your new leader, nymphs. Let the festivities now begin," Jade announced with a smile. With a loud yell from just about every person there, the party got underway for the night.

Sedah had no idea what to expect, but was definitely surprised when a group of both satyrs and nymphs started to pull out instruments and play woodsy tunes from what were obviously hand carved instruments.

Everyone was quiet at first, letting the tune seep into them as they began to move and let it take them away. At some point in the party, the food also appeared for everyone to enjoy. Before long, the crowd seemed to become smaller and smaller as the party wore on. Looking around, Sedah realized that some of the people had coupled off and were slowly disappearing on their own.

"Do me a favor and quit looking so bored," Caprika laughed as she came up from behind the tree Sedah was leaning against.

"What would you expect me to look like?" Sedah asked with a smile as Caprika stepped up to stand beside her.

"Like you are having fun. Dance or eat, something other than just standing here leaning against a tree. Please tell me that you at least know how to dance," she elaborated.

"Of course I do! I know all the formal dances."

"So, are you saying that you can't dance to this?" Caprika raised her eyebrows in disbelief.

"This is a tune unlike anything I have ever heard before. It is as if it's calling to my soul. I'm not sure I can make my body do the things that they are making theirs do." Sedah pointed towards those that were dancing on the pelts surrounding the statue of the Mother. It was like the music was their puppet master, pulling their strings to move them in ways and positions Sedah didn't think were possible. It was both beautiful and sensual. While Sedah had never had sex, she could understand better now, how its lull could be erotic to the senses and overwhelm a person.

"Then I guess we'd better teach you, huh?" Caprika said with a laugh, grabbing Sedah by the hands and pulling into the throng of dancers.

Rolling her eyes but allowing herself to be pulled along, she laughed as Caprika spun her once and let her go. Watching what Caprika did, she tried to do the same, only feeling stupid when she could see the pained expressions that a few other girls gave her.

"It's fine, you just have to learn to relax. Think about nothing but the music and let it flow through you. Just tune everything else out," she told Sedah in a serious, yet playful, tone.

Trying to do exactly as instructed, she compartmentalized everything that had gone on in her life up until then, and let the music flow over like the waterfall she had seen a few days ago. Everything left her mind but the music. Her body responded instinctively to the rhythms before her mind could process the sounds.

MELAM HAD BEEN FOLLOWING ALONG AT THE BACK OF THE pack, just as bitter as ever for still being with the satyrs. He had no idea why he was there, or if he would know where to go when the time to act would come. While he understood that his mission must be very important to his grandmother, he missed his home and his family. His only solace in this exile was that there was another myk'tu there. He had asked

Anoi earlier if he needed to attend the gathering that night, since he wasn't one of them.

The insult on her face that he had presumed to ask had caught him off guard. "I made a promise to my mother, who was told in a dream from Mother Earth herself, that you were coming and could not be harmed. Just letting you into camp is doing you a favor. Don't insult us by rejecting our ways," Anoi had retorted. He knew she had been ordered to show him kindness and hospitality as well, but she had purposefully omitted that part. Knowing then that he didn't have a choice in the matter, without offending her or revealing who he was, he had been forced to drop the subject.

It was for that reason alone that he was there that night. He surveyed the scene from a branch, taking stock of all the nymphs below, and what each of them were up to. Some of the satyrs had also chosen to see the festivities from different branches high in the trees, while some chose to mingle with the food and dancers immediately. Melam had chosen a branch that was low, but farther away, in order to better look out for any humans that one of the guards might have mistaken for a nymph. Although unlikely, it was possible. Melam had just returned to his branch with some fruit, when one of the fyk'tu named Kohl sat down beside him.

"You know you can go down there and join them. You are supposed to feel like one of us, so you're allowed to participate in most of the things we do. Go dance, chat up the girls, anything. All you can't do is have sex with any of them. Although, from what I have been told as far as boundaries with myk'tus, there's nothing stopping you from making out and having some fun." Kohl smiled conspiratorially.

"Who knows. The night is still young," Melam said in agreement. Kohl had just unknowingly answered a question that had been on his mind. He had been a widower for almost one hundred and seventy years. If his mission didn't start soon, he might just go native, minus the lamb fur, horse ears and deer hooves.

***

SEDAH'S APPREHENSION GREW AS THE SATYRS JOINED THEM on the dance floor. Caprika gave her a reassuring smile.

Sedah had no problems showing that she was uncomfortable with other guys coming up to dance with them. She only knew only what the girls had told her about the celebrations, but after what had happened with Kohl the other day, she didn't want to accidentally piss off any more of the nymphs, especially any that she considered friends.

While Caprika had stayed with her for most of the night, Sandy, Freil, and Amy had all taken off, returning periodically to have a little fun with them before disappearing again. In fact, Amy had just come back, with another female in her wake, as more men arrived on the scene.

She couldn't help but notice how good looking most of them were. The human parts of them anyway. The guys seemed to just want a nice, good time, for the most part. They chose to dance with Caprika, moving slow behind her in a caring and romantic way as the music suggested. As that song faded into the next, more lively song, even Sedah laughed as a few particular satyrs spun around Caprika to the center of the dancing girls and did outrageous moves that she had never seen before.

As they quickly became the center of attention to more than just Caprika and Sedah's little group, Sedah became aware of two things: one guy pulling his dancing partner away towards the woods, and the familiar feel of a male body pressed tightly against the back of her body a moment or two later. Thinking it was Kohl, because he had done that once before, Sedah turned and found that, instead, it was the guy that had embarrassed her the day before.

Her tormentor was smart enough to back away before he began to taunt her.

"Thought I might return to the scene of the crime and see if I could get into any more trouble," he told her, getting a cocky grin on his face.

His comment inflaming her further, Sedah started after him as he kept backing through the mingling partygoers. "I told you I would get you back, you mangy little goat," she said as she made her way through the crowds and took off after him in blind fury.

No one seemed to notice when she chased after the male, intent on doing him harm. She caught up to him surprisingly fast. She grabbed his bicep from behind, turning him around, again, too easily. Something in the back of her mind was warning her, but she couldn't determine why. She began to beat his chest and try to slap the smile off of him. When she went to kick him in the shins, he quickly made a move that sent them to the ground, her straddling his body at the waist and him firmly holding her by the wrists to stop any further assault.

"Let my wrists go, you goat, so I can beat your ass!" she yelled, turning a dark red from the severity of her anger.

"Well that doesn't make much sense, now, does it? You are only going to end up getting yourself hurt." He smirked up at her as she struggled.

"Fine," she sighed in exasperation. "Let me go so I can get up off the ground, you filthy goat!" She struggled against his tight grip to get up.

"Now my feelings are just hurt. First you call me a goat, and then you can't even have the decency to say please?" As she squirmed, she felt what was stirring under his loincloth.

Sighing in frustration, Sedah counted to ten before

looking him in the eyes. "Would you please let go of my wrists so I can get off?" She glared at him.

"Now those are the right words, indeed," he told her. Confusion crossed her face a second before he rolled them over, using his own body and hips to pin her under him. There was no mistaking his arousal pressing hard against her stomach.

"What are you doing?" She struggled underneath him, becoming panicked when she couldn't get herself free. "I thought if I said please that you would let me go."

"No, you said to let go of your wrists, so that you could get off." He grinned, the gleam of anticipation in his eyes. "That is exactly what I plan on doing, too," he told her, then laughed. His voice grew throatier as she continued to squirm, trying in vain to get out from under him. "You really are ignorant, aren't you?" he whispered in her ear.

"Of what?" she asked in barely more than a whisper. The sudden change in his voice hinted at something evil, causing hers to be low and breathless in panic. Surely he couldn't want to have sex with her.

"Of what?" he mocked as he took her imprisoned right hand and led it down to the side of her body. "Of this of course," he told her as he moved his body just enough to put his thickness in her trembling hand, forcibly guiding her to stroke him repeatedly, despite her trying to pull her hand away. He moaned and looked down at her with heavily lidded eyes. Tears fell silently down her face and she shut her eyes firmly.

"This is what gets us both off, baby. This is what you women beg us for time after time at these things," he said without ever letting up on guiding her hand. "Tell you what, I will finish for you this time, since I have no idea how to get those clothes off of you, and when you come back for the next party, you make sure you come and see me, dressed as one of us, and I will show you why it is that you want me to get you off." He stood suddenly, replacing his hand where hers had been and walking away into the night with a laugh.

Oblivious to where he might have gone, but afraid he might come back, all Sedah could do was lie there in a crumpled, weeping mess on the forest floor as the adrenaline ebbed and the panic and fear took over. She had no idea how long she lay there before she felt strong hands suddenly picking her up. The thought that the vile satyr might be back to take her off and finish what he'd started by force brought her to life, kicking and flailing about, trying and hoping to be put down and forgotten about again.

𝒮 10 𝒮

"**S**hh, it is okay. I have you. You're safe," a new, unknown male voice spoke down to her—a voice that most certainly did not belong to her attacker. Hearing the difference, she instantly stopped struggling and settled. A calming sensation filled her. Her mind struggled for control, even as she felt her body snuggling deeper into the warm, bare torso of her rescuer.

She half dozed through the rustling of the leaves around her, the sound of inhuman whispers, and the familiar sounds of animals. The next thing that passed through the haze in her mind was the feeling of the comforting warmth disappearing. Sitting up with fears anew, Sedah groaned as the familiar room began to spin.

"Calm down meve, I haven't gone anywhere," came the same male voice from earlier. To her, it seemed to be coming from her right, yet she found the man sitting to the left of her bed, leaning back in a chair. He had been talking towards the ceiling which was throwing off where he was in the room.

"See something interesting up there?" She asked, smiling

weakly as she attempted to steady her spinning brain with her hands.

"Sorry, good acoustics."

Finally, the room stopped spinning enough so she could get a good look at him. "You're not a satyr! What are you?" she blurted out before she was able to stop herself. Instantly embarrassed, she slapped her hand over her mouth to try and prevent any other stupid remarks or questions from coming out.

"Like you, I am an outsider, hiding in the mountains with the woodland creatures, learning earth's ways," he repied, setting the chair back on four legs.

"So what is your name then?"

"I am Melam. I'm not a satyr obviously, I am just . . . visiting, I guess you could say. What happened to you out there?"

"How did you get into camp? Men are not supposed to be able to get into camp, human or otherwise."

"I guess they took pity on me helping you. Would you care to tell me why you were sleeping on the forest floor?"

"Does anyone know? Did anyone see you carry me back?" She looked towards Dusty and Caprika's hammocks. Sedah found herself glad Caprika had decided to give the bed to Sedah and take the hammock for herself a few weeks ago, after continually waking up to Sedah having fallen out of it.

"No one from the party, and only one or two of the younger girls here, why?" He kept pushing.

"I just don't know what I would tell anyone about what happened." She averted her eyes, choosing to look at her hands instead.

"And what did happen exactly?" he asked in a calm, reassuring voice, coming to sit on the bed next to her. "If you don't talk about it, it will fester inside and eat away at you. I promise that I won't tell a soul. Just between us myk'tus." He grinned, causing a small smile pull at the corners of her mouth too. Playing with the covers, she told him everything.

She rushed it all out, her words getting faster as she told him her story. At the last two words, her emotions caught up, causing her voice to crack as tears rolled down her face. Melam said nothing for so long that she risked looking over at him. His eyes were as blue as the Arctic Ocean, so much like hers. They were such a contrast to his black hair. It was obvious that he was used to it being shorter, as he kept pushing it out of his eyes every now and then. He had a hard face that spoke of authority and exuded confidence, and yet he was looking at her with such concern that it softened his features.

"You were lying there in the fetal position because he tried to force you? I didn't see anyone," Melam said, his voice low and pondering. "I wonder if the satyr told you to stay there and incited fear in you before I got there."

"I know nothing of mating, but I know it should never be forced. He said that the only reason we didn't go farther was that he could not figure out my clothes." She started crying in earnest at the thought of what could have happened.

"First, animals mate. Humans have either meaningless sex, or, if they care for the person they are with, they make love to one another. Secondly, you are saying that he did not have sex with you. So, what part has you so upset?"

"I was forced to touch him!" she yelled in a whisper in case there were prying ears around.

"Okay, but you cannot do anything to change what has already happened. Why not just try to forget about it if you are not going to tell anyone?"

"Because I'm gonna start wearing their clothes, and he will try it again at the next party. He said he would." Tears rolled unbidden down her cheeks at the thought.

"So you make sure not to be alone at the next party, have a

person with you at all times, or just don't run off. You will figure it out. You seem smart enough." Melam's heart hurt for the scared girl. He wiped at a tear on her cheek.

"Okay, so what am I supposed to tell the girls about the strange man who came into camp, carrying me to my hut?"

"That's easy: nothing. I will make those who saw us forget that they did. Just say that you got sleepy and came back early. All the dancing wore you out, right?" Melam winked as he continued to stroke her cheek.

"How do I explain if I think about what happened and turn grey or black?"

"What do you mean turn grey or black?"

"You mean you haven't seen the multitude of colors I have been turning during our conversation?"

"No, I've been looking at your beautiful eyes, not at your skin color," he told her in a seriously sexy voice. She had no idea what to make of her body responding to someone who was simply giving her a compliment. Just the sound of his voice filled her stomach with butterflies.

"Um, okay. Well I guess I'm fine here, if you want to go back and have more fun while you still can." She tried not to sound as depressed as she suddenly felt, failing badly.

"I do actually have to go. Before I do though, I feel like I need to do something, so you don't have nightmares tonight. Do you trust me?" he asked.

"I barely know you," she admitted apprehensively.

Melam leaned toward Sedah, putting his arms on each side of her body, bringing himself closer to her and effectively caging her in so she had to lie down. She was sure he could hear her heart beating out of her chest as he leaned toward her. She slowly sucked in and held her breath as she watched him lean closer. Scant inches separated their lips as he spoke softly, almost reverently to her. Instead of feeling trapped or scared, she felt acutely aware of how close her arm was to his hand. One slight movement and he would be touching her.

"Will you trust me then, just this once, to help you forget, so you actually end the night on a happy note?" He used his right hand to push a piece of hair off her face.

Lost in his eyes and sweet, caring tone, Sedah could only nod. Her voice failed her as soon as he touched her face.

"Close your eyes," he whispered. Somewhat nervous, Sedah stared at him for a minute before doing what she was told with a long sigh. It was hard to close your eyes when all you wanted to do was stare at something so beautiful.

Having her eyes closed made her focus on her other senses. She could hear that he was still there, yet his stillness made her want to move to find him. She tried to wait patiently for him to begin his treatment to help her forget. Lying there, she could only inhale his unique scent to try to keep herself grounded. It was like freshly washed linen, mixed with something she couldn't quite comprehend.

She was about to speak when he finally touched her, again causing all rational thought to blow away like smoke. She could hear the sheets rustle as he leaned away from her, but she still jumped when he wrapped his fingers between each of hers. Slowly, he moved her arms from her sides to above her head, crossing her arms at the wrists.

Slowly unlinking their fingers, he very lightly ran his nails from the inside of her wrists, down her forearm to her triceps. She almost jumped as his breath met her right ear. Saying nothing, he simply laid a slow kiss where her lobe met her cheek. Starting there, he kissed a line down her jawline to her chin, and pausing a moment, repeated the slow process on the left side.

Smiling as he looked down at her, Melam watched her skin slowly turn pink. He could feel her body getting flushed, her breathing increasing with each kiss. He paused between moving the lines of kisses from one side of her beautiful face to the other to see if she would become wary of what he was doing. When her eyes remained shut, he finished her other side.

Beginning at the base of her throat, Melam used his tongue to trace a line down her sternum to the base of her v-neck shirt, before planting a kiss there also. Sedah's breath hitched and she began to squirm under him. She was about to move her hands when he grabbed at her wrists, holding them in place. He could tell that she was beginning to panic on him, so he gentled his hold, linking their fingers again so she would not feel held down like earlier.

"Open your eyes for a moment," he said softly to Sedah. She blinked up into his sapphire gaze. He continued, his voice calm and smooth "Trust me. I won't do anything to hurt you. No clothes will be removed. Just breathe and allow yourself to feel," he told her.

Staring into her eyes, he could see the understanding of the truth he spoke. Once she closed her eyes again and settled back down, he touched the base of her throat with his lips, kissing his way down to her shirt again. Once there, he followed the trim of her shirt as he kissed along the neckline, where shirt met skin, until he reached her shoulder. Without pause, he kissed from shoulder to collar bone, nipping once on the bone, causing her to jump slightly.

"Now, I am going to kiss your lips. If I begin to scare you, all you have to do is say stop."

He chuckled when her eyes flew open to pin him with a scared, yet confused stare. "Why would you do that?"

"I just wanted you to know a nice, innocent kiss—one given to you, not taken from you." "Well, I—" she began. Melam held a finger to his lips and smiled down at her.

"Others are coming. I hope that your mind has been sufficiently diverted for now. That kiss will have to wait until another time." He winked at Sedah before standing and slipping quietly out of the hut. A few feet from the hut, Caprika, Amy and Dustie walked up to stop his progress out of camp.

"How did you get into camp, and why are you in our hut alone with my charge, sir?" Caprika asked in a threatening and accusatory voice as she crossed her arms and puffed up in a show of intimidation. Melam almost laughed at the display.

"The forest let me in, while I carried her in my arms, so you can stop threatening. She fell asleep while we were talking at the party, so I figured it only right to bring her home. The forest seemed to agree, so I fail to see a problem here."

"Is she awake now?" Dustie asked from behind Caprika, making it more of an accusation than a question.

"Yes, and we were talking some more," Sedah jumped in, coming from the hut. She was not sure if she was defending Melam or herself, but she had heard the commotion and was not about to let him take all the heat.

"Well, we're here now, so you may go." Caprika stepped out of the way of his progress. All four girls watched until he had disappeared through the mist that separated the camp from the forest. Sedah wondered if they enjoyed the view as much as she did.

"There, he's out," Dustie said, exhaling like a thorn had been removed from her foot. "Why was he here, and how the hell did none of us here know it?"

"I told you. He told you. I don't see the big deal here!" Sedah retorted.

"You're going to get a reputation here as someone who goes off with men willingly. If you were one of us, it would be nothing," Dustie began explaining only to have Caprika cut in.

"But you are not one of us! You are a myk'tu, who went off with the only other myk'tu around! Someone had to have seen you go off together, and it can only lead to talk. You need to focus on training, and nothing but that, while you are here. There will be plenty of time to see and talk to Melam later, but not while you are here training for your outside life," Caprika finished explaining. "Get some sleep. We will train all day tomorrow." She sighed.

Wanting to ask some more questions, but seeing in Caprika's stance and voice that she would not get any answers, Sedah sighed and turned her back to them. "Goodnight girls."

❧

DUSTIE MOTIONED TO CAPRIKA SILENTLY BEFORE WALKING away from the hut.

"What little sister? I'm tired," Caprika said, rubbing both hands over her face in exhaustion.

"What we wonder, is what aren't you telling us?" Amy asked from behind her. She turned to see Amy leaning against the shed, right knee bent to support her weight, should she need to stand quickly.

"I don't know what you mean," Caprika told her, holding Amy's stare with confidence.

"You're not that good at it, Caprika, so don't lie to us. The only way for this to fully work is to let us in, so we can help. Who is this other myk'tu, how do you know his name, and why was he allowed into camp? We all should've felt the disharmony the very second he crossed the barrier." Amy's voice was as hard and cold as steel.

"He said he was carrying Sedah, so it let him in. I have no reason not to believe that." Caprika threw her hands up in resignation.

"It doesn't even let her in yet, so try another one," Amy reminded them.

"I felt the initial disruption in the forest barrier. Then I heard a lulling whisper to ignore it. Difference is, I know Sedah can't come in alone like everyone else assumes. So, imagine my surprise to see a male myk'tu leaving our hut as I walked up to see how her first party went," Dustie chimed in.

"I'm still not sure how he got in. Caprika acted like she expected to see him though," Amy agreed.

"Fine. You wanna know? That myk'tu," Caprika pointed to the fog, "is an unknown that we have been told to accept, but not told why. All I can figure is that it has something to do with that myk'tu in there and the deals her father has dealt for her!" She pointed towards the hut where Sedah slept, unaware.

"What are you talking about exactly, Cap?" Dustie asked.

"One part of her time here is to see if she can find love by herself. Otherwise, she has to serve any one of Poseidon's children that he chooses, in any way he sees fit. I guess that Melam is one of those sons being considered, since we are told to accept him. I am not exactly sure, to be honest."

"Why is he here now then, instead of giving her time to acclimate? Is he the son chosen for her to serve?" Amy asked.

"Again, I don't know. If he is the son of Poseidon, he is an unknown son. Since Poseidon and Hades are sure she will end up serving one of them anyway, I guess Melam was sent here as someone Sedah could get to know so she wouldn't feel like she was alone out there, serving complete strangers. We haven't been told anything other than the deal for her to find love or become a servant and that we had to accept him being here, without being told who he was or why we had to."

"She either has to find love or she becomes a servant mermaid?" Dustie was flabbergasted.

"So we are supposed to let them get to know one another in addition to training her to pass as a human? Do either of them realize they are being manipulated?"

"Yes, we have been told not to stop whatever happens

between them. As to whether they know—I don't know about him, but she has no idea who he is . . . that I am aware of anyway. That is, unless she found out tonight, which I doubt. Even if he is a son of Poseidon, I don't see how he got through the barrier."

"We assume that he is a son, but we do not know for sure. I'll ask him a few questions the next time we come across him and see what he says. I don't think any of us are getting the full story tonight. The only one that will be hurt from not knowing is Sedah, and that is unacceptable to me," Amy said pointedly. "Sedah maybe an outsider, but she's grown on me, and I'm not going to just do what I'm told without a good reason."

"Okay, just so we're clear, no more hiding things from us. Otherwise, we won't help you anymore." Dustie glared at her older sister.

"Agreed." Caprika looked them both in the eyes to show she was being honest.

"Then goodnight, ladies." Amy shoved off the wall with her foot and headed in the direction of her tree.

৩৯৩

AFTER LEAVING THE WOMEN'S CAMP, MELAM WENT BACK TO the party to watch the men and women and see how out of hand these parties could get. While most of the satyrs were having a great time, drinking, dancing, and cavorting with the ladies, Kohl, and a few of his most avid followers, silently slipped from the party. Melam's gut told him something was off. Kohl wasn't the type to miss out on one of the few nights he could be with as many females as possible, just to hang out with his male friends he could see every day.

Following his instincts, Melam allowed some of his energy to follow them silently until they returned, seemingly unnoticed, some hours later. Once he'd gathered all the information on the party that he felt he needed, Melam went back to the satyr camp and to his bed.

Sometime during the night, Melam became aware of a familiar presence in the room with him. Opening his eyes slowly, his ears alert, he slowly sat upright, making sure his body was covered with a sheet as he swung his legs over the side of the bed.

"Mother, Grandmother, to what do I owe the pleasure of your visit?" Seeing these two imposing women at such a late hour couldn't keep him from remembering his manners.

"The Goddess has come to me seeking your help in matters that may need your intervention, since you have more knowledge with humans," his mother explained.

"More knowledge? I'm afraid that I do not understand." He looked back and forth between the women.

"My sons have alerted me to some behavior tonight within the satyr's ranks that I cannot condone. Those in charge have turned a blind eye to my objections of how humans are being treated by otherworldly beings. The Mother of the Earth will not be ignored." His grandmother said in a determined, steel tone. As if to accentuate her meaning, a rogue wind blew through the camp, into his room.

"Why do you think this is going on?" Melam dared to ask.

"This is why I wish for your help. I need to know the satyrs' role in this, as well as know the names of those involved," Gaia told her grandson.

"I am only to watch and be a messenger, then, and not deal with the problem as I usually do? What is the issue that I am to watch for?" He looked to the Goddess and his mother. The only problem he could think of was with Kohl. But he did not know what had happened yet.

"It was your trail of energy that alerted Hyperion and Crius to a problem involving several satyrs. They let your grandmother know what they found, and that it had not been dealt with." His mother's brows furrowed.

"But how did you know there was a problem but not what the problem was, yet you have already told the head nymphs to take care of it?" Melam directed toward Gaia. He heard his mother gasp with surprise that he had been bold enough to ask.

"I do not always have the proof, as I have other places to be and issues to deal with, although my word should be enough. It is the cries of pain coming from my children that I hear in the air and the very soil," Gaia chastised Melam. "Although you are not my child, you are my blood, and I do care. I heard your heart's sadness and distrust even before you came here. Is it just one creature, or is it more than one that is causing you these feelings as of late?"

"It was originally just one satyr, but I believe now that it may be more," he admitted, looking down and running his hands through his hair.

"This is why you need to be the watcher. Just be attentive of all and I will have the proof I need when I return next."

"How will I get the proof needed without people getting hurt?" Melam asked, looking up at the two women. He was almost certain that people already were, but he would have no proof until he followed his energy trail in the daylight the next day.

"I will have the proof, if you will be my eyes." She slowly walked two steps toward him. Without warning, her hands went to his head, her thumbs covered his eyes. He lost his sight for a moment as the rest of her hand rested at his temples. Almost as soon as his vision went away, it returned, leaving him confused about what had just happened, but still smart enough to not question it. Looking up, he saw his mother was alone in the room with him. He quickly looked around but saw no one else.

"She will be back in a moment, but there is something that I must tell you, with everything that's happening," Rhea told Melam in a rush.

"What is happening? You make no sense mother." Melam barely kept himself from rolling his eyes in irritation.

"The other myk'tu that is here, the female that you were allowed to see safely home tonight? You need to know, first, that it was one of your uncles that decided to let you through the barrier, as he is in charge of them. But you do need to decide whether you like her, or you will need to begin avoiding her."

"And why is that? What would me liking her or not have to do with anything?" Melam had no idea where his mother was going with this.

"She is not, nor can she become, aware that you are not some level of human. I have been told that Poseidon and her father made a deal to bind her to one of Poseidon's children to keep her a secret from Demeter. I would hate to see you become attached to her and then lose her." His mother's eyes held concern.

"Why would she be bound to one of them, unless she is half Mer? Did her family cause dishonor or simply promise their daughter to Poseidon? Why should I care what deal these Gods have struck with one another? I still do not know why you were told to send me to this archaic planet to begin with." Melam knew that he sounded like a petulant child, but he would rather be home with his daughter than there, literally being the eyes for his grandmother.

Before he could put enough rational thoughts together to ask any more questions, the Mother Goddess appeared out of a black mist.

"We will leave you my son. Just watch and listen to all around you." Leaning down, his mother kissed the top of his head before stepping back. She took the hand of Gaia, and dissolved them both into purple particles, which sparkled, then evaporated into nothingness.

Melam could do nothing for the rest of the night but stare at the roof of his lodge and think. All he knew for sure was that he had to take care of Kohl and his minions. While he would admit the little goddess was pretty, she was obviously not his mission. His wife had died a long time ago, and he was not looking for a replacement. Not knowing how long he lay staring at the ceiling in contemplation a hummingbird landing on his naked chest finally alerted him to the approaching dawn.

"Now that your hand is healed, and you're going to start dressing like us, we're going to practice traveling like a nymph. That has to start today if you're going to make any progress. The sooner we get started, the sooner you can act like one of us, so we can have more time for your lessons of the outside world. Get up," Caprika said the next morning, while poking at a sleepy-headed Sedah.

Freil burst through the door, a set of reed clothes in her hand. "I made you a longer skirt than we wear, and a less revealing top, considering how you feel about our clothes." She handed them to Sedah, who took them into the curtained off area to change.

In the end, she had to let Dustie show her how to get into the tank top shirt and reed skirt before going to breakfast with Caprika. Afterward, they met up with Amy and Dustie in the central clearing of the camp.

"Okay, now let's get to the forest and turn you into a monkey woman," Caprika told her as they walked, which caused Dustie to laugh.

"Fine, Dustie. Go show me how it's done, since you think this is so funny." Sedah blurted out in agitation. That someone much younger would be so much better made her feel incompetent. In that moment, it didn't matter that she'd had no way to learn it at home.

Not reacting to the bite to her voice, Dustie scaled the nearest tree and sat down on the lowest limb. "You just need balance and to be limber, see?" she stood up and hopped from tree limb to tree limb all above them, giggling the entire time in happiness.

"She's showing off, but she is right. Balance is a must. Being limber will come with time and practice," Caprika reassured her as they reached the spot they used when they didn't care if anyone stumbled upon them or not.

"Okay, this'll do for now. Do what Dustie did when you get to the tree. Since you're new, you might need to run up to it to have enough momentum. Either way, let's see if you can do that first. We'll worry about walking the branch later." Caprika took to the tree beside her, giving her an example, getting herself a good seat.

Sighing, Sedah looked at the tree two yards in front of her. "Time to put up or shut up, I guess," she muttered Amy's common phrase as she backed up one more yard. Taking a deep breath, Sedah ran toward the tree. She kicked out one foot to push off the trunk. She bounced off it and landed back on the ground. Gaining confidence, Sedah backed up to her starting point and tried again. Bouncing off like last time, she growled in frustration.

"Don't get mad, Sedah, your powers might kick in." Amy warned her softly, wrapping an arm around her shoulders.

"Look, you have the gist, you just need the forward lift. When your foot hits the tree, bend like you are going up the steps of the camp tree. When you do that and push off the trunk, you should go up instead of out." Caprika positioned her foot against the tree in demonstration. She started from beside Sedah and Amy, showing what she meant, in action, landing back on the ground without a sound.

Confident that she could do it, Sedah ran forward, everyone yelling in encouragement as her foot hit the tree. She was able to gain a little more height before hitting the ground.

"Okay, try again. This time, if you get close enough, see if you can touch the limb and still land on the ground on both feet," Caprika said as all the girls clapped.

With a confident nod, Sedah took a deep, calming breath, shaking her hands to help her relax. Finally feeling ready, She took off toward the tree.

Just as her left foot was about to connect with the trunk, a root grew from under the dirt, catching her right one. Instead of landing solidly, her left foot slid down the bark of the tree. Her right knee went to the ground hard enough that she could feel something audibly crunch.

Still falling forward, Sedah had no time to throw her hands up to keep herself from hitting the left side of her head against the trunk, as the world went black.

❦

MELAM, WHO HAD HEARD THE DISTANT SOUND OF MULTIPLE women and been curious, broke through the trees just in time to see Sedah crumble to the ground. Not thinking, he blinked to her side before the girls could register what had just happened. All they would have seen was that one second their friend was falling, and the next, Melam was pushing hair and dirt off Sedah's face. He checked to see if she was still breathing.

The girls were silent until he nodded his head in confirmation that she was still alive. The girls moved closer, gingerly, as if they were afraid of causing more damage. Once there, Caprika, Amy, and Dustie sat on their knees surrounding her.

Melam closed his eyes as they sat down. His initial shock and fear quickly became anger. These girls were supposed to protect this Godling and had just failed miserably at it. He had to calm himself before his anger got the best of him and he shed this human form. If that happened, Heavens help him, he would end up killing them all. The entire forest of nymphs and satyrs alike would burn before his anger abated.

"Don't touch her," he managed to get out through clenched teeth as he felt the air move. A few more deep breaths and he was in control enough to look at them again. "Anyone care to tell me how this happened?"

"We're not sure really. She was finally getting the hang of it." Amy shrugged helplessly.

"We were taking it slow, training her like I did when Dustie was little and just learning. She was running, then falling, I don't understand it," Caprika tried to explain.

"Why isn't she waking up?" Dustie said softly. Everyone turned to see tears running down the little nymphs face unbidden. Caprika motioned for Dustie to come sit between her and Amy so they could comfort her. This put Melam on the right side of Sedah's prone body with all three girls on her left.

"She isn't waking up, little one, because she took a very nasty hit to the head when she fell. Her brain needs time to heal before it can process the rest of what was hurt," Melam said, looking straight at her. While what he said was true that moment, he didn't tell them that he would keep her unconscious purposely, so he could evaluate her for himself.

This innocent minor goddess was becoming an enigma for Melam. What exactly did the fates have in motion that made her need to stay hidden? Who hated this beautiful girl so much that she was going to be forced into servitude?

Caprika stood, taking charge. "We need to get some water to clean her up some. Amy can go do that. Dustie, go grab a couple of the blankets we use for covering the animals. Melam and I will look over her injuries." Without question, the girls got up and took off toward their tasks.

"How did you get to her so fast? It was literally in the blink of an eye."

"Is that really what you want to know nymph?" Melam's face was an expressionless mask.

"Not really, but I bet you won't give me a straight answer to what I *really* want to know, so I'll ask what you probably *will* answer," Caprika shot back. "I know the games of the Gods, and how to spot one. Which one are you and what's your game?"

"Not won't, can't answer, and by a power higher than you could fathom. Just leave it alone. There are going to be things I can't or won't explain, and as her protector, you need to back me up on them without question, especially in front of the others. If you can do that for me, I will answer what questions I can. My name is the one I gave you. There is no deception there. I am no one you would have ever heard of."

"Fine," Caprika agreed. "Now for Sedah. Don't we need to try to bind anything that's broken and roll her over so she's more comfortable?"

"Watch for others and I will see what's broken. What I do might damage your eyes, so don't look, seriously," Melam told her. He waited for her to decide whether to believe and trust him or not. Slowly, she nodded to him, got up and walked a few steps away, keeping her back turned. Once he was sure curiosity wouldn't get the better of her, he started his assessment.

Sending his energy out of him, he encompassed Sedah's

upper body within it like a bubble. As she breathed it in, he willed the energy to surface through her skin wherever there were injuries. Time slowed as she took more of his energy into her system. She had many small cuts and abrasions, and her face was a scratched, bloody mess. Most of the energy flowed out through her right ankle, right knee, and her head wound. Her right shoulder was also injured, though thankfully not broken. Melam let go of a breath he hadn't known he'd been holding. When he had come through the branches to see her falling, he'd feared she had snapped her neck or broken her back. Thank the Gods, he had been wrong.

Slowly, he retracted his energy, her body expending what it needed, and releasing the rest. The last of the energy was returning into him when Caprika let out a cough in warning. Melam checked Sedah to ensure no lingering energy could be seen escaping, just as Dustie and Amy came through the foliage. Freil was also behind them with supplies.

"Man, you weren't lying, she really is hurt bad," Freil said when they all got closer.

"What are you doing here Freil?" Caprika looked from her to a guilty looking Amy.

"She asked how it went, so I told her. She brought food for us and helped create a cover story of camping with Sedah so she wouldn't be missed. She helped buy us some time. How bad is it?" She nodded her head to where Sedah lay. Caprika looked at Melam, who cleared his throat to focus the girls' attention on him.

"Her worst injuries are to her head and her right leg. The knee and ankle to be specific. Her right shoulder is fractured, but not broken. We can clean her up, carefully turn her over and splint the leg. The rest is just up to her to heal naturally. She is lucky that she will heal faster from this than a human would," he explained.

Quickly, the girls cleaned a few scrapes. Melam helped

support her head and shoulders while the girls held her bad leg steady to roll her onto the clean blanket. The girls got to binding her leg, letting Melam clean the head wound and face lacerations.

Melam took his time, wanting to be thorough and gentle. They were all determined not to miss a speck that could later get infected. The girls had covered her with the blanket and gotten a fire started by the time he was satisfied with his work and stood.

Looking over the busy girls, he sent a small stream of energy to tickle Caprika's cheek to get her attention. When she looked to check on Sedah, he motioned her to him so they could talk in private. He wasted no time when she walked over to where he was standing over Sedah.

"I assume you trust these girls—that none of them have done anything to help this accident happen?" He crossed his arms over his chest, staring at her to gauge her honesty.

"With my life. All of these girls are helping me teach Sedah and look out for her. None of them would do this." She stared back, letting him see her resolve.

"Okay, then only you four can watch her now. There is something I have been tasked to do elsewhere in the forest, so I will have to leave from time to time. If anything happens, no matter how small, call to me in your mind like you would to your mother. Tell me what has happened, and I will hear you. I will either reply, or come, depending on the issue. I need to leave for a little while now, actually."

"We're going to stay here tonight; in case she wakes. Do what you need to do. She is ours to protect anyway. You have done more than enough," Caprika reassured him, while letting him off the hook. His eyes boring into hers said exactly what he thought of her saying that.

Without another word, Melam walked away, disappearing into the trees. While he wasn't one hundred percent confident that the girls could keep Sedah safe, he had no other choice. If he really was the eyes for his grandmother, there was no telling when she could be watching or what she could be seeing.

❦

AFTER A FEW MINUTES IN CAMP, MELAM'S SUBTLE INQUIRIES earned him very little knowledge, and a whole new appreciation for parents with endless patience. Gods knew, Melam felt ready to strangle every satyr there.

Watching the party the night before, it was obvious that the nymphs were as close knit as the satyrs were clueless. Not a single satyr knew where their brethren hung out.

Deciding plan B was his best chance, Melam went to where the trail of energy from the night before started. Not knowing how far they had gone, or how often they used the trail, Melam walked at a leisurely pace so it would appear as if he were simply wandering, should he come across anyone.

Melam wasn't sure how using his energy to follow someone had projected loudly enough that his grandmother, of all people, had decided to step in. Although he loved her dearly, she was the type of woman that tended to let her children watch over Earth while she took care of running the universe. Melam just hoped he didn't disappoint her.

Maybe, if he pissed her off, she would send him to help his brother. He missed Phail fiercely. Starting to feel depressed, Melam stopped, the trail of energy passing beyond the opening in the trees ahead of him. Melam could see that the opening was actually the edge of the forest that surrounded Nantahala Lake. The energy from the night before was everywhere. He could see it around fire pits, lounge chairs, and even the water's edge. So Kohl had come here the night of the party, like Melam had suspected.

Right now, there were couples, single adults, and even families at the lake. They were either swimming, playing ball, or just hanging out, enjoying the sun and each other. While it was somewhat noisy with kids and adults occasionally squealing, Melam could only guess how loud and crazy it was at night with fire and alcohol involved. No children and no inhibitions could lead to some dangerous decisions.

Stepping back into the cover of the trees, Melam put his hand over his heart, releasing enough energy as he ran his hand down the front of his cotton shirt and reed shorts to change them into more suitable beach attire to blend in better. Leaving the protection of the forest, he tried to get into the center of all the energy traces he could see.

Hoping he would not seem too weird sitting down in the sand alone, Melam had no choice but to close his eyes and concentrate. Slowly, he was able to let the sound of the people around him disappear. He focused only on the sound of the waves lapping on the shore, and the energy surrounding him. Silently, he willed the energy to come to him. It started, hesitantly at first, a grain or two being sucked into him. It began to pick up steadily, siphoning into his body at a constant rate until not a speck remained from outside the forest line.

Opening himself up to the information, the image of a proverbial Pandora's box opened to show him what had occurred there the night before. Just like the damned souls that had opened the real Pandora's box, he quickly wished he had not.

A satyr had the ability to enthrall whomever they wanted with their heavenly instruments. It seemed that one satyr had stood at the edge of the forest and started playing a haunting tune. Once they had the entire beach front near Wayah Road enthralled, the tune had changed to a dance timbre as the small band of satyrs exited the forest to join the party. It didn't surprise Melam at all that Kohl was the one who led the group.

The single satyr, Melam recognized as Danny, played in the background as Kohl and his hoard partied alongside the people, pretending they were human. They sat at the bonfires laughing and telling jokes, dancing provocatively with women, and other random, innocent things Melam had observed humans to do. Melam could not really turn them in to his grandmother for such a thing, either, since they'd had the foresight to enthrall the area first. But the question became: why was it such a secret if it was so innocent? Something just didn't make sense. Melam was about to let go of the energy when Kohl let out a whistle from where he had been sitting at a bonfire that night.

As if it had been previously planned, Kohl and one other satyr led a girl behind them, heading east as all the other satyrs silently filed back into the forest behind them with a human or two, going under a bridge that passed over a small creek.

The vision blurred out as the last of the energy Melam had collected from the area was used up. Melam blinked as the present came back into focus. He looked around slowly, searching every face he saw, in order to determine if anyone from the party that night was at the beach that moment. They were not.

It was Melam's mission to find out what had happened to those girls, but the vision had cost him a couple hours and it was obvious that there was still more of the energy trail that needed following. It was getting late and he wanted to start heading back. He knew that the nymphs would camp with Sedah, but he honestly didn't trust anyone to protect her like she needed anymore.

He had seen to her injuries and believed Caprika when she said they would all watch over her, but he hadn't been able to stop himself from adding protective energy feelers around her body before he had left. This energy lay underneath her entire body. When someone stepped close enough to touch Sedah, feelers came out from under her body like the arms of an octopus to test the person's intentions. Only those looking to cause Sedah harm would ever know that the feelers were there.

At home in Ava Carina, this was known as a locni datera, which translated into locked spider in English. Once a person with malicious intent was caught by a feeler, it would shock the person as it wrapped them up, in wait for the owner to return. The wait was usually never that long since each locni datera was linked to its creator through the energy, and while Melam had felt nothing negative so far, he still felt the need growing within him to get back to her.

Thinking about where he had been standing at the edge of the clearing when he had seen her fall, he set his entire being of energy into bending time to get there in less than two seconds. The need to be with her was becoming paramount.

Materializing, Melam looked around slowly. Two dead animals lay near the encampment. The four girls surrounded Sedah protectively, facing outward. Melam's senses went on high alert as he approached the group. They had already shot a fox and a hog, but were still at attention like they were expecting more.

"Anyone want to tell me what is going on here? *And why was I not called immediately?*" Melam asked, the last being directed solely at Caprika.

"*Because we had it under control.*" She lifted her chin in defiance as she answered back mentally as well.

"I have never seen anything like it," Amy explained, "The forest got really silent. It's nothing new to see a fox in the open at night, but both animals came from opposite directions, running towards Sedah, snarling. Neither animal could be distracted, no matter what we did."

"Seems she has been discovered by someone, then," Melam thought aloud.

"Get ready, I feel more coming! Why aren't they listening to my mental commands?" Freil almost whined in frustration. She did not want to have to hurt another innocent animal.

No one had time to answer as bats flew over them and insects seemed to pour out of the ground. Melam hastily threw up a one-way shield so the animals could be forced out, but not able to reenter.

"What's happening?" Dustie asked panicky as the bats beat at the barrier until they fell to the ground. The continual thumping noise was almost deafening.

"I wish I knew." Caprika pulled Dustie to her so she could help comfort her little sister.

Melam watched the creatures trying fruitlessly to get through his ancient barrier. Just as he was about to trace the energy from a bat back through to the culprit, the animals were released from their thrall. The area was quickly cleared as the animals and insects all went on their way once again.

As if on cue, a young male and female shimmered into view about ten feet away as Melam was taking down his shield. While the boy had a human appearance other than his eyes, the girl looked dressed for a costume ball.

The entire left side of her body, from toes to hair, was as black as if she had been dipped in soot. On her right side, she was as white as cotton. These two contrasting sides were split right down the middle of her body, as was evident when Melam saw how the separation of color continued up her neck, to her nose and forehead before continuing into her hair. Her eyes were the only thing that suggested a familial tie with the boy. Hoping the girls knew to stay put, Melam walked forward to greet the pair.

The closer they got, the more power rolled off them. Not to be outdone, yet not wanting to reveal himself either, Melam raised his power to the surface some, so they would not mistake him for human.

"Did you need something, Godlings?" Melam tried to sound as bored as possible. Internally, he was transmitting this encounter to his mother. Who knew how important this might be for whatever was going on.

"That is our sister those nymphs are supposed to be protecting. We wanted to know what happened to her." The boy pointed to where Sedah lay.

"How did you know something had happened?" Melam's alertness picked up at this. Were they all being watched, despite his abnormally high senses telling him differently?

"Let's just say the sandman couldn't help her, so I knew something was wrong," the male said very guardedly. He shifted uncomfortably for a moment. The relief was evident on his face when his sister spoke like nothing odd had just been said.

"I was actually on my way to give her my support for her first meeting with her betrothed when I bumped into my brother. I'm Melinoe, by the way. This is my brother Sephir." She indicated the male beside her.

"I am Melam. Why is her betrothed coming here?" Melam motioned with a sweeping gesture for them to follow him as he turned to go back to the girls.

"Apparently, Mother convinced Father to get Uncle Poseidon to agree to them meeting a month or so before she goes for her first visit, so she wouldn't feel so awkward. Our oldest sister, Makaria, will be bringing him from the lake any minute, which means I need to leave. Once they are gone again, I will come and see my sister," Sephir explained.

"Yes. I have a feeling you and I need to talk when you are here next." Melam's right hand grabbed Sephir's left arm in a warrior's farewell, which allowed a little energy to flow through them both. While Melam saw what Sephir knew, he decided right then to let Sephir see Melam for who he truly was. This revelation had the Godling gasping, his eyes flying up to lock with Melam's. Melam's arm forcefully keeping him standing was all that kept Sephir from kneeling.

"I will come back directly; you have my word," Sephir said hastily, even as he was becoming translucent, slipping into nothingness.

Deciding not to question at the moment why he had just disobeyed his mother again, Melam sent a message on the wind to Caprika. Thankfully, she quietly motioned for Freil and Dustie to sit where they were, on either side of Sedah's shoulders without questioning Melam first.

"They are coming." Melinoe touched Melam's shoulder and pointed to the right. Stepping beside him, the tension could be cut with a knife as everyone waited to see the son of Poseidon in the flesh.

❧ 12 ❧

As if on cue, the second couple of the night broke through the thicker part of the forest, walking straight up to Melam and Melinoe. Triton had dark long curly brown hair and looked like a younger version of Poseidon, with his diamond shaped face and ocean blue eyes. He carried himself with what should have been an air of authority, but came off as pretentious to Melam. He supposed the two could be confused if one didn't know whom they were dealing with.

"Melinoe, I did not know you would be here. Who is your friend?" Makaria asked her sister, making a show of looking Melam over from head to toe as if she was deciding which part to kiss first.

"Makaria, this is Melam. Now I've shown you mine, you can show us yours." She smiled sarcastically as the sisters locked eyes.

"You knew I was bringing Triton to meet Sedah. Where is she?" Makaria attempted to look around them to the nymphs.

"Someone, or something, tried to kill her earlier. I healed her the best I could and put her in a deep sleep for tonight, so she could heal more," Melam supplied while gauging both of their reactions.

With a gasp, Makaria ran around Melam, straight to her baby sister. Triton strode directly up to Melam and Melinoe, stopping when he was mere paces from the pair. He looked between them, not at them, and cleared his throat.

Melam squared his shoulders, as he took a deep breath in. While he didn't smell deceit in the air, this merman's actions did nothing to help Melam think he was innocent either.

Both Melam and Melinoe slowly took a step back to allow Triton to walk between them when he took a step forward instead of going around them like Makaria had.

As he walked through them with plenty of space, he grazed Melinoe's breasts, causing a ghost to pop out of Melinoe's side, becoming corporeal enough to grab Triton's arm to stop him from moving forward.

"Tell this thing to unhand me. How dare it touch me." Triton tried, unsuccessfully, to get his arm free.

"Listen closely, dolphin tail. I might be two toned, but don't think I would entertain the idea of even being acquaintances with your half animal, half ass-hat, spoiled rotten, twenty shades of green self. You think one ghost is bad? You ever mentally or physically hurt my sister, and I will show you what the Goddess of Ghosts can really do, are we clear?" She stared him down without blinking.

"Yes," Triton bit out through gritted teeth. Any tighter and he would chip a tooth. Melam had to hold back a smile as he watched them. It was clear that Triton had never met his match before now.

The ghost let Triton go, staying close just in case, as they all walked over to Makaria and the nymphs. While the nymphs had stayed where they were, Makaria was sitting at the end of Sedah's head, with her legs folded.

"The little one said it was safe for me to stroke her hair

since her neck was uninjured." Tears rolled unchecked down her face. "Do you know who hurt her?"

"Not yet, but I will find out," Melam said with conviction. "The incident itself was simply strange. But afterwards, someone possessed animals to try to harm her while she was lying here vulnerable."

"When will you wake her up so that we can be introduced, and I can leave?" Triton asked. Slowly, while trying to keep his temper in check, Melam turned his eyes on Triton.

"You have no idea how badly she was injured, and you want me to wake her, intentionally causing her pain, just so you can say hi and then leave? I guess one royal ass really can beget an even bigger royal ass." Behind him, a couple coughs tried to cover the snickers from the youngest nymph. Triton glanced at the nymphs, then at a pissed Makaria, before turning to his right to face Melam.

"How dare you speak with such hostility against me, much less about a major God such as my father! Who the hell do you think you are?" Triton shook from his anger, and Melam knew why. Triton was the son of the God of the Sea. People knew better than to question him, much less make fun of him or openly show any hostility.

Melam answered with a step forward, making them toe to toe as they stared one another down. Both were red from holding their anger in check for very different reasons; both wanting to kill one another but knowing they were not allowed to.

"*What* are you?" Triton amended his question in a hushed tone as they locked eyes in a stare down. Melam knew what Triton could see in them: the cosmos.

"Honestly? Your past." Melam smiled slowly, answering at the same volume as Triton. He could tell that he was getting to this minor god, and he couldn't help but enjoy it a little.

"I'm going to go scout." Melam told Caprika mentally, turning his back on Triton in a blatant show of disrespect.

◌✦◌

CAPRIKA CROSSED HER ARMS AND FROWNED AS THE awkward mess tried to untangle in front of her. Triton took a step to follow Melam, only to be stopped by a line of impenetrable ghosts. He growled, just loud enough for Caprika to hear it, spinning to glare at Melinoe for an answer.

"Just thought I would save your hide. You can sit down and wait for my sister to take you back, or I can call a ghoul to escort you. Your choice, but you will be leaving tonight." Melinoe shrugged as if she was talking about the weather. Her return glare spoke of evil deeds directed at the prince.

"I can take him now." Makaria wiped at her eyes. Kissing Sedah on the forehead, she stood. "We will come back when she is healed. Let her rest for now." Her hand jumped back slightly when she reached for Triton's arm, as if everything in her rebelled at touching him. Taking the same calming breath Caprika frequently used, she placed a hand on his arm. Skin replaced scales where she touched him. Something in the prince seemed to soften at Makaria's grief and his posture relaxed slightly. With a nod, they were on their way, the forest swallowing them up quickly.

Even as Melinoe began walking toward her baby sister, ghosts of every age and gender were left in her wake. They multiplied quickly and quietly, surrounding the forest and protecting everyone in the small clearing.

Dustie's head darted back and forth at all the ghosts and huddled closer to Sedah instinctively. Melinoe's smile at the innocent girl carried the same warmth Caprika herself felt. She wasn't even sure if Dustie knew she had done it. It wasn't like she could actually protect Sedah if the need arose.

And in her current state, Sedah certainly couldn't protect anyone.

"My ghosts will help Melam protect you all. They will act as an advanced warning system around the perimeter. Can one of you tell him that for me? I have some mischief to find."

Caprika silently relayed the message. "He said he will send them back when he is done with them," she answered. Melinoe shimmered out of view. Before Sedah had showed up, only Demeter had ever done such a thing in front of them. Now, it seemed to be an almost daily occurrence. Caprika had to clear her throat to get the girls attention, making all them jump.

"If the ghosts are here as protection, that means that we can get some sleep without worrying. Just to be safe, though, I am going to take first watch in case Sedah wakes up." Caprika looked at each of the girls. Freil still looked shaken, probably still wondering why the animals hadn't listened to her and Amy. She had the type of mind that would try and figure it out. Dustie cuddled next to Amy as they lay down, clearly not comfortable with dead people around, despite Melinoe's words.

❦

As much as he hated leaving, Melam did his patrol, then went in search of Kohl and his gang of satyrs. The replay he'd seen earlier had been insightful. Chances were, if they did this often, tonight would be good pickings for them. Not only was it summer, but it was the weekend. It was still early, but it would give Melam enough time to conceal himself.

Bonfires and laughter could be heard through the trees as Melam looked for a good vantage point. Leaning against the tree, he watched the humans get bolder and louder as the night wore on. Some women danced to radio music together, some played their own music by the fires along to the radio, and some couples were wandering off and returning some time later. Melam was so busy watching, he didn't see when the satyrs arrived until they were already spread out mingling.

Melam had to search for the flute player, as there seemed to be no disruption in the music. All six satyrs were with humans, yet the humans seemed to not care that they were laughing and dancing with things that were half human and half animal.

There had been a human playing a flute earlier, but Melam had not thought anything of it he admitted to himself, as he now searched for the man. He was now regretting that over-sight. At some point a satyr had given a human male an enchanted flute of theirs to play before their arrival.

Instead of Kohl signaling for them all to leave at one time tonight, each satyr picked out a girl and coaxed them down the beach and away from the crowd. A little persuasion got each girl to call out to another, urging them to catch up.

Once they were under the bridge leading to the forest, the five satyrs pushed the girls against the arched wall. They said suggestive things to see if they could get the girls to make out with one another as the satyrs felt them both up. The three that were willing went with the satyrs into the forest, while the other two were told to go back to the party.

Melam stayed where he was, watching as Kohl found two men drunk enough to follow him as they went after the other group. Disgusted with their treatment of defenseless humans, Melam sent out energy to follow Kohl so he could find out what happened. As much as he wanted to follow now, he had no idea if there was enough cover to keep him hidden. If they were caught now, he might never find out what was going on for his grandmother. It killed him to walk away, but all he could hope was that that time would be the last time, and that nothing too bad would happen that night.

The coast clear for the time being, Melam let himself imagine Sedah. Her spirit guided him as he teleported from the lake, straight to her side. It was telling that the ghosts never moved an inch as he shimmered into solidity.

Caprika on the other hand, gasped, having to throw her hands behind her to keep herself from falling over, she backed up so fast.

"Don't you know better than to do that without warning? Is doing that at home considered normal?" she huffed in frustration as she righted herself and watched Melam sit down.

"I'm sorry little one. Thank you for watching her, but it is not necessary, if you would like to sleep now."

"Any hope of sleep left with you scaring the sacred mother out of me." Caprika smiled sarcastically at Melam. A comfortable silence stretched over them, each lost in their own thoughts. Some of Caprika's thoughts needed answers though.

"Melam, why are you here?" Caprika laid down a body length away from Sedah and stretched out, using her hands behind her head as a pillow.

"I was sent here to keep an eye on my sister. She does not need me at present, so I decided to explore and come north," he lied. "Now I am not so sure why I am here. I am being told it is for one reason yet feel as if I am held here for an entirely different one," he said softly as he looked down at Sedah's still form.

"I figured that much."

"Thank you, by the way," Melam said some time later.

"For what?" Caprika mumbled, having been on the verge of sleep.

"For being her friend. And for being there to protect her when I couldn't be," he said solemnly. Her falling because of a root, and later lying there helpless, would play in his mind and haunt him forever.

"She makes the friend part easy. And as for her protection, I keep telling you it's my job, not yours. But you're welcome anyway." She winked at him before going back to sleep.

Once he was sure all the girls were sound asleep, Melam encased himself and Sedah in a dome of energy. It would allow him to work on healing her battered body without it spreading onto any of the nymphs.

His hand cupped the side of her face, where his fingertips rested at her temples. He sent a little tendril of energy through the pads of his fingers into her to wake her up slowly. He woke up her mind but held her body as still as if it were wrapped in an iron blanket.

He smiled as her eyes slowly opened. He hadn't known his soul could become a little lighter just by looking at something so normal, and at the same time extraordinary.

"Hi," was all he could say. He felt like a blubbering human, or an idiot.

"Hi." Sedah's voice was raspy from disuse. He could tell she was assessing her condition before continuing. "Would you mind telling me why I can't move?" she asked. Melam was surprised not to hear an inch of panic.

"Do you remember what happened at all? When you hit the tree, your left leg slid down the bark when your right foot caught on the root. Your right shoulder is fractured, and your right knee went to the ground hard enough that you severely fractured it as well. You also hit your head pretty hard and knocked yourself out."

"How long have I been out?" Sedah was horrified at the fact that everyone had had to take care of her. She tried to look around, but Melam's voice brought her back to staring at his beautiful eyes.

"I put you under almost immediately, so you couldn't move or feel the pain until we knew how badly you were injured."

"You put me under to protect me, so I'm guessing you are responsible for me being incapacitated right now?" Sedah smiled as Melam nodded. He had this childlike, guilty look about him that made Sedah want to laugh. "Why did you wake me then, if I am just going to lay here immobile?"

"I never said I would keep you that way. I want to heal you some, using my energy. It is easier with you awake since I already know where you are hurt. You can tell me when I have healed it to a bearable point." Melam explained.

"Which means the pain will be unbearable when you first let me feel everything again. I was born in Erebos, so I think I have a much better pain tolerance than most." She pinned his gaze with a look of fire and determination.

"Okay, but I have placed a protective shield around us, so if you need to yell, feel free to yell. No one but me will know, and I will definitely not hold it against you, okay?"

Sedah just nodded, waiting for it. Pain was a second friend when you lived in hell. It almost felt like she was back home when he finally released his hold on her body. The pain washed over her like a second skin so that she only grunted aloud. She could definitely feel every injury he had mentioned.

Melam watched her until he was sure she wasn't just putting on a show of bravery for his benefit. Once he was convinced, he closed his eyes, allowing his strong celestial energy to flow towards Sedah like a slow brook. He could feel the energy cling to her injuries like bandages, leaving some behind while moving the rest to the next problem.

Once every external issue had been addressed, Melam moved the remaining energy to Sedah's face, so she could breathe it into her like the time before. Sedah stared at

Melam during the entire process. She could feel the energy seeping into her very pores where it was attempting to heal from the outside.

As she breathed the energy in, it was potent enough to actually lift her torso off the ground. She wondered if this was her body's response, or if Melam had something to do with it. Suddenly, it felt as if mini incendiary devices were going off within her.

"My energy seems to be mixing and yet clashing with yours quite violently. I don't understand. It didn't do that last time. It is like storm clouds are fighting within you before they mesh together to create the perfect lightning bolt." Melam seemed amazed and confused as he looked within her being.

"Then get your energy out before it kills me!" Sedah felt suddenly clammy. It was getting hard to stay calm, and Melam's words hadn't helped matters.

"Fine, but you need to heal. It won't kill you; it will just hurt like hell." He floated her body above his sitting form.

Ignoring her protesting, Melam closed his eyes and concentrated on slowly pulling his energy out of Sedah. While most of it came back, allowing her body to slowly descend back into Melam's lap, some of the energy would not budge. It seemed to have bonded with her own, like a protective coating.

Behind him, Melam materialized a rock so he could lean against it to rest.

"You can lay me down on the ground if I am too heavy." Sedah blushed slightly. There was a buzzing going on inside her as she sat there in his lap, which she couldn't fully blame on the energy.

"You are as light as a feather." He did a curl using her body, causing her to giggle and grab at his shoulders. "Why?

Do you prefer the dirt to my lap?" He made a show of frowning.

"I don't care either way, but you are safer. The ground has bugs," she stage-whispered the last, as if it were their secret. There was no way she was going to tell him how much she enjoyed being held by him.

"I don't know about *safer*, but we won't go there. How are your knee and ankle feeling?"

"Better, but still painful. How are you able to do the energy transfer, and materialize yourself and objects. Only the major Gods and their direct offspring can do those things. Even then, they can only do one or two things. Like, I can materialize objects, but not myself. Other than that, all I can do so far is shrink and enlarge objects, and when I am mad, I can levitate objects."

Melam didn't know what to say. Even if he wanted to tell Sedah the truth, his tongue would be held by either his mother or his grandmother, then he would get in trouble later for even attempting to tell her. Knowing his grandmothers temper, she was just as likely to send a few dozen Erinyes, or Furies, as modern humans called them, to torture him until she could come do it herself.

"I have always had these powers. I am not sure what levels of power are given to which children, only what I have been born with," he answered honestly.

Melam turned the line of questioning back to Sedah, keeping it there for the rest of the night. Every time she would ask him a question, he had to try to find a way to be honest, yet as vague as possible, before turning the questioning back to her.

They talked about her home, siblings, parents, schooling, and even about herself. By the time the first ray of light created a kaleidoscope of color across the morning sky, Melam felt as if he knew Sedah as well as he knew himself.

He caught her cute attempt to cover a yawn as he took down the protective barrier. She involuntarily shivered as the cool morning air hit her skin. Feeling it through her, he instantly had a prepossessing blanket draped over her. Her eyes widened in awe as she looked at it.

"Where did this come from? It's beautiful!" She spread her arms out underneath the blanket to get a better look at it. It looked like the vanishing night sky had been captured and turned into a blanket just for her. It was probably just her eyes playing tricks, but Sedah could almost swear it was moving too.

"From my bedroom at home. All you have to do is think about how hot or cold you want to be and the vosan, as we call it, will make it so," he told her. Melam could have gotten her an earthly blanket, but a vosan was so much more than that. He had learned that the best earthly translation for the word would be *convert*. Vosan was the name of the material because of its properties that allowed it to be converted by thought into anything.

Knowing the girls would wake up soon, Melam material-ized a padded blanket, laying Sedah on it and covering her up with the vosan again.

Amy was the first to stir a little while later. Seeing that Sedah was awake, she rushed over, smiling ear to ear.

"How are you feeling? Oh my goddess, we were so worried about you!" she spoke rapidly in her happiness. She realized what she had been doing when both Sedah and Melam laughed at her excitement.

"Calm down. Breathe." Melam made the motion of exhaling and inhaling with his hands as he did it in slow motion. Their banter seemed to stir the other girls, who immediately rushed over, all speaking at once in their excite-ment. Melam watched them, smiling, until Caprika could get them all to quiet down.

"I'm fine guys. Thank you all for being so worried about me. Melam told me what happened, though I confess I remember nothing past starting to run, then pain. Melam helped move me so I could be more comfortable, but I'm not sure I could move myself right now if I had to. People will come looking for us, won't they?" Sedah looked at Caprika, then to Amy. If anyone would know, they would. The girls exchanged worried glances.

"Eventually, yes, Lilac will send a party when someone notices you gone more than the two days that we said we were taking you out for. Hopefully you will be better by tomorrow since you heal fast if it is sunny, and we won't have to worry about it," Caprika answered.

Dustie laughed. "If they do come, we'll just let your sister's ghosts handle them."

"We could send Freil back to camp to say that we are further away than we are to watch how humans act or something," Amy suggested.

Caprika nodded. "It could work."

"They sure took Triton down a peg or two," Freil said under her breath, nudging Dustie in agreement. "I could go to camp and do that," she answered to Caprika's suggestion.

"Wait, what? My sister, ghosts, and Triton all here?" Sedah exclaimed in a shriek. Caprika and Melam pushed her down by the shoulders as she tried to get up on her elbows to look around. She got a glimpse at the ring of ghosts before Melam captured her gaze with his. Slowly, he ran his hands along her shoulder blades, and up her neck. His fingers glided into the silky flames of her hair as his palms cradled her face. He smiled slightly at the feel of her pulse increasing at his nearness.

"*Do you trust me precu?*" he smiled as her eyes widened in shock.

"*Oh my, I hit my head harder than I thought. Hot or not, I should not be hearing his voice in my head."* Sedah thought to herself.

"I'm hot, huh? Listen, I'm going to put you back to sleep for now so you can heal, and I can go take care of business." He smiled at Sedah as her blush spread from having been caught calling him hot. "Do I have your consent to put you to sleep?" he asked aloud, for everyone's benefit.

Too embarrassed to speak, Sedah nodded her head. Her eyes closed and her head went limp as Melam sent her under. The second she was asleep, Caprika turned on Freil and Dustie.

"Did you really have to go and mention that stuff? Did you even think to ask if we thought she might need to know that yet? She already hit on our biggest current problem, and you guys are adding to her stress. I don't know if it will hinder her healing, but it could definitely call other gods to her." She almost shouted from frustration. Melam cleared his throat to get her attention.

"Everything inside Melinoe's circle of ghosts is undetectable by human or God alike. Anyone looking will see a landscape without people. For now, you all are safe." Melam walked over to Freil. "Wear this at all times until Sedah is healed. When you go into camp, think of anyone here, and their image will be walking beside you. Should they need to do or say something, imagine the real person doing it, and the body double, or niyt neuk, as we call it, will become corporeal enough to do it just as the real girl would." Dustie and Amy looked at the gear shaped necklace in wonder at its power despite its simple appearance.

Caprika sent Dustie home to care for the animals and report back while Freil and Amy took care of their jobs. Amy was instructed to come back to them at noon and help guard, while Dustie took over for her until dinner. Hopefully, it would be the next day before Freil needed to worry about using her special necklace.

Melam was just turning to speak to Caprika when they both witnessed the ghosts kneel and part for what looked like two human girls.

"So they can be moved! All the girls were too afraid to try so they've been using the branches to jump over them." Caprika laughed nervously. Kneeling ghosts did not bode well for Caprika if it meant she'd been protecting Sedah poorly.

"Calm down. They're here to speak with me. Go sit with Sedah, and I will be back shortly, hopefully." Melam's eyes never left the two females, trusting that Caprika would do as he had said. Just in case he was wrong on who these women were, he wanted Sedah protected.

When the two humans were nearly three feet from Melam, they stopped. While big grins covered their faces, they said nothing, choosing to let Melam go first.

"Smile all you want, but you do not fool me. I would know my daughter and sister anywhere. Come here baby." Melam held his arms wide so Skylu could run into them for a hug.

"Tesir pre sko serl kalec, ge ni mevid niyt, bas precu meve." *Your pure spirit shines brightly, even in a human host, my precious child.* He looked down at her and spoke in their native tongue with gazes locked so she would know he was seeing the real her.

"And here she thought you would never guess! You owe me three adenons, arhe Nonnis." Skylu smiled from her dad to her aunt.

"I don't understand though? Why are you two here? Is The Ether okay?"

"Everything is fine. Skylu wanted to see her hecu and I had to come oversee events for The Ether Major so they 'would know how to proceed on another matter.' At least that's the line that I got told. I thought I would bring her along to see you and experience the essence that is her great grandmother, The Ether Major," Nonnis explained.

"I'm glad you did, then. Although I should be mad at you both for making me miss home even more now." He smiled, giving his daughter a noogie as he pushed her away from him. "I gotta say precu, I don't like this look on you though. This human looks nothing like you. I miss your chocolate curls." He ran a hand through the human's straight blonde hair.

"I'm just borrowing, hecu. We found them in the woods behind their house talking and stuff."

"Just don't forget to erase their memories when you leave them. People forgetting is how the term 'skinwalkers' came into being. You girls get to wherever you need to be, I have things to do today. Tell The Ether that I will have their answer soon." He gave his daughter one last hug before watching them disappear through the ghosts and back into the forest.

Turning and walking back toward Sedah, he saw that Amy had returned, and was sitting by Sedah, building a fire. With Caprika having Amy for backup, Melam could go chase down his latest energy trail. The problem was, Melam wasn't so sure he wanted to see what he was almost certain he was going to find.

❧ 13 ❧

After informing Amy and Caprika that he was leaving, Melam flashed over to the bridge the satyrs had used to take their humans into the forest the night before.

Melam followed his energy trail with confidence, as he had the first time. Satyrs may not like to work, but they had to. Kohl and his gang would not risk being seen here during the daytime hours. When he had watched the night before, the satyrs had managed to round up three girls and two guys that seemed susceptible to what they were being manipulated into. Mind numbing music that made a human revert to their base instincts could open a person up enough that they would do many uncharacteristic things they secretly wanted to try.

The problem was, most satyrs were civilized. Their worst antics were the equivalent of teenage humans'. They played pranks, messed with neighbors' livestock, and were general menaces, yet never hurt anyone. Melam got that adolescent feeling from most of the satyrs in camp. The six satyrs he was put in charge of watching gave off an entirely different vibe, and not a good one.

The energy trail followed Wine Spring Creek for about two miles before taking a sharp left up an incline on the side of the mountain. As Melam climbed, he began to hear a human snoring. Reaching the top of the incline, Melam saw that there was a cave set in the side of the mountain, and a small clearing with boulders and stumps to sit on. To the right of this area, a man sat crisscrossed, sleeping, his hands tied around the tree trunk behind him. Melam knelt by him, patting the man on the cheek to try and rouse him. Other than to cease his snoring for a moment, nothing happened.

Standing, Melam started for the cave. The scent of sex as soon as he reached the cave's entrance was something he expected, but the added smell of blood had him instantly on high alert. He snapped his right thumb and middle finger together twice to create an ethereal fire big enough to help him see.

At the back of the cave, two of the girls lay cuddled on each side of the second male for warmth. All three appeared to be in good health. Looking around more closely, Melam found, lying in the shadows of the rock, the third female.

Melam attempted to wake the girl up. Nights in the mountains were cold, especially without added layers of clothing. Even one layer would protect better than being in a corner off by herself, fully nude.

Using his light, Melam inspected the girl for injuries as his left hand went to her shoulder to try and shake her awake. In the darkness, he couldn't tell if what he was seeing was dirt or perhaps more.

When shaking the girl did nothing, Melam felt for a pulse. The girl had a heartbeat, but it was thready and slow. Opening his right hand to extinguish the ethereal flame, Melam quickly picked up the girl, carrying her to the mouth of the cave. While the man outside might have experienced the satyrs' domineering side during the night's festivities, this girl had obviously been on the receiving end of their depraved and vicious side.

Not only was she probably in hypothermic shock, but her swollen right foot hung at a weird angle, and almost every inch of what Melam could see of her body was covered in bruises of varying colors, sizes, and shapes.

Knowing she would never make it until one of the others woke up, Melam materialized another vosan and wrapped the girl in it as best as he could. He held her in his arms as she started to shiver, then twitch as her core temperature began to rise. Melam breathed a sigh of relief when her eyelids began to flutter, and she began to mumble and moan incoherently.

Seeing she would live, Melam tried to remember what this girl had been wearing the night before and have the vosan replicate it onto her body. Melam sat her down on the rock outside the cave, placing his arms on her shoulders to keep her upright.

"I need you to open your eyes, little one. I need to see inside for just a moment." Melam spoke softly. He didn't want to startle her, but he had to know if Kohl and his band had erased her memories of last night. Judging from the gasp and immediate look of fear when she complied, against her wishes, to open her eyes, they had not.

Immediately, Melam had no choice but to view the horrific details of the night through her memories as her mind replayed them all, one after the other, like flash cards put together to create one long video. Even though he had expected it to be bad, Melam didn't think anyone could ever unsee something so vile, once it had been seen.

As each memory played, Melam took it away by simply collecting all the energy from the memory and taking it into himself for his mother and grandmother to see. If this wasn't enough evidence to damn this group, then he didn't know what was. Had he not come across this human when he had, the other humans would have woken up to find a dead body.

Disgusted with what the satyrs were capable of doing to a human, Melam tried to keep his emotions down as he held this innocent in his arms. He felt so bad for how they had abused her, and yet he was having to be almost as bad by going into her memories and altering them.

Feeling that he had done all that he could, Melam pulled out of her mind after catching her address and sending her to sleep. She had been healed of the smaller bruises when she was wrapped in the vosan, but Melam planted memories of her falling hard and breaking a bone in her foot. Such a break would not swell and reveal itself until hours later.

Sending the vosan back home to the palace on Ava Carina, Melam used the human's memories to flash them both into her dorm room at West Carolina University. Still sleeping, Melam laid her down gently, mindful of her injuries.

A thread of energy would now link the human woman to Melam, since he had merged with her mentally to help heal her. He would know if she experienced any nightmares or trauma in the future, and could come to her aid if needed.

Flashing back to the mouth of the cave, Melam looked up and sent a *nemg samn*, or mental message, to his mother, the queen of the Avaan people. He didn't know if she would come alone, or with her mother, but he was ready to let them see all the deplorable things that were done the night and the things that had been planned for the next.

It didn't take as long as he had expected for Queen Rhea and the Mother Gaia to receive the *nemg sanm* and arrive. He expected the Goddess of Earth itself to be too busy to deal with such a matter personally. Melam bowed in respect as the women solidified.

"You have sent us a message, so I assume you have the evidence that we need, in order to know what has been going on and who needs to be punished," his mother started as he rose to his feet.

"I have, Ether. There are three mortals in the cave behind me, as well as one sleeping against the tree." Melam pointed to the man on his left, still tied up. "There was another who was hurt, almost to the point of death. I have her memories for you as well," Melam explained thoroughly.

He watched as the Mother Goddess closed her eyes and slowly put her hands out in front of her, palms up, as if she was waiting on a surprise to be placed in them. Melam knew better than to question what was happening, so he stood, waiting silently.

As if it was sand being shifted around by the wind, energy began to come from all around the area, moving into his grandmother's waiting palms and being absorbed into her skin. First was the dark blue, older energy from all the times this area had been used before.

Once she had collected all of that, Melam could see the memories coming first from the man outside, then from the three individuals inside the cave, flowing from each of them, into one stream of light green feeding into the Mother. Once she had collected all the evidence, she opened her eyes and turned to look at Melam. The depth of sorrow in her eyes could almost drown a person.

"Although I have much more than I need, would you allow me to take your memories from the girl to get the full picture of last night?"

"As atrocious as they are, could you only view them my Goddess, and take them when I return home? I want to keep them in case the human needs me. I will want to know why we share a bond and have no explanation if you take them now." Melam bowed his head.

"Of course. You may keep them for as long as you like," she told him.

Closing her eyes, Gaia placed the palm of her hand in the center of Melam's forehead, letting her fingers rest in his hairline. It only took a minute for her to view the images. It felt to Melam as if she had viewed more. While Melam was not comfortable with that, perhaps it was necessary that Gaia knew how he had tracked Kohl down, so she may better know how he had happened upon his information.

Feeling the absence of her hand, Melam opened his eyes, only to find the Mother of Earth gone. He looked to his mother; the question was obvious.

"I assume she was called away to take care of something else. She has what she needs and will deal with it when she can. Since this was caused by satyrs and not a wayward danmoc from our realm, you are now free to go anywhere you please until your sister needs you. Nonnis is back home and Skylu is with Saiph, who is going by Symee, in Mississippi," Queen Rhea told her son.

"While we are alone, I have to ask you, what is it that makes you want me to keep my distance from the myk'tu? I will be honest, I feel a pull to her unlike anything I have ever felt before."

Rhea sighed. "She has a dangerous path ahead of her, laid out by the Fates, my son. I hoped that you would feel nothing for her and that it would be easy to keep your distance so that your fate would not doom her path, or change it in any way. You know how the Fates work, so you know that I can't tell you what it is. That's why I told you to be careful, which is still all I can say to you. All I can do now is wish you good luck and hope that it works out for the best. With Phail missing, you are next in line for the throne, as you know, and I would hate to lose you to three women's machinations." She stood, giving him a long, heartfelt hug.

"*Seuc les stri gui tes bas reher.*" Melam told his mother.

"Son, may the stars guide you too. I fear you may need

their guidance more than I do right now." She kissed his cheek and disappeared quickly.

❦

It was almost dusk when Melam was finally able to get back to the girls. Sitting with them by the fire was one of Sedah's brothers—the same one that had come with the ghost sister and had left in a haste when Triton was near.

Melam had been hoping for a few minutes' peace, to wake Sedah up and talk to her. Something about being near her seemed to calm his head and heart as nothing else could since his wife's death.

Melam stood at the forest line for a moment, just to watch. Here was the simple, carefree sensation that most humans should feel, if given the rare opportunity to meet any otherworldly entity. He wished with all his heart that the human he had helped would have been introduced to beings such as these girls and Sedah, instead of Kohl and his vile crew. Sephir was laughing at something Amy had just said. They were being nice to him, despite him being a myk'tu, or outsider, as they called non-woodland creatures.

Sephir and Caprika were the first to see Melam as he made his way to them at an unhurried pace. Both stood and started toward him, leaving Amy and Dustie to watch Sedah. Sephir and Caprika met Melam halfway. Sephir tried immediately to bow but found himself physically unable to.

"You were gone a long time. Is everything okay?" Caprika asked. You've never taken this long on your trips, nor have you looked so sad and drained afterwards."

"No, but all will be revealed whenever the judge feels ready. Can I have a few moments alone with this godling?" Melam asked out of a newfound respect for these girls.

"*Sure, can you wake Sedah again, I made her some food,*"

Caprika asked into his mind. Both knew she didn't have to, but Melam found himself smiling that she was asking mentally, in order to hide from Sedah's own brother, that it was only Melam holding the sleeping state. A silent nod and it was done.

"So, godling, why are you back?" Melam crossed his arms.

"I told you I would return, sir, thus I have. I wish you would allow me to show you the respect you deserve though."

"Tell me this, young one. Your father is King of the Underworld. Why do people not want his job, over Zeus or Poseidon's?"

"They fear him. They think he controls who lives and who dies. He is hated for tricking my mother and pissing off my grandmother," Sephir explained quickly.

"Now what do you think would happen if those people were to know he was in a human body, hm?" Melam allowed the comprehension to light Sephir's eyes.

"You mean you could be—" Sephir stepped back, mouth agape in shock.

"Killed? No. This body would die, but then I would be in my original form, and no one could see me, lest I blind them. I am telling you this for one reason alone. You know beings far more powerful than Zeus, Poseidon and your father put together, do you not?" Melam's eyes bored into Sephir's, waiting.

"How do you know about them? Even my father is scared of them, which has always fascinated me, since he's not even scared of Hekate, who is the queen of witchcraft.

"Let's just say that they are family. One of them has a soft spot for Sedah. Probably because you speak of her so much, is my guess." Melam raised an eyebrow to Sephir, daring him to deny it. Instead, he had the decency to blush and look at the ground.

"What do you need of me, my Lord?"

SEDAH SAT BACK, LISTENING TO THE GIRLS RECOUNTING TO her and Sephir how Triton had acted when he'd come to visit. They told her how Melinoe's ghosts had gotten a rise out of him, and finally how he had acted like such a pompous ass, Melam had shamed him into leaving.

During the entire retelling, Melam sat opposite of Sedah, on a similar rock, on the other side of the fire. He would be lying if he said that he was not a little jealous that her brother was beside her instead of him. But if he were beside her, he would be missing the amazing experience of seeing the riot of emotions and subsequent colors that he was privy to at this angle.

She was indeed a kaleidoscope of color. As his mission was now complete, he could get to know Sedah more, without the added encumbrance of his mother and grand-mother watching. His eyes met Sedah's across the dancing flames, the glow of the fire bathing Sedah in shadows, enhancing her own natural beauty.

Dustie fell asleep first, as they caught Sephir up on every-thing Sedah had been doing since she arrived. When Caprika asked if his mom helped when Sedah had depleted herself in practice, Sephir said he had no idea who would have given his sister such a boost. Melam made a mental note to ask later why he had so obviously lied.

After the story, Amy excused herself to go to sleep. Caprika wanted to take first watch, leaving Sedah and the boys alone. Melam flashed himself to where Caprika had been sitting, to the left of Sedah. Sephir jumped high enough to fall backwards at seeing Melam move so quickly. Melam grinned when Sedah laughed at her brother.

"Don't worry big brother. You're not the first one he has gotten that reaction from. I would bet you won't be the last either," Sedah said through laughter. Melam could tell that the action hurt her, but she was doing a good job of not showing it, so he tried not to help her. Instead, he created a soundproof bubble around them like he had for Sedah the night before, so that he could be sure no one would overhear their conversation. Nothing was going to stop the answers tonight.

"Do your parents know Sedah is hurt?" Melam got right down to the thick of the questions. He heard Sedah gasp beside him but ignored it.

"Mom new right away somehow and told dad through their bond. He sent Melinoe to check it out since Makaria had already left to go get Triton, and when I couldn't reach Sedah, I asked to tag along and see how bad it was." He turned his head to his baby sister, who held a single tear in her left eye.

"You could have been seen." She made it more of a statement than an accusation.

"It would have been worth it. So what if dad has to drag another immortal to hell to drink from the river Lethe! You're my baby sister." Sephir scooted closer and gave her a light hug. "I might not have bothered if I knew you had . . . him here to protect you." Melam took every incriminating word from Sephir's mind right then, leaving 'him' as the only usable one. Melam didn't want Sedah to know what he was either.

SEDAH LOOKED BACK AND FORTH IN OBVIOUS CONFUSION between Melam and her brother. One of them was hiding something big, she just couldn't tell which one. Melam reached over and began to rub Sedah's neck with his right hand, continuing to talk, like he had no idea what he was doing to her in that moment.

"Who was it that really gave her all of that energy that day? She said she felt like a lightbulb for days," Melam pressed.

"Hey! I never told you that. Melam, how did you know I felt like that?" Sedah turned to Melam so fast she winced in pain.

"I got it from Caprika when she was telling the story. A byproduct of being mentally linked," he told Sedah, holding her glare with an understanding one of his own. His confession changed her skin from red, to a blueish grey as comprehension dawned. For him to tell something, even that little tidbit, in front of her brother was something she would forever remember. Because Sephir was family to her, Melam was trusting him with things he would not with others. She tamped down the feeling of jealousy at the thought of Melam being linked to a female other than herself.

Melam's big throaty laugh had her looking back and forth between the men wondering what she had just missed. She was a little relieved to see her brother sharing her confusion.

"Never play the human card games, Little Fire, you could never win. I trust no one, as a rule, not even my own family. I reveal what I do, to whomever I do, because I know that they are well aware of the consequences if they were to ever tell." He turned his gaze from Sedah to Sephir. "Your brother probably has more to lose than any other immortal alive should he ever cross me. Hate them or love them, family usually protects family."

"I don't understand," Sedah said, willing either to answer.

"Yes, Helios gave her the energy boost, at my request. He told me she was drained, and that mom had asked for his help."

"Next question. Why did you run off from Triton? Are you scared of him?"

"I am not scared, but I could not be seen. Daughters marry and leave, which would leave Hades his miserable self when Persephone is gone. The curse placed on him by Demeter, was for daughters, and never sons, to be born. No one knows what allowed it, but something happened and the three of us boys were born, and then Sedah," Sephir explained.

"Those few that know or have found out, are forced to drink from either the river Styxx or the River Lethe," Sedah chimed in as she yawned.

"Get rest, little sister. I'll come back when I can. Maybe by then you will stay one color again," he teased her as he leaned over to give her a hug. A quick kiss on the cheek and he was gone.

※ 14 ※

Melam chuckled as Sedah's brow scrunched in irritation at yawning again.

"Why am I so tired? You've had me asleep half of the day, so shouldn't I be wide awake?"

"Your body is still healing. You used a lot of energy staying up and chatting with everyone." Melam explained.

"Talking doesn't use *that* much energy, Melam." Sedah smiled.

"No, but hiding your pain and discomfort for that long does." Melam raised his eyebrows, daring her. "Why didn't you say anything?" He caught her chin with his index finger to stop her from dropping her head. Their eyes locked, trying to read what the other was thinking for what seemed like forever.

"I didn't want to seem weak. To admit my pain would make me seem . . . less, in the nymphs' eyes. And maybe even in yours." Sedah tried to hide the insecurity in her voice. She had no idea why it mattered to her how he saw her, but it did. She wasn't strong enough to stop the tear that rolled down her cheek as he let her go, stood, and faced the fire, giving her his back. It was a long moment before he finally spoke.

"There are many things people do on this planet that I would say makes them less, even weak. There is not one thing about you that is not admirable, Sedah." He turned and looked back at her. "Going somewhere you have never been, where you know nobody, learning their ways and customs the best you can, without a single complaint, is something even I couldn't do. And that shit the night of the party? You fought back with everything you had until you won. That's not less. That's more, in my book."

"Thank you Melam. I guess I never saw it quite like that." She tried to hide another yawn. Seeing everything she had done through his eyes painted her as more confident than she felt that she was. Knowing that he saw her that way made her want to cry.

"Do you want me to send you to sleep and try to heal you some more?" Melam offered, sitting beside her again.

"Can we try healing me with me falling asleep naturally?" Sedah asked. With a nod, Melam wrapped his arm around her shoulders to hold her up, and mentally pushed the rock out of her way. Laying her down, he materialized a normal blanket over her for warmth.

"Can I have a pillow?" Sedah almost whispered. She didn't want to ask for too many things, afraid of depleting his magic like it did hers by conjuring too much at one time.

"I do not know this word. You will have to materialize it yourself," Melam admitted. He frowned when Sedah began to laugh.

"It's about time you didn't know the answer to something. A pillow is a cushion that goes under your head, supports your neck, and keeps it off the ground. I don't know how I materialized the only two things that I ever have. I only know how to duplicate things I touch." She said.

Sedah watched Melam move closer to her, pick up her head gently, careful of her injuries, and lay it in his lap once he had arranged himself to sit legs crossed with her head in his lap, his knees touching her shoulders, careful of her injuries.

"That is called a *weki* in my language. I have never used one here to know the word. You have now taught me something new, and I thank you for expanding my understanding of this world." He smiled.

As if sensing her tension, he began a light circular massage at her temples. As tired as she was, it didn't take long for his hands to lull her to sleep.

Melam could feel her barriers dropping as she fell deeper into the abyss. Closing his eyes, Melam released only a handful of his energy in case her body didn't accept it. The last thing Melam wanted to do was to cause her harm again.

The energy fell slowly, settling on her like dust. Gradually, he could see it disappearing, meaning her skin was absorbing it like before. Hopeful, Melam released another handful, directing it to hover above her just enough to be inhaled as she slept. Melam held his breath as she took the whole handful into her at a steady rate, without problems.

Melam smiled and breathed a sigh of relief as she sneezed in her sleep. Concentrating, he directed his energy to finish healing her wounds. When she woke in the morning, she would be completely healed, and could go on with her life.

Content that he had done all he could to heal every ache, Melam pulled the remaining energy back into himself slowly, to avoid a repeat of last time. With his energy returning to him, pieces of her energy came back, connected to his somehow—something entirely unheard of to him. He would normally be worried enough to call his mother and ask her what it meant and if it had ever happened before. This time, he felt like he should keep this to himself. He had to admit, he liked the thought of having a piece of her essence in him and his within her, which would strengthen their bond further.

Like the previous time, Sedah and Melam's energy seemed to have fused together, which was what normally happened in the areas that energy was sent to heal. It was a type of aloe vera band-aid, his daughter had called it once. He had no idea what that was, but he also knew that he had never seen a fused cell leave the host body.

Instead of the fusion causing her pain when he went to remove the excess, this time it had just taken random pieces of her energy back into his body. There wasn't enough energy to give him any images, just the fleeting emotions of love, anger, and a giddiness that was a new emotion, for her. As old as he was, Melam had never heard of this sort of thing happening. While he knew he should do his princely duty and inform his mother about it, something held him back from seriously considering it. Melam found that, no matter how small the piece, he more than just liked having a part of Sedah with him.

Knowing what the next morning would bring, Melam watched Sedah all night. He watched her dreams, rubbed her arms when the blanket wasn't keeping her warm enough, and even found himself running his fingers through her hair, where it fell over his leg like a waterfall of fire. As dawn crept into the sky, it was this feeling of safety and security that had Sedah smiling and looking up at Melam as she stretched.

With a sudden gasp, Sedah quickly jumped to her feet. Spinning in a circle, she looked all around to be sure.

"Where are Melinoe's dead? I knew I felt her here last night, why did she take them?" Sedah couldn't control the fear and hurt in her voice at her sister's actions.

"They were almost translucent, *varela*. Your *meta* came skipping through the woods. As she made the circle, they seemed to be sucked right back into her." Melam held his hand up to her. Taking it, Sedah allowed him to pull her back down slowly, seemingly unaware she had been standing. "She waved, blew a kiss, I'm assuming to you, and laughed as she disappeared again. We were still protected though. I put up a barrier behind them on day one." He rubbed the top of her hand absently with his thumb as he spoke.

Pulling her hand out of his, Sedah smiled as she got back into the position she had awoken in. She had liked that view. With an answering smile that did not quite reach his eyes this time, he went back to finger-combing her hair. There were a few minutes of quiet while Sedah worked up her courage.

"You were able to heal me totally last night, weren't you? I didn't feel a single stitch of pain when I jumped up in such a hurry. I feel so good that I actually forgot I had hurt myself for almost a full minute, to be honest. My mind didn't know whether to process the fact that there was no pain, or no ghosts, literally." She giggled.

"Yes, I was able to heal you. Now try to stay that way." He tapped her nose with his right index finger quickly, with a smile. "Go wake the girls up one by one and freak them out. They'll love it." He nudged her head. If she stayed in his lap a moment longer, he would have some explaining to do. She was too innocent to understand her hold over a man, and he didn't want to give her the wrong impression after all the shit that she had already been through while on earth.

It only took Caprika's squeal of surprise and delight to wake up Amy and Dustie. Soon, he couldn't tell who was saying what, as every girl was talking at the same time, like she had been in a coma instead of just immobile for a couple days. He smiled, although it didn't quite reach his eyes. His standing up seemed to remind the girls that he was still there. He inhaled deeply, his heart breaking at what he knew was the best thing for both of them, even though it would kill him. He had to take his mom's advice. He would not be the reason fate went wrong for her.

"I will see you girls later. It has been an experience I will not soon forget." Before any of the girls could respond, Melam's body seemed to vaporize and be carried off by the wind.

Sedah stood there, simply staring at the spot. She couldn't believe he had left without a word. She had somehow become used to having him there when she was scared or hurt. Without him around, she was beginning to panic. Dropping to her knees, she tried to control her erratic breathing. The girls crowded around her asking questions, but all she heard was the hum of their voices as she began to grow lightheaded.

"She's having a panic attack. Go ahead and we will catch up," Caprika told the girls as she got down on her knees, rubbing Sedah on the back. "Humans have these when they become overwhelmed, but I've never heard of a godling having one."

"This is Melam's fault," she growled, as she continued to rub Sedah's back, holding her in a side hug and rocking her. "I'm going to kick his ass next time I see him."

"Do you want to talk about it?" Caprika asked as Sedah began to finally gain control of her breathing again.

Sedah looked around, noticing for the first time that the other girls had left them alone. As much as she wanted to talk to Caprika, she wondered how she could explain something that didn't even make sense to her. The second that Melam had disappeared, she had felt both as scared and helpless as she'd felt in the dream of the net of vines. When he'd left, she felt like he'd taken her strength and courage with him.

Determined not to be so weak, a plan began to form in Sedah's mind. She would prove that she was still strong and fearless. She was the daughter of the King and Queen of Hell, after all. She decided right then, that she would no longer be afraid, to start taking after Melinoe and make others fear her. It was now painfully obvious, by his departure, that she had meant nothing to Melam, but she would to others.

"Not really." Sedah slowly straightened up into a sitting position, turning to Caprika. "But I need your help."

"You're cherry red, and your face has that same determination you had when Amy was pissing you off on purpose. I'm afraid to even ask, but go ahead, lay it on me." Caprika sighed. Better to know the plan and be on Sedah's good side. Sedah began explaining, and by the end, Caprika agreed. "I feel sorry for Onyx and Lilac right now. This is either going to draw out the person that had hurt you and sent the animals after us, or it'll show that person that you're not someone to mess with."

Caprika did as Sedah planned and ran ahead to tell their friends so they could be ready to help. They would all know what to expect. Sedah was more confident that she would be both prepared and protected from all sides.

When she was sure Caprika was gone, Sedah said the ancient Greek words to bring Melinoe to her. "Apó tin kólasi sti gi, to paidí skoteinó apó to myaló, na fereis Melinoe se ména." *From Hell to Earth, the child, dark of mind, bring Melinoe to me.*

Instantly, Melinoe's half snow white, half jet black hair shone bright as slowly, first one side of her body, then the other, became solid from nothing.

"The problem of being born of heaven and hell; they don't like to play well. Why go through the trouble of summoning me, sis? You could have just called. I would have come to you." Melinoe smiled, reaching out and tugging lightly on her younger sister's hair. It was her tell that her feelings were slightly hurt. Always with the hair pulling.

Sedah rolled her eyes. "Yeah, eventually. I needed you

now. Plus this way, you cannot leave until I say that you have sufficiently scared enough people." Sedah grinned cunningly.

"Oh, you have something planned. I'm in, obviously." Melinoe rubbed her hands together conspiratorially as Sedah began to fill her in. "Welcome to the dark side, little sister. I am proud of you." Melinoe grabbed Sedah by the neck and gave her a noogie. Smiling once she had been let go, the two girls started toward the hidden gate to the nymph's camp. Caprika was standing to the side, just close enough to the gate that it allowed them through. Every nymph inwardly felt a flutter inside them as the actual gate shuddered when Melinoe stepped through.

As soon as she was through, Melinoe sent her ghosts to torment, and her ghouls to wreak havoc, only on those nymphs that had not accepted or been nice to Sedah. Angry screams and frightened shrieks came from everywhere as the ghosts chased their prey and the ghouls tore through things, the nymphs trying in vain to stop them.

Caprika watched everyone as instructed. Her task was to wait and see if any of the nymphs would signal that they'd attacked Sedah before.

Dustie sat in front of her house on the ground, laughing as she held a frightened monkey in her lap. Amy was leaning against the shed post and Freil against the corner of the house, also watching.

Sedah was surprised at how long it took for Lilac and her group to come see what was happening in camp. So much for her being in charge. Lilac seemed like she had no care for her people's fears, just her own curiosity to assuage. She ignored everything as she walked towards Sedah and Melinoe, stopping when she was about four feet from them. Melinoe sent a ghost to aggravate each of the five girls behind Lilac to give Sedah more of a private conversation between them.

"What is the meaning of this, myk'tu?" Lilac spit the last word as if it were a bad taste in her mouth.

"Care to tell me who has it in for me enough to try to send innocent animals to attack me and my friends?" Sedah crossed her arms. Her emotion was clear through the deep red taking over her body, with black swirling like smoke trying to escape her skin. Sedah's anger raged, barely controlled, causing her small horns to come up through her hair. Her calm demeanor was scary enough to make her sister smile with pride.

"Maybe even the animals hate you. Have you ever thought of that?" Lilac smiled, the flash of emotions shining through clearly before she was able to school her features.

"Even those sent to hell love me. I could call one to me to prove it, if you like." Sedah moved her fingers toward her mouth to whistle for her hellhounds. Lilac quickly took a step forward, swatting Sedah's hand back down before stepping back again.

"Are you insane?! They would rip us all apart! Is that what you want?" Lilac yelled through her panic.

Melinoe made a show of rolling her head over to look at her sister with boredom. "Is that a trick question?"

"Who knows, with these six. Take it as rhetorical for now." Sedah shrugged as she stared Lilac down.

"The thing about hellhounds is that they only go after the guilty," Sedah said, softly snapping her fingers on her right. Between her and Melinoe, the ghost of a hellhound slowly came into view. "Akebar, meet Lilac." She grinned. Sedah made no show of hiding her hatred.

Melinoe took back the five ghosts she had placed on Lilac's friends. Finally free, they were about to come to their leader's aid until she raised a hand, signaling them to stop and be silent. Seeing the black dog for the first time, they wisely obeyed.

"I will only ask once, before I bring him to this realm and release him to find the truth for me. One bite from his mouth will paralyze you," Sedah warned the six girls.

"His teeth inject fear strong enough to do that." Melinoe smiled innocently as she explained it to them. "Fuljuor is the one you really need to fear." Her smile grew vicious as she snapped her left fingers, making a second, almost identical dog, appear beside the first. While the first dog was standing calmly as if it was waiting for instructions, the second was snarling and barking as it danced around like it was attempting to get off an invisible leash. Akebar nipped at Fuljuor, calming him down some.

"Fuljuor is more . . . protective of us girls. His bite is the equivalent of over fifty black mambas and his saliva has flesh eating acid." Sedah shrugged, acting like she had just been asked her preference of pizza toppings. Melinoe and Sedah had trained these dogs and knew exactly what they were capable of.

"You can't hurt us. Your grandmother wouldn't allow it and she can't know you exist." Lilac sneered, sure of her title and the protection it offered.

"She's right, I can't be found out." Sedah looked at her sister in defeat. "But I can kill them. You will take the blame for her death, right sis?" she looked back at the group of girls with an evil smile. If ever there was doubt, that one look confirmed her relation to the King of the Underworld.

"Anything for family," Melinoe said as she bent down beside Fuljuor and placed a hand on his back. The girls watched in horror as the dog began to solidify.

One of the nymphs behind Lilac pushed the girl beside her, causing her to stumble outside of their huddled group. "She was the one! She controls animals' aggression!" The girl yelled as the accused shook her head and tears began to silently run down her cheeks in fear.

Melinoe glanced up at Sedah, a sad smile on her face. Sedah felt her own triumphant smile weaken and droop. She grew sadder now that someone had confessed. She had thought that scaring the girls would be fun, but this terror in the nymphs, even the ones whom she could call enemies, wasn't fun at all.

Standing, Melinoe commanded Fuljuor, in the language of the underworld so Sedah could hear, to sniff out the truth— to determine who hated Sedah enough to harm her at the expense of the other nymphs. Hellhounds only had to sense what they were needed for and they would do it.

Fuljuor walked toward the girls, sniffing. Liking their fear, he snarled and snapped so that they whimpered and clung to one another. He felt for the person with the most anger and malice toward Sedah. No one seemed to notice Akebar weaving in and out of the girls also, feeling for intentions. Inner thoughts and feelings could only be felt by gods and shades, both needing to feed on these in order to remain on the earthly plane. Both dogs sniffed until they found the real culprit.

Fuljuor barked and growled as Akebar sat, looking from the tall green haired girl to Sedah, silently waiting for permission to be made corporeal and protect her as he always had.

Knowing that she had been caught, the girl let out a hideous half scream, half groan in frustration. The other nymphs, Lilac included, stepped back a little in surprise.

"So I did it, so what? You were obviously not hurt, so what's it matter? It was Onyx's last request of me before she left when Jade did, and I was happy to do it."

"What is your name?" Sedah asked. Knowing this girl had been asked by Onyx had made her feel better, until the girl had finished her sentence.

"She is Tutice," Lilac answered when the girl crossed her arms, saying nothing. "While I don't like you, Sedah, I'm bound by duty to dispense justice. Being Lethe's daughter won't help Tutice out of this one.

Opening her mouth to speak, Lilac could only watch in horror as a stone mallet was thrown toward Sedah with deadly accuracy that only Tutice possessed. A second before it would have hit her, Sedah threw her hands up to protect her face, and the weapon hit an invisible wall.

The sound reverberated back with an intensity that knocked the six girls off their feet, onto their butts. The two dogs were on Tutice faster than she could get up, their teeth inches from her throat. She screamed as the first drop of Foljuor's acidic saliva fell on her skin and burnt through her clothes.

Melinoe walked up to Sedah, followed by Caprika, who had seen it happen also. Both girls reached toward Sedah,nothing keeping them from touching her.

"That's new," Melinoe said in a low voice.

"That wasn't me," Sedah whispered. Her eyes were as wide as they could get, her surprise and fear so great in that moment, she was suddenly very afraid that Demeter herself would show up.

Melam sauntered through the forest and straight into camp, not even five seconds later.

"This looks like a party I would have loved to join in on. Anyone care to explain?" Melam looked straight at Sedah, holding her defiant stare. *"They are beneath you. What did you hope to accomplish?"* he chastised her mentally, showing her enough respect not to do it in front of friends, family, and enemies.

"I am tired of being pushed around and having them send innocent plants and animals to attack me. So, I enlisted my sister to help me teach them a lesson and get the truth about who did it." She tried not to let him hear the quivering in her voice from the buildup of fear, anger, and adrenaline.

"I take it you found the one behind it all then?" he walked over to stand beside Akebar, looking down at Tutice.

"*I don't know what to do now. If I kill her, I bring grandmother's wrath down on Melinoe and me. She just tried to kill me though, so I can't just let that go,*" Sedah tried answering back, unsure if he could hear her.

Melam looked at Sedah for a long moment. Hearing it said for a second time, that someone had tried to kill his Sedah, did not sit well with him. He would ask himself later why he was thinking of her as his.

"So, the question becomes, what to do with you to punish you properly, while still keeping Sedah safe." Melam stared at the girl, unconsciously petting Akebar, despite him being in shade form. Although Sedah was used to Melam doing some unusual things, she knew that what he was doing was beyond the realm of what was supposed to be possible.

"I know just the thing that will do both. Sedah, repeat after me. *Lef de les foa das ia dal, le out tes un etun dral.*" He said the words in his language, slow enough for her to repeat them. "Now say it with me." As she repeated them this time, he said the words in English so that she would be okay with what she was saying. *Here in the forest dark and deep, I offer you an eternal sleep.*

As they said the words in unison Sedah looked back and forth from Melam to Tutice. Everyone else was so focused on what she and Melam were saying, that only Sedah saw Tutice collapse as the last words were spoken. Seeing the fright in her eyes, Melam was quick to explain.

"Now that the words have been spoken, anytime you are in camp, or within sight of one another, she will fall asleep as soon as is safely possible." He looked at Sedah.

"What's to stop Sedah or someone else from harming her while she is defenseless? Will she even know what is going on around her while she is paralyzed?" Lilac asked.

"She will know what's going on, but will not be able to be injured, or moved by anyone with ill intent. If she attempts to hurt Sedah again, I will not be so lenient," Melam warned. His look brooking no arguments.

"Thank you, I think." Sedah smiled slightly before quickly hiding it. She had no idea why he cared enough to even trouble himself to show up, but she liked the butterflies it had caused when he had.

"Am I done here then, sis? Dad is calling," Melinoe said aloud, effectively halting Sedah from exploring her new feelings any further.

"Yeah, sorry." She blushed. Sedah waited for Melinoe to draw her ghosts and ghouls back within her before releasing her from their bond with the ancient Greek word, "Nostoi."

The entire camp halted from their terrified running and screaming, camp becoming as silent as the grave as everyone took stock of what had gone on and wondered what would happen next.

Sedah looked at her beloved pets. She snapped her fingers to gain both of their attention since Akebar was looking up at Melam, his tongue hanging out in contentment as he was stroked. She gave them the command to return back to hell, and to her father's great hall, "Pigaine spiti." They rushed to her, licking at her hands and face as they slowly dissipated into nothingness.

Lilac looked around at those she had sworn to protect. Turning to two of the closest girls, she pointed to the sleeping Tutice. "Take her to her tree. When she wakes, tell her what has been set upon her as punishment and what will happen if she does it again." Turning to Melam, she nodded towards the gate with her head. "I would appreciate it if you three would follow me." She looked at Caprika as she moved to deny her part in the incident. Without waiting, she walked past them, and out of camp.

The gate still shimmered in recognition as Lilac and Caprika walked through it. It finally recognized Sedah for the first time, shimmering just as it did with the nymphs, but with a few colors being more vibrant than it was with them. As Melam passed through, the gate pushed outward, creating a kaleidoscope of colors, almost as if it had to swell in order to contain them. It was no wonder the gate let him through these two times. Sedah wondered if anyone else had seen something so spectacular. A glance back told her everyone was helping each other clean up in the aftermath.

Once outside of camp and the gate, everyone traded glances, wondering who would speak first. Lilac turned to Caprika, first, taking a moment to stare at her before she spoke.

"Did you know about all of this?"

"The scaring everyone until someone confessed, yes. And I admit to standing by the gate to let her sister in, but that's it." Caprika defended herself quickly.

"Lilac, no one was supposed to get hurt. The hell hounds weren't even in the plans until you and your horde pissed me off, thinking you couldn't be touched. She tried to kill me! Technically, she's tried twice now." Sedah crossed her arms in frustration. Her horns were slowly receding, giving her a headache.

Lilac turned to Melam, pointing her index finger at him. "You did that sleeping thing to her. How long will that last?"

"Forever. It is tied currently to Sedah only, but since her first attempt to kill her included other nymphs, one more attempt to kill any supernatural, and she will fall asleep, dying within a week unless Gaia herself says otherwise. That is the law of my people." Melam's gaze never left Lilac's, letting her see exactly how serious that he was. Lilac turned her back on them, taking a few steps away and then back, obviously deep in thought.

"Okay, the deal was that we teach her until she quits changing colors. Caprika, you are now solely in charge of that. Sedah is not allowed in camp anymore. Tutice has to be able to do her job. Since Caprika will be so busy with Sedah, her jobs will get delegated to the others. The second you don't change colors, I don't care where you go, but you are not allowed to stay in my forest. This will begin at first light," Lilac told the girls. Ignoring the shock on Caprika's face and the tears running silently down Sedah's face, Lilac turned, going back through the gate and into camp.

Caprika went to Sedah, pulling the goddess into a hug to comfort her. "Your plan was innocent enough, but the nymphs had never been a species known for fighting fair. It's why I leave the woods whenever I can."

"My colors aren't gone, but they aren't as vibrant as they were before. That means they are fading. I will have to meet with Triton and stay there soon." Sedah began hiccupping through her sobs as she spilled her fears out to her friend.

"Caprika, are you a hamadryad, or are you mobile?" Melam asked quietly. The question silenced the girls. Sedah had forgotten he was there, honestly.

"Amy, Freil, Dustie, and I are all Leimoniads and Dryads, why?" Caprika asked. Sedah pulled out of Caprika's arms so they could both face Melam.

"A plan is forming in my head, but I have to go. I will meet you down at the lake tomorrow to discuss it, so tell the girls. Dustie I would leave behind, since she still looks like a child." Bowing to them, he walked into the forest, disappearing.

By the time the girls made it back to their hut, everyone

seemed to have heard Lilac's punishment on them for going about scaring everyone. Those that had never been nice to Sedah smiled in glee over not having to deal with her after that night. At dinner, those that had come to like her tried to come by and cheer her up, or were at least nice enough to come tell her bye and wish her well.

"I'm sorry for causing you to be punished too," Sedah tried to apologize to Caprika later that night, once Dustie was asleep. The two girls sat on the floor by the fire, both unable to sleep.

Caprika laughed, shaking her head. "It's not much of a punishment if you ask me. She just told me to leave my chores and all the drama to go hang out with you. I'd call that a vacation."

Sedah smiled, liking the way Caprika thought.

✦

"So how are you going to go about punishing Kohl and his gang, or at least stop him from continuing to torture humans?" Melam asked his mother, The Ether. He had called for her after leaving the girls, but when she had not answered, he had gone to bed. Two hours later, she was woke him up.

"Gaia is going to deal with them very soon. I believe she is visiting with all the Gods that have control or say, for she is not available to me at the moment, either," Rhea explained.

"But that seems like the wrong move to make in this particular case."

"Your grandmother is the all-knowing Gaia. I'm sure she has seen his intentions and will look at everything. She has never failed us before," Rhea chastised him.

"Sorry. I am not questioning her or her methods. I just worry that she will underestimate him. Not on what he has already done, but on what he will do in retaliation. He thinks he is above everyone, possibly even Mother Earth herself, instead of the lowly servant that he truly is. Grandmother likes to see the good in her children, even when they intentionally do bad." Melam said. There were many times when he was growing up, where he had intentionally done something bad, and Gaia had come to his defense, just as she often did with her earthlings.

"What would you do if you were given the choice? Would you turn him into that which he has tortured: a mortal?" Rhea asked out of curiosity.

"No, because having no powers will not stop him. The humans have enough of their own monsters without us adding to them. I would turn him into one of Gaia's most humble and loyal servants."

Rhea went to sit down beside Melam's cot, a chair materializing a second before she would have fallen.

"I will ask her to consider it." She smiled, looking at him for a long moment. Melam felt as if he was a small child again, being summoned to the throne room to answer for his latest prank gone wrong. He tried his best not to squirm in his bed.

"I approve of your plan with the nymphs, but only if this satyr is taken care of first. We will see what mother says when I am able to speak with her again. Just know that you are on a path that has many outcomes, both good and bad. You need to make sure you are okay with whatever happens if you plan on interfering with fate." His mother looked at him with a combination of sorrow and seriousness that made Melam wonder what she had seen when she had stared at him.

"*Seuc les stri gui tes bas reher.*" Rhea stood, looking down on him before disappearing as she was ascending in the air.

"Sounds like I'm going to need a lot more than the stars to guide me," Melam said aloud. From the way his mother had made it sound, one wrong step could spell disaster.

Sighing heavily in frustration, Melam threw his right arm over his eyes and tried to go back to sleep.

While his mother's visit had left him confused, his dreams seemed to pinpoint various paths he should take, looking like runway lights in the dead of night. While he still wasn't sure which route to take, it gave him hope that there was more than one good path open to him.

❀

AS SOON AS IT WAS DAYLIGHT ENOUGH TO SEE, CAPRIKA was up, showing Dustie the extra chores around their home that she would have to do to make sure the animals got fed. Dustie pouted, saying how unfair it all was.

Lilac came to their cabin as the sun broke the horizon, escorting Sedah and Caprika out. When Lilac knocked on their cabin door, both Sedah and Caprika opened the door with their necessary things already in hand, not giving Lilac the satisfaction of looking upset. Mountain nymphs surrounded the two girls as the nymph's version of body-guards. While the Oreiad nymphs usually kept to their own harsh, rocky environment, they were still forced to follow Lilac's decrees. Sedah found herself respecting Caprika a little more for living among Lilac's forest nymphs when she could live in the mountains with her sister kin, far away from Lilac's watchful eyes.

"These Oreiad will guard the gate for as long as I see fit. Caprika may be allowed in, only once a day, while the myk'tu is only allowed in extreme cases," Lilac addressed the crowd before turning to look at the two girls. She leaned in closely so only the two of them could hear. "I would never admit it to the others, but I'm slightly impressed with you, Daughter of the Underworld." She whispered.

When Lilac had knocked on their cabin that morning, she

had expected hesitancy and some tears from the myk'tu they had been forced to hide in order to get their precious Lethe back. Instead, both Sedah and Caprika had opened the door with their necessary things already in hand, accepting the guards, and walking out like it was just another day.

Lilac cleared her throat of emotion. "Do you have all of your things?" When Sedah simply nodded, she continued. "If you think of anything you might have forgotten, Caprika can get it for you on the day you can finally leave, and we get our sister back," Lilac said, effectively reminding both girls of the only reason those in charge had allowed her to be among their kind to begin with. With a smile she knew everyone would take differently than its real reason, Lilac turned around, striding through the Oreiads now posted there, and back into camp.

With a shrug, Caprika turned and headed toward the forest. Gathering her chest that she had shrunk down to the size of a boa constrictor's girth that morning, Sedah jogged to catch up.

Since everyone that mattered seemed to know its location, they agreed on the same area that they had practiced in as their camp. It had good coverage from the elements, as well as a small open area to cook and a fresh spring waterfall nearby to use.

⚘

CAPRIKA WAS SITTING DOWN ON THE GROUND, LEANING against a stump when Amy hopped down from the trees a few hours later. She paused in her focus to notice a bemused Amy and a bewildered Freil arrive.

"Are one of you doing that?" Freil finally asked when neither of the girls spoke.

"Nope. It's something she has been working on with

Amy." Caprika glanced at Amy slightly behind her, on her right.

"But she's only done it when she's mad before," Amy said.

The girls watched as Sedah had every boulder, pebble, pine cone, and limb hovering in the air, moving around lazily as if floating down a stream.

"Who says she's not?" Caprika smiled wider. "Look down girls."

Doing as she said, both looked to see that they were about a foot off the ground.

Freil squealed a little and, grabbed Caprika's shoulder below her, instead of beside her as it should have been. "Why aren't you floating?"

"I honestly don't know. I can only figure it's because she considers us both wronged and is charging the entire area. She doesn't even know you guys are here yet." She glanced at Freil before turning around to address Amy. "Guess how long she's been like this?"

Amy eyed Caprika warily. "An hour almost killed her. So, I'm honestly afraid to." Amy looked at Sedah closely, probably assessing her for fatigue.

"Try the number three on your tongue. She has slowly levitated everything except rooted trees over the last three hours. Not only is she mad about what happened to us, the forest seemed to sense her mood and try to aid her by moving things around for her. She's so mad though, that where the forest thinks it is helping, all it is doing is playing with her mind, making her think she is forgetting where she's setting things, which is fueling her anger. And instead of it draining her like before, correct me if I'm wrong, she seems to be getting brighter, like she is gaining energy almost."

"Oh, my goddess, you're right. She is glowing, and three hours is a scary new record. Should we stop this?" Amy bit her bottom lip with worry.

"Fine," Caprika exaggerated a loud sigh and an eye roll for effect to lighten the mood. She had actually been about to do just that when the girls had arrived. She had been too focused on how Sedah was still going, when she hadn't been able to before.

As Caprika stood, the three girls froze, watching as a bunny came hopping by, only with a foot of air between its feet and the ground. The girls looked at each other for a split second before bursting into laughter.

Everything dropped to the ground abruptly, the girls and bunny included, and they looked up to see Sedah glaring at them. Her eyes still held the fire from her anger, yet her brows and forehead were scrunched together, her lips tight and thin. She looked at war with herself for a moment, on which emotion she would let take over. The girls stared at her with bated breath, wondering if an angry Sedah would see friends or foes through her blinding rage.

Confusion seemed to win, as Caprika stood and the girls walked to where Sedah had been trying to set her things up by enlarging the trunk and then each of its contents.

"Did you guys just laugh at me?" Sedah asked as a grey pallor came over her skin.

"Haven't you noticed what you've been doing?" Freil asked in disbelief.

"More importantly," Amy asked as her eyes flitted in excitement, "what were you thinking about for the past three hours since you guys got here?"

"I've been pissed, obviously. Why? First, we get kicked out of camp, which may not bother Caprika, but makes me feel bad. Then, the forest keeps being an asshole and moving things so that they aren't where I put them, which is driving me bonkers. I'm so pissed and frustrated, I'm about ready to strangle someone!" Sedah yelled as her skin turned bright red, her horns came out in a rush, and flames seemed to dance in her eyes.

Freil let out a scared squeak and stepped behind Amy, not as fearless as the other girls were. Her head darted around as everything around them rose once again.

Caprika put her right hand out, palm up, to indicate what was going on around them, her eyes never leaving Sedah's as she smiled at a now bewildered Sedah. "This is what had us laughing and happy, Sedah. Until we interrupted you, you had been doing this nonstop for three full hours. Three. That's an unheard-of record for you."

"Three hours?" Sedah sat swiftly on the ground as the shock hit her like a nine-pound hammer. As she sat, so did everything levitating around her. "But I'm not drained. How is that possible?" she looked from Caprika, to Amy and back again for some sort of answer.

"That's what we were worrying about. Last time, it only took one hour of training to completely drain you, yet here you are three hours of straight levitation later, with what seems to be even more energy, instead of less.

"For the record, you can make bunnies float anytime I'm around. I thought little bunny foo foo was supposed to hop through the forest, not the air. That was both cute and funny." Freil tentatively stepped from behind Amy, a small smile forming. Sedah looked at her, tilting her head to the right in confusion.

"That's what made us laugh hard enough to break your concentration. A bunny was hopping along, only it was doing so a foot off the ground. So at least now you know that even when you are mad, your levitation doesn't hurt other living things," Caprika explained.

"Unless a floating boulder happens to land on them, so watch for those." Amy smiled, wagging her eyebrows suggestively, trying to lighten the mood.

Sedah laughed. "I'll keep that killing technique in mind. So, what are we going to do today?" Sedah asked.

"Do you have a swimsuit?" Amy wagged her eyebrows again. When Sedah shook her head no, Amy put her hands together, rubbing them up and down in glee. "Guess we are going shopping then." She looked at Caprika. "After the horns disappear anyway."

"Yes, I guess we will have to. Since she's not so bright anymore, as long as she works at controlling her emotions, this could be used as her first test to see how much she can understand how the human world works" Caprika affirmed for Amy. A slow smile appeared on her face as Sedah did breathing exercises to make her horns disappear again. "It's past time Sedah had some fun in her life."

Sedah followed the girls to the edge of the forest, where a person could just make out the water through the break in the trees. They stopped at a clearing that held four long rows of boats of various shapes and sizes. Some were well cared for, having been stored under sheds, or secured with tarps, while others sat neglected and exposed to the elements. At the end of the first row, sat a simple cottage that seemed as old and weathered as some of the boats that it stored.

Instead of heading towards the house as Sedah expected, she followed the three girls to the third row of boats. The closer they got, the greater the feeling of supernatural power became until it began to make the hairs on Sedah's arms stand. Whoever resided here definitely knew that they were on the property.

"My dear niece, I was hoping I would get to see you while you were so close!" A woman almost squealed in glee as she hopped out of the first boat. Sedah gasped in delight, running to the boat to embrace her great aunt, as the woman's feet touched the ground.

The girls watched as the beautiful young woman, dressed

in a black bikini top and aqua blue shorts, hugged Sedah. With glowing baby blue eyes and alabaster skin, she broke apart from Sedah and came towards the group, holding Sedah's hand.

Sedah was so happy she physically glowed as she looked back at Caprika. All three girls stood still, their faces showing their collective shock and surprise.

"You're kin to Hekate? But of course you are," Freil said. Sedah had to remind herself that she probably knew more very powerful gods and goddesses, even in secret, than most immortals ever met in their lives.

"Have you always been here, or do you rotate with other beings? I've been here a lot, but I've never seen you before." Caprika asked.

"How do you think I got the rumors of my dogs and I having multiple heads?" Hekate smiled at Caprika. As if she had asked for a demonstration, Hekate shook her head, causing her long, glossy raven black tresses to change to the same fiery red of Sedah's hair. Another shake gave her short, greying hair and the face of a man that Caprika had gone to often in the past. One more shake had her back to normal. "The only thing I can never change is my eyes. They're not tied to my powers, but to my true self as a goddess. Everything else can be covered by an illusion."

"So, you were the one who told on Sedah's father to her grandmother, but you haven't told on her mother. May I ask why?" Amy asked cautiously.

"I saw how everything would turn out and made a decision. Just like you are doing now, I listened to, and then followed, both my instincts as well as my heart. Keep both in sync, and you will always know what to do." The look in her eyes as she spoke to Amy and Caprika was both a warning and an instruction, Sedah knew.

She pulled Sedah against her, kissing the top of her head

as she smiled brightly. "Now I believe you girls came for a purpose." She turned herself and Sedah around, forcing the nymphs to follow behind as they walked toward the boat.

◌⚜◌

BARELY SLEEPING AFTER HIS MOTHER LEFT, MELAM groaned with the sound of the birds chirping, bringing in a new day. Even waking up in a younger body than he was used to at home, Melam still felt every bit of his true age sometimes. Sighing loudly, Melam sat up and stretched, his muscles elongating visibly under his skin, sleek, like a snake moving silently in the tall grass.

Getting up, he made sure he got to breakfast in time to see if anything relevant was being talked about. Everyone seemed to have heard what had happened at the nymph camp, but they talked more about what they thought Sedah had done to the nymphs than about how Sedah had been thrown out for it.

There seemed to be a new respect for the little goddess, and Melam could only hope that meant that they would not try to mess with her anymore, now that they knew what she was capable of.

Kohl's group sat at their usual table, barely speaking. Melam had no remorse as he looked at them. Not even bothering to ease into it nice and slow, Melam reached out mentally, seizing control of one of Kohl's demented friends. He only knew Danny and Kohl by name, but remembered from the victim's memories that this one was Kohl's second, as well as the one that had left the girl to die in the cave after Kohl was done with her.

Searching the satyr's mind was like going through a trash can of compost, but it had to be done. Melam found that Kohl and this particular satyr, Danny, had gone back that morning to untie the one male only to find all of the humans gone, including the one left for dead.

It was thralled into the humans to wake up and simply leave the area, remembering nothing and helping no one. For a thralled human to untie another, or carry someone with them, meant they had been clear minded enough for their morals and conscience to make them act.

Now, the group faced a dilemma they had never had before. Their only options were to either choose another area for their games, or to wait and see if any humans came into the woods, trying to find the area. That decision the group was leaving up to Kohl.

Pulling out of the satyr's mind, he smiled as he saw Danny's skin go green, one hand grabbing his stomach as the other pushed his breakfast away. He stood very carefully and slowly, obviously afraid of moving too fast and losing what little he had already eaten.

Now content that the group did not suspect foul play or any interference from their side, Melam felt he could move his attention to other things. Like a certain little demon goddess, bent on getting herself killed.

Melam's body shuddered, just at the thought of how close she had come yesterday. Not knowing who had given him the nudge, Melam had felt, out of nowhere, this breathtaking, all-encompassing fear grip him. Somehow, he'd known beyond a shadow of a doubt that Sedah was in trouble, and he desperately needed to get there.

It had taken everything in him to hide in the forest and throw a shield around her as the nymph produced a mallet and hurled it with all her power at Sedah. No one needed to know the kind of power he held, but if it meant saving her, Melam would have exposed himself without thought, wiping their minds later. How he had been able to saunter over to them, as if his legs hadn't felt like jello, he would never know.

He wasn't exactly proud of himself for wanting to scold her, but with his heart beating like a hummingbird's wings, his hands were itching to go to her shoulders and shake her until she had some sense back in her. Looking back, he now felt a sense of pride for what she had done too. It took guts to confront the entire camp until the culprit had come forward. It had been fun watching the ghosts terrorize people, and the innocents just sitting and getting a free chuckle out of it. He had been glad when she asked for his help, being faced with something she had not been prepared for. Melam smiled thinking about it as he made his way towards the lake.

❦

"Leave it to you to get your first piece of human clothing from a boat that transports us to another continent." Amy laughed as they climbed out of the boat half an hour later. "I'm sad Freil had to leave before she got to choose an outfit though."

"That was unfortunate. The French have some of the best clothing." Hekate smiled, turning to Sedah. "Only the best for my niece's first time among the wolves." She put her hand on Sedah's hair, absently combing through it. The girls waved goodbye, seeing Melam through the trees heading towards them. It took all Sedah had not to wrap her arms around her middle again. It was the least amount of clothes she had ever worn, and she felt naked. Even with a sheer coverup around her waist, she felt exposed.

Melam smiled in greeting as they walked towards him. He hid his slight tremor of anticipation by putting his hands to good use, holding branches out of the way for the girls as they made the short trek to the beach area. He had to work at keeping his eyes off Sedah as she walked ahead of him.

The day was nice and warm, but not to the point of

needing an umbrella or shade to keep cool. There were one or two families, but for the most part, there were only people who looked around their apparent age, and there were few of them, It was still early afternoon, when most college kids out of school are just waking up from their all-night partying.

Not wasting any time, Amy and Caprika stripped off their matching bathing suit cover ups, as they slipped off their sandals. Glancing quickly towards Sedah, they froze when they saw her fully dressed. Caprika, who had been closer to the water, picked up a handful and slung it towards Sedah, trying to make her snap out of whatever had made her stop. As the water got close, Sedah gasped, jumping back far enough to avoid it entirely.

Turning around from setting up their towels, Melam saw the worry in Sedah's eyes. Even from behind her, he could see the tautness of her body. She was as rigid as a board, staring at the water and holding her second beach towel for dear life. She had such a grip on it, Melam was afraid her fingers would break soon, the stark white tips being in direct contrast to the fire red digits.

Walking the few inches until he was directly behind her, Melam put his hands on Sedah's shoulders. When she did not react, Melam slowly turned her upper body to face him, forcing her legs to either comply or fall. He smiled when she looked up at him without being made to. Her eyes glistened with unshed tears, one escaping down her cheek as he looked down at her. His heart clenched as he saw her pain and uncertainty.

"What's wrong, *lifda fli*?" Melam cupped her face within his palms. He thought *little woman* was the perfect word for her in his language in that moment.

"What if I get in the water and Triton sees that I'm almost okay?" Her voice shook despite her trying to hide the turmoil within her attempting to boil over like a volcano.

"What would be wrong with that? You cannot stop the inevitable, you can only control your reaction to it. What part scares you?" Melam rubbed her right cheek absently with his thumb.

"That no one will be there with me. His arrogance scares me too. I don't want to be the cause of a war." Sedah searched Melam's eyes, pleading with hers, for him to reassure her. Something that they both knew he could not do.

"Okay, I was going to let us swim first, but we will sit down, and I will tell you girls of my plan." He motioned to the girls and waited until they were all seated on their towels to continue. "I don't want to wait for your colors to fully go away. I can mask your color changes, and we can get out of here. I figure that we can get a condo near the water for when he does come, but when he is not with you, you can practice being around humans." He waited for their reactions, unsure of what they might be. Some nymphs spent their whole lives in and near the forests, while others loved to explore the many different woods around the world.

As if on cue, all three girls were on their feet, rushing to hug him, laughing when he was tackled to the ground.

"I'll take that as three votes of yes. I will start looking tomorrow." He smiled as Caprika rolled off him to the right and Amy rolled off him to the left. Sedah looked at him for a long time, making no attempt to move. Finally, at his limit for how good he could be in one day, Melam rolled her off him, laughing as he got up and held his hand down to her. "Let's go swim."

Helping her up, he waited with bated breath for her to take her cover off. His breath quickened, his heart accelerating when he saw the beautiful royal purple two-piece suit she wore. Trying not to react to the heat spreading to his groin, he kept her hand in his as they followed behind Amy and Caprika. Sedah kept looking around them as their feet touched the water and they waded to waist level. He tugged on her hand lightly, to get her to look at him.

"*He lives in the Sea, not the streams, lakes or rivers. I will not let anything happen to you. Let go and have fun lifda fli.*" Melam smiled, letting go of her hand and swimming on his back a little ways away from her.

Sedah let out a breath, trying to calm down her racing heart. If she was being honest with herself, she had a feeling that it was beating fast for an entirely different reason than it had started. Standing there looking at him, all he had to do was show that half smile, half smirk, and her heart picked up speed. He made her chest physically hurt, the pressure building until she wasn't sure she could contain it anymore.

Walking forward until the water was at her shoulders, Sedah took a deep breath out, only to squeal in surprise as water was splashed in her face. Wiping her face, she locked eyes on Caprika and Amy, the latter of which had a huge grin on her face, giving herself away. Before Sedah could retaliate though, both Amy and Caprika were pushed under, as Melam bolted out from the water, winking at Sedah all the while. Melam quickly swam over to Sedah, getting away while he could.

The girls came back up, sputtering, but smiling. Melam showed Sedah how to put her hands facing out, side by side, interlocking her thumbs so that she could get Amy back. She mimicked his movements, happy that it was easy enough to understand on the first try.

The four of them splashed, dunked, and tried to evade each other, while still keeping Sedah in shallow enough water to stand, since she could not swim. Melam even let the girls take turns getting on his shoulders and jumping into the water for a little while. They were so absorbed in their fun, no one felt the change of the air, slowly driving away all the human beach goers.

Melam splashed Caprika, getting her good enough for her to retaliate by pushing him under. All three girls laughed, waiting for him to resurface. Sedah began looking around them, expecting him to resurface some distance away from them. Fear ripped through her as she became acutely aware that they were the only ones still in the water.

"Caprika," she said, turning to find no one on the beach either.

"Sedah, very naturally, get—" Caprika instructed, only to stop mid-sentence as Sedah screamed out and was pulled forcefully under the water. Above water, Amy lunged toward Sedah, trying to grab her, as Caprika dove under to try and stop whatever had grabbed Sedah. Neither girl succeeded, both surfacing, coughing up the water they had inhaled. That was the last Sedah saw of them as the thing that held her dragged her rapidly away.

❧ 16 ❧

S edah knew she only had enough air for a few minutes before she would drown. While she might not be able to swim, she was not new to the concept of breathing under water. There were plenty of dead in the Underworld who had perished from just such a way.

She tried to spot Melam, but he had been taken a few moments before her. She had to assume he was too far from her to be seen through the dark water.

Trying not to panic and lose more air, or breathe in any water, Sedah looked to her feet where a Limnatide, if she remembered correctly from her studies, was pulling her along. Almost out of air, Sedah let what was left out in a squeal as she saw the dark, underwater cave they were about to enter. Turning, she tried to swim to the surface in panic— both of losing air, and her life. For all she fought, the Limnatide easily pulled her into the dark cave as if she weighed nothing. As soon as the cavern opened, her captor released Sedah's foot, allowing her to scramble to the surface, her lungs burning in pain, screaming for release.

She broke the surface, gasping desperately for air even as

she sank below again, unable to keep her head above water. Feeling, more than seeing someone splash into the water, she felt strong hands grip her waist, pulling her back up. As soon as her head broke the surface, she began fighting her newest captor, more determined to escape than to cooperate.

"*Stop, before I drop you,*" Melam's voice brushed across her mind. Instantly, she stopped struggling, allowing him to pull her with him.

When they reached the side of the caverns, Melam made sure she was holding on tightly to a rock so he could pull himself out, then Sedah. As soon as Sedah's feet were out of the water, she hugged Melam, relieved that he was okay, but still scared. He rubbed her back as she buried her face in his chest, trying to calm down enough to get her bearings.

Melam gave her as much time as he could, allowing himself the selfish notion that she clung to him because she felt more for him than just someone to help her through their predicament. Eventually, he had to pull her away, making her realize that they were not alone.

Melam and Sedah stared at one another for a second, a look passing between them in reassurance that the other was okay. Holding hands in a show of solidarity, Sedah moved to stand on the right side of Melam.

Sedah tried not to gasp as she looked at the cavern and all its occupants. The cavern had a cathedral style ceiling and was spacious enough to hold half of a coliseum, including the cheering fans. There were shades of every color imaginable making up the cave, hinting to the types of indigenous rock that made up the region. The water reflected the colors onto the walls around them, causing waves of rainbows to flow like a flag in the wind. Every few feet, a Limnatide stood. Each one stood completely still, facing the couple silently. Another dozen or so floated in the water, also staring at the couple in silence.

They all stared and silently waited, until Sedah was about to scream. Unconsciously, she took a step forward, only to have Melam put pressure on her hand, making her stop.

Like the slow ebb and flow of the tide, a woman wove in and out of the Limnatides, approaching Sedah and Melam. While her body appeared to be made of duckweed covered water, she had hair made of water lettuce, and clothing made of various lake plants, accented here and there with Hyacinth flowers. She stopped right out of arm's reach.

"I hope we did not scare you too much in getting you here?" the woman asked, a small smile playing at the corner of her mouth.

"Not at all, actually. Our only question is why?" Melam replied. The woman stared at him a moment, trying to get a gauge on him.

"Good. Follow me and we shall have a chat, you and I," she addressed Melam. When he simply stared at her, the woman sighed. "Very well, she may come too." Nodding, Melam started forward to follow the woman.

Still holding hands, Sedah allowed Melam to lead her along, following the woman. She caught glimpses of babies playing with floating balls of water, laughing as they popped one and water splashed over them. What surprised her was how all the women seemed to be made of water, or were at least some degree of translucent, while the children looked like any human child. The other women let them pass as they entered an office of sorts.

Water flowed down a rock wall, disappearing into the floor. A rock desk sat in the middle of the room, two clear chairs in front of it. Sedah had to actually touch the chair to verify that it wasn't wet, as the chairs seemed to be made of flowing water and illuminated by some unknown force.

The woman ignored their wandering eyes and sat behind the desk. She waited until Melam and Sedah sat, to speak.

Now, before I reveal my name for you to use against me, I must know who the hell you two are. You were taken because the power in the lake was so strong that all of my nymphs had to flee the water. I do not like what I do not know, but I am willing to listen before passing judgement."

"Do you think we would then give our names to someone who has not given theirs? Give an answer, and you might receive one back," Melam countered quickly.

"Fine, I am Ingre, leader of this region of Limnatides, and you are?"

"Melam, of somewhere you will have never heard of." He looked at Sedah and nodded, giving her the reassurance to answer.

"I am Sedah, a minor goddess, and a daughter to someone powerful."

"So, names I have never heard of, from houses unknown. One, or both of you combined, held enough power to saturate sixteen hundred acres of water. I have need of someone with that much power, who can walk on land, and I wish to strike a deal. So, who am I doing that with?"

"Why don't you tell us what you want, and we will tell you which one of us could do that?" Sedah spoke up, beginning to get upset at everyone always wanting something from her without discussion.

Ingre stared at Sedah like she had lost her senses.

"Seems rational to me. It depends on the issue, as to which of us, or both of us, can do it." Melam shrugged, looking at Ingre.

Ingre scrutinized them for nearly a full minute, but neither of them would budge to give her a chance to make any more demands. "You are not really giving me a choice, so I guess here it is. We are water nymphs, obviously. We are, however, allowed four hours a day, and one twenty-four-hour period a month, on land without it causing problems to our health or the lakes' ecosystem."

"Sorry, but I'm not seeing the problem yet," Melam pressed.

"The problem is that all the babies we have are born of the species that we procreated with. A meadow nymph cares for them until the child's powers emerge. That nymph has gone missing. One of our girls found the children alone and hungry this morning," Ingre said in a short tone.

"Is that why I saw all of them here in the cave?" Sedah asked. Ingre nodded.

"So, you need us to find her. What do one or both of us get for finding out what happened to her?" Melam asked.

"One revival elixir and our backing for your protection in any lake on this continent. Will one of you do this since I cannot?"

"I could find your meadow nymph, as I am sort of living with them currently. What is her name?" Sedah asked.

"She is Lutia, younger sister to Tutice, if you know her. Lutia is the keeper of the young, born from a Limnatide nymph and a satyr." Sedah shuddered at the name of her attacker and felt the heat in her face start to rise. She pushed it down, trying not to change color.

"Well, we will try our best." Melam looked at Sedah at the same time she turned to him.

"So, which of you will I be making a pact with?" Ingre asked. Confusion wrinkled her brow as she scrutinized both of them.

"If we are right, it will take us both. Her to find your nymph, and me to get the answers," Melam replied.

"Fine, we will sort out the rewards later." Ingre stood, waiting for them to stand also.

"No, she may have both rewards. I do not need either," Melam told Ingre. She nodded once in agreement, holding out her hand for a binding handshake. Hands clasped, they waited as a golden ribbon sealed their deal, creating a branding of a key on his wrist at one end of the ribbon and half of a lock on hers at its other end. Doing the same with Sedah, she branded a key on her as well, and finished the lock on herself.

"It is done. We will get you back to the surface so you can get started. I am sorry if we frightened you, but what leader would I be if I didn't seize an opportunity when presented to me?" Ingre asked rhetorically as the three of them walked back to the pool within the cave. Two nymphs came up, waiting for Sedah and Melam to enter the water.

"May your answers be as true as the tide." Ingre said in farewell before turning her back and walking away.

Getting into the water, Melam and Sedah each took a deep breath, nodding that they were ready.

◌⃰

CAPRIKA SAT HELPLESSLY WITH AMY ON THE BEACH, NOT quite knowing what to do next. She wasn't worried that Sedah was dead; she knew that they would meet Hades and the rest of the family if that happened.

The girls pointed to the water in unison, when first Sedah's, then Melam's head popped up above water. Jumping up, Amy and Caprika ran to the water, lifting their legs high, to reach their friends faster.

As soon as Amy got to Sedah and Caprika reached Melam, the girls began pulling at their friend's arms to try to get them onto dry ground quicker. Melam's light laughter and Sedah's reassurances of being okay fell on deaf ears until they all reached the shore.

Out of nowhere, Caprika slapped Melam on the chest, hard. "What the hell was all that about?"

As soon as Caprika attacked Melam, Sedah's eyes caught fire, becoming black balls with dancing flames as she stepped in front of Melam. "Hit him again," Sedah goaded threateningly. Caprika held her hands up in surrender until the flames left and Sedah's eyes were back to normal.

"To say we've had a long day is an understatement. We can fill you two in while we gather things for a fire. I need to feel heat on my skin tonight," Melam told them all.

⚜

AS THEY GATHERED WOOD, SEDAH LET MELAM TAKE THE lead of explaining everything that had happened. She wasn't sure what message Freil had gotten earlier when they were all with her aunt Hekate, but Freil had apologized to the girls for having to bail, and had asked Melam to flash her back to camp when she ran into him. Whatever had called her away, Sedah was now hoping it had nothing to do with this missing sister of the girl that had just tried to kill Sedah and been cursed by Melam. She didn't need anyone she liked to be accused of murder just because they hung out with Sedah.

"So, are you guys thinking that Tutice got so mad that she killed her own sister?" Caprika asked in disbelief as she verbally mirrored Sedah's thoughts. "To kill a fellow nymph is to be punished with death also. No offense, but I doubt she killed a blood sister just because she wasn't allowed to kill Sedah."

"Who said she would have done it on purpose?" Sedah pointed out.

"Do you think that's why Freil got called away?" Amy asked.

"She didn't act like it was an emergency, but it could have been, I guess. Who is Lutia's backup?" Caprika asked.

"You're not going to like my answer." Amy looked at

Caprika. She sighed when Caprika put her hands on her hips and waited, patting the ground with her foot. "Dustie was supposed to start training with her soon. So, someone would have to come train her early if Lutia is not available."

Everyone took a step back, out of the line of fire as Caprika kicked sand, shouting explicative after explicative for anyone to hear. Her baby sister having to take over because of the whole mess was the last straw, making Caprika blow her top. She eventually stopped, running out of bad things to yell, with her now nonexistent voice.

"We do not know anything for sure, so let's just calm down. The reason behind it would suck, but Dustie learning a job wouldn't be the worst thing. Let's just hope it doesn't come to that," Melam said, in an attempt to calm the situation. "Let's sleep here and we can go to camp and see if there have been any developments first thing in the morning."

Grabbing the collected wood, they found a spot on the sand and got a fire going just as night set in. Amy propped herself up on a rock, Caprika's head in Amy's lap, with Amy running her hands through Caprika's hair to help relax her. Both were lost in their own thoughts until Melam helped them sleep, giving them a small mental nudge. He looked over at Sedah, who was jabbing the fire with a stick.

Melam took a moment to watch the young Goddess while she was unaware. Even in anger, she was more beautiful than should be possible. He mentally sighed, thinking about how her simple beauty was just as alluring as his late wife's pristine looks had been. More so, when he added in all her other qualities, if he was being honest with himself. Melam had a feeling that if he didn't distance himself now, he would be in pain later, when he was forced to give her to Triton.

Refusing to go down the rabbit hole his mind was heading, Melam picked up a pebble and threw it, letting it hit Sedah gently in the back. He smiled when it bounced off her bottom, causing her to squeal and turn as she grabbed her butt in surprise. Turning, she saw Melam failing miserably to hide his smile. She sat down on the log beside him, nudging his shoulder with her own.

"What are you thinking about?" Melam asked. He was just beginning to realize how little he knew about her. If their combined power was enough to run water dwelling creatures out of their homes, he needed to know why. Simply being the child of a God and Goddess did not always guarantee a lot of power.

"It's silly really," Sedah stared into the flames absently, "but I was just wondering what happens to us when we die. I was trying to remember if I had ever seen a paranormal being at home or heard someone mention it. I don't think I have." She frowned. For some reason, the idea made Sedah sadder than she would have thought. The light tinge of blue to her skin told Melam that her time among the nymphs was growing shorter, which saddened him more than he would admit.

"This is something only a handful of beings know the answer to, and for good reason. They are judged and sent to where they belong, to put it simply," Melam tried to vaguely explain. He waited for her to argue, or to ask questions, but she did neither. Melam ventured a look to her, more curious about her than ever.

"What, no questions?" he asked, watching Sedah dig her toes in the sand, her hands at her sides, resting them on the log.

"I'm used to not understanding what is going on around me—having to accept that it will make sense when it needs to," she said. Her long, wavy red hair hid her face as she continued to stare at her feet, now buried in the sand. She sounded so forlorn, yet so wise in that moment, Melam wanted to grab her and make it all go away. With a sigh,

Sedah pushed herself off the log and lowered herself to the sand, using the log as a back rest. Knowing she must be tired, Melam dropped down beside her, wrapping his arm around her, urging her closer.

At that angle, Sedah was able to lay her head comfortably on his shoulder and fall asleep quickly. What she dreamt about, Melam didn't know. All he knew was that every contented sigh made his heart soar. When her fingers roamed his chest, her arm wrapping around his neck loosely, Melam had to fight to keep from responding.

Instead, he placed a lingering kiss on her head, before slowly unwrapping himself from their entangled bodies, so he could get up.

Once he was free, he turned and stared back at Sedah, who was still asleep, but against the log now. Taking a deep breath, he let it out slowly, running his hands into his hair, intertwining his fingers and letting his hands rest on top of his head. His head and heart had not argued with his libido since he lost his wife, and he was determined not to give them a reason to now. Throwing a barrier of protection and invisibility around the girls, Melam got to work on finding them all a beach house.

❀

FREIL WAS ALREADY SITTING BY THE CAMPFIRE SHE HAD stoked back to life, eating a pastry, by the time the girls woke up some time later. Groaning and stretching, they slowly joined her around the fire, sitting in their previous spots from the night before. Not one girl said a word until they were on their second sugary confection.

"Why did you have to leave yesterday?" Caprika asked, sitting back down from grabbing a drink from the lake.

"I was called to the village to be questioned, then given

instructions." Freil looked down at her hands, sadness evident on her face.

"Why would you be questioned? Freil, what's happened?" Sedah asked, already hoping that her speculations had been wrong.

A tear dropped from Freil's cheek as she spoke. "One of our meadow nymphs was murdered two days ago. She was found right outside of camp, torn up like a rabid animal had mauled her, and yet she had also drowned, both of which make no sense."

"So why would they . . . they wanted to know if Sedah did it." Caprika sat up straight, like she had been struck.

"Her hell hounds, more precisely." Freil turned to look at Sedah. "Lutia was never a fan of you being here. Probably because her sister wasn't."

"But obviously they don't believe this theory, or they would have come for her by now. What were your instructions?" Amy stood, pacing in agitation.

"To get the children back, and begin training Dustie until an older, more experienced person can instruct her. Then I will take over for Caprika on top of my duties. So, I cannot take off with all of you as we planned." Freil's tears ran freely. "I'd been looking forward to getting out of here for a little while. It seems fitting to be made to stay—like a punishment for my own selfishness." Caprika and Amy held Freil to comfort her.

"Seems Ingre was right, however wrong I was praying to the Mother that she was," Sedah said softly, staring down at the key branded on her.

When Freil looked at them all questioningly, Amy sat back down, beginning the story of what had happened, with Sedah filling in the middle, and Caprika finishing the story.

"That means you've technically found her and now you

have to tell her. Then it'll be up to Melam to find out what happened," Freil stated.

"I don't want to go back down there alone." Sedah looked at Caprika, hope in her eyes. Caprika sighed, shaking her head.

"I can't go with you. But you shouldn't have to go under water this time either. This has been asked of you and Melam to accomplish, and you must be the one to give them the news." The compassion and sorrow made Caprika's voice thicken as she spoke.

Taking a deep breath, Sedah only nodded. Giving herself a moment to steel herself, Sedah's eyes took on a far-away look as she stood and waded knee deep in the chilly morning waters.

Expecting to be pulled under again, Sedah squealed in surprise, almost falling in her haste to retreat, as the head Limnatide rose up out of the water.

Ingre looked at Sedah, then glanced quickly at each of the nymphs behind Sedah, seeing all their sullen expressions and tear tracks running down their faces. She had no need to ask the fate of the nymph.

"Do you know how?" Ingre looked at Sedah.

"No, but Melam will get you the answers you seek." Sedah tried to sound calm and determined to keep her voice from betraying her emotions.

"Are our children to be cared for by someone else then? Is it even safe for them to be kept on land?" Ingre glanced at all of them.

"I will be training the next in line until another can be sent for. They will be safe. You can bring them at first light tomorrow. We will be ready," Freil answered, taking a step forward as she did so.

"So be it." Ingre nodded at Freil before holding out her arm to Sedah. "Place your key on the lock that is on my arm."

Doing as she was told, Sedah felt the brand lift from her arm. When she moved her arm away, the key was no longer on her arm, and the lock on Ingre was unlocked, but still there. With a nod, Ingre turned, disappearing back into the lake.

୬୯୫

MELAM SAT ON A BEACH, FAR FROM THE LAKE WHERE HE'D left the girls, his feet in the sand, staring into the ocean with no clear thought on his mind. The Atlantic Ocean was a simple body of water, yet it was fast beginning to be an object of hate to Melam. As screwed up as humans were, it seemed to him that his grandmother's children were far worse. What the satyrs were doing to humans was deplorable, and the hatred that the nymphs had for Sedah, who was an innocent victim in all of this, was downright shocking. Hatred being passed down for a crime committed long ago just seemed pointless.

Feeling the sudden charge in the air, Melam made no move to look at or speak to the newcomer as they sat down on his right, mirroring his buried toes and his arms resting on his elbows. It was a comfortable passtime, making it a long while before either decided to speak.

"I feel your mixed emotions. It is strong enough to call me here. Do you wish to speak about it?" Gaia asked her grandson.

"May I speak freely?" Melam asked hesitantly. He wanted to make sure he would be addressing his grandmother, and not the Goddess Queen of the Universe. She gave a slight smile and a simple nod before he felt safe enough to continue.

"How do you allow all of this hurt to happen? If Earth is you, how does it not keep you doubled over in the pain, crying from the injustice and screaming from the horror of it all?" Melam's voice broke, as he thought about all that he had witnessed in his time on Earth so far.

The Goddess Gaia stared out to the sea with a blank expression, one that told of all she had seen. "The good that happens, even in the smallest amounts, adds up a lot faster than the bad. You just do not think so because it is not done publicly, nor televised, but rather behind walls, in third world countries and in labs. Where I see one tragedy occur, I often see one miracle happen in its place. Sometimes directly as a result, and other times indirectly, as time moves on." As if realizing how lost in thought she was, she sighed loudly, smiling as she turned to look at Melam.

"I guess, being around so long, that is probably true. I just look at what is going on and wonder how it will all be okay in the end."

"Having the knowledge of how one decision can change the outcome of something else is hard to bear. It makes you question everything you, and those around you, do, which can go either way. I'm just going to say this." Gaia grabbed her grandson's chin, turning his face so that he would look in her eyes. "Follow your heart as well as your instincts, and everything will turn out fine."

Letting go of his chin, Gaia kissed the top of Melam's head as she stood, not a speck of sand on her. "In three days, punishment will be served. Until then, *seuc les stri gui tes raleo.*" Not waiting for an answer, she disappeared into nothingness as if she were the sand the wind was brushing away.

"May the stars guide you also, grandmother." Melam sighed. Knowing there was nothing else to do at the moment, he got up and dusted the sand off his body even as he walked to the house. He would make owners think they wanted to sell to him. Something told him that he might be needing it as soon as the satyr verdict was delivered.

Introducing himself to the man who answered, Melam fed suggestions to him and his wife as they gave him a tour of the beach-front property. Melam smiled to himself. Something about this house had called to him when he had walked the beach as the sun rose that morning. Now he knew what it was. All through the home, natural elements had been used in all of their renovations.

Driftwood countertops in the kitchen with a limestone backsplash, marble tiled walls and granite counters in the bathrooms, and bamboo floors throughout, made the energy levels high, absorbing the natural energy in the air. All of this would help Sedah replenish after a long day. He could hardly wait to show her.

❧ 17 ❧

Sedah tried taking turns making herself angry, and having Amy or Caprika throw things in the air for her to stop, to practice moving objects. As the day wore on, her worry and frustration kept her progress inconsistent. She knew it was ridiculous, but she missed Melam. It was more than that though. He made her feel safe. Freil said she had convinced everyone that Sedah had not been the one to kill the nymph, but Sedah no longer felt safe. The proof of how she felt was obvious.

"Sedah, either focus or tell us what's wrong. You're so grey you're almost blending in with the rocks." Caprika stared at her in frustration.

"I'm scared, okay?" Sedah threw her arms up in the air. As she dropped them, the ground trembled slightly. Amy and Caprika glanced at one another with wide eyes before turning to look at Sedah, who was too busy staring down at her hands, to notice.

"So, with anger and frustration, you levitate things, and with fear you, what, cause earthquakes?" Caprika asked.

"I don't know." Sedah put her hands down slowly, afraid she might accidently cause another earthquake.

"Do it again," Amy dared.

Caprika took a quick step forward. "I don't think so." She looked at Amy, the promise of retribution in her eyes.

"How else are we going to know it was her or not?" Amy pouted mockingly.

"While those children are trapped under water, I guess we won't."

"Guess we won't what?" Kohl came sauntering out of the forest line, three other satyrs following behind him. Immediately, Amy and Caprika walked over to stand slightly in front of Sedah.

"What do you want, Kohl." Caprika asked.

"I just wanted to see how the training was going, then I heard she murdered a sister." Kohl made a show of covering his mouth with his hands, as if he might burst into tears, only to pull them down, his face a mask of hatred. "How horrible." He stared Sedah down.

As Sedah's color changed, Amy quickly stepped forward. "She was with us, so she didn't do it. Now, run along." She shooed at him like a child.

Kohl stepped forward in anger, only to bounce backward as he hit an invisible wall. He watched all three smiling girls for a moment before trying to advance once more.

When nothing happened, Kohl turned to his followers with a pointed look. Instantly, they all stepped forward, also placing their hands on the invisible barrier. "Find me a way in," he told them.

"It's no use boys. We may come and go, but you can't. You're not invited. You'll just have to try to kick my ass another day." Amy blew them all a kiss.

Hitting the barrier one last time with his fist, Kohl turned and left, his crew quick to follow him.

"What do you think that was about?" Amy asked, hands on her hips as she stared at the spot the boys had reentered the forest, in case they came back.

"Hopefully he was just fishing for information. My gut says something either has, or is, about to happen to his perfect world. I'm just glad Melam's barriers were up," Caprika said.

❀

It was dark by the time Melam made it back to the girls. Remaining invisible, he watched for a moment at their closeness. They had become thick-as-thieves—sisters almost. He smiled as something Amy said caused Sedah to laugh so hard she rocked backward, head towards the sky. Her beautiful hair glowed in the firelight looking like a flame all her own.

When he thought about everything she had been through, he was proud of her; she hadn't let any of it make her bitter. In his experience, all his grandmother's creatures, both human and nonhumans alike, fed off the innocence of others. This whole deal about being with Poseidon's son was crazy, but Melam wasn't sure what he could do about it.

Uncloaking himself, Melam purposefully stepped on a few branches as he walked down the beach, so that he wouldn't startle them. All three girls turned at the sound. Locating him, Sedah jumped up, running to him, full force. Stopping, Melam braced himself. Instead of simply running to him, she ran right into him, almost knocking him over as she threw her arms around his chest. Her actions momentarily stunned him. Realizing that she was also understanding what she had just done, Melam quickly wrapped his arms around her back, looking down at her upturned face.

"Well now, can't say I minded that kind of hello," He smiled.

"I'm so sorry! I don't know what came over me." She tried to pull herself away from him, only for him to stop her by keeping hold of her.

"Any time," he said, letting her go, turning them back towards the group. "What did I miss?" he asked as he sat down.

"Nothing much, Sedah just caused an earthquake, kept her end of the deal with the Limnatides, and Kohl came by, but was unable to do anything thanks to your barriers. You know, the typical since she arrived." Amy spoke quickly.

"So you found out what happened to the missing nymph and let Ingre know? That was quick. What happened?" Melam asked, directing the last question to Caprika, who filled him in on the body and about what would happen next. Melam remained quiet, secretly taking the mental picture from Caprika's mind, adding it up for himself. The nymph's death had been a warning.

"What were you saying about Kohl coming by? What did he want?"

"To be his usual thistle self and irritate us. He said he wanted to see the murderer, so I guess not everyone believed Freil that Sedah is innocent like I had hoped." Caprika sighed in frustration.

"That just means we need to start training in combat on top of Sedah's practice to blend in with humans. We can leave here before the next changeover ceremony." Melam informed them.

"Then let's get started." Amy smiled, rubbing her hands together in anticipated excitement.

৩৩৩

WHEN MELAM WAS THERE, HE TRAINED THEM IN BASIC combat. When he was not, the girls taught Sedah basic people skills and etiquette.

The more she learned, the less scared she felt about the environment around her. She felt like she could decently hold her own, should someone try to hurt her, like at the party.

That seemed like so long ago, since she had first met Melam. The lessons to appear more human felt ridiculous and unnecessary, as she would be mingling with Mers, not humans. If she were being honest, she didn't even want to go. To be some fish princess's servant was just an insult to her. Why a child of Hades was less important than a child of Poseidon was something Sedah was having a hard time swallowing. The fact that the Lord of the Underworld had agreed to it was the hardest part.

The girls were gathering wood for their nightly fire when they noticed Melam. They had not seen him come into camp, and yet he was already standing chest deep in the water, talking to Ingre. When their arms met in order to break their seal, Sedah could not stop the jealousy that came over her. In less than two seconds, Sedah was mad enough to cause a moving sand geyser, headed straight to Ingre. Staring at Sedah in shock and fear, Ingre quickly took back her seal and dove into the safety of the water. Melam put his hands on his hips as he turned to glare at Sedah. Although barely red in skin tone, her corneas had gone entirely black, with blazing flames where her pupils should be. Her body was stiff as a pole, her horns barely peeking through her hair, and her hands balled into fists at her sides. It wasn't until Melam's feet were fully out of the lake, that Sedah visibly relaxed.

Sedah allowed herself to fall to the sand as she realized what she had just done. If the barrier had not been at the water . . . Sedah paled at the thought of what she could have done to the lake nymph, though in Sedah's mind, the limnatide would have deserved it.

She wasn't surprised when Amy and Caprika didn't come to comfort her; she was a monster. Head down, she saw his bare feet approach first as Melam squatted down to talk to her. She fully expected a tongue lashing.

"May I ask what that was?" Melam asked softly. He waited a few moments but received no answer.

"Do you realize what you could have done had I not felt the power increase just in time?" This time she nodded, a tear rolling down her cheek, sizzling as it hit the sand. Melam tilted Sedah's chin up to look at him. He was met with actual flaming eyes. Eyes he had seen once before from her. Caution was fast becoming the key to this situation.

"It's okay. I'm here with you. No one is going to harm me." He held out his hand to her. Slowly, she took it. Standing with him, silently he led her away from the girls and the edge of the beach, guiding her into the tree line.

As soon as they were clear of anyone's view, Sedah pushed Melam against the nearest tree, her strength unlike anything she had ever shown. Immediately she was on him, kissing his bare chest as far as she could reach, even as he tried to push her off with a groan. His rejection only seemed to fuel her attempts. Finally getting ahold of her wrists, he quickly spun them so that she replaced him against the tree.

Melam ignored her attempts to kiss him as he looked closely into her eyes. Using his senses, he tried to find the essence of the Sedah he knew, finding only hatred and jealousy instead. The emotions were so intense, they hid the goodness that had just been there with him on the beach.

Melam closed his eyes, focusing inward. The only way to bring her back from madness was to overpower her feelings with stronger ones. Bringing his chosen feelings to the surface, Melam let them flow from him, to envelope her upper body. For a moment, he wasn't sure it would work. Slowly, he could feel her body become less tense, her arms becoming limp in his.

He watched her eyes, the flames diminishing with every intake of his chosen emotion: familial love. She felt his sense of loyalty to his people, his love for his mother, daughter, and siblings, as well as his honor to be a good ruler, if or when the time came. With the emotions came glimpses of memories that he allowed Sedah to view, to bring her back into the light. He finally let her arms go when the last of the fire and blackness disappeared from her eyes.

"Hell's bells, what just happened?" Sedah blinked rapidly, putting her head to his chest in exhaustion. She felt like she had just run a marathon.

"You became the very thing that makes people refuse to speak your father's name. You became the darkness, completely and fully. I don't know many who could have gotten you out of that and lived. You let jealousy take you over when there was nothing to be jealous of."

Sedah leaned back against the tree, covering her face with her hands. "I was going to hurt Ingre. I'm not even sure what happened. I just saw her hand touch yours, and I was gone. I knew she was just releasing you from the bond, but I went crazy!" She wiped her hands down her face, staring at the ground in shame. "I even tried to attack you. Why am I trying to hurt my friends?"

Melam took a step forward, unable to take her sadness, he leaned in, wrapping his arms around her. Surprised, Sedah stood still, allowing him to hold her, surrounding her with his presence. Too soon, he pulled back, their lips only inches apart as he stared into her eyes.

"Did that feel like I felt attacked?" Melam's lips turned up in a smile, drawing her gaze to them. He laughed, pulling her away from the tree, heading back to the beach. "I am trying to do the right thing here, Red. Help me out a little and try to behave."

"Where's the fun in that?" Sedah answered with a smile.

Melam laughed, his heart light for the first time in a very long time, as he grabbed her hand and they cleared the forest, rejoining their friends.

⚜

"WHY DO WE EVEN HAVE TO GO IF WE ARE BANNED FROM camp? They all think I am a murderer. Who's to say they won't stone me when we get there so I go back home?" Sedah asked as the girls and Melam headed towards the sacred spot that always held the changing of the Goddesses.

About an hour before, everyone in their small camp had felt a sudden pull towards the ceremonial grounds, including Sedah and Melam. Since it wasn't time for the next change over ceremony, it was unusual, but not unheard of for a group of nymphs to be called to the altar to receive advice or information from Mother Earth that they would not know about otherwise.

"Because not only would it be disrespectful to the Mother, but because the deal would then be null, and Leuce would never get to come home," Caprika explained.

"Which reason do you think they care about more?" Amy winked at them.

Caprika had timed it so that their little group would enter just as the ceremony was about to start. They had no idea how many nymphs had been called, but as they entered the area, it became apparent that everyone had. As the song ended, Jade and Lilac stood before the statue of Mother Earth. As it had for millennia, the statue seemed to buzz with energy, coming awake as the last rays of the day touched the stone. Both women gasped as their essence left them and entered the statue, which would either allow the Mother to materialize herself, or for the essence to re-enter the women with the added information from her.

Everyone sat in silence, waiting for the energy to re-enter into Lilac and Jade. When nothing happened, a murmur began within the crowd as fear began to surface. At least half of the tribe turned to glance at Sedah, whispering to one another. Just as someone stood, gasps and cries of shock filled those who were still watching the platform.

৩৬৯

As if the statue were never there, a flash of light replaced it with a woman so ethereal, she could be none other than the Mother, Gaia. With waist length glossy black hair, her glacier blue eyes held love and sorrow as she looked out over the crowd. As the light dimmed, a halo of light seemed to surround her body. She looked to be in her mid-twenties with flawless honey colored, sun kissed skin. Both Lilac and Jade took a step back, only to be halted when Gaia raised her index finger.

"There is not an animal, person, or supernatural that does not matter to me more than every speck of earth on this planet does. I have been shown atrocities that I can no longer ignore. It saddens me that the very people I have put in charge knew about these things, and did not come to me. It should not have taken a myk'tu to bring this to my attention. Those responsible will now be punished. Daughter Lilac, who will be your replacement?" Gaia asked.

"I have asked Char to act as my head nymph, Mother." Lilac's voice trembled. While a replacement nymph was immediately chosen the day after the new nymph came into power at the woman's camp, that had always been a formality, as there should be a true daughter coming next, and it was not her time yet.

Gaia nodded once, "While I am not opposed to this choice, I have another. Freil, would you step forward please?"

Heads turned as Freil stood and came up the platform. She stared at Gaia's hand as she held it out for Char to place her hand in. "As is my authority as Primordial Mother, I give you a small piece of my power, so that you may call if you have need of me."

Light came from within Gaia, floating from her to Freil as smoothly as rolling a ball. With a bow, Freil stepped back, into the crowd.

"Lilac, you are innocent, and may step forward to assume your new mantle." Gaia said. Conscience clear, Lilac stepped forward, receiving the same statement and amount of power as Freil had.

"Jade, step forward." She waited until the nymph was standing in front of her. "I will give you one chance, which is more than you deserve, to place the responsible party up here to receive the sentence with you," Gaia said.

"No one was ever seriously hurt—" Jade began, only to be silenced as a blast of energy physically hit her, throwing her back onto her butt. Her eyes were wide as she slowly got back up. Her cool demeanor was finally shaken, as the blast allowed her to feel the true anger from The Mother, Gaia.

"As your compassion and reasoning is cold and murky, so now will you be. No longer shall you hold the title of cherished nymph. Instead, you shall spend the rest of your life as a fish of my choosing, in the body of water that I choose, so that your body will be as cold as your heart."

Jade turned ashen. There was no talking the Mother Goddess out of her decision. She had passed judgement, and the sentence would be carried out swiftly. Jade bowed her head, stepping backward, off the platform, and into the crowd of stunned nymphs.

"I know you think my judgement harsh, but you are getting off light." She looked at Jade's crying form solemnly. "For those you protected, it will be worse. Kohl, and your six cohorts. Come on up and join me." When no one moved, Gaia began to raise her hands. Palms up and open, she allowed energy to release, sending it towards where the satyrs stood.

Fearing what the mist would do, people began forcefully pushing Kohl and his friends, out of the crowd, toward their fate. Smiling, with a slight nod of thanks, Gaia let the energy surround the group instead of going into the crowd. While the other satyrs looked like they were ready to pass out, Kohl, and one other, crossed their arms, defiantly waiting.

"I am horrified that this has been going on for so long without being brought to my attention. Now I am forced to hand out judgements for more than just a couple infractions against our laws. Tan, Nor, Owen, and Saun, step forward." She waited, as heads down, they stepped in front of her to receive the punishment they knew they deserved.

"The four of you were led into this, slowly becoming someone who you no longer knew. The four of you will be made human by the rising of the sun. I will place you all in different towns, where you will learn to be your own person, to either learn and prosper, or perish. This way, it will be humans deciding your fate, instead of you deciding theirs." She pulled the energy surrounding the four men back into herself. The men shivered, as they all felt a tingle within their bodies. Magic waited patiently for dawn to spark the change in them.

Not even the forest animals made a sound as the four satyrs stepped down. Surprising everyone, Kohl and Danny stepped up, onto the platform as soon as the others were off. Some gasped, while others whispered at the boldness these two were showing, for surely it would not help their case.

"So eager to accept your consequences, I see." Gaia said sadly.

"No use prolonging it, though I might ask what crime we are all being punished for, if the Mother would be kind enough to explain." Kohl said, shrugging his shoulders. He had done countless things that crossed the line with these guys, and even a few without them. If he was going to go down, he damn sure wanted to know who to take down with him for opening their trap. He'd find a way to make them pay.

"The sadness of a most beloved myk'tu brought me to see what was happening. Since then, both camps have been watched, helping to decide your fate. I had hoped to be wrong, that I could spare you all the worst of punishments. Your actions with the humans were beyond redemption. The death of a sister sealed your fate." Her face turned to a mask of stone as she spoke.

Danny's hands dropped as he turned to look at Kohl. Lutia, the murdered nymph, had been his sister. Without warning, Danny punched Kohl with all his force, on the side of Kohl's face. Blood escaped Kohl's ear as he bent from the force of the impact for a moment.

Standing back up, Kohl said nothing, crossing his arms and staring at the goddess as if nothing had just happened. Trying to rein in control, Danny also turned back.

"You at least show feeling for family, if not for strangers. I am letting you be reborn with your sister, as different paranormals. By losing one close to you, your punishment has already been served. You will be brother and sister again." Gaia reached out and lightly touched Danny's head. His body began to glow, becoming transparent, until there was nothing but golden energy left. Holding her hand out, the energy floated, meandering its way into her palm, until it formed a small ball, which she then tucked into the pocket of her shimmering gown.

"And then there was one. The one who is worse than any that I have seen in these modern times. It would be fair if I made you experience all the things you have done to those you tortured. To relive all of their pain. But I am not that cruel. It's a good thing that I know someone who is. I am going to let Sedah see her mother, who will then escort you straight to my son, Tartarus. Maybe the River of Flame will prepare you for them." She ignored the gasps and cries of disbelief. "You will go down in our history though, which should please you. The only paranormal in history to commit such heinous crimes, that The Mother no longer cared about them." Her eyes held Kohl's, watching his reaction.

On the outside, he did not move an inch. Inside, he was clawing at his face, screaming that he would change if she would give him just one more chance. Not letting any of that show, proved that Melam had been right about exactly how dangerous this satyr was.

Taking a step back, The Mother looked over the condemned. "I will be back at dawn. I suggest you say your goodbyes." Slowly, the form she had been using, turned back to stone, starting at the feet, and making its way up, until it was the same stone it had always been.

❧ 18 ❧

Sedah watched as a full five seconds passed before anyone moved. Jade broke out in a flood of tears, falling to her knees. All the nymphs came rushing to her, all speaking at once, trying to get to her, tell her goodbye, comfort her, and more.

The men mingled with the women, trying to figure out what in the name of the goddess had just happened.

Caprika and Amy never moved from their position at the back of the group with Sedah. "I don't know why that just happened, but it couldn't have been done to a nicer group. Justice is always a bitter dish to eat when one's caught. But I'm glad Danny gets to be with his sister. The two of them were always close," Caprika said softly, eyes shining with tears. She gave them a weak smile.

Sedah however, was in a cross between confusion and happiness. While the thought of seeing her mom for a moment made her happy, it had not escaped her notice how the Primordial Goddess had made the one satyr disappear. He had disappeared, slowly, as his energy was taken. His body had become transparent, just as Hannah's had when Sedah took from her. Sedah held out her hand, staring at it as she turned it over, opening and closing her fingers as she tried to figure it out. She knew her mother was the daughter of a major goddess, but how in the world did she take her energy in the same manner as the Primordial Mother? She was so engrossed in her own thoughts she gasped when a hand grabbed hers.

"You scared me." Sedah looked up to see Amy. "What is it?" Sedah asked, not liking the hard look on Amy's face. Catching on to Amy's darting eyes, Sedah looked around her.

Caprika stood behind Sedah, facing the nymphs on their right, while Melam stood slightly to the left, a shield against the men. Everyone stared at Sedah, hatred evident and injury imminent.

Amy tugged lightly on Sedah's arm. Slowly, Sedah took a step, sure that any fast movement would set them off, like a pack of wild dogs. Caprika and Melam matched Amy and Sedah step for step as they retreated from the holy grounds. Once they could see no one, Sedah squealed in surprise as Melam grabbed her from behind, tossing her like a sack of potatoes over his shoulder, choosing to travel with the nymphs at a much faster pace, in case the others had decided to come after them. He didn't put her down until they reached the beach.

"Will someone tell me what is going on here? What just happened back there?" Sedah yelled, putting one hand on her hip, and gesturing toward the woods with the other.

"They were all about to kill you, that's what," Caprika said, standing up from where she had been bent over, hands on her knees, catching her breath.

"Yeah, somehow, they think you outed Jade and the men to The Mother, since all this started when you arrived," Amy said from her spot, laying down in the sand, also panting.

The girls turned, looking at Melam as he cursed. "A few

are stupid enough to try to follow us. We need to get out of here, now." Melam was pissed at his grandmother for the way she had handled that. She'd had no reason to say that a myk'tu had tipped her off. While he was as much of an outsider as Sedah was, the woodland creatures only seemed to associate the word with her, leaving him alone.

"Did you ever get us a place to go?" Caprika asked. He nodded. "How do we get there?"

"I can only transport two at a time, so I will have to come back for one of you." Melam said, hating more than ever that the earth and his mortal body limited his powers.

Caprika pulled Amy up, pushing her toward where Melam and Sedah stood. With a quick nod, Melam pulled both girls to him, wrapping his arms around their waists. One second, he was pulling them to him, and the next, he was gradually releasing them, letting their vision and minds catch up before he let go.

Just as Melam took a step back, a bright flash of light revealed Caprika, on her knees, holding her neck while coughing violently. Melam and the girls raced down the beach to her, Amy patting her on the back, while Sedah asked Caprika what had happened. Slowly, as to let her see his intentions, Melam put his hands in place of where hers had been, as she dropped them to allow him access. Melam gave a sad smile, glad that she trusted him, but sorry about the situation. His hands warmed, glowing subtly as he healed her swollen throat. He could sense the intent and those responsible for trying to kill Caprika. Melam sighed as he released her neck, feeling like a failure.

"You will be fine now. I guess they were closer than I thought." Melam told her.

"It's not your fault. What I am assuming was The Mother, teleported me here, and told me to tell you she would 'fix it.'"

Caprika used air quotes. "I assume you know what she means."

"Yeah, I do."

"Where are we? I see we are by the ocean," Sedah shivered visibly, "but where exactly?"

"We are, from the looks of that lighthouse, not far from Tybee Island, in South Carolina." Caprika answered.

"Very good. We are on Wilmington Island, actually. The house is this one right here." Melam pointed at their new home as he realized that his grandmother must have heard his questioning her word choice that put them in their current situation. The girls looked towards the pale green, two story house on stilts, with balconies on every level, including the one room attic at the top.

Sedah's hands flew to her mouth. She had no idea what she had expected, but what she saw before her was breathtaking. The homes she had glanced at on their way to the lake had seemed so cold. With their brick exterior and dreary colors, Sedah had not had high expectations. While the beach house was simple and modern, it gave off the same relaxing feeling that Sedah got when she sat in her mother's garden. She looked toward Melam, realizing he was staring at her, a certain indiscernible look in his eyes.

"What?" she asked through her fingers.

"Is it okay?" he asked her.

"It's beautiful." She smiled, seeing relief in his eyes. He was afraid she wouldn't like it? Sedah was just about to ask him about it when Amy grabbed her hand, half dragging Sedah as she ran toward the house, yelling to Sedah to hurry up.

"Why didn't anyone see our spectacular arrival? This beach is always crowded in the summer," Caprika asked Melam. She fell in beside him as they walked more sedately to the house.

"Why ask when you think you already know the answer?" Melam countered with a sly grin.

"Because I know you are something more than what you want us to believe. The Mother wasn't talking about Sedah, was she?" Caprika raised one eyebrow, daring him to lie to her.

"How are you so knowledgeable, while others of your kind are content to never leave the forest?" Melam answered her question by ignoring it and asking one of his own.

"One of my siblings, Dionyskle, is a minor god. I have gone off with him a few times, getting away from the drama." Caprika smiled, thinking of her older brother, whom she affectionately called Dio for short.

Melam gave her the key, letting her ascend the stairs before him. Sedah stood patiently by the door while Amy had already bound and scampered to the attic balcony like the house was nothing more than another tree, testing the doors and trying to peek through the blinds. Melam watched Sedah's face as Caprika opened the door and the two entered. When she entered the front door, the open floor plan allowed the living room, which sat to the right, to flow smoothly into the kitchen without hindering the natural path from door to stairs.

Apart from her eyes growing wider, for once Melam could not tell if she liked it or not. He almost groaned in frustration. Usually, she was an open book to him, but at that moment, he could not even feel her emotions. Glancing toward Caprika, he could feel her appreciation of the place, and Amy's excitement of getting out of the forest was almost overpowering as she hit the threshold.

While Caprika had already reached the stairs, Sedah was still fixated on the main floor.

As soon as she had stepped into the house, a small hum of energy seemed to settle around her. Almost reverently, Sedah internally reached for it, not quite sure if it was a noise, or a feeling. Letting everything and everyone around her disappear to the background, Sedah focused. When she opened the front door, the open floor plan allowed the living room, which sat to the right, flowing smoothly into the kitchen without hindering the natural path from door to stairs. The buzz led her to the left, into the kitchen.

Letting her left hand trail beside her, Sedah looked around slowly, taking in the white cabinets and the counter, made out of driftwood that had been sliced and fit together like a jigsaw. Sedah ran her hands over the surface. While there was a small amount of power within the wood, it was not what she was looking for. Sighing in frustration, knowing it was somewhere, Sedah almost missed it.

Between the counter and the stairs, was a frosted pantry door. Sedah gasped, jumping back until her butt hit the island, stopping her retreat. Instantly, Melam was there, pulling her to him, his hands going around her shoulders.

"What's wrong? Are you hurt?" He began trying to look her over, even as she swatted his arm away, finally pointing to the pantry. "It's a pantry door *varela*, what-"

"It's a gateway home!" She interrupted. She didn't have to look at him to know he was questioning her sanity. The energy in the room changed. Feeling it, Caprika and Amy came running down the stairs, looking like Amazonian warriors, searching for the enemy. Sedah turned, half facing them.

"What do you mean, it's a gateway, Sedah?" Melam asked slowly, cautiously.

"I felt a steady energy when I entered the house. It was . . . familiar, yet not." She traced the outline of the door, where the molding was. "I don't know if you guys can see it, but above the door is carved writing, which in English, says Damos. If I say it in the ancient language, it will become a doorway for anyone to walk through and come out somewhere in the Underworld, either in or near my house."

"I don't see anything," Amy said.

"I don't feel the power you say you do, either," Caprika agreed.

"I see it, but I couldn't feel the power, nor could I feel your emotions of the energy itself, until I touched you just now." He let her go, stepping back. "It is dormant, but it hinders my abilities to feel your presence, like it is neutralizing your energy."

"Is that a bad thing?" Sedah smiled, a hint of mischief in her eyes.

"I don't know yet." Melam smirked. He was beginning to wonder if he had had "help" finding the house.

"How would someone know to put that word there?" Amy asked, cocking her head to the side.

"The word, alone, will only let you enter. The wood that makes up the door frame comes from my home, and allows you to leave. The two together create a portal that stays open once someone enters, until they either exit, or they die.

"Then we will make sure no one says the word," Melam said matter-of-factly. "Other than this, what do you think? You didn't even get to finish exploring."

Sedah glanced around, noting the limestone backsplash in the kitchen, and the cedar mantle in the living room. "It is beautiful. All the natural elements will help me keep my power up easier. It's perfect."

Growing quiet, the girls explored the rest of the house. Amy discovered that the beach level held a storage area and a mud room, complete with a shower to wash away the sand that was tracked in. They had already discovered that the first livable area contained only the kitchen, with its own personal door to Hell, and living room.

Running up the stairs and stopping at the top step, Sedah

looked to the left, where there was one light yellow bedroom facing the front of the house, the open doors carrying the breeze through to the pale blue bedroom on the right, which faced the beach, complete with its own double doors and balcony.

Amy was already leaning against the balcony in the blue bedroom, taking in the beach, while Caprika had already claimed the front bedroom that had a clear view of the entrance. Walking the distance to the next flight of stairs, Sedah gasped, quickly covering her mouth to keep from squealing in delight as she hit the landing. Twinkle lights were interwoven within a sheer material, placed on a midnight blue ceiling, to perfectly represent the night sky. A blood red duvet, with a black panel in the middle, lay on a bed frame that was ornate and intricate with scrolling metalwork. Sedah found tears streaming down her cheeks.

Three cathedral style peaks made up the high headboard and both the headboard and footboard were connected by tall posts. Arched ironwork crisscrossed, to connect the two together. Black sheer fabric, wound with lights, covered the overhead iron, flowing down the four posts to the floor. It was the most beautiful blend of her Underworld home, and her temporary forest home, that she had ever seen. She said nothing as Melam came up silently behind her. She had no idea how she knew it would be him, but she was happy when he stayed silent.

No one outside of her family had ever done anything for her without having something to gain for themselves. There had never been a shortage of tutors, trying to get her to choose them, thinking that, if or when they were done with their teaching, they would receive a gift, usually a second chance at life, more time of solidity, or any other thing they thought her father might bestow on them for thanks. Judging by the rest of the house, even Sedah knew that there was no way something this beautiful was here before they arrived. Somehow, this held no notes of selfishness. There was nothing he had to gain by doing this. She bit her lip as he placed his hands on her forearms.

"Do you like it?" Melam asked softly. His voice tickled her ear, sending goosebumps down her arms. Her body felt weird, like it was being warmed from within by him, despite his body not being near hers.

"I said the house was perfect, but I was wrong. The house is no comparison to this room. How did you come up with this? It's unimaginable that something could be balanced so perfectly. It sums me up so completely, I don't even know how to describe it," Sedah replied, more to herself than to him.

"I thought of you, and it just came to mind." Melam smiled. He was glad that she liked it so much. He knew how it felt to miss home, so he wanted to make things a little easier for her. He felt the storm coming, and she deserved to have a place she felt safe.

"Well, I don't know what I did to deserve it, but thank you." She took a half step forward in order to turn around and look at him, only for him to use his hold on her arms, to pull her body backward, inches from his. In that moment, she thought that she could feel his every emotion, all of them warring for supremacy. Sure it was just her imagination, she tried to step backward.

"Don't. Don't move," he whispered. His forehead lay on her shoulder, his voice gravelly and light, like he had just run a marathon. Sedah stood there trying to figure him out. One thing she did know was that when he had pulled her back to him, she had felt him more than when he had first pulled him to her. Something she had done had aroused him.

"Did I do something wrong?" she asked. Her breathing became quick at the thought of him and her imagination ran wild. She was a little surprised at herself at the images, unaware before that moment that she even could conceive of some of them.

"No, but if you keep moving towards that bed, then *I* might." Melam admitted. He sighed as Sedah gasped at his honesty. Knowing she was meant for another was all that kept Melam in check. He would not ruin her chance at happiness. Using his right hand to brush her hair off the left side of her neck, he allowed his incisors to lengthen. As slowly as he could manage, he ran them down her neck to the base before leaving a long kiss. One second, she could feel his breath on her neck, and the next she felt the movement of air his quick absence created. Sedah hugged herself as she looked around in confusion. Ignoring the view, Sedah threw herself down on the bed, trying to replay everything that had just happened.

❧ 19 ❧

Sedah was glad her room faced the setting sun instead of its evil brother, the rising one. It allowed her to wake in a nice glow, instead of harsh rays streaming in her room every morning. They had been there two months, and had been able to set up a nice balance of training, to keep developing her powers, and sightseeing, which was as much about developing her human skills as her other training was.

True to what her mother had said, she needed Melam's help to hide her color change less and less. While that should have excited her, she knew what it meant. She had a feeling Caprika did too, by the way she had begun to watch Sedah when she didn't think Sedah was looking.

"We are going to have to let Triton know soon that your colors are fading so that we can figure out when you are going to go down there for your first visit," Caprika told her over breakfast one morning.

Sedah set her fork down noisily. "As soon as you do that, Poseidon will have me fetched like a dog! Caprika, I'm not above begging here! I'm terrified of the water now. I can't go live in it and be a servant to them! I can't!" Her eyes became wider, glassy with unshed tears as she spoke.

Instead of speaking, Melam watched Sedah pick up her fork and try to eat again, only to push away her plate and head to her room. After everyone was done eating and getting dressed, they hailed a cab and headed for town. No one spoke, and it was driving Melam crazy. He had bit his tongue to keep from telling them all that he would never allow her to be harmed, but that would mean confirming Caprika's suspicions that he actually did have some pull with Mother Earth, the Primordial Goddess herself.

"Do you know how Poseidon will know that you are ready, exactly?" Amy asked after paying the taxi driver through the window. Sedah looked around, taking in the energy of the humans around her. She wasn't sure if she was surprised or not, to see paranormals walking around among the humans.

"I don't know exactly. Father only said that he would be notified. I'm sure Poseidon has spies everywhere, even on land." Sedah sighed in defeat.

"Well, we'll just have to deal with it when it comes." Amy grabbed onto Sedah's shoulders from behind, using her as a springboard to propel herself into the air. She laughed, roaming around among the mix of old colonial buildings and massive newer ones, pointing things out to Sedah that might be interesting.

Caprika tried to push them into some sort of direction by handing her a credit card that she had been given when Sedah had first arrived at the nymphs' camp. Jade had explained that it had been sent to her by Sedah's father in case they needed human money while she was there, not letting on about Sedah's budding powers. As they went perusing through town, Melam hung back and had fun just watching their antics. He made sure, though, to blur his image to anyone that looked their way, in case anyone tried to tamper with any bystanders' minds later.

❦

"I can't believe your dad put that much money on the credit card we were told to give you! Didn't he know it would make you rich in human eyes now?" Amy asked at dinner, smiling.

"Money means nothing to us. He probably didn't even look to see how much anything in the human world costs." Sedah said sarcastically.

"He gave you five million U.S. dollars, to make sure you were taken care of," Melam said as he cut into the porkchop he had grilled for them. "Sounds like what any good father would do."

Caprika dropped her plastic silverware. "Five million?" She choked out as everyone turned to stare at her. "I know you guys don't understand, but that's more money than human millionaires give colleges to overlook any small infractions their kids make."

No one wanted to talk about the elephant in the room, meaning that after dinner, video games took over instead of conversation. Caprika kept Sedah occupied until well after dark, until Sedah admitted defeat and headed to bed.

Melam watched her ascend the stairs, uncertain what to do with himself. He had done what his mother and grandmother had asked of him, so why was he still here? Staying here was not helping his sister find their brother, yet his grandmother's *sanm*, or message, did not specify who or when he was to help, just to stay with the satyrs. But was Kohl his original mission, or was he only staying with the satyrs until another mission was supposed to happen? Until he was told otherwise, he was going to stay there and enjoy the company and the view.

Not needing sleep, Melam decided to go down to the beach so he wouldn't disturb anyone. Imagining what his workout course at home would look like on earth, Melam smiled to himself as, piece by piece, sand came from all around him, spinning together, to create the necessary obstacles. Jogging down the beach, he took one quick pass to assess the course and get his heart rate up before tackling the course with gusto. He was in the middle of doing his drill for the seventeenth time when a tingle of awareness came over him. It didn't feel threatening, so Melam finished the course before focusing in on the source. Sensing the energy's signature, Melam's brows rose in surprise. He had expected Sedah, but he had gotten Persephone instead.

Not in the mood to pretend, Melam simply flashed himself to Sedah's balcony, leaning against the railing, arms crossed, like he wasn't wanting to ask her a million questions. He had to give it to her, if he had surprised her at all, she barely showed it. Instead, he watched her eyes widen slightly as she felt his enormous power, before looking back at her daughter's sleeping form from her place at the balcony door.

"She looks like she has no care in the world, yet she has the weight of it on her young shoulders, and she doesn't even know it." She sighed. "When we became pregnant with a son after my mother decreed that we would only ever have girls, the fates said that there would be consequences for deceiving her. This is not what I expected. I expected the consequences to fall on Pluton or myself, not one of the children."

"Why is Sedah here? Be honest," Melam said. It was Persephone's husband who had made the deal. A good mother, as Melam had no doubt Persephone was, did not let that happen without at least knowing the details.

"Don't get me wrong, I hate her being here, but I have no choice. She has always wanted to see earth, so at least she gets that out of all this." She smiled sadly. "She was forever bugging the professors that had only recently come to us with question after question. It is part of why she was taught only by the original inventors and history makers."

"Then what changed?" Melam stood, coming to the other side of the doorway. He told himself it was to better gauge Persephone, not because he had to see Sedah's form and know that she was safe.

"Sedah's middle brother, Lexur, snuck out with Hermes and got caught by Poseidon. He came to some sort of agreement with my husband, in exchange for not telling my parents. The fates said—" Persephone's voice broke, tears trying to overflow the dam.

"Let me tell you something about the fates. Their prophecies were once seen as good things, believe it or not." He smiled at the look of disbelief Persephone shot him. "The Primordial Mother used the three women to send *sanms,* or messages, to all of her children. Then, as her children began to misbehave, her anger at her children turned the *sanms* vague, and the Mother's sheer power began to shred the three women's minds. The Titans were misbehaving at the time, and the *sanms* that humans and immortals received were so vague that they were perceived as unreliable also. The fates will never admit it, but they do not hold control over your life. That is all on you," Melam told Persephone with sincerity as they held eye contact. He had no idea why he had come so close to oversharing. He only knew that he wanted to comfort her. She was looking at Sedah so sadly he felt that he had needed to give her something to lighten her heavy heart.

"I just don't want to lose her," Persephone whispered.

"She's just a baby." A single tear escaped, rolling quickly down her cheek.

Melam knew that nothing he could say would make Persephone feel better, so he remained silent while she lost herself in her thoughts.

"Why are you helping the girls? It is obvious that you do not belong here," Persephone asked, turning to rest her back on the door jamb so she was facing him.

Melam was silent for a long moment, as he thought about how he should answer her. He thought about all the lies that he could tell her, but just as quickly decided against them. She had given him the truth. He would do the honorable thing and do the same.

"I don't know. I was sent here to complete a mission, without being told what the mission was. I thought that I had completed it; the more I think about it, the more I believe that either your daughter, or this deal, is the real mission. Though, I have no idea what role I am to play in this cruel game," he said, his brows furrowing together with derision, as he looked heavenward.

"I swear, you look almost like my grandmother when you do that," Persephone said. "Well, whatever the reason, thank you for being there, and now here, to protect them. There is great power in you, so although I am more than mildly curious, I choose to believe that you being here is a good thing." Pushing off the frame, Persephone went to her daughter's bed, leaning over to brush her daughter's hair out of the way so she could kiss Sedah's cheek.

"I used to tell her that she had hair so red because of the fire my mother ignited within me when she said that if I were to have another demon-spawned child, The Underworld would be relaxing compared to the bite from the ice that she would unleash. Of course, she had no idea that I was pregnant with Milos at the time. So, every child from then on has stayed a secret, no matter what I had to do to make it so." She sat on the bed, still combing Sedah's hair as she looked at him.

"Don't worry. I have more secrets than you ever could. Believe me when I say that your secret is safe with me."

"Good." Persephone stood, walking to the balcony again. She stared out at the slowly growing storm over the ocean for a moment before looking over her shoulder at Melam. "Take care of my baby. According to my husband, Triton will most likely come for her this week sometime. And if he is anything like his father, I would not put it past him to be as devious as my husband and his siblings. Protect her?"

"Again, you have my word, *meve,*" he said. Her audible gasp told him immediately that he had screwed up. He saw recognition when he used the old language, calling her a child out of habit. She caught and held his gaze, tilting her head as she searched for something within his eyes. Melam tried to keep from squirming like he was the meve, caught red handed for doing something he shouldn't have.

Apparently satisfied, Persephone bowed her head regally, even as she let the wind sweep her away, allowing it to carry her away like she had been made of sand, just like the major gods, and like his own people. Melam smiled at her strength even as he let out the deep breath he hadn't been aware he was holding.

SEDAH SWUNG HER BLADE IN THE AIR, LOVING THE FEEL OF it as she swung it at her best friend's shoulder, forcing Caprika to duck, then just as quickly, jump backwards as Sedah followed up on the swing with a thrust to her midsection. When Amy had suggested archery and sword training that morning to change up the training, no one had understood the smile that had come across Sedah's face. Five minutes into practice, they no longer needed to guess.

"Switch!" Caprika yelled as Sedah thrust once more, causing Caprika to fall over a limb sticking up from the sand. Amy, though more skilled with a bow and arrow, rushed in to take over.

Caprika walked towards Melam, even as he left his spot on top of the sand dune where he had been watching them.

"*She is kicking your butt,*" he told her telepathically, eyebrows raised. He would never give away Persephone's secrets, just in case she had kept it from Sedah as well. There was only one sure way to know, and judging by those clouds, he didn't have much time left.

"Bet she's had formal training," Melam said, more to himself, as he grabbed Caprika's blade and started forward.

Sedah seemed to be teasing Amy, more than actually sparring with her; laughing when a bluff would make Amy jump. Although the blades were the real thing, summoned from Melam's own collection from home, he had used power to place a protective *lavh*, or barrier, on them so that no one would be injured. When Amy saw Melam coming towards them, sword in hand, she took the opportunity to dramatically run away screaming towards Caprika. By the time she made it into the nymphs waiting arms, all of them were in full laughter.

Trying to settle themselves down, Melam and Sedah bowed, before readying their stances. Digging her bare feet into the sand, Sedah rushed forward in an attempt to gauge Melam's style. She tried a few different moves, all aimed at reading him.

"Warm up is done. Don't hold back now, *varela*." Melam smiled. They fought as gracefully as if they were dancing. Melam barely moved, no matter which maneuver she used. He even succeeded in enraging her when a few attempts on her part landed her a kick to the backside, or a headlock where he would kiss her cheek before letting her go just as quickly. It was one such headlock, where he asked who had trained her.

"Would you believe me if I said William Marshal?" she asked, jumping out of the way of his blade.

"The Earl of Pembroke? You don't say. Should have asked for Flamma or Aristodemus, although they might have been a little too bloodthirsty for a beginner. Neither had much patience, I fear." He slowed his assault as she realized what he said and lowered her weapon, using it to lean on.

"Melam, how did you know these men? You mean that you heard they had no patience, right? You read about how bloodthirsty they were, right?" She took the steps toward him unconsciously as she spoke, eating up the space until she was standing toe to toe with him. She sounded hysterical, even to herself, but the thought of Melam being that much older than her was down right mind boggling.

"My brother trained them for his army. I only met them once, where I gave my opinion of them. My brother followed my advice both times and excused them from service. I knew the Earl when he was in his first life. He was granted Earldom in his second life, for being such a good man in his first one." Melam put his hands over the ones gripping onto his shirt like a life preserver.

She looked up at him with confusion and disbelief, and maybe even a hint of hurt if Melam looked closely. Feeling a new surge of power in the air, Melam rubbed her hands, hoping that she would not be too mad at him. He looked into her eyes as he let his head come down, letting Sedah see his intent. When she didn't stop him, he confidently took her lips with his, drawing her essence into him. Her sudden intake of surprise allowed some of his own air to be drawn into her, before she was returning the kiss, and willingly taking his essence into her. Kissing her was intoxicating. With her intake of breath, he took advantage of her open mouth and plunged his tongue into her mouth, deepening the kiss. Her moan was almost his undoing as her tongue slowly dueled with his. It was hesitant, but it showed that her passion to learn and explore the explosive chemistry between them was as strong in her as it was in him. Her arms came up to his shoulders naturally, holding on while pulling his body closer to hers simultaneously.

Remembering why he had started the kiss, it took all of his resolve to break it. He had to rest his forehead against hers in order to calm him raging body and mind. This girl, who had been hidden so long from the world, had the ability to fill his universe with stars, and she didn't even know it. He opened his mouth, not quite certain what he was about to say when he heard yelling.

Caprika and Amy's shouts had Sedah's head turning towards them, and Melam's gaze went straight to the sea, to the source of the power he had just felt.

Sedah's gaze caught up just in time to see Triton come storming out of the water, murder in his eyes, as he stared straight at Melam.

"She is sworn to be mine! How dare you touch what is mine!" Triton yelled as he got closer. Melam tried to push Sedah out of the way but ended up having to grab her hand to hold her back when she lunged at Triton for his statement.

"What is yours? What is yours!" she yelled, "That is the biggest problem I have with all of you Gods! I am not chattel to be given from one person to the other. I am a person, with feelings, emotions, and a brain of her own to make her own choices. I belong to no one other than my own damned self!" she yelled at Triton as Melam held her arm, which was probably a good thing, since she was extending the sword toward Triton with the other. If he had not been holding her, she would be jabbing her index finger into Triton's chest as she laid into him or trying to run him through with the sword.

"Be that as it may, young goddess, you still have to come stay with me for a month. Perhaps by then, you may not even want to come back on land." He smiled arrogantly.

"I don't even get why this is necessary! I have made my choice, and believe me, it isn't you!" Sedah yelled.

"Time under the sea with me and mine is what was agreed on by both of our fathers. If you back out, it could be seen as a slight, and would only escalate from there. We wouldn't want to cause a war now, would we?" Triton held out his hand to her, a small smirk on his face.

A small cry escaped Sedah as she threw the sword to the sand and flung herself back into Melam's arms. She held onto him with a death grip, hoping that Triton would grow tired of waiting and leave, yet knowing that the fates would not favor her a second time. Caprika and Amy came up behind her, coaxing her to let go of Melam and let them tell her goodbye.

Slowly, Sedah relaxed her grip, throwing her right arm around Amy and her left around Caprika, hugging them both. The girls kept her in the circle they created with Melam. Melam nodded, signaling Caprika and Amy to link hands and touch his biceps. This allowed him to create a barrier where Triton could see them, but not hear anything.

"Sedah, *varela,* I need you to listen to me." He took her hands in his, catching her gaze before continuing, "Keep your wits about you at all times. Mermaids are no joke. My kiss allowed you to breathe under water as if it were air, so that you do not need him to give you gills. It also keeps you from needing to drink anything." Melam grabbed her face in his hands when she tried to look down to prevent him from seeing her tears.

He used his thumb to wipe away the tears. "The most important thing that I can tell you is not to eat anything other than fish. Anything else could be a trap to keep you there, like your father did to your mother. Do you understand? No fins, no food, got it?" He searched her eyes, imploring her to understand.

"I know you're upset, but you cannot show it." He looked stubbornly at her, hiding his own feelings of how much this was killing him.

"Be as aggravating and brazen as you are at home with your brothers," Amy suggested, trying to get a small smile out of Sedah.

"Be the girl that got us kicked out of camp for scaring the bark off those nasty nymphs who were trying to hurt you," Caprika reminded her, bringing on a full laugh as Sedah thought back on their faces.

"I'm gonna give the two of us some privacy, girls." He looked at Caprika, then Amy. Both girls nodded, looking out towards the ocean and keeping an eye on a pissed off merman.

"Listen *varela*, I'm not sure what the deal was that made you have to go with him, but I promise that I will be here when you get back."

Sedah grabbed his right hand and put it to her cheek like he had done before. She closed her eyes for a minute, allowing her face to rub within his palm, like a kitten begging to be petted.

Through her tears, Sedah opened her eyes and nodded. "I don't want to leave you, Melam. I know what the deal was contingent on, and I have made my decision." Tears running down her face like twin streams, she allowed herself to really look at him as realization hit her. She was falling in love with this man, but she had no idea how he felt about her. She knew very little about him, despite all their time together, and yet she felt safer with him than she did her own father. For him, she could be nothing but a passing fancy. Sure, she knew he enjoyed her company and the couple kisses they'd shared, but what did she know beyond that? Not much. Maybe this time away would be good for both of them. With a heavy sigh, she took a step back and squared her shoulders before looking up at him again.

He looked at Amy and Caprika so that they could hear the conversation once again.

"Make them glad to be rid of you. Then come home to us," Melam finished.

Nodding to them, and wiping her eyes, she turned to face a pissed off Triton. Unclasping their hands, Amy and Caprika allowed the bubble to be broken so that they could hear the pissed off merman.

"What just happened? The whole time you were huddled together, I have been stuck here, not able to move past this spot!" Triton yelled, the accusation implied.

The four of them stood in a line like statues. Melam was farthest to Triton's left, a mask of stone-cold hatred on his face, standing with legs shoulder length apart and arms crossed.

Sedah stood next to Melam. He could tell that the little princess was trying her best to put on a brave front, but he could feel the nervousness radiating off her despite her rigid stance. Caprika was next in line, a scowl on her face. The way her fingers kept readjusting on the hilt of the sword she had picked up, there could be no misconceptions of what she probably wanted to do with it. Amy stood beside her with an identical sword. Unlike the others, Amy seemed at ease, sword swung over her shoulder, the other hand resting on her hip as if she were bored. None of them answered him.

"Fine. Princess, are you ready?" Triton held out a hand. He'd switched to acting like a gentleman as he repeatedly glanced to Caprika's warlike stance. Sedah glanced nervously at the water, visibly shivering as she walked forward. Triton eyed her protectors nervously. Tentatively, Sedah put her hand in his. Triton began to walk her to the water's edge, where he stopped them.

"I will need to give you gill slits, to allow you to breathe under the water like one of us. To–"

"No need, Melam already did that when he kissed me. That's what you walked up on." Sedah blushed. It felt weird, yet good, to say that aloud for the first time. Someone had kissed her, and what was more, she had liked it.

Triton gritted his teeth. "Yes, I did unfortunately see that, but–"

"He did the same thing you would," Sedah interrupted him again. "His way, I don't need gill slits to breathe under water. Was there any other reason that you needed to kiss me?" Sedah asked. Although it sounded like an innocent enough question, Sedah wondered if Triton could tell that she was mentally rolling on the beach in laughter.

Melam's kiss had been soul-searing. It had not been powerful, or demanding, as she would have expected. It might have been done to give her the power to breathe under water, but it had also been more. It had felt as if he was holding her, showing her a small piece of his heart, and taking some of hers back with him. It was that sweetness that had left her more confused than if he had been aggressive. Triton's growl under his breath brought her back to reality.

"No," he said through gritted teeth. When Triton turned to continue walking into the ocean, Sedah quickly blew Melam and the girls a kiss before following him into the water, disappearing under a wave.

Melam and the girls stood on the beach for a minute, on the off chance that Sedah had a panic attack and came back. When nothing and no one resurfaced, Melam sighed in resignation. Now all they could do was wait.

Deciding to get their spirits back in order, Melam took

advantage of the girls being distracted, to grab the swords out of their hands as he ran between them. Both girls twirled towards him, their surprise allowing their bodies to twirl with the swords as Melam ran through, smiling.

Having gotten their attention, Melam threw one sword high into the air, where the sun would be in the nymph's eyes, hiding what he was doing. Melam laughed as Amy squealed, backing herself out of range for when it fell. Caprika simply crossed her arms, a slight smile on her face.

Melam's gaze locked with Caprika's as he put his sword into the sand. Amy watched as not one, but two swords safely descended from the air, as if lowered by a fishing line, straight into Melam's waiting hand.

"Is that normal?" Amy's awed whisper reached Melam even though she was still at the shoreline, trying to rationalize what just happened. When nothing else happened, she crept back to the duo, staying slightly behind Caprika.

"I have come to find that I trust you two, possibly even more than my own guards back home. For your own safety, I cannot tell who you I am, and I hope that is enough." Melam held out one sword to each girl. "We all care for Sedah, and in my world, that means being ready for anything. You now own these swords. They are my gift to you. They will always appear to be sharp but will only pierce the skin if their owner wishes it. Otherwise, they will be as dull as wooden practice swords." He demonstrated by swinging the sword out of Caprika's reach and hitting her on the forearm with the blade end. He smiled when Amy's hands flew to her face, covering her gasp.

"Are you done?" Caprika's bored tone was at odds with the smirk on her face. Melam cleared his throat and handed her the first blade, then the second to Amy, who suddenly seemed scared of taking hers. Finally taking it, the girls circled Melam, smiling.

❦ 20 ❦

Sedah was about to scream. After allowing Triton to pull her fully under the water, he stopped to show her how to regulate her breathing while she made the transition from air to water, and from lungs alone to a combination of lungs and gills. He worked slowly with her so she wouldn't freak out and take in water the wrong way. His patience as he taught her confused Sedah about his character. Once she had that figured out, however, they traveled nonstop. Sedah tried to stop, after swimming for a full thirty minutes, to ask for a break, but Triton grabbed her arm and kept going, pulling her along, without a word.

After trying to free her hand twice, Sedah decided to save her energy. Triton's massive fish tail allowed them to travel effortlessly, so Sedah took in all of the sights. Fish chased one another, sharks swam lazily, dozing, and plants drifted to and fro with the current. Triton might have been a spoiled brat, but it was clear from looking around her that Poseidon took care of his charges.

In the distance, a huge crater became visible, lights reflecting from its inner walls. Those lamps gave light to men carrying stones as big as they were. Sedah looked to the ocean floor, watching the men stack the stones onto carts, driven by a pair of hippocampi.

As Triton began their descent, the brilliance of the Palace dazzled Sedah, surrounded on all sides by the city below. Unlike most castles, Poseidon's was circular, with support columns and stairs circling the entire fortress. It reminded Sedah of the lighthouse near their new home, only grander, with no rotating light at the top. Sedah was actually surprised that she thought it was beautiful. She'd been imagining something pretentious.

They entered the palace near the middle, through the open side of the wall, which would have been called a balcony, had they been on land. Triton's fin turned rapidly into feet a second before touching the floor. The transition from swimming to standing happened so suddenly her legs buckled under her.

Triton grinned. "Falling for me already?" He arched his right eyebrow as if challenging her. Sedah made a show of scrunching her nose and lips in disgust, standing up straight.

"Never gonna happen." She crossed her arms across her chest.

"We shall see. For now, this will be where you stay. This floor and the one below belongs to my sisters who still live at home. I will come get you for dinner," Triton told her as he snapped his fingers. A servant stepped out of the wall, walking quickly to them. Unconsciously, Sedah took a step back in surprise.

"This is Navue. She will keep you safe and answer any questions you may have," he told Sedah before turning to the servant. "Do not let my sisters try anything, or boss her around. Understood?" His cold eyes stared down at the girl, who nodded her head vigorously.

Sedah was too busy scrutinizing Navue to realize Triton

was moving, until he grabbed her left hand. Her eyes shot over to him, while trying unsuccessfully to pull her hand back. Triton held her hand like a vise but showed no outward appearance of struggle as he brought her hand to his lips, kissing the back of it gently. Sedah watched in horror as his lips, as cold as his heart, touched her hand. Feeling his gaze on her, her eyes darted apprehensively to lock with his. Triton's smile, while by itself would appear innocent, promised nothing good, and everything calculated, when paired with the darkness that was in his eyes. Sedah gasped, drawing her hand to her chest, as if she had just been burned. With a smile, Triton turned on his heel and left.

Silently, Sedah followed Navue, who led her down a hallway until it came to a T. Instead of turning left or right, the servant opened the door in front of them. Sedah entered, stepping forward hesitantly. She had wondered, when her parents first told her she would be living under water, how a person slept in and decorated a castle under water, although most might ask the same thing about a castle in Hell as well.

Sedah's head moved slowly as she took in everything, trying her best to memorize every detail, in order to figure out how it worked. Somehow, fifteen leagues under the sea, was a palace that held water instead of air, and still had normal looking furniture. To her right, sat the bed, surrounded by a built-in bookshelf unit on each side that also went over the bed, so that recessed lights allowed reading while in the bed. The light golds and turquoises of the room blended nicely with the mahogany wood, adding to the opulence. The bed linen was mostly gold, with threads of turquoise looking like reeds, while the curtains were turquoise with gold embellishments hanging intermittently. A cold tile floor held Poseidon's crest in the center of each square, but not in the pretentious way Sedah expected. While guests would be left with subtle hints to remind them of where they were, the room still held the ability to be cozy and inviting.

Navue waited quietly until Sedah turned her attention to her again. Sedah took her time to really study the servant mermaid. The girl's features, odd as they were, weren't what disturbed her, but that she was a piece of the castle walls themselves. While she still appeared human, it was as if someone had hand painted fish scales on her skin in a light grey color. It was eerie and fascinating at the same time.

"It's beautiful." Sedah smiled, unsure if she meant the room or Navue.

"I will be outside if you need me. When it is time, I will come help you get ready for dinner with the family." Navue curtsied and left.

Sedah sighed, not sure of what to do with herself. She hadn't really been given time to think since she first hit the water. Going to the window, Sedah drew back the curtains and looked out. She leaned against the pillar as she admired the city below her.

She had no idea how it was accomplished, but the city was lit up like a land city. Despite wanting not to be impressed, the lights fascinated Sedah. She would never have guessed her uncle's domain could be this wondrous. Her teachers had taught her that water did not react well with electricity and gas, yet here she was, looking at lights, from a castle deep below the water, breathing just fine.

Gods, how she missed Amy, Caprika, and Melam. The corner of Sedah's mouth raised as she thought about how they would react to this. Maybe, she thought, she should act a little like they were: explore and learn as much as possible like Amy, while questioning and being observant like Caprika, yet not trusting anyone, like Melam. Sedah truly was a fish out of water there. She chuckled at the irony of that phrase, being the only one who wasn't a fish, and completely submerged in the ocean.

❧

THE ORANGE HUE OF THE SUNSET BLENDED EFFORTLESSLY with the purple tinged night like a lady held securely in her lovers embrace. Its beauty barely touched Melam as he stared out at the water, uncaring. For whatever reason, he just felt numb. Seeing someone sit in the reclining chair beside his on the beach, Melam took a deep, cleansing breath before turning.

"Hi." He said, pulling himself into a more comfortable sitting position.

"Hi." Caprika smiled. She said nothing, staring at him in silence.

"Can I help you with something?" He asked after a few minutes of increasingly uncomfortable silence.

"Yeah, go get our girl," she stated matter of factly.

"Doesn't happen that way, Caprika." He gave her an apologetic half smile.

"I know that all hell, probably literally, would break loose if anything underhanded happened to Sedah. We both know Poseidon is not about to let her go. Even if he was trustworthy, what about his son, or one of his many daughters? I don't trust them." Caprika's tone was barely in check. She wasn't saying anything Melam didn't know as she sat bristling like a caged tiger. Frustrated, she swung her legs around to face Melam.

"I don't either, but I can't do what you want me to. A vow must be kept, unless another is made to change the terms of the first one."

"So to make new terms!" she yelled, throwing her hands onto her hips in frustration, as if the answer should have been obvious. Melam sighed loudly. He knew exactly how Caprika felt. Slowly, he turned in his chair, grabbing Caprika's hands in his when she dropped them again.

"Will you trust that I have people who are helping me? That I will know if anything happens to her, or I need to go get her in order to keep her from harm?" Melam caught and held Caprika's gaze. "Can you be patient just a little bit and let me handle this part?"

Caprika stared into Melam's eyes for several moments. "Okay, but if this ends badly, it will be you that pays the price, got it?" Without waiting for his reply, she pulled her hands out of his, and walked back towards the house.

Melam wiped his hands over his face, his fingers pulling at the skin in weariness. There were so many ways this could go. To not know which one was really the best choice, had Melam worried. If this didn't go smoothly, everyone, paranormal and human alike, would pay dearly.

❧

Navue came before dinner to help Sedah get ready. Although she protested vehemently at first, Sedah eventually convinced Navue to allow her to remain in her own outfit. Until Sedah knew what was to be expected of her, she refused to dress up in some silly gown and bow to their every whim. She would be as stubborn as Caprika until she found out what the terms of the agreement between her father and uncle were. She would be the petulant child that her father always accused her of being when he was angry with her.

After letting Navue fix her hair and put some color on her lips, Sedah followed the servant to the dining room. It took all of her will not to gawk at the opulence of the room or show any surprise at the number of people in attendance. Triton had told her that only family would be at dinner.

Looking over the room with every chair of the banquet table full, Sedah had to wonder if all of Poseidon's children had made an effort to come see the hidden Princess. Holding her head a little higher, she followed Navue to the end of the table, which faced Poseidon on the other end. Sedah hesitated to sit, sure the Queen might have a very real problem with the daughter of Hades sitting in her rightful spot.

"It is alright, child, my wife sulks in her room and refuses to join us at the table. Sit, eat, meet my children." Poseidon smiled as he swept out his hands to encompass his children, all of them girls except for Triton. He introduced them all, making them stand as he said their name. She received a variety of responses before each girl sat back down. It was reassuring to see that at least most of the women did not seem to mind her being there. The ones that did, she seemed to recall, were momma's girls, which made sense to her, as close as she was to her own mother.

From her studies, Sedah knew that Poseidon had over fifty female human looking children, so she considered herself lucky that only about half of them were here. The rest were probably stuck in their places of duty.

Sedah slowly sat down, fully convinced that one of them would push the chair out from under her. She couldn't stop the sigh of relief as her body met the firm texture of the lush golden chair.

Satisfied, Poseidon began talking to Triton, who sat beside him, as he motioned for dinner to begin. All of his daughters chatted with one another, ignoring Sedah as if she had never arrived or been introduced.

Sedah perused the table, taking in not just the abundance of food, but those who were eating it. She watched the women, getting familiar with little details about each one, so that she could better remember the names. If she was going to serve one of them, it was better to start getting to know them sooner rather than later. With this many girls, Sedah didn't want to piss any of them off if she didn't have to.

Remembering Melam's instructions, she cautiously picked around her plate, not really eating. No fish meant no food, not that she was sure her nerves would let her eat anything anyway. There was snail on the plate, which she thought would probably be okay to eat, if she had the courage to try it.

Sedah jumped when she heard booming laughter come from the other end of the table. Poseidon's dark hair and celery leaf crown matched his son's. The two men laughed over something Sedah could have never heard over the chatter in the room.

"What's wrong girl? Is my feast not good enough for you?" Poseidon asked her, a knowing smirk on his face. Sedah narrowed her eyes, trying to figure him out.

Sedah tried for a modest and acceptable answer. "No, the dinner is fine, uncle. I am afraid my nerves have made me incapable of eating at the present."

Poseidon held her stare for a moment, as if he was deciding to chastise her or say more. Instead, he stood, making everyone else scramble to stand with him. Sedah was a little surprised when he crossed the room and held out his hand to her.

"Walk with me?" he asked.

Knowing it was a demand, not a request, Sedah tried her best to keep her hand from shaking as she placed it in his. Sedah glanced over her shoulder in time to see that most of the girls at the table had left as soon as their father was gone, while a few still sat and conversed with one another as if nothing had happened.

Sedah allowed her uncle to lead her out onto a balcony. She felt herself pass through something when they stepped beyond the doorway. It felt like sheer curtains rubbing over her skin, with a little bit of resistance before they went back in place.

"What has you feeling too nervous to eat, Sedah? Has anyone in particular caused it?" Poseidon released her hand, leaning against a pillar made into the railing.

"It is just general nervousness from being in a new place where I know no one. It will pass in a few days, just as it did when I first met the nymphs." Sedah tried for a reassuring smile as she leaned against the opposing pillar. "I just need to get my bearings, is all."

"Well, as you know, my wife has never been a fan of your mother, if for no other reason than she is the daughter of Demeter, and sister to one of my offspring." Poseidon's eyes grew glassy as he thought aloud. His beard and cloak moved with the ebb and flow of the water, while his clothing remained stationary.

"Sometimes, I think she'd rather your dad and I had each other's dominion so I could never wander without her knowledge." He laughed lightly, bringing himself to the present and pulling Sedah out of her thoughts as she realized what he had just said.

Not sure if she was supposed to ask questions or say anything, Sedah remained quiet. When a few moments had passed with him simply staring down towards town, Sedah cleared her throat. "My father never told me how long I was going to stay here, or what I was going to be doing exactly. Have you decided on these details?"

"You will stay here for two weeks, in which time I will see which of my children has not been poisoned against you by my lovely wife. That will determine who you serve or marry, and if by land or by sea."

"What am I expected to do for these two weeks?" Sedah asked. Poseidon was about to answer when he stopped and smiled at her.

"Duck."

"What—" Sedah began, only to be hit on the side of the face by a small fish. Reflexively, Sedah squatted as she looked up to see a school of fish swim where she was just standing. She waited for a moment after the last fish had passed, in case there were any stragglers. "A gift from your wife?"

"I would normally say no, but given her absence, I wouldn't be willing to bet either way." He grabbed his niece's hands, helping her to her feet. "Your only expectation while you are here is to get to know everyone and explore, so that you know where everything is. Just make sure that you always have a servant with you, so you do not become lost. My children, grandchildren, and my wife's sisters all come by on occasion, though the last have been instructed to stay away while you are here. I cannot force them not to tell, should they find out who you are. There should be plenty to keep you occupied. It is late; do you know how to get back to your room from here?"

Sedah nodded. Paying attention to where she was going, she succeeded in keeping her mind on track until she got into her room. Throwing herself down on the bed, Sedah stared at the ceiling, replaying the day. She had woken up happy, hanging out with people she cared for and trusted, only to be taken away to yet another foreign place, where she once again knew no one and was instantly hated, simply for who her parents were.

Sedah fell asleep, full of regrets over bugging her mom about coming above, and crying for the loss of two carefree weeks on the beach with Melam and her friends.

◈

IT SEEMED TO SEDAH VERY QUICKLY THAT HER SERVANT was going to be her only friend while she was there. Poseidon had not helped her chances by personally walking her into the girls' parlor the morning after that tense dinner, demanding that everyone give her a chance and get to know her. In that moment, Sedah had wished she could be swallowed by a whale instead of staying in the same room as these girls. Pushing her fear down, Sedah had tried to do her mother proud, standing tall, and staring straight back at the girls who openly showed their disdain for her, by the way they stared at her, their eyes full of hatred. Had she been her sisters, this would have fed her strength with all the energy that hate took out of a person.

It only took three days of being always on edge before Sedah began to feel the effects of having no sun. Every morning, Navue woke and dressed Sedah for the day before allowing her to leave the room and go to the main hall for breakfast. It was hard to tell night from day at that depth. The only indication was the shimmer of light filtered down through the water occasionally, reflecting off the animals as they swam by.

Sedah was lost in thought about how best to catch those small amounts of sun, when she felt someone touch her hand that sat on the table beside her plate. Sedah came back to the present, looking over at the young woman sitting on her left. The girl appeared to be about Sedah's age, though that wasn't saying much when all types of immortals aged differently.

"Are you okay? You seem . . . off somehow." The Oceanid held out her hand. "I'm Tamil, by the way." She smiled, her perfect bow lips stretching wide as Sedah shook her hand.

"I'm fine, just bored, I guess. I was always busy with the nymphs. It's hard to just relax all day by reading, or exploring the castle, which I have done little of, for fear of entering the wrong door and offending someone," Sedah said, cautious that she would not offend the first daughter to speak to her sincerely since she had arrived.

"I know exactly what you mean! There are lots of things to do though. I could show you around town, or we could take the Hippocampi out for a ride. The herd of whale sharks needs their feeding too. That's always fun to watch!" The joy was so evident in Tamil's heart shaped face as she suggested things, that Sedah couldn't help but smile also.

"Yes, please: to all of the above," Sedah laughed, getting up when Tamil did. The girls stopped so Tamil could get permission from her father. Poseidon stared in contemplation at Sedah for a minute before agreeing. Tamil quickly thanked him, and ran off with a squeal, leaving Sedah to have to hurry to catch up.

21

"This is amazing!" Sedah squealed as the girls broke the surface of the water with their hippocampi. Sedah had finally gotten the animal to accept her after a few hours of feeding and grooming.

The girls had the golden palace on foot, walking around town, or swam, in Tamil's case, as they got to know one another. Tamil pointed out all her favorite shops, making plans for them to visit each one while Sedah was there. While none of it sounded very appealing to her, it did beat being in the palace with people that she knew hated her.

Tamil got the guards to bring lunch to the stables, along with snacks for the animals once they returned. Tamil's green eyes sparkled as she laughed at Sedah for jumping back in surprise when a half fish, half goat came bounding up to them for attention. Once she recovered, Tamil explained that Hippocampi were not the only half land, half fish animal around.

As they sat on a blanket and ate, Tamil explained that the goat fish were known as Aigikampos. In addition to the Hippocampi, which were half horse half fish, the palace also kept Leokampos, or lions, and Pardalokampos, or leopards that were raised specifically for her father and brother to hunt.

"Why is there a need for them to kill rare hybrids, that are as much myths as we are, when there are probably billions of real fish in the sea?" Sedah asked as the girls let the animals swim lazily along the surface. Sedah could feel her body soaking up the rays as she held onto her mount's harness.

"Probably because the natural sea creatures are as much in danger of extinction as the mythological ones. Although I have never asked, so I don't know for certain, mind you. At least with the mythological ones he knows the population, because he is the one controlling it. As sea nymphs, we assist the same ways the land nymphs do. We try to help the environment and animals as much as possible, but never where humans can see us or know that we have done anything. We cannot directly interfere. Humans will either kill the sea or save it," Tamil said, sounding as if it didn't matter to her either way as she pushed her long, wheat colored, wet hair off her face.

"Can we do this often? It feels good breathing actual air." Sedah took a deep, cleansing breath, closing her eyes as the wind caressed her face.

"Sure, but we need to get these guys back. I never know when they may be needed." Tamil smiled at Sedah before kicking her mount, causing him to jump into the air before going under again. Not quite so confident, Sedah gently nudged her animal to follow their leader.

Sedah and Tamil were walking into the palace, still laughing and talking with their arms intertwined when Triton stepped into the doorway, blocking the entrance. Before anything could be said, everyone heard things crashing, and a woman screaming at people in the grand entrance of the palace. Sedah saw Triton and Tamil exchange a knowing glance before Tamil started pushing Sedah to the right, to where the servants usually entered the palace.

"What's happening?" Sedah asked as she was directed from behind by Tamil on where to go.

"She's in a mood. What is it now?" Tamil told Sedah before glancing down the stairs to her brother.

"She's been told to be present *and* tolerable," Triton smirked, as they led Sedah to her room where Navue was waiting with a worried expression. "I've had one of me trying to calm her down for almost an hour now, but you know how she—"

"Hates to be told what to do. Made only worse by it being you that she has to be tolerable to," Tamil told Sedah, a sad smile on her face, obviously feeling sorry for her new friend.

Sedah felt herself reliving everything the nymphs had done to her simply because she was the daughter of Hades. Being part of a deal she hadn't even asked for, meant that people had to tolerate her, but never get to know her before they formed their own opinions about her. If she had still been able to turn colors, she would have been bright red in frustration and anger. This was Jade and Onyx all over again!

"What am I supposed to do? This is because she has been avoiding me, isn't it?" She glanced at all three faces. "Great!" She threw her hands outward in frustration, letting them fall loudly back to her sides. She stilled at the slight tremor she felt through her feet. When Tamil and Triton ignored it, she decidedly said nothing.

"I will protect you, should she try to start anything at dinner. I doubt she will, knowing that father is watching her, but I wouldn't put it past her to put in a few snide remarks or ask pointed questions to make you lash out," Triton warned her, putting his hand on her shoulder in support.

Taking a big breath before letting it out slowly, Sedah

nodded. Tamil gave her a hug and a smile before following her brother out of the bedroom to let Sedah get ready for dinner.

"I guess let's do this," Sedah told Navue, sitting down in front of the mirror.

It had been such a nice day. To have it ruined by Amphitrite seemed such a waste. At least the little bit of sun and relaxation she had gotten would give her the energy to be ready for anything her aunt might throw at her. It surprised her that Triton wanted to shield her from his mother's temper. He had probably just been worried about his sister, not her. It was either that or he feared his father's wrath if Sedah had gotten injured.

Other than the girls that hated her just because their mother did, Sedah had to admit that her stay had not been too terrible so far. If she were being honest, other than the colors and location, it felt a little like home. It still felt weird to see fins turn to feet, and back again, and to realize that, thanks to Melam, her body somehow took oxygen, not water, leagues under the sea, in a golden palace unknown to humans.

It still bothered her, not knowing if she would end up being a servant or forced to marry Triton. It wasn't that she didn't want to one day get married and have a family of her own, but she didn't want that partner to be Triton. A picture of Melam replaced Triton in her mind, making her blush.

It had nothing to do with having a fish tail outside of the castle, or even the green tinged skin. His long curly hair and non-muscular body just didn't do it for her, when compared to Melam, who had already proven that he could take care of her when needed.

Sedah mentally shook herself as she allowed Navue to help her dress. She needed to prepare herself for a possible battle of wits. Thinking of Amy's fearless attitude, Sedah straightened her shoulders. Navue had also decided that her mistress needed armor, it seemed. Looking down at her dress,

Sedah couldn't help but admire it. Where most of the outfits she had worn so far were made from simple materials, no different from those most of the girls wore, this one was elegant.

While the slip underneath was a simple white, the sheer material over it was forest green with beautiful little rosettes scattered around the bodice. Sedah knew from experience that the gold floors would make her red hair look like living flames, while the shade of the rosettes would help with her coloring.

"Navue, it's beautiful! You have outdone yourself." Sedah beamed, unable to keep herself from twirling. She noticed the braid that made a crown shape on top of her head. She smiled a little evilly at Navue. "You did that on purpose. You know it will set her off."

"You only get one time where she will have to be on her best behavior no matter what you say, do, or look like. Might as well use it." Navue smiled back. It was clear that the servant was used to her queen's attitude, and was using Sedah's presence to her advantage.

It took all Sedah had not to kiss Tamil when she knocked on the door right before dinner. She tried not to act surprised to see Triton there as well. Some of her nerves calmed down, just knowing she had reinforcements. Brief shock made her pause. She'd just considered Triton an ally. She shook it off quickly. Triton walked behind the girls as the trio entered the dining hall. Girls were still filing in, so no one took notice of the three as Triton sat to his father's immediate left as usual, and Tamil made a younger sister move, so that Sedah sat to Poseidon's right, between him and Tamil.

As if on cue, Amphitrite entered, as beautiful and regal as she'd been described. For having thrown such a murderous tantrum earlier, Sedah would have expected her to at least act or appear pissed off. The queen said nothing as she walked to the table, looking at every one of her daughters until she found Sedah. A servant ran forward and moved the chair for the queen to sit, as her eyes had never left Sedah's.

"Nice of you to join us again mother. You have been sorely missed." Triton coaxed his mother's gaze to himself.

"Yes, well, I am here now." Amphitrite glanced at Sedah, then Triton, before staring at her husband, her vivid blue eyes filled with hatred. "Are you having any fun with our guest?" she asked Triton, spitting out the last word with disgust. Triton glanced at his sister before smiling at Sedah as he spoke to his mother.

"I am, actually. We are going to walk the gardens every night after dinner, and I plan on taking her places during the day, so we can get to know one another better." He flashed her an innocent yet determined smile.

As expected, his mother, as well as a few of his sisters, gasped in shock. The crab claws on her crown grew blood red and the current outside picked up as his mother closed her eyes and tried to calm her raging anger. It was obvious that she had not expected her son to like, much less *want* to spend time with a being lower than they were.

Amphitrite sat there, seething with rage. Tamil had explained her mother's mindset to Sedah earlier. Zeus considered Poseidon beneath him, having dominion over water and animals, instead of people. But this was the daughter of someone who spent their time with nothing but the dead. It was unthinkable that her only son would debase himself in such a way. They may both be the children of a major God, but they were not equals as far as Amphitrite was concerned.

Everyone waited with bated breath to see what the queen would do. The tension eased slightly when she said nothing, choosing to pick her spoon back up and eat. Sedah knew this would not be the end of it, but she tried to let herself relax and enjoy the food and surrounding company. The next two courses were served without anyone having to run interference. If looks could kill though, Poseidon, Tamil, Sedah and Triton would all be dead, many times over. It was right as dessert was ending, everyone beginning to excuse themselves, that the queen chose her next well-placed barb.

"Son, make sure when you are on your outings, that you explain what she might do if she becomes a servant in that area. I was thinking about putting her in the stables or out in the preserve with the rest of the untamed heathens when the time comes," Amphitrite said nonchalantly as she glided out of the hall, a handful of her daughters, trailing behind her.

Sedah stared at her hands in her lap, all happy thoughts gone, as she was brutally reminded of the reality of why she was here. She didn't need a reminder of the deal, yet again. Her food suddenly wasn't sitting well as her entire journey came rushing back to her. She had finally been having a little fun, and with one statement, it was all shattered. Like throwing a baseball through a glass window, the reverberations were deafening.

Triton came around, kneeled, and took her hands in his. He looked up at her, with a little bit of pride. He could tell she wanted to cry, her lips betraying her by quivering slightly. Without a word, he gently tugged her hands, pulling her up with him as he stood.

She let him lead her out of the palace through the back door, onto the garden grounds. They walked in silence for the entire time it took them to make one complete circle of the three-acre garden.

"If we make one more lap without you telling me what you are thinking in that pretty little head of yours, I might just have to kiss you," Triton told her honestly. He smiled and held on when his words registered, causing her to trip on her own feet as she looked up at him, clearly shocked. His huge grin caused her to giggle as she righted herself.

"Sorry," Sedah said. "I do that sometimes. You know, you didn't have to lie and tell your mother that you were having fun with me or planned on getting to know me better. Neither of us need to be on her bad side, especially if I get my duty assignment from her when I become a servant. She really will give me the worst job; I believed that part."

"It's a good thing I wasn't lying then. What little time I have spent with you has been pleasant." He grinned down at her. "And I really do want to get to know you and show you around my world if you'll let me."

Sedah stared into his eyes, trying to get a read on him, before looking up the path again. She weighed her options for a long moment, not wanting to make the wrong decision or give off a false impression.

"I'm not opposed to spending more time getting to know you and your world, actually. It fascinates me. But I don't feel like it would be right to suddenly abandon Tamil, to spend time alone with you after she has been so kind and welcoming to me." Sedah tried for the honest and most diplomatic answer.

"A chaperone, huh?" Triton glanced down with a gleam in his eye and crooked grin to match. He appeared to get lost in deep thought, as she had earlier, as he guided them to a bench in the center of the open garden. "Any other requests, demands, or questions, princess?" He laughed.

Sedah had the decency to blush, deciding to ask the two questions she hadn't had the courage to do with others around.

"Actually, I have been curious about something. How do you have lights underwater and how do you still have legs instead of a tail, even though we are out of the palace?"

Triton smiled warmly at her. "You know the White Rock Temple in the Underworld? How it leads down the River of Flame?" he asked.

Sedah nodded, wondering why she was getting a history lesson of her home, a realm she had played in since birth.

"Okay, inside the temple is an eternal flame from the river. It is constantly guarded, by one of the Hekatonkheires, and is distributed to all supernatural realms. My father said that he had to personally ask Gaia for it, and it has been here ever since. Should one of the brothers fail in protecting it, the other realms would know what had happened the second it went out," he said. Triton led her to a nearby bench, where they sat for a moment.

"As to your simpler question, I have legs because I choose to." His voice was lower as he answered this time. "All royal Mers are born with the ability to walk and swim. I think it has something to do with the strength of our bloodlines, but mother says it is so that we can find appropriate mates." He looked out into the distance as if the answer was going to swim right up to him.

Sedah put her hand on his thigh, turning her body to his in a show of solidarity. Triton turned to her, a sad smile on his face. He wrapped her hand in his two larger ones. Sedah sat back on the bench, aware of Triton rubbing her hand absently as they both allowed the night sounds and slight glow from town to surround them and their thoughts.

She wasn't sure how long they sat there. By the time Triton silently stood and, without releasing her hand, assisted her up and escorted her back to her room, she noticed that most of the staff had retired for the night.

When they arrived at her door, Triton kept her hand in his when she gently tried to remove it. Instead, he turned it to face him, laying it flat on his chest, forcing Sedah to step close to him. Their eyes met. Her breath caught in her throat, her lungs fighting for air, as her mind screamed that he was about to kiss her.

"Would you allow me to show you around? I want to take

you to a new place every day you are here. I will let my sister know that she is encouraged to join us, or your maid can act as chaperone if Tamil cannot." Honesty filled his voice, and hope shone clear across his face.

Sedah felt a small tinge of guilt for wanting to make the time pass pleasantly by spending time with Triton and Tamil. From what she had been told, he had been mean and rude the first time he had come for her, and while she wouldn't easily forget that, he seemed to be a good person once she got to know him better. Sedah couldn't help but wonder if his mother or meaner sisters had caused his attitude towards her friends that first time, and if he had come to see things differently over time.

"As long as we are escorted, as is proper, I would love for you to show me around your home," Sedah responded, her gaze never leaving his. Slowly, she eased her hand out from under his. She rubbed her right palm on her hip to relieve the itch, as she opened the door behind her with her left.

Navue was there immediately, helping ready her new mistress for bed, as she asked a million questions, not bothering to get an answer before moving on to another. Either she was used to not getting her questions answered, or her servant sensed the pensive mood she was in, Sedah thought as she was helped into bed. The fact that Navue knew everything that had happened that night meant there were no secrets there, something Sedah could not forget, for even a second.

Tamil was up and bursting into Sedah's room from that next morning on. Most of the time, she showed up before Sedah was finished getting ready. A couple of nights, Tamil slept over with Sedah, after particularly bad nights at dinner, when even Triton couldn't cheer Sedah up. It was one of these nights that Sedah accidently found that she could do something new.

It started innocently enough, when Tamil ran around the sitting area of the bedroom. She held an issue of the latest Mer gossip magazine above her head to keep Sedah from reading the article about her, the unknown palace guest. She rounded a chair, when the magazine's spine hit the sconce just right, causing the girls to slide to a stop as the ball of light plummeted to the floor.

Without thinking, Sedah dove for the ball. Her body hit the floor, driving all the air out of her lungs as she watched the ball hit the floor, a millimeter from her fingers. Neither girl breathed, waiting for it to shatter. When nothing happened, Tamil got down on her hands and knees to inspect the ball, letting out a small gasp as she did so. Fearing the worst, Sedah quickly scrambled to her feet, watching as the ball gently rolled to the floor.

Tamil picked up the ball. "Sedah, what are your powers?" She asked as she turned towards Sedah with a big smile on her face.

"Not much. I can replicate things, shrink and occasionally expand items. I don't know. Why?" Sedah asked hesitantly. While she liked Tamil, she was still unsure of how much she could tell her, for fear of what might get back to Poseidon and his wife.

"Can you stop things in midair?" Tamil pressed her.

"Only when I concentrate. But I haven't practiced since right before I got here." Sedah pointed at the ball absently. "You mean you think I kept that from shattering?"

Instead of answering, Tamil threw the ball up, letting it sail into the air before coming down. Sedah smiled, catching it with ease.

The second the ball of light made contact with her hand, Sedah knew something was wrong. While she had been about to say something witty about never learning to play baseball, there was suddenly no one to say it to.

The sight around her was not the guest room of the palace, where she had spent the last week, but a dark chamber. She stood next to an empty pedestal. The room was dark, the glowing orb in her hand letting off enough light to let her know she was not in imminent danger. She took a deep breath, trying to calm herself. Her last vision had been almost spot on, so she had no reason to believe this one wouldn't be the same.

Walking to the nearest wall so she could see with the low light, she saw huge cracks, the nearby pillars missing chunks, as if from multiple heavy blows. She ran her hands along the cracks, trying to get a sense of what weapon could have caused it. Looking down, Sedah could see the debris around her feet, mixed with blood spatter. A few feet away, a severed right hand lay in a pool of blood. When she shone the light to her left, a decapitated head lay beside yet another right hand. Sedah gagged, covering her nose and mouth with her free hand.

Needing to know, Sedah walked the entirety of what she now realized was a temple, finding a total of fourteen heads and twenty-eight hands, before finding a body. Near the door of the temple, leaning against the wall, was one of what she could only guess was a Hecatonkheire, by the multiple heads and hands. Seeing the destruction, it was obvious he had gone down fighting hard. Not knowing what it took to kill them, she stared at his chest to see if he was alive—he wasn't. If this was a Hecatonkheire, then this was the temple of Gaia and Ouranos, which held the Eternal Flame.

Sedah watched her trembling hand reach for the door, even as her mind screamed for her body to stop, begging for her to let go of the sphere and go back to the safety of the underwater palace. She forced herself to close her eyes and calm her racing heart. Summoning her courage, Sedah let out a long, slow exhale before pulling open the heavy temple door.

Sedah opened the doors and gasped as she realized that the fire in front of her was actually the Stygian Marsh. Expecting to see destruction and opening the door to see the only home you had ever known burning around her were two *very* different feelings. A sob caught in her throat as she heard Cerberus doing a combination of whimpering and barking. Looking to her right, she saw that the River Styx was on fire as well. Tears ran unchecked down her face as she looked through the fire to see only one head on her poor Cerberus instead of three. She wanted to fall to the ground and scream in grief at all the carnage around her.

Worry for her family hit her hard and fast. No longer thinking of the danger, Sedah ran, benumbed, through the fire devouring the marsh, as she headed straight north towards home. Clenching the ball of light, Sedah ran past, and even through, the forms of the Indifferent Dead as they ran and yelled for her to stop.

As the Palace came into view, she sighed in relief to see her home undamaged, ignoring her father's beloved orchards burning to the right for her own sanity. Running to the door of the Judges, she growled in frustration when it would not budge.

"Who in the Underworld locks the door to the judging chamber?" Sedah yelled with maybe a little more hysteria than she would ever admit to, as she banged against the door. She dodged as a piece fell from above her. She looked up to see that one of the decorative gargoyles had broken in half and barely missed her as it fell.

"I did, dear," a small voice said from behind her. Sedah turned around, ready to use the ball of light as a weapon if she had to. In front of her stood an older woman, about Sedah's height. "Trust me when I say that you do not want to be in there with them. They are mad as a hornet's nest and needed to blow off some steam."

Sedah looked at the woman. She was solid, with short white curly hair, glacier blue eyes, and a plain yellow floor length dress on, so she was obviously not from the Underworld. She walked closer to the woman to get out of range from the falling debris that happened with each bang from inside.

"Who is in there? Is my family safe? Who killed the eternal light? I didn't know that was possible!" Sedah asked in quick succession. This woman spoke as if she knew Sedah and what was happening, yet Sedah was sure they had never met before.

"Oh, we have met, just not with me in this particular form. Your family is somewhere safe, for the moment." A sadness seemed to envelop the old woman as she looked at Sedah. "I am Gaia. This is not a premonition as you have had before, but a future that is yet possible if it isn't corrected."

"What happened here? Who's killing guardians and tearing up my home?" Sedah asked again. She jumped as a particularly loud bang from inside the palace made the entire building shudder and the front door splinter some. She looked back to the woman, who put both her hands on Sedah's shoulders. Gaia stared directly into Sedah's fear-filled wide eyes, willing her to understand the desperation of the situation she was in.

"The Titans were willingly released in this possible future and even I will not be able to hold them off much longer. They killed the Eternal Light to weaken other paranormals before I was able to lock them in the palace. You have seen a future that is not set in stone. I exist in all possible futures, and can honestly say that I do not want this to happen as much as I love my Titan children. There's no time to explain further. Just make the decision that feels right—that leaves you feeling the most complete—and this will become nothing but a bad dream." Both gasped and turned as a portion of the roof broke, tumbling down the side to the ground as a hand became visible in place of where the piece of roof had just been. "Go back, now!" the woman commanded quickly.

"How? I don't know how I got here!" Sedah knew she sounded panicked, but she couldn't think past the fear. With a sudden flash of insight, she remembered this had all started when she caught the ball. She exhaled, trying to calm her racing heart.

"Yes, you do." The woman placed her hands on Sedah's cheeks, looking deep into her blue eyes to make sure she had her full attention. "Trust yourself, and let go."

Understanding passed between the two women, and Sedah's hand instinctively let go of the ball of light.

Sedah's eyes stayed glued to the scene before her as the ball fell towards the earth. When it shattered, the last image Sedah had was of the only home she had ever known exploding, the force within finally managing to break through. Like a flash of blinding light, it was gone.

❦

SEDAH LOOKED AROUND HER. TAMIL WAS LOOKING expectantly from the ball in Sedah's hand to her.

"What? Can you not concentrate here?" Tamil asked Sedah, then paused. "You look different somehow. Are you okay?" She put the back of her palm to Sedah's forehead.

"Here, I will take this. You are burning up. You need to get in bed and get some rest," Tamil said as she took the ball of ethereal light from Sedah. They both gasped at the second degree burn on Sedah's hand. Quickly, Sedah pulled her blistered hand away, putting it behind her back.

"I'm fine. It doesn't hurt. I think I'll go to bed now." The words rushed out as she tried to turn and usher Tamil out the door, guiding her by placing her good hand on the small of Tamil's back. Sedah ignored her friend's broken speech as Tamil tried to get Sedah to let her stay in the room. As soon as Tamil's body had safely breached the threshold, Sedah stepped back and swiftly shut the door, leaning against it. She had no idea what had happened, but she had no time to sit there and concentrate on levitating things under water, when she had just seen something so life defining. There were no other words to describe it.

In somewhat of a haze, lost in thought as the dream, or whatever it had been, played in her head, Sedah lay down on the bed to think. Her family's lives, and perhaps the world, might very well depend on it.

22

It had had been several days since Melam had given up trying to sleep like a normal human. He had tried at first, thinking that the human body he inhabited may need it. After numerous nights of doing nothing but tossing and turning, but seeing no ill effects to his body, Melam had quit trying.

On the balcony that was attached to Sedah's room, he leaned his chair against the wall, with his feet on the railing as he stared out at the ocean. He missed Sedah more than he ever thought he would. He hadn't even known her that long, and yet need pulled at his heart without remorse. He took his frustrations out with the girls, training them as often as possible. All three of them seemed to be lost without Sedah there. There was a somber mood about the house, no one really laughing or joking, as if they were afraid something bad would happen if they did. Caprika and Amy seemed to need the physical exertion almost as much as he did.

Melam found himself staring at the ocean every night, not really knowing why, but knowing that it made him feel closer to her somehow—as if, by sheer force of will, he could get her to come back to the surface faster. He couldn't let himself dwell on what she was doing down there, for fear that his own worry, or even anger, would get the best of him and he would go down there and get her prematurely. When he had said as much to her mother, her sudden fear and quickness to stop him had told him that the agreement was more than they all had been told. But what was being left out? Would his mother or grandmother actually come clean and tell him if it was something terrible? The fact that his family was keeping secrets from him was what currently had him wide awake.

He considered calling one of them to him but thought better of it as something rose out of the water, taking on more and more of a humanoid shape as it emerged, but bigger than any human. Without thinking, Melam was up, jumping over the third story balcony to the sand below. As he ran, he materialized a sword, his instincts finally alerting him that it wasn't Sedah.

As the shape rose from the water, it solidified into a man with a full black beard and mustache that went down to his collarbone. Though he looked to be in his mid-forties, this man was fit as a lumberjack, making Melam question his own strength. The water solidified into a loin cloth as the man's foot first touched the sand. An immense power, pure and raw, rolled off him like the waves he had just surfaced from, crashing against Melam with the intensity of the ocean itself. With each step, the man's power buffeted Melam, until he was forced to his knees in front of the being. This was such a powerful God that, instead of bothering with words, the man shoved his message directly into Melam's mind, using the old language. Had Melam been anyone else, he wouldn't have been able to translate.

"There is one who does not belong in my realm. I have been told you have knowledge of this." The man God pushed more power on Melam, trying to force a mental response.

"May I ask who I have the honor of kneeling before?" Melam gasped between the waves of power.

Seeming to finally realize notice the effect his power was having on Melam, the God took a deep breath, pulling some of his power back within him, allowing Melam to breathe. "I am Ophion, and you are Melam, my sister's son."

Feeling at a disadvantage, Melam simply nodded. He had just gotten his earlier question answered. Slowly, Melam stood, keeping his eyes downcast out of respect. Ophion was his uncle. He had been overthrown from his honorable post as ruler of Olympos by his younger brother, Kronus, the God of Destructive Time.

"You must get her out of my dominion," Ophion stated plainly.

"I did not want her to go in the first place. I entered the picture after the deal had been struck between Hades and Poseidon. Have you spoken to The Ether?" Melam asked. He had no idea if his uncle had any connections, or the proper seeds that were needed, to contact or travel back to their true home.

"I have asked for her to come, but she only comes in dreams to tell me that it must happen this way," Ophion growled in frustration.

"I have no authority to get her out of your realm at this time, but she is due back in three days' time. She has been there to learn their ways. Afterward, it will be Poseidon's decision if she will be a wife or servant. I can try, but I am not sure that I can stop this. She has been in your water for a small while now. What has changed to make you want her out now?" Melam asked as the thought finally occurred to him.

Ophion shuffled his feet in the sand, making Melam look the old God in the eyes.

"What's happened?"

Ophion sighed. "She has gained a new power and I am afraid of what it means."

"What power?" Melam's eyes widened.

"She can either harness an ancient power, or she can see alternate futures. I am not quite sure which. I could feel her presence in my realm, and then I couldn't. I went to investigate and saw her holding an eternal ball of light."

"Okay, all paranormals can hold them."

"Yes, but she was not simply looking into another realm. If that were the case, her presence would have still been in this realm. Wherever she was, her soul, her power, everything other than her body had gone there. When I tried to follow, I was locked out, which—"

"Should be impossible," Melam finished. "Then what?" He stood slowly, allowing it all to sink in.

☙❧

MORNING CAME TOO EARLY AS SEDAH SLOWLY GOT UP AND let Navue dress her for the day. She was sluggish from the lack of sleep, between her burned hand and reliving the vision over and over. It felt like too much work to try and function or care about the day. When Tamil came to get her for breakfast, she playfully tried to get Sedah to let her see her hand, which had healed, and also attempted to cheer her up, which seemed to do nothing but aggravate Sedah. After Sedah sent her away, Tamil told her brother, who seemed to take it on himself to try and cheer her up.

It was a gorgeous day, as far as underwater dwelling went. Triton took her to the stables, where they went on a ride around town and then out into the far pastures. He surprised her with a picnic lunch that he had arranged to have set up for them by the time they arrived. They sat on a hill that was high enough that it overlooked the town as well as the castle.

Sedah smiled as she watched the rays of sun come through the water, hit the castle, and reflect off the gold and pearls adorning it, turning the corral decor into a riot of color, casting rainbow waves over the town.

"Aw, I see that color makes you smile," Triton guessed. He loved watching the way her face moved as she watched the beauty that was his kingdom. He had always loved his home, but looking at it through her eyes, he saw it in a different light.

She had a way of bringing those around her to her level. Triton had to admit that the male had been right that first night. Triton had been arrogant and expected everything to happen when he decreed it so.

He had expected her to be as pretentious and as entitled as his sisters were, being given everything, and yet still expecting everything. Sedah made him want to be a better person, instead of behaving like his family. He had plenty to offer her, but he had no idea where to go from there.

"How have you enjoyed your stay with us? Apart from my mother and some of my sisters, that is," he quickly amended when she turned to him with a frown. Her face smoothed back into a small smile at his attempt to catch himself.

"It has been okay, I guess. Some things and some days were definitely better than others." She giggled lightly. "You and Tamil getting me out of the palace helped a lot. Being able to go to the surface to recharge helped give me the energy necessary to be able to deal with them better. And Navue is nice. She reminds me a lot of my maidservant in the Underworld."

"Do you think you'll be happy to come here in the winter? When the sun is not as bright, and the moods are not as warm?" Triton searched her face for a hint of what she might say.

"Triton, it's beautiful here, and I would be happy to see

the three of you. But no sun means no energy. I would be a sitting duck when it comes to fighting off your family's power. I will come if you force me, but I miss my friends, and I want to see them when I'm off as well. I'm hoping there's some way that you can stay on land, or just visit daily in order for us to keep our word and make this work. I'm more like my mother than my father. I need sunlight for the energy to fight off others' powers. And I want land, not water. That will be true no matter who I'm with or where I am." She looked at him with a mixture of hope, and sadness, on her face. After a minute, she looked down into her lap contemplatively.

As much as he hated that she felt that way, he was glad she could be honest with him. He was surprised that, instead of being mad that she didn't want to come back, he felt honor that she would try if he asked, in order to keep everyone happy, even at the cost of her own safety. If he was not willing to budge at all, or meet her halfway in order to keep to their parents' agreement, he would prove to her that he really was as bad as she had first thought. He'd never thought that he could like someone that was being forced upon him, but he found himself wanting to make her happy, if for no other reason than to see her beautiful smile.

"I'll talk to my father about setting something up so that we can stay on land and near your friends when you return." Triton reached out and put a finger under Sedah's chin to get her to look at him and see his resolve. "I'm sure there is something that can be done. I'd like your friends to get to know me for more than the jerk I was to them the first night we all met." He smiled in what he hoped was a reassuring manner.

That seemed to ease some of the tension that he hadn't realized was there before. They ate in a peaceful silence before getting back on their hippocampi. Once they had the animals rubbed down and settled with food, the two strolled along the streets, admiring things they came across. Triton had no idea what possessed him, but he felt like a king when he offered her his left arm as they left a shop, and she looked at him in surprise, before smiling as she placed her arm there.

She denied letting him buy her some things, having to remind him that certain items wouldn't survive a trip to the surface. He managed to talk her into a beautiful teal colored coral necklace and a matching shell hair adornment.

They tried their best to ignore all the glares, stares, or smiles sent their way as they enjoyed one another's company for perhaps the first real time since Sedah had arrived. Now that the tension and the expectations had been resolved, they were able to chat and laugh together like they had known each other forever. They ran into Tamil in a dress shop that had the newest collection of gowns designed specifically to flow with the customer's tail like a waterfall. The three entered the castle just in time for dinner, the girls taking their purchases to their rooms before joining Triton again.

⚜

THE TRIO WALKED INTO THE GRAND DINING ROOM, TAKING their usual seats near Poseidon.

"So, my dear, are you excited to get back on dry land for a little while?" Poseidon asked as their first course was being set down. Sedah looked at him and smiled.

"No dear, she wants to stay down here and have my only son all to herself so that she can rule two realms and take over, isn't that right dear?" Amphitrite asked sweetly. She smiled slightly as her daughters that had come to dine with them that night gasped, turning with fear and shock towards their father and his dumbfounded guest.

"What? N-n-no! That's not what I want at all!" Sedah stuttered as she looked quickly from her aunt to her uncle to make sure he did not believe that. She was relieved to see shock on Triton and Tamil's faces, as well.

"What are you talking about dear? We are immortal, and Sedah here is leaving tomorrow to be on land. Are you afraid that she might take your spot and the people will like her as Queen better?" Poseidon smiled, turning to look at Sedah. "Don't worry dear, she just found out that you actually had some fun while you were here. Not everyone has been thrilled that there was a visitor of such power in the realm, but I'm sure no one believes that you are here to overthrow us, or anything so ridiculous." He placed his right hand over her left, which was clutching the tablecloth.

He poured love energy into her to let her through the touch. Sedah looked at him, noting that while he may have been sending love energy to her, his moody nature had the waters moving a little faster, his long brown beard and mustache flowing with the water.

Sedah caught the glare he shot his wife. The promise of retribution in his eyes had her sitting a little stiffer in her seat. Without warning, she threw down her napkin and stood, storming off without a word.

"I hope all is well until we see you next time. Enjoy the rest of your night." He stood, kissed both Sedah and Tamil on the top of their heads and exited the hall.

The rest of the dinner was eaten in relative silence, as none of the other daughters spokw loudly enough for Sedah, Tamil, or Triton to overhear them. The three left after the second course was served, skipping dessert to spend more time together. They walked in the garden, Triton escorting each of them on an arm. Triton and Sedah explained their plan for the next time Sedah would come 'visit,' which was when the decision would be made. Tamil told them emphatically that she would help get their father to agree, especially given the scene at dinner, adding that Triton and Sedah needed to get to know one another better without all the added drama of their family.

Although Sedah was happy there hadn't been more problems with the family, she wanted to get back home. She missed her friends. She missed Melam. She felt bad that she hadn't thought about them more, but the weird dream, or whatever it was that she'd had, was something that had taken over her mind and clouded over everything in the days that followed.

Calling it a night, Triton walked the girls back to Sedah's room, as the girls had decided to stay together for Sedah's last night in the castle. Tamil went in the room ahead of them, turning and grabbing the door. Sedah and Triton laughed at the encouraging look and the kissing noises as she shut the door on them.

"I guess this is where I have to tell you goodbye." Triton took her hands in his, holding them between their bodies as his thumbs rubbed the tops of her hands. Sedah glanced at them for a moment before looking up at him.

"Not goodbye. You are going to take me home tomorrow, right?" she asked him with a slight frown. The thought of him staying behind hadn't occurred to her before now.

Triton was a good-looking young man. With his piercing blue eyes, long curly brown hair, and full lips, he would make some woman happy one day—but he didn't make her heart flutter. Although she had grown fond of him over her time there, which she would have never expected, their realms made them much too different to ever be able to meet halfway.

"I want to, but I'm not sure I could leave you without doing something that might get me killed by that guy that is staying with you girls. I don't want to start a war between families and risk a bloodbath because one of our sides gets mad and breaks off the deal." It was Triton's turn to look down at their combined hands.

"Well we don't want that, for sure. Are you saying that you won't be able to stop yourself from kissing me, and Melam might try to kill you?" She watched him nod in agreement. She liked Triton, so maybe if she let herself quit thinking so much, she might not feel so confused. While she wanted to believe that Melam had kissed her out of desire, she couldn't be sure.

"When he kissed you, just so that I wouldn't need to, in order to help you breathe under water, I wanted to as well. I thought he was denying me my right. At the time, it was out of arrogance. Before you, I never bothered to ask, or even hesitate when I wanted something. Now . . . I just want to know what you taste like, but I don't want to take anything you don't want to give. It's odd how much you've changed me in only two weeks." He let go of her left hand and framed her face with his right. He smiled when she leaned into his hand and looked up at him.

"I am not going to be mad if you kiss me, as long as you promise that it won't seal me here, or to you, forever." She looked into his eyes, showing him how much she was trusting him.

৩৯৫৩

NOT ONE TO QUESTION AN UNEXPECTED GIFT, TRITON took his chance. He pulled her to him with vigor, turning her so that her back was pressed against the wall, next to the bedroom. He tried to be gentle, guessing from where her home realm was, that she had probably only been kissed the one other time, but it took all his willpower. He waited for her to get comfortable with his lips and open hers a little more, before he pressed harder, teasing her lips with his tongue. With her gasp, he plunged in, exploring her taste, in case he never got this chance again. He pulled her closer as she wrapped her hands around his neck, almost moaning from the feel of her pressed willingly against him.

She tasted of honey and fire, an earthy combination that should not go together and be so addictive. The sweetness, followed by the smoky flavor was a taste he would never forget, and probably always crave. Fearing that he would not be able to keep himself in check for much longer and remain a gentleman, Triton pulled away with a groan, looking down at her. Sedah smiled up at him as he pulled their bodies apart and put some distance between them.

"Thank you for allowing me that," Triton breathed with a huge grin on his face. It wasn't the cocky smile he'd perfected over the years, but one of genuine happiness.

"Well, we wouldn't want you starting a war, would we?" She returned with a grin. Triton stepped forward and opened the bedroom door for her.

"No, I guess we would not." He told her as she passed him, her chest brushing against his arm slightly. As soon as she entered, he shut the door behind her and headed to his room at a brisk pace, ready for a cold bath or a hard workout.

◈❈◈

CAPRIKA AND AMY SAT AT THE KITCHEN BAR WHILE MELAM made them their breakfast. Their position allowed the girls to see out the dining room sliding glass door, so they would know the second that Sedah arrived on land. As much as Melam wanted to be out there on the beach waiting for her, he was trying to keep them calm so he could force himself to remain calm as well.

On the outside, he was fine. On the inside, he was anything but. He was excited to see her, yet afraid of what her new powers would allow her to see. He had no idea what her mood would be when she returned, and since she was surely not still changing colors by mood, he wouldn't be able to tell. Just because the *true* king of the sea wanted her out of his domain, didn't mean that she couldn't have enjoyed her time while she was down there. Had she fallen in love with Triton or some other merman while she was at the palace?

The thought had his blood boiling and his eyes changing with the power fighting to get out and do damage. He set down the skillet, snapping the handle by accident. Both girls raised their eyebrows at him as he looked up at them in surprise.

"Tense much?" Caprika smiled slightly.

Amy's grin was enormous, "Need me to cook breakfast? I can, if you're too wound up."

"I'm fine, I just got lost in my head and forgot to reserve myself," he told them, hoping they wouldn't call him out on his bullshit. They were all ready and getting antsy for their girl to come home, and yet worried. Melam had not kept what Ophion had told him a secret from them, just what he was. It took a little bit of a history lesson, of how there could be ethereal light in the ocean and the use of the eternal flame under water, but in the end, they had been as shocked as he was. To his knowledge, no one, god, goddess, or anyone else, had ever done anything even remotely close to what Sedah had done. He'd wanted to ask Persephone, but didn't want to worry her, and hadn't gotten any replies from his mother or grandmother when he had called to them either.

A shimmer of something caught his eye as Caprika and Amy both bounded up fast enough to knock over their chairs. "She's here!" They screamed as they ran out the door.

Melam had just enough presence of mind to turn off the burners before running behind them, quickly overtaking them in his need to see her again. The second she had seen the girls, Sedah had also started to run, but redirected her path when she saw Melam coming. They collided with such force, their powers created a wave that sent the sand outward, almost spraying Amy and Caprika, who came to a grinding halt, squealing as they fell to the ground, at the sight of the sand wave coming at them. Melam embraced Sedah, twirling her around a few times before setting her back on her feet, pushing her hair back, smiling and talking to her. While they greeted each other, Sedah stood so she could see the water in her periphery.

CAPRIKA NUDGED AMY AND POINTED TOWARD THE OCEAN with her head. On the shoreline, Triton stood, a sad smile on his face. When he saw the two girls looking, he threw up a hand in greeting before turning and calmly walking back into the sea, disappearing under the waves. Sedah's heart sank, realizing that Triton had watched her greet Melam with a passion she'd never have for him, and had left without a farewell.

Getting up, the girls ran to the couple who began to turn towards the house. Sedah smiled and answered when they actually asked a question that wasn't rhetorical, giving hug after hug, glad she was finally back home.

Not once did Melam let go of Sedah. The three girls were so happy to see one another that they didn't even notice. Sedah seemed to be oblivious to the fact that Melam took her hand back into his every chance he got. He knew it made no sense, but he needed to feel her, to know that she was real, that she was finally back. Going so long without her had made him realize a few things, even though he had no idea what he was going to do with those realizations.

"Are you hungry? Melam was attempting to cook us some breakfast." Amy asked as they reentered the house.

"And failing miserably!" Caprika laughed as the girls went to sit at the bar. Sedah followed Melam around to the stove, since he still had possession of her hand. She looked up at him and smiled. She was not about to tell him that that was exactly what she had been hoping for. Trying her luck, she gradually pulled her hand out of his, smiling at him when he looked down at her, a hurt look on his face. Slowly, she let her nails skim his stomach as she wrapped both arms around his waist and laid her head on his chest as she looked to gauge his reaction. His smile could have lit the sky as bright as the sun.

"Don't listen to them, I'm sure you were doing fine under the circumstances. Breakfast does sound nice though."

Melam slid away from her just enough to grab her waist, eliciting a squeal. She grabbed at his shoulders as he sat her down on the counter, beside the stove.

"I'm afraid they're right." Melam laughed lightly, picking up the bent frying pan to show her, causing her to laugh also. "I was a little distracted thinking about all the fun that you might have been having without us." He tried to keep his voice as upbeat as possible instead of letting his worry and jealousy come through.

Sedah frowned slightly, before having to direct her attention to the girls as they started asking questions about everything she had done while she had been there, and about what Poseidon and the castle were like. Sedah answered them all, glad that they never mentioned Triton, or the Queen.

Melam listened while he cooked them breakfast, correctly this time, and plated it all out for them. While he was glad that she didn't have too much trouble while she was there, there had to be some reason that she had been able to go into another realm, instead of just viewing it. He would need to find out later what had caused her to do it, or if someone else had helped her get there. Either way, he was sure he would have to tell The Ether, if she ever decided to answer his calls.

Not sure what to do, but sure that they all wanted to spend the day with her, they took turns picking out movies to watch so that they could have just one day of quality time together. None of them were naive enough to believe that they had discussed everything, but they all seemed to be in silent agreement that the heavier topics could wait a day.

AMPHITRITE STOOD ON THE SHORE, USING HER SONAR ability to see inside the structure the girl had gone into. They all seemed so happy, like the demon child had not just spent two weeks creating chaos in Amphitrite's realm. She needed to come up with a plan. This slip of a girl was not about to dethrone her, or steal her children from her, least of all her only son.

❧ 23 ❧

He felt like it might kill him, but Melam let the night progress and Sedah go to her bedroom once they all started falling asleep on the couch. He said goodnight to them and went to his room. As usual, he went straight to the balcony and lay down on the chaise lounge. He didn't particularly want to see the ocean and be reminded where Sedah had been for two weeks, but the breeze was nice and helped to clear his head.

Deciding to meditate, Melam closed his eyes and let the rhythmic sound of the Atlantic Ocean take him away. Sedah might have gone into an entirely different realm without help. She also could have developed feelings for a Mer person. The problem was, Ophion didn't want her down there, and Melam had no way to stop her without breaking a deal that had been set up with only Poseidon and Hades knowing the important details.

Concentrating, he let himself swim the hereafter to find out what the future would look like if the deal was broken. Unlike what Sedah had done, which was to jump her soul into an alternate future, most powerful Gods could see what their choices would bring them by *looking* into the future based on their decision, receiving the most likely outcomes. With himself and Ava'ans, their outcomes included what others would do, so that their view would not only be likely, but near exact. Their power used The Ether herself to channel into the people involved and look at their souls to see what they would do, to get a nearly precise outcome.

What he saw was screaming, shouting, and a whole lot of chaos on the beach he'd just been staring at. He saw Caprika, Amy, Sedah, Triton, Persephone, Hades, Poseidon, Amphitrite, Lexur, Sephir, and Melinoe. Hades and Poseidon were fighting to the death, as were Persephone and Amphitrite. Lexur held a lifeless Melinoe while Sephir held Sedah to his chest, sobbing as he watched his parents fight. Amy and Caprika sat beside Lexur sobbing over Sedah. Not seeing himself, he had to assume he was dead as well, and had turned to energy, as his kind did.

Upset, Melam was about to try to replay the entire scene when he felt something warm on his lips. Something in his present. Taking a deep breath in, Melam opened his eyes to see Sedah sitting on the edge of the lounge chair staring at him, a confused look on her face.

"Sorry, I must have fallen asleep. Did you need me?" he asked.

"I'm just trying to figure something out and it is keeping me awake. I was hoping you could help me." She blushed slightly.

"Sure, what is it?" Melam asked. He pulled her hand into his, unable to stand the lack of contact.

"I just wanted to know if you kissed me on the beach before I left because you didn't want Triton to do it." She let out a breath, glad to have gotten that out without her voice shaking.

"Yes, I did," he answered. He watched her, trying to gauge

the look on her face. He grinned when she began to get up. She let out a slight squeal when he pulled her back down. Not giving her a chance, he pulled her to him and kissed her with everything he had.

First, their lips were simply pressed together. When she realized what he had done, she opened her mouth slightly, allowing him to turn his head and plunge his tongue in. He took time exploring her mouth, moving his head this way and that, taking her in like he was starving for air. It was not meant to be a beautiful kiss like he had seen done in the movies. This was a soul stamping kiss, meant to show her what hadn't been able to say with words.

He had to change the fate that he had seen. They would not be two star-crossed lovers that died in the end like Romeo and Juliet. He couldn't tell the others, for that was not the way fate was done, but he could do everything in his power to make sure the one he'd seen wouldn't happen.

Grudgingly, Melam slowed down the kiss, wanting to give her time to come back to her senses as well. They were cuddled on the chaise, with her in his arms, though Melam had no recollection of how they had gotten into that part position.

"Does that answer the real question that you had?" He smiled as he tucked her head into the crook of his arm where she could look up at him.

"Yes, I guess it does," Sedah said as she held onto him. So, he hadn't kissed her just to allow her to breath under water. He had done it because he cared for her and hadn't wanted Triton to do it. She felt bad about having kissed Triton. There was no way she would ever tell anyone about that. Melam kissed her like he couldn't live without her, and the tingles that she got from him made her heart soar. Snuggling into him, she finally drifted off to sleep.

Melam watched her drift away, happier than before that

he couldn't sleep, so he wouldn't miss one moment of this wonderful feeling. Having her pressed against him, so trusting, made his heart soar. Feeling a familiar presence, he lifted his head off Sedah's and looked to the right, to the person leaning against the balcony railing.

"You know both of you will just end up with your hearts broken, right?" his mother said, her face sad as she looked at him. "Her destiny is not linked with yours, and yet you persist in making it so."

"What am I supposed to do then, mother? You sent me to the forest to wait. I did what I was asked. I know she is the daughter of Hades. I know there is some kind of deal that her father entered with Poseidon, which is why she had to go off with Fish Boy for a few weeks. But how do you expect me to keep protecting her and our fates not intertwine?"

"I told you not to get too close to her. She was never a mission to you. You were sent there to learn the humans' ways, so I could use you later with the chosen one and to save the human race when the time came. That was all you were here for! The deal and the girl were never meant to be part of your mission."

"Well it became that when Kohl set his sights and his depraved mind on her. You know what would have happened if I hadn't stepped in," Melam reminded her.

"Yes," Rhea sighed, looking down for a moment. "I am grateful that you stepped in when you did in that one instance. But now, you need to back off. What you see is just the beginning. I might have lost one son already Melam, we don't know. Please do not make me lose another," She pleaded. While his mother still held out hope that Phail would come home one day, Melam had long ago resigned himself to the fact that he may never know what truly happened to his older brother.

Slowly sliding out of Sedah's embrace, Melam stood and

walked over to his mother. Taking her hands, he used their language to let her know he meant it.

"*Ma, le ta ten i meve, ia le vole tsra lele ple vole tib ba fe bas meve,*" he told her while looking her directly in the eyes. What he had told her was, "*Mother, I am not a child, and I would do nothing that would take me from my child,*" and he meant it.

Melam had no plans to make his child an orphan. His wife had died in battle right after she had given birth, and Skylu would not lose her father as well, if he could help it.

"What do you know about the reason behind the deal anyway? Or about what Sedah is capable of doing, as far as her powers go, for that matter? I spoke with Ophion and he—"

"Your uncle came to see you?" Rhea looked around quickly. "What did he want? Did he know who you were?" she asked frantically, the questions coming in quick succession.

"Yes. To tell me something disturbing, and frankly I don't care, but yes, he knew me," he answered.

"What was disturbing, other than a Titan God coming out of the ocean, which he promised never to do again, in return for not going to Tartarus?"

"Sedah's soul went into another realm while she was at Poseidon's palace. She touched a ball that held eternal fire, causing time to stop for them. It sent her into a realm that even Ophion couldn't follow." He waited for what he said to sink in.

"There are only a few that could have made that happen. And she must have been aided, because there's no way she could possess that much power. It just isn't possible." Rhea stared past Melam, at the girl asleep behind him. "I am going to go investigate what you have told me and what it could mean. Just be careful *raher*," she told her son. Giving him a long hug, she disappeared as soon as they moved apart.

Not knowing what else to do, Melam turned, taking the

spot his *meve* had just vacated. He watched Sedah sleeping, a small smile upon her face.

Seeing her shiver, Melam picked her up and moved her to his bed, using his power to move the sheets.

He was glad he'd finally gotten a chance to talk to his mother, but she hadn't answered any of his questions. Instead, she'd seen fit to warn him, again, not to get too close to Sedah. The problem was, even knowing from the start that he should keep his distance, it was a lost cause that had no hope of ever succeeding.

❧

HAVING GOTTEN USED TO A ROUTINE, AMY AND CAPRIKA went to grab Sedah for their morning run and workout on the beach. She had been back about a month, so when they didn't find her in her room, they went on a search through the entire house. Once they reached the balcony in the upstairs sitting room that faced the beach, they saw her and Melam on the beach, sitting together in the sand.

Not wanting to interrupt them, the girls decided to go for their jog through downtown Savannah since it was still early enough that there were very few people, other than vendors, out yet. When they got back, Melam had already cooked breakfast for them. As much as he didn't want to leave Sedah, he needed to get supplies for the house, and the girls wanted to go shopping for some things on their own. With no reasonable argument, he walked with them into town and they set a time and place for them all to meet back up.

"So, now that it is *finally* just us, what were Triton and his family really like?" Amy asked as they entered the first store.

"At first, he was as stuck up as you all said he was. I don't really know what changed, but pretty quickly, he came around and was my constant companion whenever I didn't have his sister Tamil or my maidservant Navue around. It was almost always the three of us, and they both protected me against their mother, and gave me reasons to be out of the castle a lot so that I could stay out of the way of their sisters," she told her friends.

Caprika thought for a minute. "How mean was the queen?" Caprika wondered if they would have issues with Amphitrite trying to hurt Sedah the next time that she went to the palace, for good.

"She didn't come to any of the meals for the first few days, until Poseidon made her. And then she was particularly nasty on the last night, even going so far as to accuse me of wanting to steal Triton to my side in order to take over and rule two realms," she told them, watching their shocked faces. "Poseidon was nice to me the entire visit though."

"While she showed her true colors," Caprika commented. Sedah nodded her head in agreement.

"So now that you have met the man that can become a thousand men, as Triton is called, do you still like Melam more, or do you have feelings for Triton now?" Amy asked. Caprika knew what she had seen when Triton had been on land, but there wasn't said about the man in the sea, and it had her wondering how Sedah really felt about the Mer Prince.

SEDAH THOUGHT BACK TO THAT MORNING. AFTER HAVING fallen asleep on the balcony outside Melam's bedroom, Sedah had woken up under the covers, in his bed, with him holding out a cup of cocoa to her. Sitting up, she had taken a sip before he had asked her to come watch the sun rise with him.

As they had sat there in the sand, touching at the hip, he had wrapped his arm low around her torso, so that she could lean into him and lay her head against his strong arm. She wasn't sure, but she had felt a glow seem to form around them, keeping the wind and flying sand from bothering them. She assumed Melam had put up a shield. The morning had been perfect, and one that she knew she would never forget, no matter what happened next in her life.

"I like them both, but Triton had to try to become someone that I would like. Melam has just been himself from the beginning. Even though I know less about him than I do Triton, I feel something with Melam that I just don't with Triton. I get all tingly . . . and nervous . . . and all these things I have no words for. At least, I have nothing to compare them to, so I have no idea what to call them."

Caprika looked past Sedah to Amy, who was all smiles. While she wished she could just be happy that Sedah was happy, she still worried. She still knew next to nothing about Melam, but she felt like the two would make a good couple and knew he would treat Sedah the way she deserved. The question was, what became of the deal if Sedah did in fact find love before the year was up? Not knowing the answer clouded the happiness Caprika had for her friend and her situation.

🐉

SITTING ON THE BEACH, TRYING TO CONTACT HIS FAMILY TO see if they could tell him anything useful, Melam didn't even notice that someone had approached him until sand hit his legs. Startled out of his trance, Melam reached under the sand, materializing his sword from the ether, ready for battle as he stood. Seeing the person tripping backward in their haste to stay out of swinging range, Melam recognized who had disturbed him.

"Sephir? I could have killed you! What were you thinking?" Melam almost yelled as he dropped his sword to the sand, letting it melt away to become sand itself.

Sephir watched, eyes widening as the metal broke apart to become sand like it was a natural part of life. "Now that was cool, how did you do that?" he pointed to where the sword had been.

"Don't worry about that, why are you here?" Melam asked. The timing seemed too odd to be random after being unable to reach his mother or The Ether.

"I just wanted to see my sister. I heard mom and dad fighting about how mom didn't like that Sedah was down there with Amphitrite, and dad told her to calm down because Sedah was back home. So, I finished my duties and came as soon as I could. I was curious to see how she fared," Sephir told him. "You were so out of it, you didn't hear me call your name. You pulled a sword on me, but I'm just here to see my baby sister."

The men were walking into the house when they heard a squeal come from upstairs about a second before Sedah was jumping the second story railing of the hallway, landing in the middle of the living room floor and rushing to her brother to tackle him with a hug.

Sephir joined them for dinner, making fun of anything and anyone that Sedah mentioned when he asked her anything about her time "down under." When Sephir started settling in for the night, talking to Sedah on the couch, Melam decided it was time for him to try and sleep. He hoped he would be able to have some dreams that would give him the guidance his family wasn't.

Sleep came, but without dreams. Which was probably why he woke up easily to the slight squeak of his door opening hesitantly a few hours after the others had gone to bed.

Without looking, he knew who it was. Holding out his

right arm to her, he turned his head to Sedah. While she usually wore pajama pants and a short sleeve shirt, the balmy weather, which promised rain later, had driven her to shorts and a tank top. Trying to keep his mind on anything other than all that bare, pale, flawless skin, Melam tried to still his mind and just enjoy her presence.

Smiling shyly, Sedah crawled up on the top of the bed with Melam, cuddling up to him instantly. Pulling her closer to him, they drifted off to sleep without a word. Seeming to become a pattern, Melam came awake to a familiar presence in the room with them. Looking around, he saw Persephone leaning against one of the canopy bed's post. She looked down with a sad smile on her face at her daughter, before staring at Melam for a full three seconds before blinking out of the room. He felt like she was trying to tell him something, but he had no time to figure it out. Sedah gasped, sitting up and looking around the room, searching for something.

"Where is she? I felt her, I know I did! Where's mom?" She got up, running out to the balcony to look around for her mother, not even realizing, or caring, that it was pouring outside.

Slowly following her, Melam wrapped his arms around her, just as she turned her face into his chest and began to cry. Without a word, he walked her the three steps back inside, grabbing a blanket off the back of the chair. He quickly wrapped it around her before he could see anything tempting.

Looking up at him, she felt desperate to be with him all of a sudden. She was now determined to take control of her life, instead of always being the one instructed. Without thought Sedah threw her arms around Melam's neck, letting the blanket fall as she kissed him with every ounce of love she felt for him. She poured every feeling she had into that inexperienced kiss, determined to say, without words, what she had been too cowardly to say to him when she had first come to his room that night. She'd had every intention of waking him up and telling him how she felt, in hopes that he would tell her he felt the same way, but he put his arm out, and his smile made all coherent thought fly out the window. She was now determined to take control of her life, instead of always being the one instructed.

Emotions soaring, she wanted him to know how she felt, and though she had no experience, she would show him. His hands moved up her hips. Arms wrapped around him, she pulled him toward the bed.

When he realized what she was doing, he broke away from her lips to look her in the eyes, searching. "Sedah, baby, are you sure about this?"

"I want to be with you. You said you kissed me because you didn't want me to be with another, so this is me giving myself to you," she said, looking him in the eyes as he stared back into hers, both looking for some sort of clue as to what was going on in the other's head. When he said nothing, she pulled him back down, reclaiming his lips. When she opened her mouth at his tongue's query, he was done for.

In a fury of motion, all she could do was hold on as Melam grabbed her ass in both hands and hoisted her up before taking her to the bed. She wrapped her legs around him, forcing him to come down with her when he laid her down, his body flush on top of hers. Instead of retaining her mouth as she thought he would, he began to kiss a trail, nibbling every so often, to make her jump. He went agonizingly slow as he kissed from her mouth to her ear, then back to her nose before going down to her chin and lower to her neck.

Her hands made scratches on his back when he did something that she particularly liked, like the nibbling of her ear, the side of her neck, and her collarbone. His hands started at her navel, snaking up her body to her small but perfectly rounded breasts, swallowing her gasp of surprise with his mouth when he pinched her areola slightly. Her back arched, and her body ached below as she felt him grow against her.

Sedah wasn't so innocent that she didn't know that Melam was turned on. She knew by the hard bulge in his pajama pants, which that was causing delicious heat within her. She'd had teachers give her classes on sex education, but she had never been told about the aches her body would have, the feel of someone pressed against her like a second skin. The combination of all of these felt like being drunk on mead for the first time.

Melam caught himself while he was grinding against her perfect body. Here he was, millennia old, and he was seducing an innocent as if he were a horny teenager again. Feeling like a bucket of cold water had been poured on him, Melam detached his limbs and mouth from her and sat back on his legs, effectively kneeling on the bed with her beautiful body between his thighs. He looked down at her as she stared back at him, confusion written clearly on her face. He felt like a complete ass for having taken advantage of her when she was obviously emotional. It would be so easy to take her right now, but he would hate himself in the morning.

"What's wrong?" she asked, trying to pull him back down to her. When she couldn't, she sat up with her palms behind her to prop her up.

"I don't want to take advantage of you. You're too special, and I don't want you to think I'm making love to you so that you will choose me over him. My mother was right. You need to make this decision on your own, and me being here is just swaying that unfairly," he told her, being as honest as he could be.

"What if this is what I want? What if I have already chosen you, and this is my way of showing you that? I have no idea what I am doing, but I trust that you do." She placed her right hand flat on his naked chest.

"Then believe that the time will come for us. If you really trust me, then know this." He sat down with his legs crossed, and pulled her to him, to holding her in his arms as he looked deeply in her eyes. "I am in love with you Sedah, Princess of the Dominion of Hades. When the time is right, we will come together, and it will be beautiful. But I don't want an ounce of doubt, from you or from others, about how true or untainted your feelings are." Every word, though truthful, was pulled from him as if he were willingly ripping up his soul. He might have been throwing away his only chance to be with her, but he was determined to see things through to the very end. He could not afford for his mind to be clouded by thoughts of them being together.

Hearing his declaration, Sedah readjusted herself so that she sat in his lap with her legs wrapped around him. Although she hated what he'd said, he'd not only said that he loved her, but had proven it by not swaying her with sex. She kissed him slowly, and tenderly, to show him that she understood, as tears flowed freely down her cheeks. She wanted to be mad at him, but she couldn't. She'd never been shown the kind of love that he'd given her since they'd first met. Pulling away slowly, Sedah lay back down on the bed, allowing Melam to pull the covers over her, while he stayed on top of them, so that neither would be tempted to start where they had left off in the middle of the night.

❦ 24 ❦

Sensing his way along the rooms a little before dawn, Sephir found his way to Melam's room, opening the door slowly. Seeing his sister, he took in the view of how Melam protectively cuddled her, even in sleep. He smiled as he gently woke her up with a zing of energy between them. As she awoke, he asked her if she would take a walk with him on the beach before everyone else woke up. With a drowsy nod, she agreed, and he left so that she could go to her room and dress.

She found him waiting downstairs, arms outstretched, waiting for her to come to him so he could give her a big hug. Putting his arm around her shoulder, they started by walking around town, Sedah pointing out her favorite shops as they passed. At the end of town, they reached the beach, circling back toward their house. The wind whipping at their clothes, Sedah told her brother about Melam, and her visit to the golden castle, and that, even with Triton's attitude change, how she still cared for Melam more.

Without warning, a bolt of ice flew in front of Sedah, grazing her arm, before hitting her brother in his left side, taking him to the ground. Screaming, Sedah gaped at her brother writhing on the sand before taking a defensive stance over him and scanning the area for the source of the attack. For several moments, she could see nothing. Then, a translucent figure of a woman emerged from the water. As it did, she could feel Melinoe and Lexur materialize behind her. Brandishing a sword in one hand and an iron baton in the other, Lexur marched up beside Sedah to face the threat.

Never taking her eyes off the water, Sedah watched the translucent shape solidify into Amphitrite in all her regal, Queen of the Seas, haughtiness. Triton was on her heels, arguing with her, trying to stop her by getting in her way.

Fully materialized, Amphitrite threw another bolt of ice towards Sedah, surprising her with a second one following in quick succession. Sedah easily used her heat to melt the spear of ice but was unaware of the bolt of electricity that continued towards her, knocking her over Melinoe, who was hunched over Sephir to protect him, and onto her haunches.

As the second spear of electric ice sliced through the air towards Lexur, Hades appeared in front of his son, grabbing the weapon out of midair and throwing it back towards her. As both she and Triton ducked, Persephone materialized directly in front of her, rearing back her arm and letting her fist fly, connecting with Amphitrite's face when she righted herself again. The force of the hit knocked her under the water as she fell on her back. She bobbed back up, looking like a drowned cat, then materialized herself back upright, dry and a safe distance away, about ten feet from where she had been. She glared at the Persephone, waiting on her next move instead of making one of her own.

Protecting his mother now, Triton got in front of her, ready to defend her if necessary. Persephone exchanged a quick look with her husband before teleporting herself over to Sedah, who was getting up, even as Amy and Caprika came running from the house and Melam materialized in front of Sedah and Persephone.

"Mom, can you help Sephir? I don't know how badly he's hurt, but it was a pretty bad hit." Sedah looked at her mother with tears in her eyes as she held onto the back of Melam until she could get her bearings.

"I can try, but I'm not sure it will work," Persephone said, teary eyed. "Melam—"

"See to him," Melam said.

Persephone hastily sank to her knees next to her son. If the prophecy was going to happen, there would be no way to save him. No matter what she wanted, she was going to lose a child.

As Melam was about to offer his assistance or perhaps address Amphitrite, he felt himself being forcefully pulled into the safety of the ether.

"*Le ta solu, bas meve,*" his mother said from behind him, putting her hand on his shoulder as they watched the scene unfold before them. It played as if it was a movie, put up on a never-ending tapestry before them.

"I am sorry? Really mother? What is going to happen that you cannot have me there? There should be nothing that *your child* cannot handle. Why are you taking me out when I can be of help?" he asked as he watched helplessly.

"I cannot stop you from going, though I wish I could. Know that, by stepping in, you have taken away any chance for her to live a normal life. If you go in, you may very well upset a very delicate balance that *needs* to play itself out here."

Melam stood there, torn between knowing that his mother usually knew what was best for everyone in the long run, and his urge to protect the first person who'd brought him true joy since his late wife. His heart ached as he watched helplessly.

HADES STARED AT AMPHITRITE WITH CONTEMPT. "WHAT has possessed you to hurt an innocent child? They have done nothing to you. What did Sedah do while she was with you that would cause you to want to hurt her? To kill her?" He let out some energy to feel for his son, trying to assess the damage without taking his eyes off the enemies. A shimmer to Amphitrite's right opened, revealing his sister, Demeter, as she stepped out of her portal from Olympus.

"I told the Queen to kill her. That she killed him is just a . . . strawberry on the dish, as the humans say." She ignored her daughter's eye roll that meant she had once again misspoken a human saying. "The only children I have ever known of are your firstborn girl and that half thing you call a daughter. Imagine my surprise when dear Amphitrite came to me, telling me of her fear that you are trying to marry off your youngest daughter to her only son. A daughter that I have never seen, much less condoned. Then, I sense that the one walking beside her is a sibling? How many more of your disgusting self have you spawned?" she asked Hades, her mouth turned up in disgust as she glanced at the children there.

"None of your damn business, seeing as you want to kill them!" Hades spat back. She had never liked Melinoe, since the girl was half light and half dark, but hating children was something that even the king of the Underworld could not stand.

"Enough of this, what did you put in your spears, Amphitrite? Nothing I do is healing him!" Persephone yelled.

"You kill my brother, and I swear to you, your son will lie at your feet by nightfall," Melinoe said in a calm voice that held a promise as she stood as defense of her mother, brother, and sister, standing in front of them, and slightly behind her father. Persephone stood up, next to her daughter, her cold, hard stare piercing into Amphitrite in agreement and determination.

A bolt of lightning crashed down between the two parties, signaling a pact had been made to the fates, with them accepting whatever Melinoe had silently offered them. Amphitrite visibly paled, turning quickly to look at her only son. He returned her gaze, equally shocked.

"Mother, I told you she was not a threat! Now look at what you have done! She loves another, so there was never any way that she would have chosen me. Part of coming into her powers was that she needs light, and air, and clear skies. She can no longer live in the dark, and she will never be forced into our darkness, conceit and hate. Let this be done. Tell her what you used, or be resigned to my death, for I will not stop any blow she sends my way," Triton told her. He'd argued his point for hours, but Amphitrite hadn't listened to a single word he had said.

Amphitrite glanced to Demeter, not knowing what to say to the angry woman. Turning to Persephone, she threw a vial into the sand at her feet. "I will not tell you what I used, but this will cure him." She turned to Demeter. "Your issue. You can fix it," she said before grabbing Triton to take him to a place she knew he'd be safe.

Triton turned to go as Melam reappeared out of nowhere, stepping through a portal that was a color pattern like nothing he had ever seen. The rainbow portal opened a few feet from Sedah, as if he'd been there with her the whole time. His sudden reappearance when he should have been protecting Sedah, who had chosen him over Triton, inexplicably angered Triton like he had never been before.

Grabbing his mother's arm, he pulled energy out of her, creating one of her poisoned ice spears, and threw it at Melam's back as he was walking to Sedah. Caprika called out, trying to use her magic of nature to throw sand in front of the spear, hoping to slow it down. A wall of sand went skyward, separating everyone's view of both the spear and the culprits.

As the sand rained down, it fell like dirty confetti over Sedah and Melam. She lay with her body leaned against Melam's side, a spear between her chest and her collarbone. His arm, which he had raised up to shield Sedah at the last second, was skewered, held in place by a second spear that continued down into Sedah's side. Everyone looked up, blasting their individual energies where Triton had just been standing, but no one remained. Amphitrite had obviously snatched him away as soon as he'd launched the spear.

Melam looked down at Sedah before turning a cold glare onto Demeter. "One of these is yours," he told her, the last word slightly slurred.

"Mom always did say to come prepared for anything." Demeter laughed with pride at her handiwork. She hadn't meant to hit Melam, but two hits with one spear was not something she was going to complain about.

Melam's knees hit the ground. He was careful even then, to protect Sedah with his body, although everyone was already rushing to their side. Hades stayed behind to give his son half the potion. Sephir's wound began to heal, only to stop short, and blacken around the edges, as if not giving Sephir the full amount had made the wound worse. Hades looked at his wife with sad eyes. With a nod from her, he gave Sephir the rest of the vial, a tear streaking down his face. Being forced to choose which child would be saved was a torture no parent wished to be faced with. Knowing it was coming, and not being able to stop it, was an even worse torture.

All Melam could do was cradle Sedah to him while Melinoe melted the spear sent from Triton. Persephone pulled out the spear her mother had thrown, throwing it back at her, only to have Demeter disappear a second before it hit her, like the coward that she was.

Getting the couple apart, Caprika helped Melam arrange Sedah in his arms where they could see each other without it causing them more pain. He held her, mostly with his good arm, looking down at her beautiful, uninjured face as she tried to keep her eyes open.

Melam wanted to ask someone to kick him in the ass for being to stupid to believe Demeter wouldn't play dirty. He had been so focused on deflecting the spear from Triton, he hadn't seen Sedah until his arm hit her, as she lunged in front of him to stop the second spear he hadn't seen coming. Everyone around them was crying, they were both dying, and there was nothing to be done for it.

"Why would you do that? Do you know how much you are worth to all these people? Don't you know what losing you will cost the world?" He spoke softly to her. He ached to touch her face, to wipe the hair and tears from her cheeks. He had tried so hard to do the right thing. He'd stayed away until he thought the threat was gone. The ocean queen had agreed to back off and was leaving. It was his fault for not considering Demeter a real threat.

"Because I figured it out. The lady in my vision wasn't talking about what would happen from one of my family members avenging my death, but of what would happen if something happened to one of yours. Who else but someone much more powerful than a god could do the things you do?" Sedah looked at Melam, hoping that he could see the enormity of love she held for him. "I love you Melam. I would rather die with you than ever live without you." She touched his face, giving it a gentle caress before it fell limp at her side as she passed out from the blood loss. Persephone fell to her knees, crying as she rubbed her daughter's arm, begging her not to go.

Melam leaned forward, placing his arm that held Sedah in the sand. He could feel whatever venom Demeter had used, slowly working its way down toward his heart. His damaged hand had gone numb almost immediately, and he could detect the burn of it working up his arm the entire time Sedah had been awake.

"Persephone." He cleared his throat, the venom beginning to make it hard to swallow. She looked up at him through her tears. "I need you to promise me that not only will you not retaliate, but that you will keep Rhea from doing so as well. Promise me by binding oath."

Persephone gasped, looking at his wound for the first time. She stared at the blood, seeing the iridescence around the wound and mixed in the blood. She looked up at him, knowing, by the common way he used her grandmother's name, that he was more than a generic Greek God.

"I so swear, sir," she said, ignoring Hades asking if she was insane off in the distance.

"Caprika," he called out as well as he could. She came running, Amy behind her. The tears ran unchecked down both of their faces. "I need you to tell my daughter that I tried, and that I am sorry. Say to her *tesir hecu ne now a kalec stri*. It means—"

"It means something you will not have someone tell her, *raher*." Rhea appeared to the left of them all, coming out through the same rainbow-colored portal Melam had come through earlier. Hades bowed his head to his mother as she walked past him, more out of habit than deference at the moment. Behind her, Gaia also emerged from the portal. Her power rippled out from her, causing everyone to gasp as they felt their every intention and thought being read.

"Mother, no," Melam could only whisper as the venom set

in. If someone would not have to tell his daughter anything, then his mother was going to step in and heal him. He would not live while Sedah died. He would not survive a second loss and come out whole.

Rhea walked over to her son, bending down beside Amy. She put her hand on the young nymph's shoulder. "You are a good friend," she said. Shocked at the sheer power she felt through the touch, Amy fell back on her ass, catching herself with her arms without ever breaking eye contact with Rhea, who continued. "Help me lay him straight." Amy and Caprika hurried to obey.

"Pluton, grab your daughter and place her next to him," Gaea told Hades, using his formal name to snap him out of his grief and surprise. Grabbing his daughter out of Melam's lap, Hades placed her beside Melam, entwining their hands together, as she was mentally showing him to.

"Now wouldn't this be a lovely picture under different circumstances? As the All Holy Mother, and the Primordial Keeper of Earth, it is within my power, though I do not often do it, to interfere with what the Fates think is the best for everyone. This time, the balance of my entire self, above and below, hangs in the balance, and that simply cannot be." She walked to the feet of the couple. She looked down at Melam with pride, before turning to stare at Persephone. They seemed to have a moment between them, before Rhea spoke.

"Melam's earlier bravery, and undying devotion to a girl he knew nothing about, is admirable. Sedah willingly going into a lion's den when she entered into Poseidon's dominion was brave too." She let a little Ava'an energy snake down into the sand and encompass Sedah before stepping back.

Gaia spoke up. "Neither of these are enough to save them, even though they are family. But to lose either of them means we all lose everything." She looked to Melam, who was quickly losing consciousness. "I will say this in the mother tongue so that it is binding, and then repeat it for them. Melam, *tuk dun gife Les Ether, tsra tes atia ka atho ia nost ser zur oyo, varea tesir vele bil ka oyia, okaa ia athoa ka sie osia ia sika gife ka Ava'an kaini lat tesir huhiret itak?*" she asked him. Instead of her lowering herself to repeat it, Melam smiled a little as he felt a small amount of her power flow into him so he could speak.

"*Solel.* Yes, I, the second born of The Ether, swear to keep and honor this young woman, binding my life force to hers, seeking and keeping all laws and morals of the Ava'an people until my dying breath." He looked over to where Sedah lay motionless. He could feel his grandmother's energy searching within Sedah to see if this was what she wanted. There was no going back once the decision was made.

"Sedah," Gaea began, sending her power out to boost Sedah's strength enough for her to come back enough to be coherent. "I assume my daughter or grandson has already explained this to you, so I will ask you the same thing. Sedah, sixth born of the house of Erebos, do you swear to keep and honor this young man, binding your life force to his, seeking and keeping to all laws and morals of the Ava'an people until your dying breath?"

"Yes, I do." Sedah whispered. She gave Melam's hand a squeeze, as hard as she could. Slowly, she turned her head to look at him, smiling when she saw that he had done the same.

"Your combined energies started the binding early on. Your blood made a pact, and the words spoken here have tied you together irrevocably." She looked at the others. "You are all witnesses of this binding." With a final nod to her daughter, she blinked out of view, entering the Ether to watch in solitude.

"You might want to shield your eyes." Rhea told the group, which now included a sitting Sephir, as a light began to grow like a sapling out of both Melam and Sedah's bodies.

The light leapt from them to form the trunk, leaves falling from the branches to the injured areas of their bodies, healing and stitching everything back together. When the light reached the area where their blood had mingled, another arc of light leapt between the wounds and their owners. These arcs grew together, getting brighter as the sapling of light grew in size, making Sedah's back arch, as if the tree was pulling her into the air with it.

Internally, her body was heating up, making her feel like there was a sword being pulled out of her. The scorching pain caused her to scream so loud she thought she might tear her vocal cords. From far away, she could hear a voice trying to penetrate the pain. She tried to tune her mind to the voice, pushing the pain aside with every ounce of will she possessed. It was a woman's voice, and it was beautiful.

"I know it hurts dear, but it will be worth it in the end. You are being transformed, turned Ava'an so that you can journey home with your mate, or mer, in our language." The melodic voice told her, sending waves of love and encouragement to Sedah. Sedah opened her eyes, looking as well as she could without turning her head, trying to find the owner of the beautiful voice.

"Am I dying? Why do I have to transform to be with Melam? What does being Ava'an mean?" Sedah asked, trying her best not to sound as panicked as she felt.

"We are the originals, but we are not of this planet. I created this place we now call home, Ava Carina, to have something to do after my reign as the current Ether. You must be like him to join him on Carina. Melam and Skylu will teach you what it means to be a royal Ava'an. Welcome, my child," The Ether's voice, a voice she recognized from her vision, said as Sedah felt it drifting away. With nothing else to focus on, she could feel her body slowly lying back on the sand. Testing her limbs, she noticed that there was no more pain anywhere in her body. The voice had distracted her enough that she didn't even notice

the worst of the pain, for which she would be eternally grateful.

Feeling the healing light of Asklepios ebbing, Melam looked through the shield that his mother had put around them at everyone outside the shield. Lifting his hand up, Melam turned the outer layer of the shield into a mirrored surface so that no one would be able to see inside.

Letting go of Sedah's hand, Melam rolled over so that he could look down at her. Just to be sure, he began checking over everywhere she had been wounded as she opened her eyes and smiled up at him. He stared back for a full minute, just happy to have her still among the living.

"I almost lost you," he whispered, brushing back a strand of hair on her cheek.

"Never," she answered. Putting her right hand behind his neck, she pulled him down for a slow, sweet, exploratory kiss, which he gladly answered with all the passion he had.

"Are you okay with leaving your family? I know my grandmother told you that you are Ava'an now, but we do not have to live on Carina. We can stay here if it will be too hard for you to leave. My daughter is here, so we can at least stay until she returns home as well," he told her, laying out the options as he saw them. Her eyes widened in shock.

"You have a daughter? I'm a stepmother? Oh Melam, what if she hates me? How could you not tell me this?" Sedah tried to sit up, or at least to hide the fear on her face, only to have Melam hold her down. Her arms heated where he held her. He moved his body, caging her in with an arm on each side of her, so he still leaned over her, yet not touching her.

"Yes, I have a daughter; and she won't hate you. She'll love you almost as much as I do. You were unconscious when you could have met her. With all we have had going on, it wasn't something I was really thinking about, love. I'm sorry." He gave her a quick peck on the nose.

Sedah smiled up at him. She knew it was irrational, but she feared that he wouldn't love her the same way if she was not herself anymore.

"You are still you, just . . . different. There are things that you will be able to do at home that you can't do here, and the powers you possess naturally here will become more enhanced. Are you ready to face your friends and family? We'll see them, then go to the Underworld so you can say goodbye to everyone else. We'll grab anything you want to take with you before we go to your new home in Carina," he explained.

Sedah could only nod as this new information was given to her. Melam gave her a quick kiss on the nose before raising his hand and letting the barrier around them drop. What had been ten minutes of time for Sedah to adjust had been mere seconds for everyone outside of the barrier.

Melam helped Sedah stand, waving his hand to dress her in the fresh clothes he saw in her mind. Her mother and father were the first to come and hug her, her mother's tears drenching her shoulder as her father hugged them both. Finally, Sephir cleared his throat, making his mother realize that everyone else wanted their turns as well. Hades maneuvered his wife to the side, so Sephir could give her a huge hug and a kiss on the cheek before stepping away as well. Then Caprika and Amy took their turn.

Melam smiled as he watched each exchange, happy for all of them. It might not have worked out the way he had tried to plan it, but he was glad that it had worked out in the end, no matter who had needed to intervene.

"*So you had this big elaborate plan to keep me safe huh?*" He heard Sedah's voice in his head, laughing as she picked on him. He grinned as he looked at her, finding that she was glancing over at him, as Caprika and Amy hugged her, gushing about meeting Rhea and Mother Earth in person.

"*I did. But it was going to be hard to do with our friends around,*" he laughed. Sedah blushed, thinking about all the things he could have meant, including the other night. Pulling away from her friends, Sedah took the few steps back to Melam. She looked up at his face as she wrapped her arms around him. Tilting his head down, he kissed her forehead before giving his attention to everyone standing around them.

"I don't know about all of you, but I am past ready to get off this beach." Without waiting for a reply, he moved, Sedah secured under his arm, waking in sync with him towards their beach house.

❦ 25 ❦

Entering the house through the sliding glass door, everyone took seats in the living room. While Persephone and Hades took the couch, Sephir, Caprika, and Melinoe sat on the love seat, while Amy sat on its arm. With all the seats taken, Melam and Sedah leaned against the bar attached to the kitchen. Melam made sure that he put up some of the strongest guards and wards he'd ever woven, just in case any of his relatives decided to try to come back and finish the job, or even to listen in and see what had happened after they'd left. Everyone else seemed to think it was over, but Melam knew from experience that this wasn't always so.

"You mind telling us what it is that just happened out there, son? What just happened to our daughter?" Hades looked expectantly at Melam, then at his daughter. "She looks like my daughter, but something's different, and I can't nail it down."

"What you just saw was the Ava'an form of transformation. At home, we don't need the barrier. On earth, the energy must be contained as there is nothing to absorb it afterward. Sedah is now Ava'an. Though honestly, she was already headed that way, since I couldn't seem to stay away, despite all the warnings I was given. Every time I healed her, some of my power stayed behind and merged with hers." Melam looked at Sedah with love in his eyes. She returned his gaze with questioning eyes.

"Ava'ans have three degrees of bonding," he explained, more for Sedah, than the others, "When we combined energies, when you were hurt, we started the binding process. Today, your blood mingling with mine, when we were bleeding out in the sand, made a pact that would have mentally and physically attracted us to each other. The words that we spoke were the Ava'an wedding vows. We are mated for all eternity now. When one dies, the other dies as well," he said, looking only at Sedah. He had to make sure that she was okay with all of this, despite the fact that it would break his heart if she wasn't.

"So, where will you live? Will we be able to visit?" Melinoe asked, dreading the answer.

"I will be going with Melam, back to where he lives," Sedah said, having never taken her eyes from him. "I need to learn what I am now, and who I need to be, in order to embrace this new me," Melam looked proudly at her, happy beyond belief. He kissed her tenderly, proud of her for choosing to embrace her new life over staying safe in her old one.

"We will be back and can visit then. The Ether, my queen, has my daughter on a mission right now, so I'm sure we will be back, although time does run a little differently there than here," Melam said. "I am not sure what caused all this today, but whatever the reason for the deal with Poseidon, that deal is void, and a new one has been created. If one of your sons is killed by Amphitrite, Triton will die within a day, so I would steer clear of both of them," he warned Persephone, who simply nodded, glancing over at Sephir.

"Well, we've all had a long day and I think Sephir, Sedah and Melam all need some rest after all they've endured today," Caprika said, getting up. Nodding in agreement, Persephone, Hades, and Sephir began walking to the pantry. Sedah smiled when Caprika and Amy looked at her with questioning eyes.

"I told you I could feel a portal," she told them. "Why did you put a portal here of all places, dad?" Sedah asked her father as Melinoe walked through and Hades reached the door.

"This house is only rented out to darkly inclined paranormals. Those that Melam rented it from have portals to different parts of the world, and different realms, in different parts of the house. This one called to you, so this one was open for you, should you have needed it," he answered as if it were common knowledge that earth possessed people that rented homes to only certain paranormals. With a quick hug, Persephone followed her husband, followed lastly by Sephir, who turned around to face them when he shut the door, giving them all a goofy smile, just to see his sister's smile one last time.

With everyone gone, Caprika rounded on Melam and Sedah, her finger pointed at him.

"You, sir, were told to stay away from her!"

"I tried, remember! I went to find out what Kohl and his cohorts were doing to humans. Then she got hurt, and I helped protect her. I even left again when I felt like we might have created the first bond, but she almost got killed. Those things sealed the first stage of bonding. After that, it wasn't so much *if* we became closer, but *when*, since I'd already become invested." Melam tried to sound more like he was explaining for Caprika's benefit. In truth, he felt like a child being scolded by the nanny for getting dirty right before high court began.

"Who told you to stay away from me?" Sedah asked, looking at one then the other.

"Let's just sum it up by saying damn near everyone," Melam admitted through gritted teeth as he stared at Caprika for having brought it up. Sighing, he turned to look at Sedah, taking her hands in his. "But I couldn't help myself. You intrigued me from the start, and then when our powers mingled, I was hooked." He bent down slowly, letting her know that he was coming in for a kiss.

Instead of just waiting for him to come to her, Sedah turned her body toward his, throwing her arms around his neck, meeting his kiss head on. Caprika and Amy beamed before walking around the counter and grabbing things to get dinner started for them all.

A thought occurred to Sedah as they all sat down to watch a movie after dinner that night. "Do we have to go right away? I haven't gotten to see a lot of this world, but I just said that I'd go back home with you and learn what it means to be an Ava'an."

"Did you want to see the rest of this world? We can post-pone going home for a little while. You can learn how to be Ava'an while you're still here. You're already royalty, so that part shouldn't be too hard."

"And being a mother? When do I learn that?" she looked up at him from where she was snuggled in his arms on the couch.

"We can take you to meet Skylu tomorrow if you like, honey. We aren't on a tight time frame." Melam kissed her on the nose eliciting a giggle out of her.

"I don't know about either thing, honestly. Let me sleep on it."

. . .

Later, Melam lay in bed, wondering what could have been done differently to change the outcome of what had happened that day, so Sedah might have never gotten hurt. It was a pointless thing to do, but he had to wonder if it was how things were meant to turn out. Maybe the Fates knew more than they wanted to admit about their ancestors. After all, it wasn't until recently that the Ava'ans had consciously decided to interfere with the lives of both the human and inhuman earthlings.

Every creature that populated Earth had its origins with the Gods, and thus with the Ava'ans and Ava Carina, their original home. He made a mental note to ask his mother about it when they finally did travel back home.

A creak of the old door gave away the fact that he wasn't alone, as if he hadn't known that Sedah had been lying awake in bed all night wondering what to do about so many things. He had yet to tell her that they could feel what one another were doing, and even thinking, at any time they wished to. He'd wanted to talk mentally to her, to try and comfort her, but knew that she needed the time to come to her own decisions.

Without a word, she came in, lay down, and cuddled up to him. He put an arm around her, holding her to him, happy as a kid with a lollipop.

"So, we are basically married now?" Sedah finally got up the courage to ask.

"Yes. In the eyes of our people, we are a bonded, mated pair. We are what humans call married," Melam answered.

"So if we stay here, no one will think it's weird if we sleep in the same bed? I just feel like part of me is missing when I am not near you. I felt it before, but it seems to be stronger now. After everything today, I feel safer when I'm with you." Sedah snuggled up to him more, looking up at him to see if his answer was genuine.

"That's what comes with the bonding. It'll be like that for a long while. We're meant to not be without our mates for very long, because it increases the risk of danger to the family."

"Then I have made my decision. I want to take a trip to gather my things and say goodbye to my family, then I want to go to my new home and learn about who and what I am now. Once your daughter isn't so busy, maybe I'll feel more confident in myself. Right now, I feel like I'm the child, with so much still to learn."

"It will come with time love, you just have to play the part until you feel comfortable. I'll be right beside you the entire time, either physically, or mentally," he told her.

"The way we did earlier?" she asked, getting excited when he nodded. "Can you show me?" She looked at him with sparkling, excited eyes. Smiling, Melam held his left hand up. Grabbing his hand, she placed her palm in his.

"Now, focus on finding your inner calm, and listen. Always listen for my voice, for I'll always be just a mental call away," Melam said as he stared at their combined hands. He let his power flow, watching as she followed his lead. She gasped, seeing that her power, while still grey, had bits of what looked like rainbow confetti in it.

"This is our link. Now imagine you are talking to me, but say it in your head." Melam waited, seeing if she could do it when she was consciously thinking about it. She had done it on the beach without meaning to. To do it on purpose was something totally different.

"*I love you,*" he heard from what seemed like a mile away.

"What? I think I heard something, but it sounded like static. Try again."

"*Why can't you hear me? I am saying I love you.*"

"It still sounds far away. Can you say it again?" Melam tried to hide his smile.

"*I said,*" Sedah began only to catch his chest rumbling as he tried not to laugh. She hit him on the arm, rolling over to pin him down with a stare that was meant to be intimidating. "Am I always gonna have to keep you in line when you try to make jokes?" She kissed him soundly.

"By the Ether, I hope so." Melam dragged her down for an all-consuming kiss. "*I love you too, my princess of darkness.*"

ABOUT THE AUTHOR

I have been writing for as long as I remember. I don't think there is an author out there that wasn't that way. I was on the edge of when you could use a computer to type, and printing meant tons of paper that you had to tear apart afterwards. My first unofficial published book was a class assignment in the fifth grade where we had to write a story, and our teacher was awesome enough to get them bound for us. That was when I really felt the awe that comes with holding something in your hand that you created without anyone's input but your own. That has been my goal ever since.

Military and life threw me some curve balls, but I am happy to be writing again, and happy to be expanding my series, The Gods of Carina Series. In 2010, when self publishing was more than just looked down upon, I decided to go that route with a company that I thought would help me every step of the way. The result of that, was a novel that I will one day go back and redo, but one that I am still glad to have had the courage to write and publish in the first place. The biggest down-side, was that the internet was young, and there were NO social media anything to help you learn and grow.

That is the main reason for my YouTube and all my social media platforms now. I told myself then, that I would help writers and readers alike, understand the process and be there to answer ANY questions that they had. I continue to try to accomplish this between YouTube and my Podcast "The Afterthought" available wherever you get your listening done.

I encourage you to leave a review of this book on Amazon and Goodreads. Also make sure you drop by my website and leave me a comment or two, read my latest Blog, and see what books and merchandise is coming out soon. I love to receive snail mail as well, so make sure you check out all my information below.

My Website:
www.amberscraft.com

Mail:
21301 State Route 410 E #148
Bonney Lake, Wa 98391

Thanks for reading! Please add a short review on Amazon and Goodreads and let me know what you thought!